War Song of the Wild

Silent Skies

Book 3

Rebecca L. Fearnley

LIGHTNING HYENA PRESS

First published through Lightning Hyena Press in 2022

Cover image © by Getcovers.

Chapter images and final image Copyright © by LovedDesign, licensed via Shutterstock.com .

Map image Copyright © by Rebecca L. Fearnley, created using Inkarnate Pro.

ISBN: 978-1-915124-07-4

First Edition.

Drifter Island
No
Blind Desert Province
Skyheart Village
Valley Province
Last River Province
Heart
Light Island
Westwater Province
Hallow Island

Alphor
...ip Province
East Delta Province
Whisperer Council
Landlock Province
Black Earth Province
High Savannah Province
...ert Province
Southtip Province
Last Coast Province
Sand's End Village

Contents

Early Winter

Frost bites the grass this morning. The old woman pulls the blanket tighter around her shoulders. Beneath her, the rickety chair she wrestled from the porch creaks as if it, too, aches from the chill. The old woman pats the chair's arm, like she's comforting an old friend. She turns to stare at the house behind her. The house that used to belong to a girl she loves dearly. No one lives there, now. The old woman has kept it in order as best she can, but at her age, she's barely capable of keeping one small house clean, let alone two. She sighs and turns back to the distant horizon, where sunlight creeps into the sky.

Autumn was brief this year and winter came swiftly on its heels. The temperature dropped and the rains arrived early, ruining the last of the summer crop. The old woman frowns. Soon, the Fei field workers and Oritch orchard hands will rise from their beds.

There's still work to be done on the land. Windfall must be gathered from the orchards. There's veg to be harvested from the glasshouses and the Fei workers will be doing their best to salvage the last of the crop. The old woman is too arthritic for such work, but that's ok. She's Aldren. Elder-caste. Her back might not be strong enough, anymore, to dig or plant or cajole a plough horse, but her tongue is sharp enough to scold unruly children and her eyes haven't failed so much, yet, that she can't thread a needle when clothes need mending.

The sun lifts above the horizon and the old woman squints at its brightness. She doesn't know why she still bothers to sit out here, behind the haphazard dwellings, staring out across the grasslands to where the village territory ends and the world seems to go on forever. But she's been doing it a long time now. She's hoping someone will appear on that horizon. Three someones, actually. A ruddy-cheeked woman with a mouthful of sass, a boy who'll be nearly nine now, with meadow-green eyes and a power that took even the old woman by surprise, and a girl who was once a soldier but became a hero. A girl with dark hair and eyes and clear, pale skin that tans easily. A girl taller than the stocky, red-haired, freckle-flecked type normally seen in the village. Who walks, proud, on a prosthetic limb. The old woman murmurs her name, as if the wind might carry it across Alphor to draw the girl home.

"*Solma.*"

But it's barely more than a whisper. And nothing happens.

The old woman sits back in her chair, remembering. Remembering Solma as a solemn youngster just after her parents died. Remembering when Solma first joined the Gatra—the soldier-caste of Alphor. It was the old woman, six years ago, who tramped across Alphor, to ruins of the old-world, to find the prosthetic limb Solma wears. She remembers nursing Solma after she lost her leg, holding her hand while the girl drifted in and out of consciousness. The old woman had told her, "Don't you dare die, girl. Don't you dare."

Solma didn't die. And the old woman is mighty glad about that. But now, with everything that's happened here in the last year, the old woman thinks the village needs her back. So, she waits here every morning, watching the horizon.

And hoping.

Movement to her left and the old woman stirs, glancing aside to see two figures, dressed in the black uniforms of the Gatra, loping towards her. She huffs a sigh and returns her attention to the horizon. The soldiers stop a few feet away and she casts them a narrow-eyed glance. A boy and a girl. She knows them. She doesn't want them here and so resolves to ignore them. The boy-soldier hooks his thumbs into his belt and stands silently. The girl nudges him.

"We should go," she says.

The boy nods but doesn't move. His rifle is slung over his shoulder, but the old woman eyes the wicked hunting knife sheathed at his hip, and the pistol holstered beside it.

"Up early again, Gerta?" the boy-soldier says. His voice is soft, but it still makes Gerta bristle. She sucks irritably on her few remaining teeth.

"What's it look like?"

The boy-soldier chuckles and Gerta glares at him. "Don't you sass me, Aldo," she snaps. "Remember, I cuffed your ears enough times to knock at least a little sense into you."

The girl-soldier turns to say something sharp but Aldo touches her arm. The girl mutters and turns aside.

Aldo, though, smiles. Gerta studiously avoids looking at him. She spent a good six months furious with this kid, back when he'd been a shy, allergy-ridden thirteen-year-old, freshly recruited into the village guard. Both these kids had been in a squad with Solma. And they, like many others, had turned on her when she'd needed them. They'd sided with the Steward—that vile snake of a man. Like everyone, they'd been scared and desperate. Gerta stares past Aldo to the girl-soldier he's with.

"Still can't look at me, Ilga?" Gerta croaks. "Two-faced coward."

Ilga rounds on the old woman. Her lank, red-brown hair falls across her eyes, half-masking the furious gleam in them.

"Don't you dare—"

Aldo grips Ilga's wrist. Not hard, but firm enough to give her pause. She glares at him as he shakes his head.

"Not the time," he says. Ilga bares her teeth.

"Never is," she says, casting Gerta a dark glance. "Thinks she can say whatever she wants and there ain't no consequences. She's trouble."

"She's hurting," Aldo says. He says it quietly, perhaps expecting Gerta not to hear. But she does. And a painful lump forms in her throat.

"She sided with the traitor," Ilga growls.

Traitor. Gerta flinches at the word and bites the inside of her cheek. That's what they call Solma. They don't say her name anymore. Never mention how often she risked her life for her people. *Traitor.* Because she told the truth and was exiled for it. Gerta grips the arms of her chair, resists the urge to hurl insults at the pair of them.

Aldo sighs. "The others are late," he says. "Go knock on their doors. We got patrol."

"But—"

"*Now,* Ilga."

Ilga's glare darkens. She wrenches her wrist free of Aldo's grip and stalks away, disappearing between the patchy houses.

Aldo stands in silence for a bit, until Gerta finally turns to look at him. She's startled by the changes the last year and a half have wrought on him. He's stronger. Tougher. A proper soldier now. His eyes are still blotchy from allergy, but his arms ripple with muscle. Life as a soldier has hardened him. And he's not as bad as some of the others.

Gerta had been hopeful last year, when Solma and her brother had exposed Blaiz, the Steward, for the tyrant he really was. But they'd been cast out. Blaiz's son, Maxen, has been in charge since then, minding the village for when his father wakes from the coma those bee stings put him in. He's mad, Gerta reckons, to think his father will wake. Mad to run this village the way he has.

More and more youngsters recruited as soldiers. The Fei and Oritch working the land under constant guard. Dissent quashed at gunpoint and rebels vanishing without a trace. He rules like his father. Gerta's fingers itch at the thought. That young wretch. She's been dying to rap the back of her hand across his face for some time now, but she knows where that would get her.

Exile at her age? She wouldn't even make it five minutes.

Actually, she would. Gerta's more resourceful than people realize. But in the face of a hungry wildwolf ... Gerta's no fighter.

Aldo's still standing beside her, saying nothing.

"What you want, boy?" Gerta asks. Aldo shrugs.

"Nothing," he says. "Just thought I'd wait with you."

Gerta wriggles in her chair. "Don't need babysitting," she growls. "Sun's up. Ain't you got Fei to terrify?"

For the first time, Aldo looks uncomfortable. Gerta allows herself a small smile. So, he sees how he's being used to tyrannise the village, does he? Good. Let the guilt of that fester in him. Maybe he'll grow brave enough to stand up to the teenage dictator.

Aldo lifts a hand to shield his eyes, squinting at the horizon. Gerta frown, then follows his line of sight. She sits up straighter, gripping the arms of her chair so tightly her arthritic knuckles scream.

"Can't be," Aldo says, dropping his hand. "I ... oh, Gerta ..."

Three figures have appeared on the horizon. One tall and imposing, walking with a swagger. The other two smaller, just kids. One of the kids grips the other tightly by the arm. As Gerta watches, the tallest figure lifts his hand to the sky and *fire* appears in it, burning red against the pale, morning blue.

Gerta swears. As quick as her stiff joints allow, she's out of her chair, leaning heavily on her cane, hoping against hope that it isn't—

But there's no mistaking those figures. Gerta's heart constricts. When Maxen sent those two raiders—the violet-eyed man and his son, who can make fire with nothing but a thought—on a mission out of the village, Gerta had hoped, guiltily, that they might die out there.

But here they are, both smirking in that smug, triumphant way Gerta has learned to hate. More figures appear on the horizon. Gerta counts twelve others in all. They have weapons slung over their shoulders or holstered on their hip. Gerta shields her eyes as they come closer. They're all in black, but she doesn't recognise most of them. Young, arrogant. They were soldiers somewhere, at some point. What have the Fire Maker and his boy been doing this past year?

As they draw near, the violet-eyed man spots Gerta. His lip curls. The sun glints off the flame tattoo above his eyebrow.

"You're up early, old woman," he rumbles. Gerta glares at him.

"Vulkan," she says, spitting his name. "I hoped you'd died."

Vulkan laughs. His son, Ignis, flattens a mop of black hair over his forehead, still clinging to the arm of the boy beside him. "Stop wriggling, will you?" he snaps.

The boy he holds will not stop wriggling. Tears pour freely down his face. His clothes are ragged, torn and caked with dirt. He swears at Ignis, hate shining in his eyes.

Meadow-green eyes.

"Warren," Gerta breathes. She drops her cane and gathers the boy into a hug. "Bless the Earth! I never thought I'd see you again! Where's your sister? Your aunt?"

She pulls back so Warren can talk, but he just hangs his head and sobs. Gerta's heart flutters and she scowls at Vulkan.

"What d'you do?" she demands. "What happened?"

Vulkan shoulders past Gerta with a grunt. "Our job," he says. "And get off that kid. He's a prisoner."

"He ain't!" Gerta yells. "He's one of ours! How dare you—"

Vulkan's hand lands hard across Gerta's face. Without her cane, she loses her balance and stumbles, only avoiding a fall because Aldo catches her. There's a mutter from the twelve soldiers gathered behind Vulkan, but no one steps forward to help.

Gerta's too shocked to cry out. Instead, she clutches her face and stares at Vulkan with wide, frightened eyes. Aldo helps her upright and hands her the cane she dropped, by which time she's regained enough of her senses that she's no longer frightened. She's angry. Batting Aldo away, she glares at Vulkan.

"You let that boy go," she says. "He needs his sister."

Warren has stopped crying. Instead, he looks at Vulkan with hate in his eyes. Ignis tries to grab his arm again but Warren twists away. Vulkan rolls his eyes.

"I don't care what he needs," he snarls. "He's here now. He's ours. Maxen's orders."

Gerta feels the anger building into something deep and bitter in her chest. She bares her teeth. "Maxen," she says, "Can go and—"

Vulkan raises his hand again and Gerta flinches. Vulkan laughs, turning his back on her. He grabs Warren's arm in his huge hand and drags the boy away.

"Gerta!" Warren cries over his shoulder. Gerta says nothing, just watches the kid being hauled towards the village centre. Towards the Steward's house. The soldiers follow, ignoring Warren's sobs. Gerta wipes her eyes, hating the wetness she feels there. She turns on Ignis.

"Proud of yourself, are you?" she says.

Ignis glares and shrugs. "Just doing my job, lady," he mumbles. "Ain't my fault, is it?"

He meets her gaze, his own full of defiance. But Gerta searches his face and finds a flicker of uncertainty there. She draws herself up to her full height, which isn't much. She isn't even taller than this jumped-up kid.

"We all got choices, boy," she says. "You made yours, and it'll come back to bite you one day." She pushes her face close to his, pleased when he takes a step back. "I don't like this," she says. "And I'm betting half the village won't like it, either."

Ignis' lip twists into a sneer. "Ain't their choice, is it?" he says. "They ain't in charge. And when the crop gets pollinated next year, I'm betting they won't complain much."

He steps close to her again. Gerta smells burning and Ignis lifts his hands so she can see the flames dancing on his fingertips. "You keep your beak outta this, old lady," Ignis says. "Don't reckon Maxen'll miss a doddery old sack of bones like you. One less mouth to feed."

Gerta glares. She wants to slap this boy. He deserves no less. But a hand touches her shoulder, and she turns to see Aldo. The soldier boy stares hard at Ignis.

"That's enough now," he says. "Like you said, Ignis, you got a job to do."

Ignis glowers, then turns on his heel and stalks after this father and the soldiers. Gerta catches him cast one last glance over his shoulder and she reckons there's fear in his eyes.

Good. Because she's got no intention of letting this go. And if she knows Warren and his family, that sister of his won't be far behind.

Aldo's hand is still on her shoulder. He guides her back to her chair. "Bad idea, Gerta," he says softly. "Those two are dangerous. 'Specially Vulkan, he—"

Gerta twists out of Aldo's grip and rounds on him. "Solma would never've let them treat her brother like that," she hisses. "Solma would've fought. None'a you are fit to lick the dirt off her boots. Call yourselves soldiers? Reckon you're brave?"

Aldo stares, saying nothing. Gerta shakes her head.

"You, standing there, doing sod all, it's just as bad," she says.

"Gerta—"

"Leave me," Gerta says. Aldo hesitates.

"I said, *leave!*"

Aldo trudges away. Gerta eases into her chair and touches her stinging cheek. As the rage ebbs, despair sits heavily on her chest. She wipes her eyes again and peers at the horizon.

"Come on Solma," she mutters, almost in prayer. "Hurry up."

One

Solma's breath mists in the air. The morning is crisp and frosty. The grass under her prosthetic leg crunches, making her wince. The rest of the forest is deathly silent. Here, the trees are thin, and sunlight penetrates the canopy. But there are enough shadows that the raider Solma's tracking has evaded her for the last twenty minutes. Solma clenches her jaw as she scans the shade between the trees. Clusters of mushrooms sprout among roots. The broken remains of dead ferns rustle in a soft breeze.

Solma slips between the trunks of two vast oaks, their branches entangled in their endless race for the sun. She presses her back against the rough bark of one tree and unsheathes her hunting knife. She listens. Her heartbeat drums in her ears. It's a struggle to calm her breathing. But …

There's the skittering of a startled rodent, the shiver of feet on grass, the strange pressure of a body moving through the trees. The raider. She's close.

Solma braces her back against the oak, waiting. She needs to be fluid. Relaxed but reactive. This raider's no scrawny exile from some impoverished village. She's muscular, swift, powerful. And she's eluded Solma this long.

The footsteps draw closer. The raider's not running anymore. She's come to fight. That means she feels cornered and that's never a good sign. Cornered people fight like crazy. She'll be twice as deadly.

Solma waits, battling her pulse into submission. She tenses, holds her nerve. The raider's close now, close enough that Solma hears her breathing. It's steady. Confident. She thinks she can best Solma.

She's going to learn differently this time.

Solma forces herself to wait until the raider's footfalls sound less than a metre behind her. She's close enough for Solma to smell, now. That familiar, gunpowder scent she's been chasing so long. She braces an elbow against the oak's trunk.

Closer. Closer.

The raider's footfalls stop. There's a moment's pause, then a gasp as she realizes her mistake. But by that point, Solma's already moving. She springs from behind the tree and slides across the grass on her hip, hooking her blade foot under the raider's ankle. The raider yells and goes down, landing hard on her back and rolling away. Solma leaps up and lifts her blade-foot, ready to bring it down on the raider's belly. But the raider grabs it and twists, sending Solma sprawling. She grunts with pain but is on her feet in moments. The raider's already up. Her face is obscured, mouth and nose covered by a neckerchief, and a black scarf wrapped over her head. Her green eyes gleam, fierce and determined. She's got a knife in one hand and a wicked-looking sickle in the other. She faces Solma, body tensed. They circle, blades flashing in the morning sun. The raider's eyes narrow.

But there's no way Solma's letting this girl get away again.

The raider lunges and Solma dodges left. The raider curses and stumbles as Solma throws a punch into her ribcage. She grunts, but absorbs the blow, twisting so she lands in a crouch. Solma resists the urge to charge. She's done that before and this enemy is too smart for it. She's ended up doubled over and gasping while the raider disappears into the forest again.

This time, she feints left, then right, jabbing with her fists and knife. She drives the raider back against a cluster of trees, where a knee-high wall of brambles blocks her escape. The raider growls, punching and blocking, but Solma doesn't let up. She needs to trap the raider against the brambles so she can incapacitate her. She sees the raider's eyes widen and knows she's worked out Solma's plan. Solma smirks.

The raider's blocks become more desperate. She stumbles backwards, deeper into Solma's trap. She feints left, then right, trying to dodge past Solma's blows, but Solma's wise to her. She blocks one escape with a punch to the jaw, and another with an elbow to the sternum. The raider grunts in frustration and backs away. She's surrounded on three sides by trees and brambles, now, with no clear path of escape. Solma advances and relief floods her. She's won this time. She'll bring the girl down and take her back to camp. Finally.

She curls her fist, ready to deliver a final blow.

But then the raider springs. With a shout, she propels herself off a tree stump Solma hasn't seen. She braces her foot against a tree and twists, leaping at Solma. They both go down in a tangle of limbs. An elbow lands in Solma's gut and the wind goes out of her. The raider rolls away, springs upright, and suddenly her knife is at Solma's throat.

Solma freezes. Something hot and wet drips from her lip and she knows she's bleeding. She glares at the raider kneeling above her, having won. Again. She rolls her eyes.

"That was a mean trick."

The raider chuckles. She lifts her knife away from Solma's throat and sheathes it, pulling off her scarf and neckerchief to reveal a braid of flame-red hair and a pale face with constellations of freckles. It's a face Solma loves dearly, which is why she'd told Olive to cover it—and her hair—before they sparred. It's hard to throw a punch at a face you'd do anything to defend.

Olive raises an eyebrow as she tucks her raider disguise back into her belt. She stands, offering Solma a hand. "You've had all winter to learn, and you never do," she says, hauling Solma to her feet. "You reckon you've won and you relax. If I can see it, so can a real enemy. If I ain't unconscious on the ground, you ain't won."

Solma scowls. "I ain't gonna knock you out."

Olive glares. "Why not?" she demands. "We're s'posed to be practising for war, right?"

Solma shakes her head. "It'll be different when we get there," she says. "I'll—"

But she can't finish. Her brother's face bursts into her head again. She's lost count of how often she's thought of him while she and her friends have travelled all winter. She's lost count of the nights she's lain awake, wondering if he's ok, if he's still alive. Earth, she misses him! She replays the memory of his cries last summer, just audible over the roaring flames, as he'd begged her to abandon him so she could save their friends.

Help them, Sol!

And she had. She turned her back on her brother. She left him.

But she's going to fix that. She's going back for him. And this time, she's not leaving him.

The days are lengthening now. Spring is stirring. And the relentless march across the continent is almost over. They're weeks away from Sand's End. Solma's home—if she can still call it that. Her brother's prison.

And yet, Solma feels as if Warren is half a world away.

She hits the heel of her hand against her head until the echoes of his voice fall silent. Olive draws her into a hug. Solma lets her head fall against Olive's neck and breathes in the other girl's scent. She closes her eyes as Olive kisses her cheek.

"He'll be ok, Sol," she says. "Maxen won't hurt him."

Solma doesn't ask how Olive knew what she was thinking. Olive always knows.

She lets her fingers entwine with Olive's and they fall into step. There's going to be hell to pay when they get back to camp. Bell disapproves of their training sessions. *Games,* she calls them. Only, this isn't a game. It never has been. It's preparation. They're not exactly expecting a warm welcome at Sand's End. Maxen has squads of trained soldiers at his disposal and all Solma has is—

All Solma has is hope.

The sounds of camp drift through the trees. Already, the sun is high and warm. Solma's come to expect that in High Savannah Province. Sweat prickles on her brow and she wipes it away. Olive winks at her.

"You'll get me tomorrow," she says. "You gotta stop assuming you've won. That trap was a good idea, but you never scanned the ground when you cornered me. You can't do that in Sand's End—"

Solma's heart feels as if it's made of lead. She lets Olive chatter on. But who are they kidding?

They're a sorry band of tired travellers against a village stronghold. Four weary women and a bunch of kids. Mamba and Cobra, the lead Earth Whisperers, might be adults in the eyes of Alphorian law, but they're still teenagers really. Barely seventeen and sixteen, they're still gangly with puberty and neither of them are fighters. Solma's Aunt Bell is terrifying with a rolling pin but that's useless in the face of a flying bullet. And Roseann's a doctor; trained to save lives, not take them.

And the others? They're just kids. Ana is barely fifteen and Taipan and the boys haven't even made it to double figures. They can't fight.

Or at least, they can't win.

Solma closes her eyes against tears. Behind her eyelids, her brother's face comes into focus.

Blink and he's gone. In his place is the snarling face of a boy she once thought loved her. A boy she once loved. She knows better now, on both counts. Maxen was always his father's son, and he used her. She'd been ready, last year, to turn away from all that. To bury her hurt, her anger, and leap, with her whole heart and her whole self, into Olive's arms.

But Maxen was never going to let her do that. He'd come for her brother last summer, sending his servants, Vulkan and Ignis, the Fire Makers, to do his bidding. And with only a thought, they'd lain waste to an entire forest. Burned a glade full of Alphor's precious insects just as they were building their numbers. Solma remembers the scorched bodies of bees and butterflies littering the ground, the shrieks of the Keeper children—whose power linked them to the insects—as the creatures died. Smoke filling the sky, the screams of her friends. She shudders.

How are they supposed to win against a power like that?

Eleven exhausted travellers against an entire village Gatra? Against the Fire Makers? Impossible.

Olive pushes through a tangle of branches and they emerge from the forest. A modest stream gurgles nearby and a few ground squirrels skitter into the grass. Here, the land is wide and flat, with only scrubby trees and bushes breaking the endless expanse. Just visible against the horizon is the village they found refuge in a few days ago. The only village for the last month and a half that has given them shelter. Solma expected to be driven away, like they were with all the others.

For some reason, villages don't think they need Earth Whisperers anymore. They don't trust them, so they've driven Solma and her friends out.

Two villages ago, they found a Whisperer hanging from a tree. Dead. They'd put as much distance between themselves and that place as possible.

A few feet from the stream is a cluster of tents. The camp was quiet when Solma and Olive left it that morning. Now, it's bustling with activity. Aunt Bell, red-faced with her flyaway auburn hair drifting in the breeze, tends a fire over which a pot of something delicious-smelling bubbles. She uses both hands to stir the pot with a stick, and Solma sees her grit her teeth in concentration. She was injured during the battle last year, a nasty burn to her right arm, which has left her with numbness. She rarely mentions it, but Solma knows it frustrates her. Solma smiles at her aunt as she and Olive pass. Bell looks up and nods. Roseann sits cross-legged beside her and the two bicker amicably. The three Whisperer boys—Krait, King and Habu—squeal as they chase each other in circles, tripping over the hems of their green Whisperer robes.

Ana stands a little way off, her bow slung over her back, feeding the two tan ponies, Burdock and Poppy. Burdock pricks up his ears as soon as he sees Solma and nickers a greeting. Solma smiles. That pony might be only small, but he's mighty. Without him, Solma would never have been able to save her friends last year. He braved fire, smoke, and death for them. She counts him among her dearest friends.

Mamba and Cobra emerge from a tent just as Solma and Olive flop down beside the fire. The two Whisperers hold hands and Mamba strokes Cobra's knuckle with his thumb. Solma smiles. Those two are good together, though Mamba always looks like he can't believe his luck.

Cobra shields her eyes as she steps out of the tent. Solma notices that the freckles on her usually pale face now stand out against a deep tan. Cobra spots Solma and her green eyes light up. She heads over, kissing the top of Solma's head and wrinkling her nose.

"You two smell awful."

Solma laughs. She's still amazed her friend forgave her, even after all this time. A lifetime ago, little Kobi was exiled from Sand's End because of Solma's betrayal. She became Cobra, the Earth Whisperer. But before all that, they'd been two misfit children playing together, trying to find their place in the world. Kobi had been a girl everyone believed was a boy, and Solma had been newly orphaned with no idea where to turn.

Mamba settles down beside Olive. Sweat shines on his dark-skin and he wipes his brow. "Hot this morning."

Solma nods agreement. "It's always hot here."

Bell passes round bowls of soup. It's always soup when their supplies are running low. Smelling breakfast, the Whisperer boys tumble over.

"Krait!" Bell shrieks as the little boy wraps his eager hands around the wooden bowl she hands him and mushrooms sprout all over it. Krait and Bell both let go of the bowl at the same time and it drops, spilling its contents. Krait looks up, red-faced.

"Sorry."

"*Control* yourself!" Bell snaps. Krait hangs his head, but Habu stands up, his eyes fierce.

"He *can't!*" he retorts. "It's *hard!* We can't just turn off the mycelia whenever we feel like it!"

Bell rounds on him. "Well, *learn!*" she barks, pointedly placing another bowl at Krait's feet. She glowers at Habu until he sits, then places bowls in front of him and King, too.

"Complete mess," she mutters. "Mushrooms sprouting out of everything, wood rotting whenever they touch it, those damn silver thread-things growing over every surface! You lot have gotta learn to control this!"

Mamba sighs. "I know," he says. "We're trying."

Bell harrumphs and heads back to the fire. Solma and Olive exchange glances. Last summer, their Whisperer friends discovered a remarkable new secret. A fungal network, deep underground. Slender, silver filaments that link all life in Alphor. A new way for them to use their power to communicate with Alphor's plants. The mycelia. It saved them last year. Solma doesn't think they'd have got out of the burning glade without it.

But since then, it's been a problem. Solma often sees them with their fingers or toes dug into the soil, glassy-eyed as they struggle to extract their minds from the network. Mamba warned them that only the strongest Whisperers can withstand such a link. Younger, less experienced Whisperers lose themselves.

Go mad.

He'd told them a story about a Whisperer who'd linked with the mycelia and lost himself, ended up locked away by other Earth Whisperers.

Solma shudders. She couldn't bear that happening her friends.

She and Olive finish breakfast and head to the cart to do their morning ammo audit. Solma counts three pistol magazines and no more than ten rounds for the rifles. They're running low. And, with villages driving Earth Whisperers away, it's becoming more difficult to trade.

She glances up, catching Olive's eye. The other girl's brows knit together. "We'll have to be careful," Olive says. "Hunt with knives. Ana can use her bow. Arrows we can make on the road. Bullets ..." she shakes her head. Solma says nothing.

There are few people, now, with the expertise left to craft bullets. Fewer who can make weapons to fire them. That knowledge is precious, jealously coveted by villages. Solma feels a stab of fear in her core. They're going into battle with barely enough bullets to take down a single squad of soldiers.

They return the ammo to the cart, tucking it safely under sacks of grain. Olive frowns and looks around. "Where's Taipan?"

Mamba and Cobra exchange glances. "Um," Cobra says. "In the mycelia."

Olive's eyebrows lift. "Still?" she asks. "Is that healthy?"

Cobra bites her lip. Mamba's face darkens. "No," he admits. "I'm worried."

Ever since last summer, when Taipan connected with the mycelia to save the bees, that girl's been different. All the Whisperers have, but Taipan's connection to the underground fungal network seems deepest and strongest. For a year, Solma knew her only as the cheeky, orange-eyed Whisperer girl. Her brother's best friend.

Now she's something different.

A crease appears between Mamba's brows. Cobra squeezes his hand. "I'm sure it's nothing," she says. Mamba doesn't reply. Everyone else busies themselves with their soup. Solma feels worry claw at her insides.

Behind the tent, Burdock flicks his tail and nickers softly. A breeze stirs Solma's hair, and she remembers she hasn't bathed in weeks. Her dark hair is lank with grime, her skin mottled with sunburn. She looks around at the others, at the grubby Whisperer boys. At Bell, with dark craters round her eyes. At Cobra and Mamba, whose shaved heads are sunburned and whose faces are gaunt. Everyone is exhausted. It doesn't matter how often she and Olive train, how much they hope.

They're just a sorry band of starving exiles.

Solma lowers her bowl, having suddenly lost her appetite.

"This isn't working," she says. Everyone looks at her. "We need a plan."

No-one says anything. Krait whimpers at the bowl in his hands, which is now empty but covered in mold growing from his fingertips. Bell snatches it away with a dark look, places it by the fire to dry out and comes to sit beside her niece. She puts an arm around Solma's shoulders and Solma leans into her aunt's warmth.

"Yeah," Bell agrees. "We do."

Two

Solma closes her eyes and rubs her temples. Her head aches. This is getting them nowhere. Bell's voice has risen to such a pitch, the children wince every time she speaks. Mamba's tried reason, but then he got cross and stalked off, mushrooms bursting from his footprints. Cobra followed to try and talk him down. Now, Roseann and Bell bicker furiously and won't stop when Olive yells expletives. Ana says nothing. Solma watches as the Whisperer girl rolls her hazel eyes and gets to her feet. Silver filaments creep across the grass under her toes. She pulls a face, hitches her bow onto her shoulder and trudges towards the horses.

Perhaps she's got the right idea. Solma's not sure she can cope with this nonsense either.

"And *what,*" Bell screeches, "are we s'posed to do even if we somehow sneak into the village? Reckon we can recruit a bunch of allies without alerting Maxen and his cronies? We got no idea what's been going on in that village. I ain't risking my niece and nephew—"

"They're already at risk!" Roseann growls. "You're being an idiot, Bella—"

"Don't you call *me* an idiot! You—"

Solma winces as Olive marches between them, swearing. Her mother cuffs her around the head and the two fall to arguing. Bell shoves her hands on her hips.

"*I am still talking!*"

Yeah, ok. Solma's done. Sighing, she gets to her feet. The Whisperer boys look at her, pleadingly. Solma mouths, "go play." No sense in them suffering, either. Relief written all over their faces, the boys scurry behind a tent.

Solma wanders after Ana and finds the girl standing with the horses. Solma's always liked Ana's company. The girl's gentle and quiet, but Solma knows she's capable of real bravery. Whisperers name themselves after snakes they rescue from frightened villagers, as their strange connection with the Earth makes them resistant to snake bites. Solma had been impressed by Mamba's story of being bitten by an extremely poisonous snake, and she's since learned that the Inland

Taipain—the snake little Tai got her name from—is even more deadly. But nothing was more shocking than Ana's story. Ana is short for Anaconda. Solma still has no idea how this quiet, diminutive teenager once wrestled the largest snake in Alphor into submission. She's a bit scared of finding out.

Burdock pricks his ears as soon as he sees Solma. She smiles and strokes his velvety nose. He nibbles gently at her fingers, nudges her for treats. She chuckles and Ana glances over.

"You're still his favourite," she says. Solma shrugs.

"Well, after what he did last year," she says, "he's my favourite, too."

Burdock lowers his head so Solma can scratch behind his ears. Solma's spent over a year with these ponies now and, all through this winter, she's paid more attention. Poppy's an anxious thing, all twitches and nerves. Solma doesn't blame her. The world's a harsh place. But Burdock's different. He's got this quiet strength to him, as if he knows everyone around him is terrified and so he'll stay calm and show them the way. Like he did last year. Solma closes her eyes against the memory of that roaring blaze. Trees wreathed in flame, smoke choking the air, the cries of her friends within the inferno. And Burdock, tethered to that cart, willing Solma to drive him through the flames so they could rescue those trapped inside.

Solma glances down at his left hind leg, where a patch of his hair has never grown back. The flesh there is mottled. She hadn't realized he'd been burned until well after they'd put out the fire and left Skyheart village. He'd never even flinched. Brave thing.

She lays her forehead between his eyes. "Could do with your courage again, buddy," she says. "Any ideas?"

Burdock huffs a breath but offers no further insight. Ana chuckles and hands Solma a fistful of oats. Solma holds them out for Burdock to gobble.

"This feels so hopeless," Solma says. Putting it into words makes the ache behind her eyes deepen. What the hell can they achieve against a tyrant determined to take every precious thing for himself?

Ana sighs. "I know," she says. "And everyone's tired. We should—"

She stops suddenly, staring past Solma as one of the tents is drawn open. Solma turns to see a diminutive figure step into the sun. Taipan stretches and stares around camp. Her sun-blaze eyes, orange as the dawn, come to rest on Solma, Ana and the horses. Solma sees those dark rings standing out around the girl's irises and flinches. All the Whisperers have those rings since connecting to the mycelia, but Taipan's are the most prominent. The little Whisperer girl's blazing gaze was always unnerving, but with this new power, Solma finds she can no longer hold the girl's eyes.

Or maybe it's nothing to do with that. Maybe it's the memory of her brother being dragged away. Maybe it's knowing Taipan has missed Warren as much as she has.

Help them, Sol! You got to help them!

Solma shudders, pushing that memory aside as Taipan trudges over.

"Hey, Sol," she says, her voice soft and distant. "Hey, Ana."

"Hello, little one," Ana says. "You alright, today?"

Taipan stares at her for a very long time. Ana squirms under the girl's gaze. "Yeah," Taipan says. "Just been listening."

Ana's eyes sparkle with concern and Solma looks away. She shares Ana's worry. Sometimes, it feels like Taipan's already slipping away from them, her mind falling into that ever-muttering network of silver threads beneath the soil. Just like the Whisperer in Mamba's story.

Solma can't bear the idea of that. What would she tell Warren?

Taipan glances over her shoulder. "Well?" she says. "Don't you want to hear my idea?"

She wanders in the direction of the raised voices, stumbling over the hem of her emerald robe.

Solma and Ana exchange glances.

"Right," Ana says. "Let's hear what she has to say."

They head after Taipan. Ana taps Solma's arm as they follow and points down. When Solma looks, she sees that Taipan's footfalls leave a trail of red and white mushrooms, shining mold and many-coloured lichens in their wake. Ana's brow creases with worry.

Roseann and Bell's argument falls silent as they notice Tai. Something about Taipan and the way she's changed makes everyone behave differently. There's a reverence in the way they talk to her now. Whether Taipan notices, Solma's got no idea. The girl always seems to have half her mind in the earth nowadays.

Taipan sits cross-legged by the remains of the fire. She runs her hands over the stubble on her scalp and closes her eyes. The Whisperers helped each other shave their heads a few days ago and Solma's beginning to realize that it's more to do with hygiene than aesthetics. Her own hair hangs in a dark, greasy braid over her shoulder and she fingers it nervously. Bell, Roseann and Olive have frozen, watching Taipan as if they're watching a real snake, not sure if it'll strike or slither away.

Solma sits beside the young Whisperer. She smiles at the girl and Taipan blinks distantly back. Solma looks away quickly. Ana kneels on Solma's other side and, taking their cue, the others sit as well.

Taipan looks at Bell. "May I have some breakfast, please?"

Bell hurries to oblige, slopping soup into a wooden bowl. When she hands it to Taipan, she does so gingerly, and snatches her hands away as soon as the girl has taken it. But no mushrooms sprout from the bowl, as had happened with Krait. Though, Solma notices, the grass around her now puckers with little yellow fungi. No one speaks, and Solma can't help the sense of foreboding that kindles in her gut. She wonders what her brother would think if he was here.

The thought sparks the old guilt that Solma thought she'd managed to do away with last autumn.

The ache that reminds her of the mountain of failures she's racked up.

There's a shuffle from behind and the three Whisperer boys traipse over. Krait lower lip trembles. King looks thunderous. He sees Taipan and his frown deepens.

"We don't *want* to argue more, Tai!" he protests. "We just want to—"

"We won't argue this time," Taipan says, patting the ground beside her. "C'mere."

King rolls his eyes but does as he's told.

Bell twists the hem of her dress between her hands. "Should we call—"

"No," Taipan says with a smile. "I called them. They're on their way."

Ok, it's unsettling how she does that. The Whisperers talk through the mycelia now. It means they can talk without opening their mouths. Like some mind power Solma thinks shouldn't be possible. The others are a bit erratic with it, but Taipan's got this new ability down to an art.

Cobra and Mamba appear from the woodland behind the camp. Mamba's still frowning, but Cobra holds his hand, drawing him towards the fire. He sighs as he sees Taipan.

"Ok," he says, crouching beside Cobra. "What're you thinking, Tai?"

Taipan licks her spoon clean and hands the bowl to Bell. "That was yummy," she says and, for a second, she's the sweet girl Solma met two years ago. Her brother's best friend.

Then she presses her hand to the ground, her eyelids flutter, and that girl is gone.

"We can't rescue Warren with just us," she says. Mamba sighs.

"We know, Tai, that's why—"

Taipan gazes at him and he falls silent.

"Maxen's got an army," Taipan says. Fear stabs in Solma's throat.

"An army?" she demands. "How? When?"

Taipan covers Solma's hand with her own. "It's complicated," she says. "But he has allies. People from across Alphor are heading to Sand's End. Maxen's promising them trade if they defer to him. Lots of the Stewards have sent soldiers to support him. It's a small army, but it's more than we've got."

Solma stares. It seems impossible, but she knows better. Taipan has heard this through the network of the Earth. The mycelia telling her the way Alphor's people move, hinting at the shift in politics.

"If Maxen has an army," Taipan says, "then we need an army, too."

Mamba throws up his hands. "And where the hell are we s'posed to get—" his eyes widen. "Oh, Earth, this is a terrible idea."

Solma frowns. Cobra's mouth twitches and Ana looks stricken. The boys squirm. Solma huffs a sigh and sees her frustration reflected in Olive, who folds her arms.

"Ok," Olive grumbles, "most of us can't do that weird mind thing you do. Care to share?"

Mamba covers his eyes. "It's so obvious." he says. "It would answer everything, but it's ... really dangerous."

"What is?" Solma and Olive demand at the same time.

"Maxen has an army of villagers," Taipain says. "So, we need an army ... of Whisperers. And there's one place to get it."

Mamba nods. "The Whisperers have a camp in the north," he says. His voice is hesitant, troubled. "It moves about every so often for protection, but it's where our Council lives, where decisions are made and where Whisperers go when they're sick, injured or need to train."

Solma blinks. "How come we never heard of this?" she asks. Mamba shrugs.

"We don't spread the knowledge around," he says. "You've seen how villages treat us. Our way of life is secret to protect it. Only Whisperers know about the camp and the Council."

Solma gives him a withering stare. "Right," she says. "And you never bothered to mention it during eighteen months of travelling together?"

Mamba looks sheepish, but Cobra touches Solma's hand. "Don't take it personally, Sol," she says gently. "We haven't ..." she pauses, her face pained. "We haven't been back there in ages. It's complicated."

Solma's about to argue, but Taipan wriggles impatiently. She fixes Mamba with those big, distant eyes. "We need more than an army," she says. Mamba starts to shake his head.

"Tai, you know our rules. If we go back now, they'll punish us—"

"What for?" Olive demands. Cobra gestures around the circle.

"*This,*" she says, indicating the fact that where they sit is now resplendent with more kinds of mushroom than Solma's ever seen. "This is against Whisperer law," Cobra continues. "If we go back, they'll know straight away. They'll—"

"We need one Whisperer in particular," Taipan interrupts. Everyone looks at her. "We're strong now. Stronger than all the others. But we gotta learn how to control this, or we don't stand a chance. We need *training.*"

Solma frowns, puzzled. She catches Olive's eye and sees the other girl is just as perplexed. Krait starts to cry. Mamba shakes his head.

"No, Tai," he says. "No, no. It's too dangerous, he's—"

"He's exactly who we need," Taipan insists. "He's been connected to the mycelia longer than anyone. He knows how to use it. He can teach us."

"He can't, Tai!" Mamba insists. "You know the stories. You know how he lost himself—"

"He didn't," Tai insists, her face darkening. "He didn't lose himself. They're not telling the *truth,*

Mamba. Those stories they used to scare us. They're *lies.* He's strong. He's got power, but they're stopping him from using it. We need him."

Mamba and Cobra stare at each other. Solma feels Ana stiffen beside her. She narrows her eyes, searching Bell's and Olive's faces, but they look nonplussed.

"Who?" she asks. "Who're you talking about?"

Cobra's cheeks flush with worry. "She's talking about someone dangerous. Someone the Whisperers locked away a long time ago," she says. "She's talking about Python."

Three

WARREN'S FEET ARE COLD. Now that he thinks about it, he doesn't remember the last time they were warm. He can't feel his toes and when he pokes at them, pain shoots along his sole. It's a strange compulsion. It hurts, but he can't help it.

It's been raining for three days and the damp creeps into this horrid stone room. The only window is too high for Warren to see out of, but level with the rain-slick village path. Warren didn't know the Steward's house had a basement until Maxen threw him in here all those months ago. Figures that Maxen would use it as a prison cell. Warren learned last year, when he was Vulkan's captive in the Earthroot Mountain caves, that he can't connect with his insects when he's underground. Of course, that meant Maxen learned it too. Half Maxen's face is covered in puckering bee-sting scars where Warren set the bumblebees on him almost two years ago. He's in no hurry to give Warren a chance to do it again. It's no wonder Warren's been locked down here all winter, barely even aware what time of day it is.

Warren summons all the horrible words he ever learned from Olive and thinks them about Maxen, hoping Maxen might be able to feel his hate. But the effort is too much. He's tired and hungry, and he runs out of hate after a few minutes. His shirt feels heavy with old sweat and the ragged remains of his pants scratch his knees. He's lost count of his sores. He feels like a single raw nerve.

He gets to his feet, wincing at the pain. The numbness in his toes sharpens to pins and needles as he hobbles the five metres across the room to hammer on the heavy door. It's locked. It always is.

He beats his fist against it. "Hey!" he yells. No answer. "Hey! I'm hungry! And can I have a blanket?"

There's a moment's silence, then someone on the other side of the door swears and shuffles off. Warren sighs, leans his back against the wet stone wall and slides to the floor, hugging his knees. The cold has settled into his bones and it's going to take ages to get warm, even if they do bring a blanket. At this rate, he'll get sick and die before Maxen needs him to talk to the bees. Serve Maxen right, that would. But Warren doesn't want to die.

The thought sends a flash of panic through him and he's on his feet again, beating the door, screaming.

This time, there really is no answer. No swearing, no shuffle of feet. There's no one there. They don't care.

Warren wipes his eyes and feels how grimy his skin is. They barely give him enough water to drink, let alone wash with. The dirt's probably embedded into his skin now. Aunt Bell will have a fit when she sees him.

That thought prompts a small laugh, a flicker of hope. *When.* Because Solma will come. He knows it as clearly as he knows the sun will rise, and the sky is blue, and the bees are back. She'll never give up. She'll burn the world, or save it, to reach him.

But it's been *months.* A whole, long, cruel winter with biting cold and little sun. He's growing thinner, weaker, paraded round the village every so often so Maxen can boast that he's brought the Beekeeper home. Warren is no more than a tool in his vile politics.

The worst of it is, Warren sees the hope in their eyes. These people he's known all his life don't see him as little Warren El Yuen, anymore. He's The Beekeeper. The miracle kid who can talk to insects. Not a boy. A symbol. And they don't care he's cold and hungry. They just need him to live until spring so he can Whisper the bees into doing what Maxen wants. So Sand's End can get rich.

Because never mind the rest of Alphor, never mind the future, if Maxen gets what he wants.

Footsteps sound outside and Warren springs to his feet, fists clenched. Whoever's coming, they'd better be bringing a blanket.

The door creaks open and a small figure, taller than Warren, slips inside. A quick scan tells Warren there is no blanket and his heart sinks.

"Where's the blanket?" he demands, hating how his voice croaks.

The figure steps into the light and Warren shudders. The boy before him has a messy mop of black hair to match the Gatra-black uniform he's wearing. He has no weapons. He doesn't need them. His fringe is swept aside to reveal a flame tattoo inked above one eyebrow. His eyes sparkle violet in the meagre light and a sneer twists his lips. Ignis. The younger Fire Maker.

Warren remembers this boy burning half a forest last summer. Conjuring fire with nothing but his hands, laughing as it engulfed everything.

But he also remembers the boy Ignis had pretended to be last spring. Clumsy little Ig, eager to please but always getting it wrong. A boy Warren had considered a friend. A boy who'd never existed.

"What do *you* want?" Warren growls. He raises a fist, as if to punch.

Ignis laughs. "I don't want nothing," he says. "I'm checking the room. In case you're planning on trying anything."

Warren frowns. "A Gatra normally does that," he says. Ignis throws him a withering stare and gestures pointedly at his uniform. He marches over to the pallet and kneels, flicking his finger upwards. A flame bursts to life at its tip. Warren jumps. He knew Ignis could do that, of course, but seeing it still reminds him of the burning glade. The bodies of charred insects. He shakes his head to rid himself of the image.

Ignis scours the stone walls, shakes the moldy sheets, and scans the floor. Apparently satisfied that

Warren isn't hiding anything untoward, he turns to face his prisoner. Warren notices he doesn't extinguish the fire from his finger. Instead, he opens his hand and lets the fire spread across his palm. He takes one, menacing step towards Warren.

"We gotta go," he says. "Now."

"But—"

Warren wants to cry. Is nobody listening? He can barely feel his fingers and his feet ache. At this rate, they'll find his stone-cold corpse huddled in the remains of those moldy sheets tomorrow. Doesn't Maxen care?

"I need a blanket," he insists. Ignis glares.

"Like I care."

Anger flares in Warren then. He's too cold, too tired, too *desperate* to deal with this boy's taunts. It's all wrong. He misses his sister, and all he's asking for is a stupid *blanket!*

Before he knows what he's doing, he's stormed towards Ignis, ready to push him. For a moment, surprise shines in Ignis' eyes, but then he dodges aside. Warren loses his balance, falling across the pallet. His arms whirlwind to find his balance and he catches

Ignis' flaming hand with his elbow. Heat sears up his arm.

"Idiot!" Ignis yells.

The fire from Ignis' hand catches and spreads up Warren's sleeve. Warren feels the heat of it tighten his skin. He cries out, but his flailing only makes the flames worse.

Ignis curses. He throws out his hand, fingers splayed, and makes a motion, as if drawing the fire to him. Immediately, the heat on Warren's arm cools. He sees the fire sucked from his clothing in a glowing orange rope towards Ignis' hand. Ignis shudders as his palm absorbs the fire. He flexes his fingers.

"Well, that was dumb," he says. "You could'a got hurt."

Warren reddens as he gets to his feet. His sleeve is charred and now there's a big hole in it from wrist to elbow. Great.

"I never knew you could do that," he grumbles.

Ignis glares. "Useless waste of power," he says. "Dja hates it."

Warren says nothing, just searches Ignis' face. His eyes snag on the constellation of pale scars across Ignis' cheekbone. Bee stings. Warren's fault. He'd called his bees to sting Ignis, to distract him, so Solma could save their friends. Warren should feel satisfied at the sight of those marks. But he doesn't.

Ignis catches him looking and glares. "You're welcome, then," he grumbles.

"Thanks," Warren concedes, lowering his eyes. "*Please,*" he begs. "Can I just have a blanket?"

There's a long pause. Ignis shoves his hands in his pockets. "Not now," he says. "Maxen sent me to get you. The bees are waking up. He needs them working."

Warren's scowl deepens. "If he needs me so much," he says, "He can come tell me himself."

Ignis' sneer disappears. In a flash, he's grabbed Warren's upper arm. The skin there is still tender from the fire and Warren cries out. Ignis snarls.

"You don't got a choice, y'know," he says, baring his teeth like an animal. "C'mon."

He drags Warren to the door, not caring when Warren falls and grazes his knee on the stone.

"Get up!"

Warren's lost all his bravado. His heart stutters. He wants to cry but that seems pointless. He stumbles after Ignis as the older boy hauls him into a narrow hallway, past two teenage Gatra and up some narrow, stone steps.

Warren feels carpet under his feet and knows he's now in the main part of the Steward's house. Maxen's house. But Ignis doesn't stop. They head down a corridor lit with electric lights—it's the only house in the village with solar panels—and towards the open front door. Warren struggles but Ignis shakes him into submission. Warren doesn't have the strength to fight. Not really.

And the truth is, he wants to see his bees. He wants to hear their soft tremolo, sense their scent-language, connect his mind with them.

He's missed them so much.

Outside, the cool spring air makes Warren gasp. He fills his lungs with freshness instead of the dank air from the basement. He follows Ignis, catching his feet on loose stones and gravel. The day is grey. Although it's not raining, there's a dampness to the air that refreshes Warren's grimy skin. Ignis pulls Warren down the path from the Steward's house and into the main village, where haphazard, mismatched houses cluster together with clothes lines strung between them. It's early, still. The Fei and Oritch workers are emerging for the day's work. They stare as Ignis drags Warren past, their eyes lighting with hope. A Fei worker tips his straw hat at Ignis. His grey uniform, designed for working the fields, is already covered in dirt. The blue-clad Oritch workers head to the orchards. The Gatra are out in force as well, with pistols and knives in their belts, rifles slung over their shoulders and a mean look in their eyes. They prowl the streets, calling the other castes to work.

Warren frowns. The Gatra are supposed to be protectors, not enforcers. But it seems Maxen is using them to keep the villagers under control.

Those not able to work the fields—the Aldren elder caste—take up places on porches, ready to care for the Yuen—the children too young to work—or commence the tasks needed to keep the village running. A few settle with needle and thread to mend clothes, or set to whittling weapons or fixing tools. Yuen scamper between the houses, waiting to be wrangled by parents or minders. Warren watches them longingly. They're too young to understand how dangerous the world is. With no caste color, they're not tied to any responsibility. Sure, their clothes are patchy hand-me-downs, but why should they care? They're free. At least until they're old enough to head out with their parents to work.

It seems a lifetime since Warren was that carefree. He's not Yuen anymore. He hasn't been for a long time. He's a Beekeeper, now. His responsibility weighs heavier than anyone's.

Warren sniffs, fighting the shivers that wrack his body. He looks up and meets an old woman's eye. A shock goes through him as he realizes it's Gerta. He hasn't seen her for months, not since she met him being dragged into the village by the Fire Makers. She's sitting on an old bench outside one of the Fei houses, watching a couple of toddlers tumbling in the grass. She's older, thinner, with more wrinkles and even fewer teeth. She's not smiling, either, which is unusual. Warren remembers Gerta smiling a lot before all this happened. She might be old, but she's always been tough. Always able to find joy in the smallest things.

Now, though, she holds his gaze, and there's sadness in her eyes. She nods at Warren, and Warren feels as if there's more than a simple greeting in the gesture. There's an unspoken solidarity. He imagines her voice, what she'd say if she was able.

Don't give up, boy. There's always hope.

Warren nods in return and the corners of Gerta's mouth twitch upwards. She struggles off the bench and grabs her cane.

"Guess that's my cue," she mumbles. Warren frowns.

He's about to ask what she means but Ignis feels Warren slowing down and tugs him sharply. He stumbles.

"Hurry up!" Ignis snaps.

Warren doesn't argue. Ignis is short-tempered today. Usually, the older boy enjoys lauding it over his prisoner. Today, he's distracted and irritable. Warren watches Ignis' face and see his violet eyes darting. Something's wrong.

Warren turns back to Gerta but she shakes her head. Warren bites down on his questions.

Gerta follows as Ignis hauls Warren down the path winding to the west. The houses and their crowd of workers fall away and Warren stares at the glasshouses ahead. He was never allowed round here as a Yuen, though he snuck out with a few friends, years ago, when he didn't know any better. Glass is hard to come by in Alphor, and difficult to make. Only a few villages still have the knowledge, so the fact that Sand's End has five of these structures, all made of glass, is a point of pride. Warren frowns as he stares at the structures. He's certain he remembers at least one was smashed in a raid two years ago. But there, standing before him, are five glass buildings, intact. The precious plants they house are a burst of green against the grey day.

Fixing it must have cost Maxen a fortune. Warren's stomach tightens. If he's got that kind of wealth, now, it's because other Stewards are paying him. It's because Maxen is the only Steward with insects and a means to control them.

It's because of Warren.

As they draw closer to the glasshouses, Warren hears that tremolo he's missed all winter. The industrious buzz of waking bees. His breath catches and he quickens his step. Their scent-language drifts through his mind, waking parts of him that have been dormant for too long. He needs to be with them. It's where he belongs.

Nestled between two glasshouses, Warren sees two boxy structures, almost as tall as he is. One leans slightly, the other stands proud. Both have slit openings at the base, leading out onto a short wooden platform. Warren's eyes widen as he sees hundreds of tiny bodies clambering over each other, scurrying across the platforms.

Honeybee hives.

How did Maxen get these? How does he know to house them like this? Warren's step falters, and Ignis drags him forward.

Warren throws a questioning glance at Gerta but now the old woman won't look at him. She's staring at the ground. Are those tears in her eyes?

"Where did he find these?" Warren demands, pointing towards the hives. Gerta chews her lip.

"He used to have three," she starts to say, "but—"

Ignis makes a sharp sound and ignites his hand. "Shut up!" he growls. Gerta glares but clamps her mouth shut.

Warren frowns, but a new insect-scent prickles his senses. He closes his eyes as that familiarity wafts over him. Buff-tails. They've made a nest inside a strange structure Maxen's had half buried beside the honeybee hives. It's a wide, shallow dome with a long, tubular entrance. There's no activity at the entrance, but Warren knows the young queen will be incubating her first brood in there. If he sends his scent out far enough, his mind brushes against hers. He frowns.

That makes no sense. It's too early in the year for her to have chosen a nest site. And why would she choose here, of all places? Beside two honeybee hives that could rob her nest?

Behind the honeybee hives, there's a huge wedge of rough wood shoved vertically into the ground. It's wreathed in chrysalides, and a few newly hatched butterflies. Warren's mouth falls open. He recognises the species. Peacock butterflies, like the ones his friend Addie can Whisper to. It was Addie's capture, last year, that he and his friends were trying to solve. Her butterflies were dying without her and, now that Warren looks, he doesn't think these ones are faring much better.

"Why aren't they flying away?" he demands. "And why," he adds, pointing to the shallow dome of the bumblebee nest, "is she in there? She shouldn't be nesting yet. It's too early."

Denial swirls in his mind. It's wet this morning, after all. The air is heavy with moisture. Maybe the butterflies are huddling together until the clouds pass. Maybe the bumblebee queen isn't laying yet, perhaps she's just sought shelter to wait out the rain.

But Ignis shatters that. "Chemical barrier, obviously," he mumbles.

Tears sting Warren's eyes. The butterflies' haphazard language wafts over him and he feels their frustration. Chemical boundaries are how the village controls wild animals, discouraging them from entering the village. The substance produces smells that either draw or deter animals and the Gatra put it in a ring around the village. But Warren knows insects talk through scent. A chemical boundary will be twice as strong for them as for other animals. He can feel it now.

He feels how the chemical ring around these insects is small, limiting them to this tiny circle of land until Maxen's ready to use them.

Warren wrenches his arm free of Ignis' grasp. "You have to open the chemical barrier," he says. Ignis rolls his eyes and makes to grab him again, but Warren dodges away. "They'll starve."

Ignis clicks his tongue and points to the little lavender shrub and a few barely open crocuses nestled behind the honeybee hives. Warren's eyes widen.

"*That?*" he demands. "That's not enough! You can't feed all these insects on one plant! It won't work—"

Ignis moves so quickly, Warren barely has time to register it. The older boy snaps forward, cuffing Warren around the head. Warren yelps, raising his arms in defence. Ignis grabs his wrist and drags him forward again. There's an urgency to him now, frustration gleams in his eyes.

Gerta hobbles after them, her cries of protest carrying on the air.

"You leave him alone!"

Ignis ignores her. He keeps hold of Warren's arm. Warren wriggles, fighting all the way, but Ignis is strong. He throws Warren down at the entrance of the first glasshouse. Warren winces as his other knee grazes. He pushes himself up onto all fours.

Gerta finally catches up with them. She rounds on Ignis, clearly intending to give him an earful. Ignis scowls and his fingertips begin to smoke.

"Don't start, old woman," he growls. "Or I'll—"

"You'll *what?*" Gerta snarls, pushing her face close to his. Ignis bares his teeth and lifts his hand. Flames dance across his palm. Gerta bristles and Warren stares in dismay as they square up to each other.

The glasshouse creaks open and they both fall still. Someone steps out. Warren stiffens. He recognises those rough-toed shoes, the hems of pants that don't bear any caste color. He squeezes his eyes shut.

"Get up," says Maxen's voice. "There's no time for stupid games."

Warren feels his face heat and he pushes himself up, too shocked to resist when Ignis grabs his arm. The sound of honeybees intensifies and a few of the butterflies flick their wings. They can sense his distress. Warren tries to quiet himself, but he can't. His pulse is a maelstrom, his breath gone. He feels blood rush to his face. Maxen's had this effect on him since he first returned to Sand's End.

The gentle, soft-spoken boy he'd known two years ago has changed. Those pale-blue eyes that had once looked at his sister with such love, now glare at him with disdain. He stands tall, a pistol at his hip. He's not in Gatra colors anymore. With his father still co-matose from those bee stings Warren gave him, Maxen is Steward, now.

And he didn't escape the onslaught of Warren's bees that summer, either. Half his face is a livid red, puckered with scars. His left eye doesn't open properly and the ear on that side of his head is damaged and misshapen. Warren lets himself feel guilty about that for a moment. It had been his bees, after all, that attacked Maxen and his father.

But the guilt doesn't last long.

Maxen smiles. It isn't a nice smile.

"How's your accommodation, kid?" he asks. His good eye gleams. He already knows the answer, but Warren can't help himself.

"Rubbish," he says.

Maxen chuckles. "Well, if you do well today, perhaps I'll try to make it more comfortable. Or," and his face darkens, "I can make it a whole lot worse."

Warren forces all his hate into his glare. Maxen is unmoved.

"You can let go of him, Ignis," Maxen says. "Warren's got work to do."

Four

IGNIS PINCHES WARREN'S ARM before releasing it. Warren yelps but says nothing. He stares at Maxen, chewing his lip.

"What do you want me to do?" he asks, hating how small his voice is. Maxen gestures to the insects.

"They're not behaving as they should," Maxen says. Warren's cheeks flush with angry heat.

"They need more space," he says. "They're hungry and cold. It's too early. How'd you get the buff-tail to nest here anyway?"

Maxen's eyes widen. "The what?"

Typical, Warren thinks. He doesn't know what they're called. He wants to control them, but he's not got the faintest interest in understanding them. These insects don't stand a chance. Scowling, he points towards the domed structure where he knows a bumblebee queen broods her first clutch of daughters.

"The big, fluffy bee that lives in there."

Maxen shrugs. "I didn't give her a choice," he says. "They're very compliant when you want them to be."

Warren folds his arms. "'Cept for now," he says, glaring. Maxen inclines his head.

"Yes," he agrees. "Except for now."

"They ain't got enough space," Warren insists. He can feel how tightly the chemical barrier holds the insects in. "They'll die if you keep trying to control them like this. They need more room—"

"Well they can't have it!" Maxen snarls, shoving his face so close to Warren's that Warren stumbles back. Maxen breathes deeply and pinches the bridge of his nose. "Look," he says, like if Warren would just *be reasonable* this would all be so much easier. "The situation with the other Stewards is delicate. I need them compliant for when my father wakes."

Warren blinks, nonplussed.

"Wakes?" he repeats. He quails as Maxen fixes him with a thunderous glare.

Blaiz, Maxen's father and the real Steward of Sand's End, had suffered so badly from bee stings that he'd fallen into a coma. Is he still alive? *Could* he wake up? Warren doubts it. And, from the way Ignis shifts uncomfortably, Warren thinks others might doubt it, too. Maxen doesn't notice. "I've got the Stewards making deals right now," he insists. "But any inkling of weakness and the trade will fall apart."

"*Everything* will fall apart if you don't let them go!" Warren yells. Heat shoots through him and the clamour of insect scents intensifies. Their panic, their hunger. It's too early, too cold, and there's no space. He's still perplexed as to how Maxen acquired these insects, but he's certain they'll be lost if Maxen doesn't listen.

But Maxen shrugs. "I can't let them go," he says. "There's too much at stake, and this is what Dja wants. You'll have to find another way."

"Another way to what?" Warren asks. Maxen frowns.

"Make them work," he says. "We need to start producing crop and to do that, we need these things to reproduce. Get them out and get them working."

Warren shakes his head. "It's too early," he protests. "There ain't enough sunlight—"

"Don't concern yourself with that," Maxen says, casting a significant glance at Ignis. "My—ah—*ex-*

pert has been upgrading the chemicals we use for the boundaries."

His eyes flicker upwards. Warren follows his line of sight, realising he's looking at Gerta. The old woman shuffles and won't look at Warren.

"I never said it'd be alright to make 'em stay in a space this small," she grumbles. Maxen waves a dismissive hand.

"Shut up," he says.

Warren stares at Gerta. Understanding drops on him like a mountain falling from above. He reels.

"*You?*" he splutters. "*You* made them like this?"

Sorrow shines in Gerta's eyes. "I never wanted it, kid," she says, quickly. "He promised he'd not harm you if I—"

"I said, shut *up!*" Maxen snaps, his face reddening like that of a petulant Yuen. Beside him, Ignis raises his hand and fire dances across it. Warren and Gerta both shut up.

Questions spiral around Warren's mind, though. Gerta's always been a mystery. He remembers when Solma lost her leg and the old woman had disappeared into the wilderness for weeks. Everyone had given her up for dead until she'd returned with the prosthetic limb Solma now walks with, made of some lightweight old-world material. Gerta tinkered with it until it was what Solma needed. And as Solma grew, so Gerta adjusted the leg to ensure it still fit. Warren's never understood how she knew what to do, or where to find it. He never asked.

But Gerta, Maxen's chemical expert? That sort of scientific knowledge has almost died out in Alphor now. If Gerta has it, it's no wonder she's kept it secret. Other Stewards would likely kill for it.

But she's chosen to reveal it now. To Maxen. And use it to *help* him. Warren scowls, turning away before she can mouth an apology at him. He feels her eyes on him, how she wants him to forgive her. He won't. *She* did this. Because of her, the insects are going to die.

Oblivious to the new atmosphere, Maxen's still talking. "The barrier's effective," he boasts. "It should wake them and get them started, but I need *you*, Warren, to keep them going."

Warren's mouth falls open. "I can't—"

"You can," Maxen says, voice stiff with impatience. "And you will. Now."

He gives a careless twitch of his finger. Ignis steps forward, reaching his burning hand out towards

Warren. Memories from last summer flash in Warren's mind. The glade on fire. Heat searing his skin. His friends screaming. His sister staring through the smoke, tear-tracks visible through the ash on her face, as he'd yelled at her to leave him, save their friends instead.

He shrinks away from Ignis. "Don't!"

Ignis pauses, smirking. Maxen sighs. "Then do as you're told, kid."

Warren glares. He wants to shout. To swear. Say something clever. But his throat constricts, and all he can manage is, "I *hate* you."

Maxen rolls his eyes and looks away.

Warren turns and closes his eyes, attuning himself to the insects, searching until he senses it. The sharp, cruel stab of a scent the insects find distasteful. An invisible barrier they won't cross. The thing keeping the insects in is also messing with them. It wakes them early, makes them hatch. It's like a drug, pushing them to behave against the way nature intended. A heaviness settles in his gut. It's all gone so wrong and Maxen's not listening. The same way Blaiz wouldn't listen. He doesn't care if the insects die. He just wants them to stay alive long enough to make him rich.

Warren opens his eyes to find Maxen studying him. The young Steward shoves his hands in his pockets. "I'll leave you in Ignis' capable hands," he says. "Don't mess it up."

He stalks past Warren, heading up the path back to the main village, then pauses and turns.

"Gerta," he calls, making the old woman jump. "My father will need tending this afternoon. You're not to be late, today."

Gerta scowls as Maxen disappears up the path. Warren watches him go, tears stinging his eyes. Gerta's strange knowledge is keeping Blaiz alive, too. And she's given Maxen a power over the insects that no other Steward has.

Warren's brain buzzes with insect fear and he clutches his head to try and hush the noise. It makes no difference. He glances up to find Ignis frowning at him, arms folded.

"Well?" the older boy says. "Get on with it, then." He turns to Gerta. "You can go now."

Gerta shakes her head and plants her cane firmly in the earth. "Don't think I will," she says. "Think I'll stay. Make sure you don't do more'n your jobs worth."

Warren scowls. He doesn't want Gerta to stay, not after what he's learned. But he eyes the flames in Ignis' hand and thinks perhaps having the old woman watching over him might not be a bad idea. He's still furious with her though. He glares at her, so she knows that. Ignis turns his back on Gerta.

"You got work to do, kid," he says.

Kid. Warren huffs a frustrated sigh. Ignis is only fourteen but stick him in a soldier's uniform and now he thinks he's a grown up. Thinks he's important. Ignis is an idiot.

Warren can hardly believe he'd once thought this boy was his friend. He clenches his fist against the memory of his real friends; the orange-eyed Earth Whisperer, Taipan, who he misses desperately. Yennevieve, the Keeper girl he'd met last spring, who could talk to honeybees. Mamba and Cobra. Ana. Roseann and Olive. Bell.

Solma.

Oh, Sol.

He wonders if they're ok. If they're alive. He pushes that thought aside before it can take hold. They *are* alive. They *must* be. He turns to Ignis.

"You don't got to do this, y'know," Warren says, wondering why he's bothering. "You're powerful. You don't got to do what Maxen says, it's—"

"Shut up," Ignis growls, and there's venom in his voice. Warren shuts up. He searches Ignis' face and sees loathing written into it. But there's a flicker of something else there, too. Warren sensed it in Ignis' snappishness this morning, the way he seemed impatient rather than cruel. He's scared. Why's he scared?

Warren sighs. He shakes the cold from his numb feet and trudges between the glasshouses to where the insects are being kept. His insect senses surge and he feels the stab of something noxious behind his eyes. He reels, spluttering as he staggers forward, but as suddenly as it came, the sensation is gone. Warren blinks, looks behind him. There's no sign of anything abnormal. He glances at Ignis and sees the other boy smirking. The realisation drops like a stone.

"*That* was the chemical barrier?" he says. He stares pointedly at Gerta, who won't meet his gaze. "It's horrible. They hate it."

Ignis rolls his eyes. "That's kinda the point," he growls.

Warren scowls and turns back to the insects, despair growing in his gut. The barrier is strong. There's no way the insects will cross it.

A few honeybees cluster around him as he moves closer, their buzzing desperate and anxious. Warren holds out his hand so they can land. They dance urgently. Warren watches them, his frown deepening, but their messages are nothing he doesn't expect.

There's not enough food. They're too close to another hive. They want to swarm and go elsewhere but something's preventing them. And it's too cold. They should be sleeping but they can't. What's happening to them?

Warren closes his eyes and shifts into that part of his mind where the insect language lives. He feels his senses sharpen and change and, when he opens his eyes again, the color of the world is different. Blues and purples stand out, reds and oranges are muted. Everything is fringed in a strange light made of colors he can't name. It's sharp and bright and confusing, as if his power strengthened during the winter. But how can that be? He pushes that thought aside for now and concentrates on the bees, trying to calm them. He tells them that everything's fine (even though it's not) and the humans are trying to keep them safe (which is a lie).

But it's difficult to lie to a bee. No matter how you phrase things, the truth has a smell you can't mask. The bees fold their antennae back, dissatisfied. He doesn't smell like honesty, and he needs them to trust him. He tries again, hoping a different approach might work.

I'm trying, he tells them. *I know you need more space. But our leader doesn't understand.*

The bees can't comprehend this. Why would a queen not listen to her workers? Why would one bee stop the others from doing what's needed? The hive is unity. The dance is democracy. The dance is life. Warren needs to tell the truth, the bees say, and his leader will understand. Warren feels his face crumple with dismay.

It ... doesn't work like that with humans, he tries to explain. But the bees are adamant. Warren feels the pressure behind his eyes intensify. He rubs his forehead. This is pointless. He promises the bees he'll try, but the thought of facing Maxen again makes him feel sick.

The honeybees power off. They fly in frustrated circles around the hive, unable to cross the invisible barrier laid around them. Warren tries the butterflies next but they're lethargic. Many of those that hatched early are already dead. As Warren watches, another butterfly loses her footing. She floats, like an autumn leaf, to the damp ground. Warren cries out and crouches, scooping her up. But she's lifeless. The tears that have been threatening for a while finally spill and Warren lets himself sob. He lays the butterfly gently on the ground and turns towards Ignis and Gerta, unashamed of his grief.

"You did this," he says. He doesn't even try to keep the meanness out of his voice, and he sees Gerta flinch. "You lot and your stupid plans and money and everything. It's your fault. You're gonna kill them all over again and you don't even *care!*"

Ignis shoves his hands in his pockets, but he's gone red, and something Warren doesn't recognise shines in his eyes.

"Just fix them, yeah?" Ignis mumbles. "Stop fussing so much."

Warren clenches his fists. He resists the urge to stamp his foot. He's nine now. Nine-year-olds aren't supposed to have tantrums. And yelling and screaming won't help the insects. But what can he do? He's powerless. Just a kid with a talent everyone wants to exploit. He's not strong like Solma or fast like Olive. He's not clever with words like Cobra or a good leader like Mamba. He wishes they were here.

Something whispers at the edge of his mind. He closes his eyes, feeling the tug of insect scent. It's a pull he recognises. His eyes fly open in surprise. He whirls round, almost tripping over himself as he crouches by the entrance to the bumblebee nest. He peers into the dark tunnel. A little shape emerges.

Bulbous and fluffy, the bumblebee queen lifts her antennae in greeting, huddling just inside the entrance to her nest. Her fur is lustrous, a healthy black and gold, and her strange eyes reflect the early spring light.

You shouldn't be out here, Warren tells her gently. *Go back inside.*

But she doesn't. She waggles her antennae, wafting scent in Warren's direction. Warren shuffles closer and gives himself over to that part of his mind, listening to the bumblebee queen.

Buff-Tailed Bumblebee Queen

Darkness. The nest is empty except for the nectar pots I managed to make. The world is small, fringed in this vicious smell, darkened by heavy clouds. I don't understand. I clamber through the dried moss and scraps of fur I found in here. It keeps me warm, provides padding for my brood. I laid days ago and keeping the eggs warm takes everything from me. I nestle on top of them, shivering my flight muscles to keep them warm. My antennae burn with fear-scent, the too-close fragrance of other bees nearby, of petal-winged insects hatched too soon. Something's wrong. I'm tired, but the vicious smell at the edge of the world keeps me awake, urges me to lay and brood and work.

Outside, the scent changes. The ground vibrates with something huge approaching. I tense. Poison gathers on my sting. Every bee I've ever known is gone now, but I carry memories from a lifetime ago, memories gathered by my long-dead sisters.

Cruel teeth.

Ripping claws.

Hunger.

Destruction.

Chaos.

I smell the memory as clearly as if it were unfolding in front of me. A huge paw raking through the earth, rending the nest apart. A great mouth scooping bees and pollen. Eggs and nectar disappearing in moments.

But the sounds and smells outside don't seem like that. There's something strange out there. It smells like bee. But not. I lift my antennae and catch the tendrils of that odd scent. The air stinks of argument. A tang of anger. The sharp, pungent stab of fear. I fold my antennae back, waiting. The air trembles and I search my sister-memories for an explanation.

There is one, hazy with age, not from my sisters but from an age before, from my mother's mother, hatching into a beeless world two lifetimes ago. I dig into it, searching the memory for clues.

Blinding sunlight.

A riot of scent.

A giant creature crouched in the dirt.

A clammy hand laid out, a bee climbing onto it.

The strange, thunderous language of humans and ...

Then this boy spoke bee.

And everything changed.

My antennae quirk up. Could it be? I've felt stories of this boy-who-speaks-bee passed down in the scent of mothers, daughters, sisters. And now, perhaps, he's here. The need to understand drives me towards the entrance tunnel. I hurry for that circle of light that means The Outside. I buzz my flight muscles as the cold air squeezes my joints, stings my antennae. The light blinds, despite the heavy layer of cloud. I feel wetness against my fur and recoil. My feet brush a blade of grass. The odour that marks the edge of the world wafts towards me and I shudder.

Then, another scent cuts through, soft and friendly. A huge shadow blocks the sun and a two-legged crea-ture towers over me, his footfalls making the ground quake. I feel poison budding on my sting, but the creature only peers at me.

The friendly scent washes over me again and I hear the creature speak. In bee.

You shouldn't be out here. It's too cold. Go back inside.

It is him! I shiver my wings as hope seizes me. Perhaps this boy can fix everything. Perhaps he can save me, save my future before it drifts into nothing in the cold air. I shuffle out of my tunnel, lift my antennae, and hope he understands.

He does. He lays down a hand so I can climb aboard, then lifts me closer to his face. I study his features. Eyes of meadow-green, hair of nectar gold, skin spattered with sun blotch freckles and sticky with grime. He smells of sadness, loss. But he also smells of bee. Of safety.

I push my scent towards him, trying to explain.

But he already knows.

A honeybee zips by, too close. I feel her wings flutter the air and I tense, my sting poised. She senses my distress and swoops higher, wafting an apology scent towards me.

I mean no harm. There is so little space.

I try to relax, but it won't be long before the honeybee nests swell to full strength. Tens and tens of thousands, all clamouring for food. When that happens, they will mean harm. They will compete with my nest for flowers. There will be battles. And what can a few hundred of my daughters achieve against so-many-thousand honeybees?

I feel the bee-scent-boy shudder as he smells my despair.

I know, his scent says. *I'm trying to fix it. I'm trying.*

Behind him, something shifts, and I catch another scent. Cutting, cruel, uncanny. I recoil in disgust, antennae folded back.

There's someone here with you.

The bee-speak-boy stiffens. I feel his fear quicken. *Yes.*

It's someone that strikes fear through his heart as well as mine. I trundle to the edge of his palm and peer round him, trying to find the source of the harsh scent.

And there it is. Another human, standing a behind my bee-scent-boy. This one is all angular sharpness. Hair black as badger fur. Eyes the color of violets. Skin pale as snowdrop petals. And in his hand, writhing like a living thing, is a flame.

I buzz my wings in horror.

What is that?

The bee-speak-boy feels my fear. He lowers his hand so I can retreat into the safety of my nest tunnel.

It's a Fire Maker, the bee-speak-boy says. *He ... won't let me make the world bigger for you.*

Anger. Sharp and bright as spring sunshine. My wing muscles shiver with the will to battle. I feel the bee-speak-boy's fear of this ... *Fire Maker.* I am ready to challenge him. How dare he?

And what use is the bee-speak-boy if he can't over-come this Fire Maker? I search my memories, sifting through images my grandmother embedded into the genes of her children and her children's children.

He saved them, then. He found them flowers. He protected their nest. He found males for the virgin queens to mate with. And when the nest was under threat, he called a swarm of my ancestors to protect the daughter-queens. He defended the future.

Can this be that same boy? Stinking of fear, beaten down by despair.

No, it can't be him. Perhaps it was, once. But this boy doesn't have the strength of the one my grandmother called friend.

This boy is broken.

I turn away from him and head back into the darkness of my nest. I fold my antennae back to dull the scent of his sadness.

Five

EVERYTHING IS ON FIRE. The world is heat and smoke. Maxen's face looms out of the shadow. Grinning. Snarling. Solma can't move. When she looks down, great vines have slithered from the earth and tightened around her legs. She tries to scream but smoke claws her throat. She's burning.

Maxen's face softens for a moment, and she feels a glimmer of hope. Perhaps he isn't the man his father wanted him to be. Perhaps he'll let her go.

He reaches for her, fingertips brushing her throat. It's a touch she knows. She remembers his tenderness, back when she'd thought he loved her. Maybe it wasn't a lie. Maybe ...

His fingers tighten and she knows it isn't true. He's killing her. He's killing the world. And there's nothing she can do—

Solma.

A voice she recognises. Harsh, demanding, loving. Solma tries to shout for that voice, but she can't.

Sol, wake up.

She can't wake up. He's killing her, he's—

Sol, wake up. Breathe.

She can't.

It's ok.

It's—

Her eyes snap open. She lurches upright, gasping for breath. But she's fine. There is no smoke. No fire. No hands around her throat. There's only the gentle movement of the tent canvas around her, the heat of her sleeping bag, now clammy with sweat. There's only the midnight darkness and Olive's hand on her back.

"Breathe, Sol, you're ok."

Solma breathes like she's never realises how wonderful air is. She draws it inside in huge, greedy gasps until she feels dizzy. Tears sting her eyes, but she wipes them away. Olive pulls her close, kissing her forehead.

"Another bad dream?"

Solma lets out a manic laugh. "Nah, this one was bloody great," she says. Olive squeezes her tighter and Solma nuzzles her neck.

"Maxen again?" Olive asks. Solma stiffens. She's still bad at this part. The honesty. Laying her fear out like a carcass to be butchered. But she promised Olive last year. No more secrets.

"Yeah."

"Wanna talk about it?"

"I—"

Solma pulls back. Now that she's back in her own body, the dream is fading. But Maxen's face stays, snarling, behind her eyelids every time she blinks. What is there to say? It's been the same almost every night for two weeks now. Since they decided to head for the Whisperer camp. Every step away from Warren feels like a betrayal. Every harsh gust of wind seems to carry his voice, begging for her help.

Olive rubs her back. "You don't got to talk about it 'til you're ready, y'know," she says. "Just ... don't keep it hidden, yeah? It ate you up last year. I don't ... wanna watch that happen again."

Solma grabs Olive's hand and squeezes it. She slips her fingers around the back of Olive's neck and pulls her in for a kiss, breathing in that familiar gunpowder musk. They huddle together, arms around each other.

"C'mon," Olive says, pulling the tent open. "Let's get some fresh air."

Solma hesitates, then sighs and grabs her prosthesis. Once it's secure, they head into the night. In the light of a full moon, a breeze ripples through the plain's grasses. Stars stud the sky and Solma puts her head back, breathing the night air. She feels Olive's fingers lace through hers and lets herself be guided around the camp. She stares at the outlines of three more tents, thinking of the people sleeping inside them. Her friends. Her family. Between the hastily pitched tents is the remains of a fire. The cart is parked nearby, its contents covered by a canvas sheet. Beside it, the ponies doze. Solma scans the area for Bell, who should be on watch. She finally spies her aunt leaning against the cart, chin on her chest as she snores softly. Solma allows herself a small smile, but then the memory of the dream returns, and the smile disappears.

"I'm ... I dunno if I can do this," She admits, startling herself.

"Do what?" Olive asks, stroking her hair. "Sol, we been through this. You don't gotta do it alone. You're not a one-girl army. You're amazing, but you're just human. We're here with you. All of us."

Solma leans into Olive's hug, feeling the other girl's steadiness, the rise-and-fall of her ribcage. Olive rocks her gently and Solma lets herself be soothed. It's still hard to be weak. Still hard to show her vulnerabilities, even though all Olive does is calm them. Solma feels her eyelids drift closed. She's so tired of all this fighting, all this—

Maxen's face flashes behind her eyelids again. Snarling. Murderous.

Her eyes snap open. Olive hushes her softly. "Easy, Sol. You're ok."

But she's not, is she? How's she supposed to admit it's not that she doesn't know if she *can* do this, it's that she doesn't know if she *wants* to? How can she stand in front of the boy who kissed her, said he loved her, and put a bullet between his eyes?

Movement behind them and Olive whips round, a knife drawn. But it's only Bell. She stretches and rolls her shoulders, tucking her rolling pin—her favoured weapon—into her apron. She trudges towards Solma and Olive. Moonlight falls across her face as she raises an eyebrow.

"Can't a woman nap in peace?" she asks. Solma rolls her eyes.

"You're s'posed to be on watch."

"Don't you sass me, girl!" Bell says, but there's a twitch to her lip that makes Solma smile.

Bell glances towards the camp, frowning, then turns to Olive.

"Mind if I borrow my niece, Liv?" she says. "Reckon we got some stuff to discuss."

Olive shrugs. She gives Solma's hand a squeeze and hands over her knife. "Stay vigilant, yeah?"

Solma nods, kissing Olive's shoulder, and watches as the girl who loves her always—saves her, *always*—heads back to their tent. Without Olive beside her, Solma feels exposed. She hugs herself. Moonlight glints off her knife.

Bell stares at the blade, frowning, then slips her arm through her niece's. They turn from the camp and walk out a little way into the plains. Bell says nothing, and Solma glances at her, wondering what on Earth her aunt wants.

"I been hard on you in the past, girl," Bell says finally. It's such an unexpected thing to hear that Solma stumbles over her own feet. Only Bell's grip stops her from falling face-first into the grass.

"What?"

Bell raises both eyebrows. "You gonna disagree?"

Solma shakes her head quickly.

"Thought not," Bell says. They come to a halt at the summit of a little hillock. Solma stares out over the darkened landscape. The dark smudges of lone, scrubby trees dot the otherwise featureless land. Bell shakes her head.

"Truth is, Sol, you're tougher'n all of us," she says. "Strong. I known that all your life. All your brother's life. You're the strong one. You was always gonna do the right thing. Even if it took you ages to figure it out."

The words should be a comfort, but Solma feels them like rusty iron through her heart. *Strong.* A weight settles on her shoulders, so heavy she can barely breathe. She feels her aunt's eyes on her, and the heat of that expectation burns.

She shakes her head, not to deny it, but as if she's trying to shake off the mantle Bell's placed round her shoulders.

Bell squeezes her arm. "I know you're worried," she says. Solma lets out a derisive snort. That's an understatement and a half. Bell frowns.

"I got faith in you, girl," she says. "When it comes to it, I know you'll do the right thing. You'll make the right choice."

The right choice. What does that even mean? A chill that has nothing to do with the night settles in Solma's bones.

"You mean when I face Maxen," she says. His name catches at the back of her throat. Bell doesn't answer, and so Solma says the thing she dreads. The thing that makes sweat prickle on her forehead, her breath quicken, her heart race.

"I gotta kill him, don't I? It's the only way to end it."

Bell says nothing for a bit, just stares into the dark. Solma snatches a glance at her and sees moonlight gleaming in her eyes. A breeze cools Solma's skin. She untangles her arm from Bell's, hugging herself. The silence is too much.

Then, Bell says, "He's a tyrant, that boy. Just like his Dja. If he don't get what he wants, he'll set the world on fire to stop anyone else getting it."

Solma nods. She's thought the same enough times. In her mind, she's tried everything. Reasoning. Pleading. Bullying. But in every imagined scenario, Maxen won't relent. He's set on Blaiz's legacy. He's got to be stopped. Alphor needs to know that men like Maxen and Blaiz don't get to take what they want anymore. Not just for Warren, but for the world.

Bell takes Solma's hand. She turns so they're facing each other and cups her other hand under Solma's chin, lifting it so Solma is looking directly at her.

It's amazing how Bell manages to look so fierce. Those ruddy cheeks, the sharp glint in her eye. Not for the first time, Solma thinks how Bell has fought, too. Moment after moment, day after day. Fought to keep her niece and nephew safe. Fought not to let the grief of losing her sister overwhelm her. Fought for the truth. For what's right.

"I trust you, Sol," she says.

She turns back to face the dark expanse. Cold prickles Solma's skin again. Olive's knife feels heavy in her hands and her mouth is dry. Because what is *right*? And how can Bell be so certain when Solma is plagued with doubt?

Maxen is a tyrant. He does need to be stopped. Solma needs to take him down. And what other option is there, even if it makes Solma sick? It's not like she's never killed before.

But when it comes to it, when it comes to facing him—

Bell kisses the top of her head. "You're a fighter," she says. "You'll do what you need to do."

Solma says nothing. She's terrified Bell can read her mind, can see the truth she hopes no-one will ever see.

That in every dream for the last two weeks, every time she's met Maxen, she can't pull the trigger. She can't even lift her pistol. Years of training, of fighting, and it all goes out of her in an instant when she stares into his face. The face of a boy she's known all her life. A boy she once loved. The gun hangs limp in her hands while he comes towards her, wraps his hands round her throat and squeezes.

She lets him win. Every time.

Six

Ignis shoves Warren so hard he sprawls in the dirt.

"Ow!"

"Shut up."

Warren bites back a retort and rubs his stinging hands together. At least it's not wet today. For once, Sand's End had a damp winter, but the chill meant the insects' early waking has been hard on them. Gradually, the cold is giving way to a tentative spring. A few clouds waft across the sky this morning but it's otherwise clear. Warren closes his eyes as the sun touches his face. For the last two weeks, he's been dragged to the tiny chemical cage nestled between the glasshouses, every day.

"Sort them out," Maxen keeps saying.

Warren tells him they want more space.

Last time he said that, Maxen backhanded him across the face and left his jaw bruised. He hasn't mentioned it again.

The only thing he did manage to get Maxen to concede to was setting up a wooden platform inside the chemical barrier with a shallow bowl of sugar water. Warren is allowed to refill it daily. It's not much, but it's keeping most of the insects going. For now.

Warren's eyes flick towards the two Gatra stationed outside the chemical barrier. Aldo and Ilga. He's seen them here a lot lately. Ilga stares at the ground, refusing to look at him, but Aldo steps forward, offering Warren his hand. Warren scowls, pushing the offered hand away as he gets to his feet. If Aldo's offended, he doesn't show it. He stands quietly as Warren brushes soil from his clothes. Warren fixes cold eyes on Ignis.

"You didn't have to push me," he says. "I want to see them, y'know."

Ignis shuffles and looks away. Warren frowns, noticing the shadow of a bruise around the other boy's eye. Ignis catches him staring.

"What?"

"Nothing."

Ignis grumbles under his breath. He slides the canvas bag he's been carrying off his shoulder and throws it to Warren.

"Here."

Warren hesitates, eyeing the bag as if it might be full of snakes. Ignis rolls his eyes.

"Ain't gonna bite you, is it?"

Warren glares. "Dunno," he says. "Depends what you put in it."

Ignis' cheeks flush crimson. He blinks and flattens his fringe over his flame tattoo. Warren's stomach clenches. It's the first time he's seen Ignis do that since he stopped pretending to be Ig, the goofy orphan kid Warren met in Skyheart village.

"Ain't nothing," Ignis mutters. "Just shoes."

Warren has to stop himself from spluttering. *Shoes?* He opens the bag and finds a grubby pair of too-big boots. The stitching is torn in places and the soles are peppered with holes but they're better than nothing. Warren slips them on, wincing as his cold-stricken toes brush the leather.

"Thanks," he says. Ignis shrugs.

"No good to no-one if you can't walk. I ain't doing it for *you*."

Right. Warren laces the boots in silence, glaring at Aldo when the soldier boy bends to tie them for him. For the second time, Aldo backs away. Warren hears Ilga mutter something under her breath that might include the word *ungrateful.* Aldo hushes her with a look.

"How do they feel?" Aldo asks as Warren walks a few tentative steps. Warren frowns. They pinch a little at the heel and are too long in the toes, but who cares?

"They're good," he says. He looks at Ignis and tries to smile, even though smiling at this kid is the last thing he wants to do. "Great, actually."

Ignis reddens further.

"Finished?" he demands. "Only, we got to take the bees to the orchards."

Warren freezes. "What?"

"The apple trees are blooming and Maxen's got trade orders to get ready. We gotta get them pollinated."

Warren's mouth falls open. "You can't just—"

In a matter of seconds, Ignis covers the space between them and jabs his fist into the side of Warren's head. Warren's too surprised even to cry out. He goes sprawling backwards, landing on his rump in a wet patch of dirt.

"Ignis!" Aldo scolds, stepping between Warren and the fire boy. Ilga's hand goes to her knife. Her eyes dart between Warren and Aldo as if she's not sure whose side to be on. Ignis glares but Aldo doesn't move.

"Ain't no need for violence," Aldo says. "We're all friends here."

Friends, are they? That's news to Warren. He sits, too dazed to cry. What's the matter with this kid? He gives him a pair of boots with one hand then punches him with the other? Warren bites back the anger clawing his throat. This time, he doesn't reject Aldo's offered hand. Aldo pulls Warren to his feet and Warren glares at Ignis.

"What was that for?"

He expects Ignis to snarl at him like he's been doing all winter. But the other boy looks uncertain, as if he wasn't expecting himself to do that. He shakes out his fist.

"For ... being annoying," he says. He points towards the hives. "Can you call 'em?"

Warren looks at the bees. The honeybee hives are more energetic, with workers zipping about the wooden structures. The butterflies still look dazed and more of their delicate bodies litter the floor. Over the last two weeks, Warren's persuaded a few to feed. He holds his breath as he pushes through the chemical barrier, but that awful, noxious scent stings his nose. The part of his mind that connects to the insects screams with alarm. He staggers through, gasping for breath. Behind him, Ignis tuts loudly.

"Ain't got all day!"

Warren ignores him. He checks the bowl of sugar water and finds a lone honeybee floating in it. Dead. Biting his lip, he scoops her out and lays her in the grass. Nothing he can do for her now.

He checks the honeybees first. The queens are both young and inexperienced. They remind him of Orchid, the honeybee queen he'd met at Skyheart Village. Her bees had been sick, but they'd also led his sister to the place Vulkan and Ignis had been keeping him prisoner. That bee and her colony tried to save him. He'll never forget that. He's given these two queens names as well. Willow is a soft soul. She's cautious and Warren feels this ripple through her daughters. They don't like being close to the other hive.

The other queen, Indigo, is Warren's favourite, though. She's clever, impatient and adaptable. Her personality thrums through the hive and her workers are more inquisitive.

Both the hives are alert, warmed by the early spring sun, but Warren feels tension coloring their scents. There isn't enough food. Warren senses the workers from each nest turning their attention to each other, testing each other's defences. If he doesn't persuade Maxen to widen the barrier soon, they might attack each other. The thought makes his throat tighten with fear.

Warren lets a few bees from both hives gather on his hands, waiting to see if they dance. They don't. There's nothing to dance, is there? No new flowers. Nowhere to forage. He lets them fly away and crouches by the entrance to the bumblebee burrow, pushing his mind out for the queen.

He's called her Clover. It's weird, but he still feels shy of her.

She's Blume's granddaughter. He doesn't know how he knows this, but he's certain. And it means the precious, beautiful bee he discovered two years ago lives on.

He remembers the feel of Blume's mind against his, how she'd trusted him. Loved him, he believes. She'd been so brave, his Blume. So special.

Clover feels different.

It's been two weeks since he first brushed her mind and, since then, she's been distant. It hurts that she's indifferent. But he's trying to understand.

She has a nest to grow, eggs to lay, a future to protect. A few of her first brood have hatched and are ready to fly and forage. But fly where? Forage what? If this nest fails, perhaps the whole of Blume's line disappears. She has a legacy to protect. And much as he loved Blume, much as he connects to their way of life, he isn't a bee.

He isn't important. Not to her.

He closes his eyes and brushes her mind. She buzzes an irritable scent at him.

Tired.

He tries to be gentle, ignoring the way her scent stings his nose.

There are flowers. I need your help.

She perks up.

Where?

Warren thinks. Bumblebees don't dance like honeybees, so he tries to push pictures into her mind; the path around the village, a long stretch of grass, rows of trees with buds just opening.

Clover dismisses him with a harsh scent. *Can't go that way,* she reminds him. *Stinks of anger and death.*

Yes, the chemical barrier. How's he supposed to get them through that? He withdraws his mind, feeling a guilty relief to be free of Clover's accusing scent. He turns back to Ignis.

"They won't move through the chemical barrier," he says.

Ignis huffs a frustrated sigh. "I know that," he drawls. He unclips a silver cannister from his belt and waves it at Warren. "I got the neutraliser."

Warren stares at it and is clearly too late to disguise the hunger in his eyes, because Ignis hides the cannister behind his back. "You can't have it," he snaps. "Maxen's orders."

Warren lowers his gaze. "Where'd you get it?" he asks. Ignis snorts.

"Gerta," he says. "She makes it, don't she? Now shut up your questions. I'll open the barrier. I just need to know you can control 'em."

Warren frowns. "Why?" he asks. "They just need food. They'll come back to the nest at night. They'll—"

Ignis steps forward, his fist raised again. This time the threat is enough to shut Warren up. He winces, but Ignis' eyes flick towards Aldo. He lowers his fist.

"'Cos we got to make sure they don't wander off and pollinate nothing else!" he growls. "Just the apple blossoms. Got it? Nothing else."

Warren gapes. Nothing else? *Why?* That makes no sense. Does Maxen seriously want Warren to control the bees so tightly he tells them where to forage and feed? Doesn't he understand that they need more than one single type of flower to survive?

For a moment, frustration overcomes Warren's fear. He growls, shoving the other boy hard. Ignis staggers back, surprised, whirling his arms to keep his balance.

"You're going to kill them!" Warren growls. "You and Maxen and all the other stupid people who think they got a right to own everything! Don't you get it? They're gonna fight each other if you don't *listen to me!*"

The surprise drops from Ignis' face, replaced by a look of thunder. Warren tenses, expecting violence.

But when Ignis meets his gaze, those violet eyes are misty with something Warren doesn't understand. He takes a step forward, but Aldo's hand is on Warren's shoulder.

"Breathe, Warren," he says. Warren shoves him off.

"You ain't no better!" he growls. He points at Aldo and then at Ilga, who stands red-faced, staring at her feet. "You're *letting* it happen! You're *helping!*"

Aldo's face falls and Warren sees hurt in the soldier-boy's eyes, but he doesn't care. It's true, isn't it? He feels the scent of aggression in the air, the way the bees begin to see each other as the enemy. And no-one's listening. Furious, he plants both hands against Aldo's waist and shoves hard. He's not strong enough to move the other boy, but Aldo takes a step back anyway.

"Easy, Warren," he says.

Ilga finally looks up, hand on her pistol. "You shouldn't let him push you," she says, though her voice is uncertain. Aldo shakes his head.

"He's angry," he says softly. "He's—"

"Can you do it or not?" Ignis interrupts. His voice is no more than a growl but everyone else falls silent. His eyes fix on Warren. Burning. Angry.

Warren sighs, hating Ignis. Hating himself. "Yeah," he says. "Probably."

Without another word, Ignis waves Ilga and Aldo aside. He opens the cannister and sprays a thin mist. Warren feels the bees' excitement as they sense a gap in the edge of the world. He pushes his mind towards them, feeling each little bee like a point of light in his consciousness. He grits his teeth. It's a lot of bees to hold onto at once, and he doesn't like controlling them like this. Bee colors fringe his vision. Blues and purples, strange hues he has no name for. Warren's come to think of this as the *bee-vision,* when their minds and his link so tightly he sees how they see.

A new scent touches his mind, and Warren stares at the entrance to the bumblebee nest as three young workers clamber from within. They're small, their gossamer wings catching the sun. He scoops them up and places them on his shoulder. One fires her flight engine and powers upwards to hover by his ear, but the other two stay put, content to ride.

Now, Warren turns what little space there is left in his mind towards the butterflies. They're easier to manage than the bees, but they're disparate in nature, more erratic. By the time he's gathered all the insects into his mind, he barely remembers where the noise of their language ends and he begins.

"Ok," Warren says, his own voice sounding distant. "I'm ready."

Having this many insects connected to him makes his head hurt. His vision is a strange, swirling mass of blues and purples and his nose stings with the scent of three chemical languages.

Through the haze of bee-vision, he sees Ignis staring at him strangely.

"Let's go then," the other boy says. "Keep them under control."

He heads off, expecting Warren to follow. And Warren does. Sullen, furious with himself, he follows. He looks back once, to see Aldo and Ilga staring after him, their faces inscrutable as they watch Ignis lead him away.

Seven

SOLMA KEEPS HER PALM against Burdock's shoulder, listening to the tan pony's breathing as he plods along. Occasionally, he nuzzles her, as if to encourage her. On Burdock's other side, Poppy's more skittish. Bell holds the mare's lead rope and Solma tries to tune out her aunt's nattering.

"Come on, you daft thing!" Bell says. "Walk on!"

Poppy prances sideways, but Burdock lowers his nose and nudges her in the shoulder. She settles but her ears lay flat against her head. Bell rolls her eyes.

"What's wrong with you?" she demands, as if she's expecting an answer. Solma suppresses a nervous grin.

"It's the mountains," she says, nodding towards the silhouette of several looming peaks piercing the eastern clouds. Bell frowns.

"What about them?"

Up ahead, Olive turns, raising an eyebrow. "Really?" she says. "You forget our ridiculous trek through the Earthroot Mountains last year? All those darkcat tracks we found? You forget the *actual darkcat* we had to see off on our way back through those same mountains?"

Solma's gut tightens at the memory. They'd been lucky the first time, but racing back through the mountains, hoping to catch up to Vulkan, Ignis and Warren, they'd been less lucky. That cat had been huge, reaching Solma's shoulder, though she's taller than everyone else except Mamba. Its paw looked like it could have crushed a human skull. And those teeth …

Solma shudders. She remembers Olive firing a warning shot, then a second when the cat ignored the first. Two precious bullets wasted, and the cat had kept coming. It was Ana's arrow that finally saw it off. It hissed, turned, and melted into the shadows.

It's no wonder Poppy's so anxious.

Solma glances back and sees Ana traipsing along with the kids. Taipan stumbles over her own feet and Krait rubs his eyes.

Solma calls to the head of the group. Mamba and Cobra pause.

"Might be time for a break," Solma suggests.

Mamba gives a frustrated sigh. "Yeah, alright," he says. "Let's give the ponies some water."

They unpack a few preserved morsels from the cart and sit the kids in a circle. Bell and Roseann see to the horses, but Solma can't relax. Her eyes are drawn to the mountains, to the horizon, to the clusters of trees where every rustle could be a predator. Or worse.

From the tension in Olive's body, it seems she feels the same.

Solma trudges over to her and their hands brush.

"Something don't feel right," Olive says. Solma agrees.

"I'm gonna do a quick perimeter check," Solma suggests. "You stay with them?"

Olive nods, eyes fixed on the distant mountains. Solma leaves her and heads west, pistol drawn. Footsteps sound behind her and Solma turns sharply, but it's only Cobra.

"Thought I'd come with you," the Whisperer says. "Two pairs of eyes are better than one."

Solma smiles, letting Cobra fall into step beside her.

They crossed the border into Landlock Province a few days ago and the landscape has changed from vast, flat plains of tough grass to undulating hillocks dotted with woodland. There's a river close by and the land is greener. But the rolling landscape means there are plenty of dips and troughs for attackers to hide in, which Solma doesn't like. They walk round the little camp in widening circles, keeping an eye on the horizon whilst also scanning the ground for anything unusual. Nothing gives Solma alarm.

"Think it's clear," she says.

Cobra nods. "Yeah." She hugs herself, though it's not cold. Solma watches her, frowning.

"You ok?"

Cobra jumps at the question. Her cheeks flush. "Er …" she says. "Yeah. I mean—"

She bites her lip, staring at the ground as they make one last circle round the camp. Solma sighs. "Out with it," she says. "I know you got something to tell me."

Cobra's shoulders slump. "It's just—" she says, "I reckon you and the others ought to know. Whisperer ways are a bit … odd."

Solma raises an eyebrow. "I know that already," she says with a sly grin. Cobra gives a nervous laugh.

"I mean," she says, "you might find them shocking. Our leaders—we call then The Seasons—they aren't like village Stewards—"

"Thank Earth," Solma mutters. "I had enough of those to last a lifetime."

"No, I mean—"

Cobra's voice is strained. She's having a hard time trying to explain, which is unusual, for her. Solma frowns.

"You sure you're ok?"

Cobra opens her mouth to reply but a breeze wafts past them and, with it, comes the sound of voices, rumbling cart wheels. Solma tenses, peering at the horizon.

Coming over the crest of a distant undulation, she catches the silhouette of a caravan. Five carts pulled by powerful horses. They're flanked by a squad of tough-looking men and women wearing Gatra-black.

She swears, grabs Cobra's arm, and they pelt back to camp. They skid to a halt beside Roseann, who's holding a bucket of water for Poppy to drink from. The mare startles and Roseann throws Solma a fierce scowl.

"Great," she says. "I only just got her to calm down."

Solma ignores her, pointing back the way she'd come.

"Caravan coming," she says.

Instantly, everyone's on alert.

Bell ushers the youngsters onto the back of the cart. Krait cries softly. Mushrooms sprout from the side of the cart where his fingers grip it tightly. Habu prizes the younger boy's hands off the wood and holds them. The ponies paw the ground. Roseann takes the rifle Olive hands her and Ana nocks an arrow in her bow. Only Cobra and Mamba don't grab weapons.

"If we look hostile, they'll be hostile right back," Mamba says. "Calm down. They're probably just a trade caravan moving between villages."

But Solma hears the uncertainty in his voice, which isn't helped when Taipan jumps down from the cart and lays her flat palm against the soil.

"They're not," she says. "I mean ... they are, but. Oh, I dunno. It's different."

"How?" Mamba demands. Taipan shoots him a glare.

"I'm reading the mycelia," she says, "not their minds."

Olive lets out an impatient grunt and holsters her pistol. "Keep your weapons ready but outta sight," she says. "We're just a band of Whisperers and their protectors moving between villages. They ain't gonna hurt us. And—" she turns grave eyes towards Mamba and Cobra. "Try *not* to grow mushrooms as far as the eye can see, yeah? Reckon that might throw up some alarms."

Cobra laughs nervously, then kicks over the toadstools blooming under her toes. Olive smiles. "It'll be fine."

But even she doesn't sound convinced. The old code that villagers don't harm Whisperers hasn't held true for the last couple of years. Things are changing. And not in a good way.

It doesn't take long for the approaching caravan to crest the nearest ridge, spot the travellers, and pull to a stop. The five wagons are massive and covered in thick canvas. They're pulled by horses twice the size of Burdock and Poppy. Burdock tosses his head and neighs what Solma hopes is a greeting, and not a challenge.

There's a shout. The Gatra draw their weapons and form a bristling perimeter around the caravan.

"So much for a peaceful greeting," Cobra grumbles. Solma and Olive grab their pistols and Ana aims her bow. Mamba holds up his hands, trying to placate both sides.

"State your business!" someone yells from the other caravan. Solma frowns. Isn't their business obvious? There's a reason the shaved heads and emerald robes of the Whisperers are so distinctive. No-one's going to mistake a Whisperer. Nowadays, Solma's not sure that's a good thing.

"We're travelling north," Mamba says, which is true. "Many villages need help this time of year." Also true. "We only want to pass safely into Landlock Province. We'll offer our gift wherever we can."

Solma struggles to keep her face under control. She's always marveled at how Mamba manages to hide the truth whilst also telling the truth. It's a Whisperer thing.

The caravan of strangers mutters among themselves, then a young Gatra holsters his pistol and trudges towards them. Mamba signals for the others to lower their weapons. Ana complies, but both Solma and Olive keep their pistols trained on the approaching soldier. Old habits and all that.

The soldier glares when he approaches but doesn't reach for his own weapon. He's tall, Solma notices, white-skinned with crisp, blue eyes and sandy blond hair. He looks like he's native to Northtip Province, where Solma knows it's often cold. But his companions look like they hail from all over Alphor. Solma sees skin and hair colors of all shades, clothes of patchy cotton, hemp, and even silk. These people aren't all coming from one village. Solma frowns. Why would a trade caravan of many different villages be heading east to—

Oh.

The realisation sends a jolt through her and Olive casts her a sideways glance. "What is it?" she hisses as the soldier approaches Mamba. He stands a little too close.

"They're heading east," Solma whispers back. "From different villages."

Olive raises an eyebrow. "So?"

"A trade caravan?" Solma says. "This time of year? From different villages, heading in the direction of Sand's End?"

Olive's swears. "You're right."

Solma knows she's right. This isn't an ordinary caravan. It's the first wave of a new struggle for power that Solma had hoped to stop. They're going to trade with Maxen.

Mamba holds out a hand to the soldier. "Good to meet you," he says.

The soldier doesn't reply. He doesn't take Mamba's hand either, just keeps staring at him with cold, blue eyes.

Ana steps up to Mamba's side, her bow still drawn.

"That's a bit too close," she says. On her other side, Cobra gestures urgently for her to lower her arrow, but she doesn't. Solma and Olive exchange glances. This is going badly.

The soldier looks Ana up and down, his eyes wandering to places they shouldn't. Ana's cheeks flush pink, but she holds his gaze and keeps her bow steady.

"Cute," the soldier says, an edge of sarcasm in his voice. "Whisperer kid with a bow and arrow. That a new thing?"

Olive closes the gap between her and the soldier before Solma can stop her. She steps in front of Ana, blocking the soldier's view of the younger girl. She holds her pistol an inch or so from his temple.

"It a new thing for traveling trade folk to leer at teenage girls?" she demands.

A cry goes up from the caravan. There's the sound of Gatra soldiers readying their weapons.

Solma swears, holsters her pistol and jogs to Olive's side, a hand on the other girl's shoulder. "Easy, Olive," she mutters. But Olive either doesn't hear or pretends not to.

Fear flickers across the soldier's face. He glances at Olive, then the barrel of her pistol. "You ain't a Whisperer."

Olive raises an eyebrow. "Well spotted," she drawls. "Now step back from my friends. I ain't afraid to shoot you."

Solma casts Olive a warning glare but Olive keeps her gaze fixed on the soldier. Someone from the caravan yells something threatening. A horse whinnies. Solma's pulse roars in her ears. She grips Olive's shoulder, willing the other girl to lower her weapon. She doesn't.

The soldier sneers.

"Your lot," he says. "You been controlling the world too long. Freedom of Alphor and all that crap." He spits on the ground, narrowly missing the hem of Ana's robe. "You reckon no-one'll hurt you 'cos you travel with Whisperers. Things're changing. Won't be long before Whisperers are no better than the rest of us. 'Til I can shoot you and nobody'll stop me."

Solma can't stop her jaw from falling open. Her grip on Olive slackens in surprise. "What're you—?"

"Shut up," Olive hisses, though Solma's got no idea who she's addressing. Olive lowers her pistol and holsters it. She gestures for Ana to lower her bow. The Whisperer girl curls her lip in disgust but complies. Olive folds her arms.

"Off to Sand's End, are you?" she asks. The soldier's eyes widen in puzzlement. To Solma's surprise, he fidgets like a naughty child.

"Yeah?" he says. Olive raises an eyebrow.

"When you get there," she says, "you remember I told you this: Maxen Camber is a snake, just like his Dja. You think he's saving the world. He ain't. He's killing it all over again, and he'll take you down with him."

She gestures to Ana. "Go to the cart," she says. "Make sure the kids're ok."

The soldier blinks. "You got kids with you?"

Solma folds her arms, mirroring Olive's stance. "Would've shot them just like the rest of us, would you?"

"I—" the soldier shakes his head, chastised.

"Let us go without a fight," Solma says. "It'll be better for everyone."

The soldier mutters under his breath. He brandishes a finger in Solma's face. "This time," he says. He turns and stalks back to his caravan. Solma catches Olive's gaze. They both let out a half-hearted chuckle, but it sounds flat in the cool spring air.

That was too close.

The caravan rumbles by, Gatra soldiers glaring as they pass. Burdock tosses his head and whinnies, posturing. Solma wonders if he understood what just went on, but that pony's smarter than most humans, she reckons. He probably does.

The Whisperer children watch with wide eyes as the caravan disappears down a dip in the landscape. In their fear, they've managed to grow mushrooms of all colors across most of the cart's wood and some of the beams are rotting. Bell swears, ushering them down. She starts tearing mushrooms from the wood.

"'Least you didn't rot the wheels," she mutters, glaring at the three shame-faced boys. Taipan puts her little hands on her hips, glaring, but even she knows not to antagonize an already tightly-wound Aunt Bell.

Ana slackens her bow, slotting her arrow into her quiver. Cobra and Mamba clasp hands.

"Well," Cobra says. "That was horrible."

Mamba nods. He looks like he might be sick. Solma unsheathes her hunting knife. She's keeping a weapon in her hand from now on.

"We need to stay alert," she says.

Olive nods agreement. "And we'll take turns on watch at night," she adds. "That lot won't be the last heading to Sand's End. But they might be the friend-liest."

Solma catches Cobra's eye and the Whisperer girl's face pales. Mamba shakes his head.

"Sooner we make it to the Whisperer camp," he says. "The better."

Solma sneaks a sideways glance at Cobra. Worry shines in her friend's eyes. Solma frowns, but she's not sure she can take any more bad news right now. The five of them stand in heavy silence for a moment, until Bell's voice drifts towards them on the still air.

"Boys, will you get your grubby hands *out* of the food bags! It is not lunchtime!"

Solma manages a smile. She takes a deep breath and wills herself to relax, but her shoulders are bunched with fear. She closes her eyes and feels Olive's hand grab hers.

"You ok?"

She nods. "Yeah," she lies. "Fine. Let's get moving." The ponies are eager to be off. Bell and Roseann bicker good-naturedly and the kids stay huddled in the cart. Solma tries to pretend, as they make their way through the undulating landscape, that everything is fine. That they'll find safety soon.

But she fancies she hears voices carry on every breeze. Over every ridge, she imagines another caravan heading east. Next time, weapons might be drawn and fired.

Eight

WARREN CLOSES HIS EYES—JUST for a second—and receives a shove in the back. The jolt loosens his hold on the myriad insects he's trying to control. The bumblebees huddled on his shoulder take off with a surprised buzz. Warren resists the tears that sting his eyes. No-one will have any sympathy if he cries.

Instead, he takes a moment to catch his breath and reconnect with the insects. He hates it. Every instinct tells him to just let go, let them fly free and spread their song across Alphor. Who cares if the bumblebees wander beyond the orchards? Who cares if the butterflies sip from wild crocuses instead of apple blossoms? (Not that there *are* any wild crocuses).

Maxen cares. Maxen cares a lot.

Gradually, Warren gathers the insects, feeling them as points of light and scent. The purplish-blue hue of the bee-vision pulses in his eyes as he turns to glare at Ignis.

The other boy shrugs. "You stopped," he points out. "We're late."

"We're two minutes late," Warren retorts, "and twenty metres away."

Ignis shrugs again, and looks past Warren, up the dirt path to where it divides, leading to the fenced off fields. Orchards of apple and pear trees stand in neat rows, gooseberry bushes line the perimeter and red- and blackcurrant plants huddle in the corners. The Oritch workers wait at the gates. Their blue overalls are covered with dirt and mud, but they've taken off their straw hats as if in reverence. They gaze hopefully at Warren.

Amongst them, stand several of Maxen's Gatra. They watch Warren, too, but not with reverence. Their weapons are ready, their black uniforms pristine. Warren scans the crowd and sees several faces he recognises. People who once smiled at him, ruffled his hair, fed him when he was hungry. These people raised him. Now, they stare at him with fear and hope. It's too much. Warren shoves his hands in his pockets so no-one will see how badly they're trembling.

He looks away from the crowd and catches sight of Ilga and Aldo. He's surprised to see them. For the past few days, they've been stationed at the insect nests but, today, their duties are here. Where Warren is. Warren's mouth twitches. Maxen clearly thinks Warren is more of a danger to his plans than any potential insect thieves. In the last few weeks, Warren has learned that Maxen now has a dozen Gatra squads, each ten soldiers strong, and he counts five of those squads here. Despite himself, Warren feels proud.

Maxen believes he needs fifty soldiers to control one unruly nine-year-old. Warren squares his shoulders.

"I can get there myself, thanks," he snaps. Ignis rolls his eyes, but follows Warren as he trudges up the path, insects drawing orbits around him.

The crowd of Oritch workers parts as Warren draws near. Warren sees a few of them take in his grubby clothes, pale face, and sunken eyes, before they look away. They know how Maxen's treating him. Know what their teenage Steward is like. But look at them, standing there, doing nothing. Cowards! Warren clenches his fists. The insects detect his tension, landing on his head, arms, shoulders. There are gasps from the gathered crowd and some of the youngsters stare openly. Warren's face feels hot. These are kids he knows, people he's grown up with. Now, they stare at him like he's some kind of prophet.

He glances at Ignis. The older boy scowls.

"What?" he asks. "Just get on with it. Start with that one." He waves towards Orchard One and Warren heads for it, feeling the tug of insects on his mind. They've caught the scent of early blooms and what's the use of fences and numbers to them? They don't care that Orchard One needs pollinating when Orchard Five is also in bloom. They want to spread out, to feel the warm spring sun on their gossamer wings. To explore.

Warren keeps hold of them. Just.

This way! A honeybee begs.

That way! Suggests a bumblebee.

The butterflies draw their erratic flight around Warren's head, trying to pull free of his influence. Warren clenches his jaw as he tries to keep control.

The crowd closes behind him as he heads into the first orchard. They shuffle after him, staring.

The Gatra are less awe-struck. They scowl as Warren passes, getting out of his way a beat too late, so he keeps having to stop and ask them to excuse him. They touch their weapons as they step aside. Warren feels the skin on the back of his neck prickle.

A butterfly lands on his collarbone, its wings a whisper-breath against his skin. He feels its feet flutter against him, the almost-not-there feel of its antennae under his chin. He stops just inside the gate of the orchard, closes his eyes and homes in on that little butterfly.

A female. Hatched that morning. Hungry.

Afraid.

He tries to plug into her mind while keeping a tight tether on the other insects. The honeybees fight him, but he keeps them close. He bites his lip in concentration, tasting blood.

Are you alright? He asks the butterfly. Her language is still strange to him. It's more erratic than the bees. Each butterfly's scent signature is different and sometimes they clash. He can't always get it right.

This time, though, the butterfly hears him. She shuffles her feet.

Afraid, she insists.

He reaches a hand to his throat and persuades her onto his fingers. *I know,* he says. *It's ok. There are flowers here. Explore.*

He lifts his hand so the morning sun gleams across her scarlet wings. She's like a living jewel, vibrant and precious. Warren smiles as she pumps her wings and lifts into the air, effortless as a windblown leaf. She flutters into the orchard to join her brothers and sisters. Warren sways, gripping the fence for support as waves of nausea sweep through him.

The Oritch workers let out noises of awe. Yuen chase the insects through the trees, lifting their hands in the hopes a butterfly might land there. Everyone's smiling. Many eyes glisten with tears. Someone grabs Warren's hand and squeezes it. He looks up into a gnarled face under the rim of a straw hat.

"Thank you!" the Oritch says. "You've saved us."

Warren blinks blearily but the Oritch doesn't need a reply. He lets go of Warren and wanders through the orchard, eyes wide with awe.

Warren's vision throbs purple and he feels bile at the back of his throat. "I just need to ... sit down," he mutters to no-one in particular. He slides into the dirt, his back pressed against a fencepost.

The insects pull at his mind, but he can't let them go. It hurts. Pain like bee-stings sear his mind. There's a throb behind his eyes. He's not supposed to use his power like this. As a tether. His heart screams against it, against what Maxen's making him do.

A hand lands on Warren's shoulder and he jumps. Through the purple haze of his vision, he squints at the figure standing above him.

"Why you down there?" Ignis asks.

Warren closes his eyes. "Feel ... sick," he mumbles.

Ignis grasps Warren's hand and pulls him up. Warren sways, clutching the other boy for support. He realizes, suddenly, that they're almost the same height. Ignis is a little taller, but Warren's catching up. He can almost stare directly into Ignis' eyes and, despite the purplish interference at the edges of his vision, he thinks he sees concern there. Whether it's for Warren's wellbeing, or his own skin, Warren doesn't know.

"Gotta stay standing," Ignis mutters. "Steward's coming."

Warren groans but tries to hold his own weight. He peers towards the orchard gate where the Gatra stand to attention. A ripple of excitement passes through them as two figures head up the path. They salute as Maxen approaches, followed by a figure that makes Warren's gut roll with horror. He'd forgotten how huge Vulkan is. Barrel-chested and thick-necked with powerful arms and a murderous stare. He's got the same dark hair and violet eyes as Ignis, the same flame tattoo inked above one eyebrow. Warren tastes something foul at the back of his throat.

"I can't ..."

His hold on the insects wavers. Sensing a falter in his control, a honeybee makes a break for the edge of the orchard. Warren clenches his jaw, throws out his consciousness and grabs the little bee. Wrapping his scent around her, he pulls her back to the orchard. His heart hurts.

I'm sorry he tries to say, but he's not sure how well apologies translate into bee. It's a strange notion for them, to act in a way you know you'll regret.

The bee doesn't understand. She tries to shake off his hold and, when she can't, he feels her aggression. Poison glistens on her sting. He hates this. He's turning the bees against him. They won't trust him if he treats them this way. It won't work. It—

"How many trees have they visited?"

Maxen's voice behind Warren makes him yelp and whip round. Maxen stands over him, flanked by several of his guard. His arms are folded. He frowns out over the orchard. Those bee-sting scars look worse in the sunlight. Painful. Warren stares, guiltily, until Vulkan cuffs him across the back of the head.

"Answer your Steward!"

Warren presses a palm to his stinging scalp and glares.

"I dunno," he says through gritted teeth. "It ain't easy to count while I'm trying to keep hold of them."

Maxen's jaw tightens. "You'll need to work on that," he says. "I have several trade delegations arriving in a few weeks and I need to know what I can offer."

Warren fixes Maxen with the most hateful glare he can manage. Maxen doesn't notice. He's still watching the orchard, the shooting stars of bees zipping between apple blossoms. The scarlet flash of butterfly wings. The awe in the faces of his Oritch and Yuen. Warren wonders whether Maxen sees how precious this is; the insects, the hope for the future. Probably, he wonders how much profit he can make from it. He studies Maxen's face, watching the veins in his temple pulse. Is it just Warren's imagination or does Maxen look ... out of his depth?

Scared?

"What happened to the third hive?" Warren demands suddenly. Sickness roils in his belly, but he folds his arms and tries to look brave. Maxen turns towards him, surprise in his eyes.

"What?"

"I know you had three hives," Warren pushes. "Now there's just two. What happened? Did it die?"

Maxen throws a furious glance towards Ignis. "That's none of your concern," he says.

Warren opens his mouth to retort but Ignis grips his arm.

"Don't," he growls.

Warren wrenches free, but his stomach rolls again. He leans forward, hands on knees, trying to steady his rebellious gut.

Maxen turns to the gathered Oritch, spreading his arms wide with a wolfish smile.

"Didn't my Dja promise you?" he says. "He promised we would never go hungry again. When he wakes, we will be the strongest village in our province."

Maybe only Warren is close enough to notice, but there's an edge to his voice. A manic desperation like, if he says it loud enough, means it deeply enough, he can make it true. Warren snatches a sideways glance at him and sees colour rising in Maxen's cheeks, wildness in his eyes.

The gathered crowd shift and mutter. A few look at Maxen with reverence, but many glare at him darkly. Somebody in the crowd says something Warren can't hear, but it's obviously mutinous because one of the Gatra reacts with lightning aggression. He smacks the offending Oritch to the ground, aims his rifle at the downed man.

"Apologize to your Steward!" the Gatra barks. Warren steps forward, enraged. This isn't how it's supposed to be! The Gatra are protectors, not—

Ignis' grip on his arm tightens. "Stay still," the other boy growls. "You don't wanna get involved."

The Oritch on the ground lifts trembling hands. "I'm sorry," he mumbles. "I'm sorry."

The Gatra smacks him around the back of the head. "Ungrateful wretch!" he snarls. "You forgotten how our Steward worked for us last year? Gathering those insects? Finding the Bee kid?"

The Bee kid. As if they've all forgotten Warren has a name.

"No," the Oritch says, shaking his head. "No, I haven't, I—"

The Gatra smacks him again. Warren looks at Maxen but the young Steward just stands, watching. Is he going to let this happen? Is he going to let his Gatra bully his villagers? His *people?*

"Stop it!" Warren yells and receives a rough shake from Ignis.

"Shut *up!*"

But Warren's not having this. He wrestles against Ignis' grip. "Let go! I ain't just gonna watch this happen—"

But in the end, he doesn't have to. Another soldier steps forward. Tall and confident with a sergeant's insignia on his chest. Aldo. He grabs the other soldier's wrist as it's raised to deliver another strike. Ilga hovers behind him. For the briefest moment, Warren catches her eye and sees she's … afraid. Uncertain. He scowls at her. How is it so hard for her to make the right choice?

"That's enough, private," Aldo says softly. "You've made your point."

The soldier glares. "But he's—"

"Your superior just gave you an order," Aldo says. "I suggest you follow it."

The soldier wrenches his arm free and stalks back to his squad. Aldo helps the Oritch man to his feet. Warren watches as the Oritch workers cast hateful, frightened glances at the Gatra. A mutter passes among them. Maxen's clearly bored by the whole spectacle. He turns his back on the workers.

"Vulkan," he says. "Get the Oritch back to work."

Vulkan's lip curls, his eyes flick towards Warren. He smirks. Warren wriggles.

"Yessir," Vulkan rumbles. He nods at his son. "C'mon, Ignis,"

Ignis lets go of Warren but hesitates, biting his lip. Is Warren's vision playing tricks on him or is that the ghost of concern in Ignis' face? Ignis jerks a thumb towards Warren.

"He's feeling sick—"

Vulkan grabs Ignis' arm, twisting it awkwardly. Ignis winces. He doesn't cry out, though, and a coldness creeps through Warren at the sight. This has happened before. Ignis knows not to yell, not to cry. Only a slight twitch of his mouth betrays that he's hurting. Vulkan's face is inches from Ignis.

"What do you care?" he growls. Ignis glares.

"I don't, do I?" he says. Vulkan grunts, letting go of Ignis' arm.

"Then get moving," he says.

He stalks off towards the apple trees, voice booming across the orchard. Ignis throws Warren a furious glare, as if that whole incident had somehow been Warren's fault. He trudges after his father. The Oritch workers flinch at the sound of Vulkan's shouting. They're as scared of him as Warren is. Some of the Yuen start crying. Frightened parents hush them. Eyes that had been filled with wonder now look dull with fear. Warren shakes his head, glancing up as a cloud passes across the sun. He shivers as the air becomes chill.

Maxen watches him, one eyebrow raised. "I know you think I'm cruel, Warren," he says.

"You are," Warren snaps, surprising himself. Maxen's eyes widen but he recovers quickly.

"I'm not," he insists. There's a whine in his voice, like a child protesting his innocence. "Sometimes, difficult decisions must be made for the good of the village. When Dja wakes, he needs to see I've cared for our people as best I can."

Warren doesn't know what to say. There's a mad gleam in Maxen's eyes, as if he needs Warren to agree with him. To side with him. To *love* him. Warren clamps his mouth shut and says nothing.

Maxen sighs. "When you're older, you'll understand."

"I won't," Warren insists. "I won't never get how you just take things and think that's ok. People like you are why the insects died out in the first place."

Maxen shakes his head. Warren scowls at him, thinking how Maxen's become so good at lying, he's even managed to convince himself. But then he sees that manic shine in Maxen's eyes again and thinks maybe there's still doubt there. Maybe he's not quite his father yet. Then again—

"No, Warren," Maxen says. "People like me are going to save Alphor. My father and I, we're protecting the insects—"

"You're not!"

"We *are!*" Maxen crouches in front of Warren, meeting his eyes. "They are safe here, under the watch of our Gatra, controlled by you. No one will try to take them—"

"*You've* taken them!" Warren says, stamping his foot. His vision pulses midnight blue as the insects sense his distress. A few honeybees zoom towards him, stings gleaming with poison. Warren takes a breath and tries to calm them.

"When my sister gets here—" he says. Maxen rounds on him so fast that Warren stumbles backwards, landing on his rump in the dirt.

"No!" Maxen growls. "Don't involve your sister! She's a traitor. I exiled her."

"You exiled me, too, remember!" Warren points out. "You and your precious Dja!"

"Yeah, well," Maxen says, uncertainly. "I've fixed that now, haven't I? And when Dja wakes up, he'll see ..." He runs a hand through his hair and looks away. "Your sister's a traitor," he says again. "A criminal."

"No," Warren says, getting to his feet. "She ain't. She's a hero. And she's coming to—"

"No, she's *not!*" Maxen insists, eyes wild again. "She can't come back. If she comes back, you know what I'll have to do?"

A sudden sickness claws Warren's throat. Triumph flashes in Maxen's eyes.

"I'll have to kill them," he says. His voice is ragged, wretched. But Warren can tell he means it. "It's what Dja expects of me. I'll ... have no choice."

Warren stares at him. He's losing his mind. He must be. Blaiz isn't going to wake up. It's a miracle he's not dead yet, locked in that bee-sting coma for more than a year. How Maxen has managed to keep him from starving is beyond Warren's understanding. He must have raided some old-world hospital, threatened poor Gerta into using her knowledge to keep his father alive.

Maxen stands, turning his attention to the orchards. The manic gleam in his eyes flickers out. He looks in control again. The perfect politician.

The Oritch return to their duties. They're quiet and subdued, ignoring the insects that zip around them. Every so often, they cast wary glances towards Ignis and Vulkan. The Fire Makers patrol the rows of trees, glaring at everyone.

"We'd both better hope your sister doesn't try to rescue you," Maxen murmurs. "I don't want to have to kill her. But ..." his lip trembles. "But I will. If I must."

Warren's throat closes and he struggles to breathe. This has all gone so wrong.

There's no way Solma will abandon him. Warren's got no doubt she'll set the world on fire to save him, if she must. But if she comes here—

No. Warren can't let that happen. He needs to find a way to rescue himself.

He turns his back on Maxen, trying to control the roar of blood in his ears, and heads out into the orchard.

Nine

SOLMA CAN BARELY LIFT her head. Her shoulders bunch. There's a lancing pain behind her eyes. Her right knee is swollen, which often happens when she travels a long way on foot. Her flesh-and-blood leg compensates for the fact her left leg is half prosthetic, taking most of the weight. Several times over the last week, her right knee has threatened to buckle, and she's had to ride on the cart to rest.

She should do that now, but Krait and King are sleeping on the cart beside the rolled-up tents. The ponies are exhausted and she doesn't want to add to their load. She can cope. She must.

The undulating northern plains roll around them, though they've left the eastern mountains far be-hind. Tussock grasses and scrubby shrubs dot the landscape, catching the cartwheels occasionally. The constant up-and-down is helping no-one's mood and

Poppy has expressed her irritation on numerous occasions. Bell's nursing a bruised shoulder where the mare kicked her two days ago. Roseann patched her up and, by some miracle, nothing was broken. Poppy took an age to calm down and, to no-one's surprise, it was Burdock that managed it. He had touched his velvety muzzle to hers, standing calmly until she stopped prancing and accepted his comfort. Clever boy.

The spring sun rides low on the horizon. Mist clings to the ground, making it harder for Solma to judge her footfalls. She stumbles, and feels Burdock pause beside her while she catches herself against him. He turns, those liquid eyes watching her carefully. She smiles.

"I'm alright, boy," she says, patting his side. "Thanks."

He sets off again, nudging Poppy into movement beside him. A hand touches Solma's shoulder and she jumps, but it's only Olive. The other girl's green eyes shine with concern.

"You ok?"

"Yeah," Solma says, then bites her lip. Why does the lie always come so easily? "No. I'm knackered. My knee hurts. How far did Mamba say it was to this damn camp?"

Olive loops her arm through Solma's, taking a little of Solma's weight. "He reckons we'll be there by this afternoon," she says. "It ain't far, now."

Solma nods grimly. This afternoon is hours away. She stares ahead, past where Ana walks with Bell, where Roseann trudges, holding hands with Taipan and Habu, to Mamba and Cobra. They walk at the front of their little procession, their hands interlocked. Solma frowns. Is it just her, or is the line of Mamba's shoulders tighter than usual?

"He looks tense," she says. Olive's eyes darken.

"Yeah," she agrees. "He's been weird since we packed down camp."

"Hmm," Solma says, remembering Cobra's strange conversation from a few days before. "They've all been weird since we decided to head this way."

Something nags at her, some warning in the back of her head. She eyes each of her Whisperer friends in turn. Ana has removed her bow and arrow. She must have stashed them amongst the supplies in the cart. Why would she do that?

Olive turns her gaze on Solma, a smile tugging her lips. "I ever tell you, you look really cute covered in sweat and grime after months on the run?"

Solma nudges Olive playfully, but can't help the grin that comes, unbidden, to her face. "Don't tease."

"I ain't!" Olive protests, hand on heart. "It's the truest thing I ever did tell."

Solma laughs and leans her head on Olive's shoulder. Olive plants a kiss on her temple.

"Mmm," Olive says, wrinkling her nose. "Dirt, rain and body odour. Delicious."

Solma casts her a withering glare but can't maintain the pretense. The pair of them collapse into ridiculous giggles. Solma squeezes Olive's arm. She knows what Olive's doing. Already, her knee feels a little less sore. The laughter helps invigorate her. With Olive at her side, perhaps the next few hours won't be so painful.

Gradually, the sun climbs, its warmth growing. At one point, there's a sudden, brief rain shower. The kids shelter under the cart, but Solma tilts her face up to feel the drizzle against her skin. Once the rain has finished, and they push on. A river gurgles in the distance. They haven't seen anyone for miles.

Finally, they crest a ridge and Mamba points into the distance, towards a little area of woodland stretching across the rolling landscape.

"There," he says. Solma, still supported by Olive, comes to stand beside him. She squints and shakes her head.

"There what?" she asks. All she can see is the forest, a few tussock-grass mounds lining its edge. "There's nothing there."

Mamba grins. "Keep watching," he says. Solma does as she's told. After a while, something amongst the tussock-grass mounds moves. Solma stiffens, reaching for her hunting knife, but Mamba hushes her. From this distance, it's hard to see, but now that Solma thinks about it, the tussock-grass mounds are arranged in a kind of circle against the treeline. They're almost uniform in size and shape. As Solma watches, one of the mounds opens. A figure creeps out, dressed in green robes. Solma's eyes widen.

"Oh," she says. "Clever,"

Mamba winks. "One of the great things about being a Whisperer," he says. "Camouflage is easy." The smile falls from his face. He casts an agitated glance back towards the cart where the youngsters huddle. Solma follows his gaze and realizes he's looking at their feet. Trails of mushrooms bloom in their footprints. Silver filaments spiderweb across the cart where their hands touch it. He frowns.

"We gotta be careful," he mutters. Solma opens her mouth to ask why, then closes it again. She remembers his fear of connecting with the mycelia last year. Remembers what he said about how only the strongest Whisperers are allowed to attempt such a thing. She's sure there's a punishment for breaking that rule. Given the look of fear in Mamba's eyes, she's not sure she wants to know what it is.

It's downhill to the Whisperer camp. Solma's right knee throbs. Roseann ushers the boys down from the cart. They complain, but it isn't far. Roseann hitches Krait onto her hip and holds King's hand.

Quiet as she always is nowadays, Taipan wanders along between Cobra and Mamba, holding Cobra's hand. Toadstools and lichen sprout wherever her bare feet touch the earth. The heady scent of truffles follows in her wake. Solma thinks they've probably left a trail of fungi all the way across Alphor. But it hasn't escaped her notice that the youngsters struggle to control their new power when they're angry or frightened. And it's got worse the closer they draw to the Whisperer Camp.

The land levels out and the river comes into view. As they descend into another dip in the landscape, Burdock snorts and draws to a halt. Solma touches his neck. "What's up, boy?" she asks. "C'mon, we gotta keep moving—"

Mamba holds up a hand. Suddenly, where there was no-one, there are five figures moving towards them. All with shaved heads, dressed in emerald robes. Two carry bows, with quivers of arrows at their hips. A third carries a short, wooden javelin. But it's the fourth and fifth figures that draw Solma's eye. An older woman stands at the front of the group, glaring at Mamba with a look on her face that suggests she's just found something vile stuck to the sole of her foot.

Beside her stands the biggest, burliest Whisperer Solma has ever seen. He's unarmed, but Solma eyes his solid fists and thinks he can do plenty of damage with those.

Solma chews her lip as she watches the figures approach. Mamba turns, beckoning, and the six Whisperers of his little troupe gather at his side. Solma sees him muttering urgently to them and thinks she catches the word *mycelia*.

Not good.

Solma and Olive hang back with Bell, Roseann and the ponies. This is Whisperer business. Though Solma's desperate to hear what's going on, something tells her it'll work out better if she stays back.

The five strangers are all older than Mamba, the youngest looks at the end of his teenage years. The oldest doesn't look like she's much younger than Aunt Bell. They are three men and two women, a mix of heights and skin-tones, with eyes ranging from deep, brown-black to piercing gold and verging on pink, which Solma finds disturbing. The woman standing at the front of the procession grows more agitated as she and Mamba converse. Solma reaches for Olive's hand.

"I don't like this," she mutters.

Olive shakes her head. "Me either."

Solma studies them each in turn, the tense line of their shoulders, the hostility in their stance. These don't look like the gentle Whisperers she knows Mamba and his troupe to be. They look like warriors.

She glances again at the burly Whisperer at the centre and balks, hand snapping to her pistol. It's him! How can he be here? She tries to unholster her pistol, but Olive's hand is on hers, keeping her still. Solma can't take her eyes off the Whisperer, off the dark stubble covering his scalp, the sneer on his lips, his hulking outline. He's huge, rippling with muscle and power. His face turns, his eyes meeting hers. It's Vulkan. It's—

No, it's not Vulkan. There's no flame tattoo above his eyebrow and his eyes are blue rather than violet. He has a tangle of vines tattooed up his neck, over the back of his scalp. It's not Vulkan. But Earth, it looks like him.

"Sol," Olive mutters. Solma forces herself to let go of her pistol. The huge Whisperer smirks and Solma thinks he's enjoying her fear. She glares.

Finally, Mamba beckons Solma and the others over to join them. A frown creases his brow. Solma helps Bell lead the ponies over and Mamba introduces the group of strangers.

"Sidewinder," he says, indicating the older woman in the centre. "The Seasons charge her and her troupe with the law and security of the Camp."

Solma glances sideways at him and sees fear in his face. Sidewinder lifts her chin, staring down her nose at the newcomers. She's white-skinned but with a deep tan and a smattering of freckles across her nose. Her head is shaved but Solma can see from the stubble across her scalp that she's blonde. Her eyes are a deep, unfathomable black, and full of disdain. It takes everything in Solma's power not to bristle. She gives a curt nod of greeting. Sidewinder gives no acknowledgement.

Mamba gestures to the man and woman holding bows and arrows. The woman is a little older than Solma and Olive, black-skinned with sunburst yellow eyes. Mamba introduces her as Cascabel. The man is so pale-skinned, Solma wonders if he's ever seen sunlight. His eyes are amber, and he looks to be somewhere around Bell's age. Keelback, his name is. Solma offers them both a tight smile. Neither of them return it. The final Whisperer—the man-boy with the javelin—is Copperhead. He doesn't take his gaze off Mamba, a look of deep disdain in his almost-pink eyes. He's white-skinned with sun-blotches across his face. The stubble over his scalp is dark.

Solma turns her attention to the burly Whisperer who looks so much like Vulkan. He meets her gaze and Solma resists the urge to reach for her pistol again. She holds Olive's hand tightly instead.

"This," Mamba says sullenly, "is Urutu. The Camp's tracker."

Tracker? Solma can't stop her lips parting in surprise. Back in Sand's End, the best trackers in the Gatra had been wiry and slight, nimbler than shadows. This man is built like an old-world war machine. Solma can't imagine him moving anywhere quietly. He catches sight of her surprise. His grin widens. Solma scowls.

Sidewinder squares her shoulders. "This is a waste of time," she snaps. "You know what my answer's gonna be."

She stares imperiously at Mamba and Solma hates how the boy who has led them across Alphor, taken Solma and her family in as his own, now can't even raise his gaze to meet Sidewinder's. He stands before her like a scolded child and Solma bristles. She turns a furious glare on Sidewinder, wondering who this woman thinks she is.

Sidewinder glares back, unflinching. She searches Mamba face. Her jaw tightens.

"Look at me, boy," she says. Mamba winces. At a gesture from Sidewinder, the other strangers raise their weapons. Urutu clenches his fists. Solma's hand goes to her knife and, beside her, Olive does the same.

"Look at me!" Sidewinder says again. "All of you!"

There's an edge to her voice. Is that fear? Solma feels her gut tighten. She unsheathes her knife but forces herself to keep it lowered.

Finally, Mamba raises his eyes. The frown falls from Sidewinder's face, replaced by open shock. Suddenly, Solma understands. She's seen the dark rings around his irises. She knows. Frantically, Sidewinder searches the faces of all Solma's Whisperer friends. Her gaze darts to their feet, where, in their fear, they've been unable to contain their power. White-dotted redcaps shoot from the ground, sprouting before their eyes. The silver filaments of the mycelia draw glistening threads across the grass. A musty, fungal smell fills the air.

Sidewinder's face darkens. "*What have you done?*" she growls.

Mamba's shoulders tense. He averts his gaze, like a scolded child. Cobra steps in front of him, eyes ablaze.

"What we had to," she says. "And it turns out, you and The Seasons have some questions to answer."

Sidewinder sneers. "You've disobeyed our oldest rule, kid," she says. Solma stiffens at the way she calls Cobra *kid*.

"Easy, Sol," Olive murmurs. Solma realizes she's raising her knife. She lowers it.

Cobra straightens her shoulders, an arm around Taipan. "We had no choice," she says. "If you'd been there, you'd—"

"I'd have stuck to the rules!" Sidewinder retorts. "You're not an elder, you can't contain that sort of power. The Seasons'll hear about this."

Solma clenches her jaw. She remembers Cobra mentioning The Seasons, but Cobra never did explain who—or what—they are. From the way Mamba stiffens and Cobra blanches, it seems they're something to be feared.

At last, little Taipan steps forward. Unafraid, she gazes up at Sidewinder. The five strangers shift their weight uncomfortably.

"The Seasons are connected like we are," she says.

Sidewinder scowls. "That's different. The rules—"

"Perhaps it's time for rules to change," Taipan suggests. "Let's go."

She heads past Sidewinder and the troupe, hitching her robes up so she doesn't trip. She's not even trying to hide the mushrooms that fruit in her footprints.

The strangers watch her, mouths agape. Solma ducks her head to hide the smirk she can't suppress. Clever Taipan. Warren's picked his best friend wisely.

Furious, Sidewinder rounds on Mamba again. This time gesturing at Solma and Olive.

"Gatra?" she drawls. "You've lost your minds—"

"We ain't Gatra no more," Olive says sharply. "We got thrown outta our village. We're just protectors."

Sidewinder snorts and frowns at Mamba. "I see Python's influence rubbed off on you more than we thought," she says. "This is a new low, Mamba."

Mamba says nothing, but he lifts his gaze to meet hers. There's defiance in his eyes and Solma feels a spark of pride. Good.

Sidewinder glares, then huffs an impatient sigh. She turns her back on him. "The Seasons are expecting you," she throws over her shoulder.

"'Course they are," Mamba grumbles.

Sidewinder doesn't respond, but at a gesture from her, Urutu steps in front of Solma and Olive. Up close he's enormous and even Solma, who's taller than almost everyone she's ever known, must crane her neck to look at his face.

"We don't like weapons in camp," he says. "You'll leave them with me before you enter." He holds up a hand as Olive starts to protest. "They'll be returned to you before you leave. You have my word."

Solma's not sure how much she trusts Urutu's word, but it seems they don't have much choice. Reluctantly, she and Olive hand over their weapons and, after much persuasion, Bell relinquishes her rolling pin.

Urutu shoulders the rifles, straps the pistols and knives to his own hip. He smirks before he trudges after Sidewinder and his troupe-mates.

Solma gives Cobra a quizzical look. The Whisperer girl shrugs. Dragging his feet, Mamba leads his Whisperers after Sidewinder and her troupe. Solma strokes Burdock's velvety nose.

"C'mon then, boy," she says.

They follow Sidewinder up the shallow ridge, stopping once to pull the cart from a hidden patch of mud. Nobody says anything.

At last, they reach the circle of tussock-grass mounds, which turn out not to be mounds but domed mud huts grown over with grass and vines. Between the huts sit a few tents, covered with leaves and moss. It's not a large camp, no bigger than a village square, with several small fire pits dug out in the centre and green-robed Whisperers of all ages milling about. A few ponies graze at the perimeter, and a couple of dogs wander around, looking for food or attention. A group of a dozen children sit cross-legged while an older Whisperer, perhaps in her late teens, instructs them in the process of encouraging a seedling to life. Beyond them, two Whisperers who look to be somewhere in their twenties sit in carved chairs, mending robes. The smell of vegetable stew wafts from a fireplace where an elderly Whisperer tends a pot. Small groups, that Solma takes to be wandering troupes like Mamba's, sit together in clusters, eating or having wounds tended.

Sidewinder pauses at the edge of camp. She turns to fix Solma and the others with a hard stare. "I'll warn you," she says. "You won't find welcome here."

She's not wrong. Silence falls as they enter the camp. Eyes of all colors turn towards them. Gazes harden with mistrust. A boy from another troupe, perhaps sixteen or seventeen, gets to his feet when he sees them. He steps into Mamba's path, their faces inches apart. Mamba keeps his eyes lowered but Solma sees how he grips Cobra's hand. The other boy's mouth curves downward as if he's smelled something unpleasant.

"Din't think we'd see you round here again," he says. "You better not be staying long."

"We aren't," Mamba mutters. He sidesteps the other boy without another word. Solma catches the boy's eye as she passes and fixes him with the meanest glare she can. He meets her stare with equal disdain. The prospect of converting this lot into an army to fight alongside them suddenly seems a childlike fancy.

Sidewinder leads them to the hut nearest to the tree line. Solma notices it's taller and broader than the others, wreathed in ivy and other leafy vines, perhaps to mark it as important. Sidewinder points to a patch of ground beside the hut.

"Wait here," she says. "I'll speak to The Seasons. You'll be given food and the ponies will be taken care of." She turns to Solma and gives her an appraising look. "One of our healers can have a look at your knee," she adds.

Solma feels heat warm her cheeks.

"It's fine," comes Roseann's gruff voice before Solma can say anything insulting. "I can see to our lot. But water, food and a few boiled bandages won't go amiss."

Sidewinder nods. "Fine. Don't move around the camp. I have no idea when The Seasons will want to see you, but—"

"Actually," comes a small voice from amongst them. Everybody looks down. Taipan stands in front of Sidewinder, orange eyes blazing. Her bare toes curl into the grass and Solma knows the mycelia are speaking to her. Sidewinder scowls.

"Actually, *what?*"

If Taipan registers the aggression, she doesn't acknowledge it.

"Actually, we'd like to see Python," she says.

Ten

WELL, THAT HAD BEEN an ordeal. Solma had known Python was kept imprisoned. She hadn't realized he was so strictly isolated.

Sidewinder and Mamba had argued for an hour about his right (or not) to see Python. Though they have now been granted permission by the mysterious Seasons, Sidewinder and Urutu aren't happy about it. They lead Solma and her friends into the little woodland with stormy expressions. Urutu keeps glancing over his shoulder at Solma, a strange light in his blue eyes. Again, Solma is struck by how like Vulkan he looks. The skin on the back of her neck prickles whenever she meets his eye. Her fingers twitch, aching for her pistol or hunting knife. But, of course, she has neither.

Solma feels Olive's fingers entwine with hers.

"This is going well," Olive mutters. Solma rolls her eyes in agreement.

"When is it ever?" she points out. They fall silent, trying to keep up with Sidewinder.

Bell and Roseann stayed with the ponies. Bell tried to get Solma to sit down so Roseann could see to her knee, but Solma wasn't going to let Olive and the Whisperers out of her sight. Her knee twinges. She knows she should be resting it, but there's no time.

The sounds of the Whisperer camp fade, replaced by the soft rustle of a breeze through leaves, rodents skittering for cover. It's not a long walk, but Solma's in enough pain that she's relieved when they reach another Whisperer hut. It's nestled in the middle of the little wood, covered in tussock-grass, vines and moss. There is no visible door. Two Whisperers stand guard outside it, each with a hand pressed against the grasses and vines that cover it, as if controlling the growth, ensuring nothing can get in. Or out.

Python's prison.

The Whisperers on guard tense when they see Sidewinder approaching. When they notice Mamba, their lips curl in disdain. Solma frowns. Why does every Whisperer in this camp look at Mamba as if he's something vile? Why does he avert his eyes and take their meanness as if it's no more than he deserves?

"Why's *he* here?" One of the guard Whisperers asks. Sidewinder holds up a hand.

"They've been granted audience with Python," she says. The guards start to protest but Sidewinder glares them into silence.

"The Seasons gave permission," she snaps. "Stand aside. Let them through."

"*All* of them?" one of the guards splutters. At a look from Sidewinder, he quails.

"Let. Them. Through." The Whisperer woman snarls.

Without another word, the guards close their eyes and Whisper. Solma's eyes widen as the hut trembles. The vines, moss and grass peel aside to reveal a door. It's pitch-dark inside. When Solma hobbles over to take a closer look, she sees the ground open into a deep, dark hole. A wooden ladder leads into the gloom below.

"You keep him down there?" she demands. Sidewinder gives her a withering glare.

"It's the only safe place," she says. "I don't take kindly to village folk questioning Whisperer ways. Your lot aren't exactly shining examples of humanity."

Solma glares, but the woman has a point.

"You have fifteen minutes," Sidewinder says. "No more. Get going before I change my mind."

Solma bristles, but a small hand touches her shoulder. She turns to find Cobra standing behind her. The Whisperer girl gives a slight shake of her head and Solma forces herself to stand down. Cobra squeezes Solma's arm.

"C'mon," she says. "We'll talk below."

Solma sits, massaging her knee, while Ana and Cobra help the children down the ladder. She and Olive follow Mamba into the darkness. Solma's blade-foot slips on the ladder and she curses as her knee throbs. But it's not a long climb and her feet soon hit soft, packed earth. She looks up in time to see the light from the door disappear, the grasses and vines creeping back into place. They've been sealed in.

No going back now.

Olive fumbles on her belt for her torch, pumps the wind-up handle and flicks it on. A weak beam illuminates the little group. Solma grabs her own torch and winds it up, too. It's barely enough to see by, but it's enough to show the fear on everyone's face.

Everyone except Taipan, who takes Mamba's hand.

"Come on," she says, pulling him into the gloom. "He's this way."

They follow Taipan down a short tunnel. The underground chamber is wide, reinforced with wooden beams that loom out of the darkness every so often. Roots dangle from the ceiling and protrude from the walls. The ground is soft underfoot.

Cobra and Solma walk side by side. In the weak torchlight, Solma sees the Whisperer girl is ashen.

"You ok?" Solma murmurs. Cobra nods, then hesitates and shakes her head.

"It's just ..." she whispers. "He's been down here. All this time ..."

Solma grabs her friend's hand again and holds it tightly. Whoever these Seasons are, she thinks, she'll be having a word with them about this later. It seems cruel to cut a Whisperer off from the world above. Plants thrive in sunlight. To never see the sun, never feel its growing power, must be hellish.

"Co," she says gently. "I think ... if you can ... we might need some answers."

Cobra nods, though her expression is pained.

"It's difficult to explain to anyone who's not a Whisperer," she begins. "But our ways have always been there to protect us. We don't ... have the best life expectancy, see, so anyone who makes it to a ... a certain age, has the right to become an Elder. They store their knowledge in the Earth, become more powerful to ensure the Whisperer community survives. Only the strongest of us make it that far, and that's when we might connect with the mycelia. But it's a difficult power to control. Our rules are strict. No Whisperer under the age of thirty can connect and, even if we reach that age, we must be granted permission based on our abilities and our histories. The Seasons almost never grant permission.

"When ... when Python reached into the Earth five years ago and connected, they were furious. They felt it eventually, of course. Because ..." she pauses and Solma sees tears shining in her eyes.

"Because they're connected," she says quietly. "I remember Tai saying."

Cobra nods. "They sent someone after him. After ... after *us.*"

Solma swears under her breath. She should have guessed. This was more than just Whisperer history to Cobra. It's *personal.* "You were with him at the time," she murmurs. It's not a question. But still, Cobra murmurs acknowledgement.

"It was Sidewinder and her lot that came for him. They bound his hands and feet so he couldn't touch the earth. They put cloth over his eyes. It was horrible—"

She bites her lip, but a whimper escapes her. Solma feels the way her friend's hands tremble. Anger boils in her gut. Cruel leaders delivering ruthless punishments. All this sounds so familiar. Then a terrible thought occurs to Solma.

"That can't have been long after you left—" she swallows a lump in her throat. "I mean, after you were exiled from Sand's End?" she says.

"A year or two," Cobra admits. "I'd been with the troupe for eighteen months. Python found me. Without him, I'd have died. And they *took* him, Sol. Took him, and left us like we were nothing. We were so young, me and Mamba. Ana and Habu had only just joined us and ... Four kids in the wilderness. Told us we'd harboured a criminal. A *defiant.* They said we'd never find welcome in the camp. That our names would be spoken as warnings for others. They took him and ... they left us."

Solma doesn't know what to say. It's a terrible story. She imagines Mamba, no more than twelve-years-old, thrust into a position of responsibility for three young people in the harsh wilderness. She imagines Cobra's grief as Python—the man who saved her life—was snatched away. Imagines the fear of four children lost out there in a huge, terrifying world. It's a miracle they survived. Perhaps, says a dark thought at the back of her mind, perhaps The Seasons would rather they hadn't.

No wonder Mamba was worried about linking to the mycelia. No wonder he's been so afraid to come back here.

A clammy hand slips into Solma's fingers and she glances down to find Habu staring at her with big, worried eyes.

"Um ..." he says. She winks at him and tries to make her face look reassuring.

"Don't worry," she says. "I'm here. Be brave, like you were in the caves last summer."

Habu bites his lip and nods. He'd been partnered with Solma last year during the plan to rescue Warren from the Fire Makers. Everything had gone wrong. They'd failed. Warren was taken and the glade, full of precious insects, was destroyed. But Habu stuck at Solma's side. He played a part in helping her rescue their friends. Solma's got an even deeper respect for him now. Now that she knows he was with Cobra, Mamba and Ana when Python was taken. He can't have been more than four or five at the time. He might barely remember. But the fear in his eyes says he does remember. All too well.

It's not long before the tunnel opens into a small, round chamber. In the centre, something glows dimly. They've given the poor man a light, at least.

Slowly, they move inside and Solma sees the dim light pulse slightly. It glows an eerie blue-white. As they move closer, it illuminates the outline of a man. He's kneeling, barefoot, the grizzled stubble on his scalp a little longer than it ought to be for a Whisperer. He's wearing robes, but they're grey with dirt, their seams fraying. Although Solma can see he's black-skinned, five years in this underground prison have leeched the pigment from him.

When he looks up, his skin appears ash-grey, his face gaunt, cheekbones jutting.

But that isn't what makes everyone draw back. It isn't what makes Cobra let out a strangled cry, or Mamba swear brutally. It isn't what makes Ana shudder, the boys scurry behind Solma's and Olive's legs.

What makes them do that is his eyes. They're … *glowing*. The Whisperers above haven't left him a light source at all. *He's* the light source. His irises pulse a strange, white-blue, so bright it's impossible to see his pupils. His hands are knuckle-deep in the soil and his lips move soundlessly. He's looking right at Solma and, although she's frozen to the spot, she realizes he can't see her at all. Or, if he can, he hasn't registered she's there.

He's far away, flowing through the tangled silver filaments that run under this forest, that run under everything. His mind could be anywhere in Alphor right now, jumping from tree root to tree root, from grass to moss to sapling.

Because that's what the mycelia is; a fungal network that connects every plant to every other, running the length and breadth of Alphor.

And this is what Mamba meant when he said only the most powerful Whisperers can safely connect to it. When he said everyone else gets lost—goes *weird*—at its magnitude.

The man that used to be Python ... Solma doesn't think he's in this body anymore. He *is* the mycelia. He's the network of the world. Her heart constricts and she can't breathe. This was all pointless. More than two weeks' journey away from Sand's End and all for nothing.

This man can't help them. This man doesn't even remember who he is. She's abandoned Warren to Maxen for two weeks and more, for nothing.

Her shoulders sag and she looks up to meet Olive's gaze. There's a grim set to Olive's mouth. Solma knows from that flash in her eyes, she's thinking there isn't time to waste. And she's right. They won't find an army here. Python can't help them.

Cobra kneels in front of Python and takes his face in her hands, gently moving it so that she can look into his eyes. Her own are glassy with tears but Python doesn't notice. His lips still move ceaselessly.

"Python?" Cobra says. "Py, can you hear me?"

A frown creases Python's brow, but otherwise, there's no sign he's heard her at all.

"I know you're in there," Cobra says. "You need to come back. You need to—"

She chokes back a sob and Mamba crouches beside her. "It's ok, Co," he says. "Let him be. Let him go."

"Why isn't he fighting?" Cobra sobs. "Why's he just sitting there?"

"He can't fight," Mamba says, his voice cracking. "They've trapped him. The prison is ... the mycelia. They've locked him in it. Strangled his power."

He pulls Cobra into a hug. She fights him for a moment, then gives in. Her face crumples. "No. They can't have done this to him. They—"

She buries her face in Mamba's shoulder. He rocks her gently, hushing her.

Solma can't bear it. She steps towards them, reaches out a hand, then thinks better of it and clenches her fist. Cobra was under ten when she was forced out of Sand's End. When Solma, heartbroken, betrayed her to Blaiz. She hadn't been Cobra the Whisperer back then, just plain Kobi, the little girl that everyone insisted was a boy, trying to live the way she wanted.

Trying to understand this strange and precious power she had.

Solma spent so long having pushed Kobi out of her mind. A part of her always believed that little girl, the best friend she used to adore, had died in the wilderness.

But that wasn't true. She'd survived.

She'd found the Whisperers. This man, Python, had taken her in. He'd become a parent to her. And then she lost him, too. Snatched from her, by the very people she'd thought would protect her.

Solma tries to imagine what it would be like to find her own Ma or Dja down here, lost to a kind of madness, cut off from the sun for years on end. Her heart lurches and she feels a flush of anger. This isn't fair. This isn't *right*.

Olive touches her shoulder, a deep frown drawing her eyebrows together.

"Time's nearly up," she says.

They head in silence along the tunnel and reach the ladder in time to see the door open above. Sidewinder peers down at them.

"Up you come," she says.

Everyone is subdued on the walk back to the camp. Solma risks a glance at Cobra and sees tears drawing tracks down her friend's face. Mamba has an arm around her, though his own eyes look haunted.

Solma glares at Sidewinder's back as the Whisperer leads them through the wood. Behind her, she feels Urutu's eyes on her. Knowing how these two Whisperers left her friends to die in the wilderness, Solma can barely contain her rage. She clenches her fists but even that doesn't stop the tremor in her hands. She wishes she had her hunting knife. She wishes this was a problem she could solve with weapons and combat, the things she's good at. The things she knows. But it isn't.

Solma's not sure she can solve it at all.

Eleven

Solma strokes Burdock's velvety nose, smiling as the pony nudges her for treats.

"I ain't got any, remember?" she chuckles, kissing him between the eyes. "Sorry, boy."

Burdock nuzzles her in forgiveness. He stands calmly while Solma and scratches his forelock. He seems to know when she needs distracting.

And she does. She keeps her attention firmly fixed on the ponies. She stubbornly refuses to look around her, where she knows the other Whisperers in the camp are giving their group a wide berth, throwing accusing glances their way. It hasn't been a very warm reception.

Sidewinder has allocated them a patch of grass around an earthen fire pit. The group are permitted to pitch no more than two tents and were firmly instructed not to wander off, which got Solma's back up.

Bell tried to make the best of it. The Whisperers have, at least, provided them with food and Bell, unsurprisingly, had a fire going and a pot of something delicious bubbling over it in a matter of minutes. Krait's asleep in Ana's lap. King lies on his back in the grass and Taipan sits with Habu, both quietly eating their second bowl of broth under Roseann's watchful eye. Solma hasn't seen Cobra or Mamba since they and Olive finished pitching the tents. The two Whisperers disappeared inside without a word, their faces drawn with grief. Solma feels a stab of anger every time she thinks about Cobra's eyes shining with tears, Mamba's look of shock. It makes her want to lash out and she has to close her eyes for a few minutes to calm down. She doesn't know how to fix this. Not without a weapon in her hand.

Burdock's helping. Solma cups her hands around his nostrils and blows on his muzzle. Burdock blinks slowly and lets out a slow breath in reply. Solma's learned to read this as friendship. As horse for, *I care. I've got your back.*

It settles her, that slow, steady, horse-breath against her face, smelling of sweat and hay. She breathes it in, closes her eyes, pretends they're back on the road and that Warren is trudging along beside her. But, of course, when she opens her eyes, she's still surrounded by the Whisperer camp, the accusing stares. And there is no Warren beside her.

Because she left him.

She left him to Ignis and his father.

One of the tent flaps flies open and Olive climbs out, pulling her flame-red hair into a braid. Her face is thunderous.

"Any word?" she asks. Solma shakes her head.

"Nothing."

Olive's eyes flash and she glares towards the largest grass-hut at the edge of the camp, where Sidewinder disappeared four hours beforehand, promising to return soon.

"This is pointless," Olive snaps. "We tried, but it ain't gonna work. We should go—"

She stops, looking past Solma with a scowl. Solma turns in time to see the grass-hut peel open and Sidewinder emerging.

"'Bout time," Olive grumbles. Solma agrees, but nudges Olive to remind the other girl to be diplomatic. Olive refuses to take the hint. Her scowl remains fixed as Sidewinder trudges towards them. She gives a shallow bow as she approaches, but there's an irritable glint in her eye.

"They'll see you," she says. Olive tenses and Solma feels their hands brush.

"When?" Olive asks. Sidewinder gives her a withering look.

"Now. Obviously."

Olive rolls her eyes. "It's fine to keep us waiting for hours on end, but we gotta run when they call?" she drawls. "D'you not hear what Mamba told you? We ain't got time to waste! Maxen's making trade deals. Caravans are already heading to Sand's End. He's stealing *children!* We got to—"

Sidewinder holds up a hand. Olive lets out a frustrated growl and turns away. Sidewinder is unmoved. She clasps her hands again.

"If what you tell us is true—"

"It *is!*" Olive insists, whirling round. Sidewinder raises an eyebrow. Olive glares.

"*If,*" Sidewinder begins again, "what you're saying is true, we'll need to discuss the best course of action. Whisperers work the land, not the leadership. We've got the freedom of Alphor because we remain neutral. It's not our way to get involved in village politics."

"This ain't just *politics!*" Olive rages. "It's everything! Maxen's trying to take the insects so he can get rich. You get that, right? You get what will happen if he does that? It's already happening. Power plays. Then war. Then the insects die out all over again. You want that?"

She advances on Sidewinder, their faces inches apart. Solma feels the waves of anger pouring off Olive and touches the other girl's wrist.

"Olive," she says. She loops her fingers through Olive's. "Let's say that to The Seasons."

Sidewinder nods approval. "And if I were you," she says, her voice clipped. "I'd do so *calmly.*"

Olive's eyes flash, but Sidewinder turns her back. "Choose your representatives," she says. "And hurry up. They don't have time to waste."

"Why?" Olive mutters, quietly enough that only Solma can hear. "What else are they doing all day? I ain't seen them come outta that hut once."

Solma squeezes her hand. "Let's get Cobra and Mamba," she suggests, wondering how she's managing to stay so calm. Tension bunches in her shoulders and the ache behind her eyes throbs. Maybe it's not calm. Maybe it's tiredness. Maybe it's defeat.

She rolls her shoulders, willing energy through her body.

Warren needs her.

Olive fetches Cobra and Mamba. The Whisperers are both subdued but they fall into step, heading into the large grass-hut as Sidewinder Whispers the vine door open again. It's dark inside with only a white-green glow lighting the earthen room within.

Solma blinks, waiting for her eyes to adjust. Sidewinder steps in behind them and Whispers the door closed.

Somehow, the grass-hut feels bigger on the inside than it looked on the outside. They're standing in a circular room, a little like a small council hall, with no windows. The mud walls, packed with roots, seem to flow into the earthen floor so that Solma feels as if she's underground again. The air tastes thick and musty with damp. Solma's fingers twitch, wishing her hunting knife was close. Instead, she finds Olive's hand and clasps it. She looks around as her eyes adjust to the gloom, and sees that the white-green light is pulsing from clusters fungus clinging to the walls, the ceiling, patches on the floor. The ache behind Solma's eyes flares and she pinches the bridge of her nose, waiting for it to pass.

"Well?" Sidewinder snaps. "Are you gonna talk to them or not?"

Solma opens her eyes, frowning. She glances at Olive and sees the same look of puzzlement in the other girl's eyes, but Mamba and Cobra glare into the gloom at the far end of the hut. Solma follows their gaze. As the fungal light pulses, Solma sees a raised, earthen dais with four chairs packed close. Except, they're not chairs. Not really. They're twisted roots and vines, climbing plants and silver threads, tightly wound around and beneath four human figures. The figures look as if they were once dressed in green robes, just like every Whisperer, but those robes have long since fallen to tatters and now, the four figures are covered only with curling vines and criss-crossing roots.

Solma feels Olive's hand tighten around hers as the four of them draw nearer. Trepidation prickles at the back of her neck. Her pulse rattles in her ears.

The four figures have their eyes closed and their lips move soundlessly. There are two men and two women, older than every Whisperer Solma has ever met. They're suspended by the roots and vines wrapped around them. A single vine, thick and knotted, curls around each of their wrists, flowing between them like a kind of chain. Or an electric wire. Every so often, a finger or a toe twitches. An eyelid flutters, a frown creases a brow.

Solma feels bile bubble in her throat. Beside her, Olive murmurs, "this is messed up."

Solma agrees. She whirls to face Sidewinder.

"What the hell?" she hisses. Sidewinder raises an eyebrow.

"I wouldn't expect someone like *you* to understand," she says. Solma takes a breath to retort, her hand going to the empty sheath of her hunting knife, but someone touches her shoulder.

"Sol," says Cobra's voice. "It's ok. They're The Seasons."

Solma scowls at her. She's still holding Olive's hand and knows, from the way Olive's breathing has quickened, that she feels the same. This is ugly. Vile. But when she looks into Cobra's eyes, she sees shame there. Fear, too. Cobra tried to tell her about this, and Solma didn't understand. *Couldn't* have understood.

"Ok," she says, glaring at her friends. "I reckon you better tell us about this now."

Cobra's mouths set in a grim line.

"It scared me the first time I saw it, too," she says. "But it's our way. Lots of Whisperers die young. It's not an easy life. The few of us that grow old and become powerful, we need to sustain their wisdom. This is why only Elders can join the mycelia. Years ago—decades, really—these Whisperers chose not to die in the conventional sense but to ... to bind their bodies and minds to the mycelia. To flow through the earth. To keep their knowledge alive so that the rest of us benefit. They became The Seasons and they've watched over us ever since. They *chose* this, Sol, when it came to their deaths. It was their decision."

Solma raises an eyebrow, still fighting nausea. "So ... they're dead?"

Cobra nods, then changes her mind and shakes her head. "Not exactly," she says. "They're more just ... not fully human anymore. Everything they were lives in the mycelia. Their bodies are preserved here so that the mycelia can talk to us through them. They're still conscious, still *there*, just not locked in one form."

Solma stares. She's not sure she fully understands. Are they dead or not? And if they are, what the hell are she and her friends doing, asking four dead Whisperers if they can form an army? They should be in Sand's End by now. They should—

"*Come closer,*"

Solma jumps. The four figures had formed those words at the same time, and four voices had spoken, but the voices seem to come from the air, the lights, the roots, the fungus. From the soil itself. It fills Solma's head as much as her ears. The pain behind her eyes lances and she doubles over against the urge to be sick.

Olive's hand touches her back. "Sol? Sol, what's wrong?"

"*Come closer,*" the voices say again. Solma straightens, breathing through her nose. She stares at the four figures before her. This is madness. She doesn't want this.

She steps forward. The others follow, and now they're standing in a line only a few metres from the not-quite-dead Whisperers suspended in roots and vines. She has no idea what to say. What can she say to someone who's not-really-alive and not-quite-dead?

But they speak first.

"You want our help," This time, it's just one voice and it comes mostly from the figure at one end, closest to Olive. He looks to be the oldest, with a long, grizzled beard full of moss and tangled silver threads. Solma thinks his skin was probably white, once, but it looks ash-grey, now, caked with dirt and spattered with growths. A mushroom sprouts from his temple. Solma's gut rolls dangerously.

Cobra leans towards her. "That's Winter," she mutters. "He's the oldest. We think the others tend to defer to him, but it's a bit hard to tell, sometimes."

"Right," Solma says. None of that makes her feel any better. To The Seasons, she says, "Yes. We want your help."

Winter's brow creases. Beside him, the woman with hair the color of fire shifts a little in her vine confines. Though her skin is as white and ashen as Winter's, there's a strange blush in her cheeks and around her, the vines are brighter. When Solma looks closer, she realizes there are berries blooming along the vines' length. She glances into the woman's face, half-covered with lichen.

"Autumn," she guesses. The woman's head cocks at the sound of her name.

"*You want an army,*" she says. "*You want us to fight for you.*"

Solma stiffens. "We want you to fight for Alphor," she says. "The insects are returning. There's these kids with a power to talk with them. A new kind of Whispering. And some people are trying to use the insects to get rich. It'll spark another war. It's already started. It—"

She falls silent. The speech she'd prepared in her head felt grand and persuasive, as if she was a general standing before her troops. But the way it comes out felt clumsy and half-formed. She doesn't sound convincing. She sounds desperate.

Autumn's eyelids flutter. She turns to the man at her right. He's younger than Winter, but still older than any other Whisperer Solma's ever met. Like the others, his skin is clammy and grey, but Solma guesses it was once brown. Fine, black-brown hair falls to his shoulders and the vines around him swell with what look like flower buds. But they can't be flower buds. That's not possible.

This man is obviously Spring. He's more active than the others, his fingers moving, his toes twitching, a frown marring his features.

"The Earth doesn't fight," he says. *"She endures. Things begin and things end. A circle. Life to death to life."*

Solma raises an eyebrow. "In my experience," she growls. "Most living things want to stay alive. Everything fights. We're gonna fight, too. And we need your help."

The ghost of a smile tugs Spring's lips. But the woman to his right stirs and he falls still, as if deferring to her.

She's black-skinned with a crown of black curls. Flowers burst from her collarbone and moss creeps across her forehead. Impossibly, several ripe apples hang off the vines around her. Summer.

"Pretty speech," she says. *"But we are Whisperers. Not soldiers. And we—"*

She stops, her chin lifting, as if she's smelled something. A shudder passes across all four of The Seasons.

Their voices merge again, booming around the earthen room.

"*Impossible!*" they roar.

Solma reels and Olive claps her hands to her ears. The ground shakes. Solma's fingers itch for her knife but it's nowhere. Instinctively, she makes to stand in front of Cobra and Mamba, protecting her friends from this strange enemy, but Cobra holds up a hand to stop her. She ushers Solma and Olive back.

Sidewinder steps forward, smirking. "I told you," she says, casting a triumphant glance at the four friends. "Didn't I say—"

But The Seasons clearly don't care that she was right. The earthen chamber lurches, soil trickling from the ceiling. Sidewinder is thrown off her feet, slamming into the earthen wall as Solma and her friends cling to each other, fighting to stay upright.

"*We did not believe it!*" they shriek, their voices tangling in shock and anger. "*It is impossible!*"

Mamba stands his ground, determination shining in his eyes. "Not impossible!" he says. His voice sounds small after The Seasons', but he doesn't waver. "We've connected. All seven of us. And we *haven't* gone mad like you said we would. We feel the Earth. The plants. All the life of Alphor."

The Seasons throw their heads back and roar. The ground bucks beneath them. Solma loses her footing, falling against Olive. Pain blasts through her head and she crushes her eyes closed. Something warm drips onto her lip. She tastes blood. Something's burst in her nose. Olive wraps an arm round her, and they struggle to the edge of the chamber, huddling against a wall until the roaring stops.

Solma uncovers her head and wipes her nose. The back of her hand comes away red. She straightens, still leaning heavily against Olive, to find that Cobra and Mamba have, somehow, stood their ground. Cobra's hands tremble.

"*Who did this?*" The Seasons demand, making the glowing white-green fungus pulse in time to their words. Cobra clenches her fists.

"Taipan," she says. "One of our youngest. She's barely nine, and she connected."

"*This cannot happen!*" Summer says, her lip curling into a snarl. "*You've disobeyed! You've—*"

"But you lied, though!"

Solma looks round, jaw hanging open. Olive glares at The Seasons, her voice still echoing around the chamber. Even Sidewinder looks shocked at Olive's words. Olive doesn't notice. Anger blooms bright in her face.

"You lied!" she says again. "You told them it would send them mad. You made it so only the most powerful could connect. That's what you said to them, right? Well, it ain't true, is it?"

The Seasons turn towards her, eyes moving restlessly beneath closed lids. *"It is not a lie!"* they intone. *"The defiant is dangerous. He destroyed a field of crop without even realising—"*

Solma's breath catches. She remembers what Python said on their journey through the mountains last spring. *He rotted a whole field in seconds with one fingertip in the soil.* She bites her lip and glances at her Whisperer friends, but nobody else notices.

Olive steps forward, furious. "Talking about Python?" She asks, an edge to her voice. "You locked him up underground for years and then say it's the fungus that drove him mad?"

She folds her arms, and now Solma sees what she's getting at.

Power. It's like a disease. Heady and contagious, it infects everyone.

"The mycelia never drove Python mad," she realizes aloud. "That was *you*. You used him to put other Whisperers off. You ain't special. You just don't want to share!"

She realizes she's shouting. Cobra and Mamba look at her, shock in their faces. But she can't stop.

"This ain't about Whisperers and village folk. It ain't about the Earth and life and death and all that. It's about *you!* You just like being in charge!"

The Seasons twitch and fidget, frowning with consternation. *"Impossible,"* they say together. *"We are the Earth. We are—"*

"You were people, once," Olive points out. "Just like the rest of us. Just like Blaiz and Maxen Camber. Whatever you were before went into the mycelia. Ain't that right? That includes your greed. You ain't changed. You ain't wise. You're as bad as the Stewards!"

She flicks a dismissive hand towards The Seasons and whirls away with disgust. "Let me outta here," she says, marching past Sidewinder. "Open the damn door! I'm done with this. With *them!*"

The Seasons say nothing, but Solma thinks she sees puzzlement in their expressions. The vines that contain them shift and slither, tightening and loosening.

Olive drives a fist into mud wall. "Let me *out!*" she bellows. Sidewinder glares but presses her hand against the mud wall and Whispers it open. Roots, vines, and grasses peel back and daylight rushes through the opening. Olive marches into it, silhouetted against the brightness. Solma shields her eyes and follows, feeling Mamba and Cobra behind her.

Outside, Sidewinder closes the grass-hut and turns to face them. "That went well," she says. Don't reckon you'll get what you came for now. You leave at first light tomorrow."

She hesitates a moment, and Solma realizes that triumphant smirk has gone. She won't lift her eyes to meet theirs. Solma frowns, expecting a trick, expecting that self-importance to return to Sidewinder's face. But it's nowhere to be seen. The Whisperer woman looks ... uncertain.

"We'll give you supplies," Sidewinder says, then marches away.

Solma shivers despite the warm spring evening. Everyone is silent as they return to Bell and the others.

The ache behind Solma's eyes throbs again. Her fingers itch for her absent weapons, though she doesn't know what she'd do if she had them.

This is all so broken. What the hell are they supposed to do now?

Twelve

MAXEN STANDS AT THE window, hands clasped behind his back. Warren can't stop trembling. His teeth chatter and there's a cold in his bones he can't shake. The weather's warming but the cellar of the Steward's house is as cold as ever. He can't remember the last time he woke without a deep ache in his muscles. Sometimes, just moving makes him yell with pain.

Today is no exception.

Maxen sighs and turns from the window. He pulls one of the curtains across then sits at the huge, wooden desk in the middle of the room. His face is set in a frown but there are dark craters around his eyes. His skin is sallow. He looks ill.

Warren watches warily. He's only been in this room a few times, but every time before this, it hasn't been Maxen sat at that desk, sorting through that precious paper. It's been Blaiz Camber. The real Steward of

Sand's End. Maxen's father. The tyrant that Warren and Solma brought down two years ago. He's in this house somewhere, comatose, tended by a few trusted Aldren elders. Warren shivers.

Maxen steeples his fingers and peers over his fingertips. His white-blue eyes are unreadable. Warren fights the fatigue in his body and forces himself to meet Maxen's gaze.

"No fewer than sixteen insects have been seen outside the chemical confines by my Gatra," Maxen says. Straight to the point. Warren digs his toes into the deep red rug under his feet.

He's actually impressed only sixteen of them were spotted. He's managed to sneak over fifty bees out of the chemical barrier so far. Sneaking them out has been the easy bit. Sneaking them back in again—back to their nests—is tougher. That's when they get spotted.

Maxen watches him, anger gleaming in his eyes. "Anything to say, Warren?"

Warren feigns nonchalance. "It's hard to keep hold on them all," he protests. "It makes my head hurt. They gotta have space, Maxen—"

"*Sir,*" Maxen growls, baring his teeth. "I'm not your friend. I'm your *Steward.*"

Warren can't stop the shudder that passes through him. "Right," he says, making no effort to hide his sullenness. "*Sir.* Last week, more bees died than hatched. That ain't how it's s'posed to be. I'm trying—"

"Not hard enough," Maxen interrupts, slamming the flat of his palm hard on the desk. Warren jumps and falls silent. This isn't the first time he's had a conversation like this. He remembers Blaiz coming to the house he used to share with Solma and Bell, brandishing the crushed body of a bee and telling Warren he'd failed to keep them secret. That the bee's death was his fault. That he wasn't trying hard enough.

He clenches his fists.

"It's not good for them," he insists. "They gotta have space. They can't just feed off one kinda flower. They'll get sick. They'll fight each other—"

Maxen pinches the bridge of his nose. "I think you credit them with too much intelligence," he says. "They're insects. Tiny, mindless little things. Give 'em a flower, they're happy. And we've got plenty of flowers."

Warren glares. "I can hear them, remember?" he says, making his voice as fierce as he can. "I *know* that if you don't give them more space, they're gonna hurt each other. Indigo's bees are already hungry. They keep going over to Willow's to have a look. Four of Clover's bees died yesterday, trying to get into Willow's hive, and now—"

He stops. He stops because Maxen's face contorts into a snarl so vicious that Warren's afraid the older boy might launch himself across the desk and throttle him.

"You're giving them names, now?" Maxen sneers. "This isn't a game! This is my—*our*—future—"

"I know that!" Warren bursts out, shock and fury making him brave. "They need more space. You ain't giving them enough—"

Maxen's on his feet in moments, chair clattering to the floor. Warren jumps. "I'm providing everything they need." Maxen snarls. "It's you. You're not controlling them. They need to be controlled. If you can't do it ..." his eyes go big and wild. "Then, you're no use to me, are you?"

Warren's gut fill with ice. "What's that s'posed to mean?"

Maxen drags a hand through his hair. He starts pacing, like he's trying to persuade himself—more than Warren—that he means this.

"Everyone in this village pulls their weight," he says. "Everyone plants or tends or harvests or mends. That's how it works. I can't spend precious resources on someone who isn't any use to the village."

Warren's lungs tighten. He can't believe he's hearing this. "You took me away from my sister," he says. "You *stole* me, and now—"

Maxen turns his back on Warren and flicks a dismissive hand over his shoulder. "We're done," he says. "Ignis, return the kid to his quarters."

Quarters. That's putting it kindly. Warren's face flushes with angry heat. "You mean my prison!" he snaps. Maxen shrugs.

"Whatever you want to call it. Ignis?"

Warren turns to see Ignis appear from the shadows by the door. He's pristine in his Gatra uniform. There's a fresh bruise on his jaw, his eyes full of loathing.

"C'mon, then," he says. Warren hesitates and Ignis lunges for him, dragging him from the room. Maxen doesn't glance round.

Warren struggles as the door closes behind them. Ignis pulls him down the corridor towards the basement stairs.

"Let go!" he growls. To his surprise, Ignis releases him.

"You're so annoying," Ignis grumbles. "Hurry up. I gotta meet Dja in fifteen minutes."

Warren rubs his arm where Ignis' fingers have left a bruise. He scowls but follows when Ignis beckons. "Why?"

Ignis shrugs. "Maxen wants us to find more insects that got out."

Warren fights to keep his face neutral. He snuck five honeybee workers, two bumblebees and a butterfly out this morning, directing them as far as he was able in the hope that they'd be able to find help. He has no idea how far they made it, or if they'll manage to get back. He won't be able to reach his mind out to warn them when he's underground in the basement. He shoves his hands in his pockets.

"You don't got to do this, y'know," he says. Ignis gives him a sideways glance.

"What?"

Warren tries to make his face kind. This boy used to be his friend, after all. "You don't got to follow their orders and do everything they say—"

Ignis snarls. He lifts his hand, palm upward, and fire bursts from it. Warren yelps, jumping backwards. He stares at the flame in Ignis' hand.

"You're still such a baby," Ignis growls. "You don't get it, do you? Look at me!"

Warren does. Right into Ignis' violet eyes.

"You got all this hope for some kinda future," Ignis says, teeth bared. "Full'a flowers and everyone holding hands. You think there's a place for me and my Dja in that world? I stick my hand in the Earth like a Whisperer and all I do is set it on fire. I hold out my hands for bees like a Keeper and they just burn to a crisp."

"That's not true," Warren interrupts, remembering how Ignis absorbed the fire in the basement. "You can—"

"I ain't part of your *future!*" Ignis yells. "I gotta make my own. And this is it."

Warren says nothing. What can he say? Maybe Ignis is right. What would he and Vulkan do in a world with no war? For the first time, he wonders if that's even possible. He wonders how many more kids there are like Ignis. Kids who won't cope in a world they can't fight against. He thinks of his sister. Always reaching for a weapon to solve every problem because violence is her language. Her currency.

The thought makes his throat close. He resists a sob. Ignis rolls his eyes.

"You know your problem, Warren?" he snaps. "Your sister let you grow up soft."

He turns, beckoning Warren to follow. Warren hesitates. He doesn't want to go back into that cellar with its damp air scratching his lungs. But Ignis glances at him, eyes flashing, and Warren realizes he doesn't want to fight, either. He's tired. He lowers his gaze, reaching out his mind to his insects before the isolation of the basement cuts him off again.

"Can ... can you ask Maxen if I can have another blanket?" he says quietly. "A dry one?"

Ignis frowns. His eyes search Warren, taking in his torn, damp clothes. Warren waits, wondering what's been going on in that boy's head lately. Something's changed and Warren can't work out what it is. Ignis sighs.

"Fine," he says. "I'll ask, but if I get an earful, I'm blaming you."

Warren supresses a small smile as Ignis leads him towards the cellar.

But as soon as it comes, the smile is gone. Warren's mind rings with alarm. His head throbs and the ul-tra-violet colors of bee-vision burst in his eyes. Blue. Purple. Fringed with shades Warren can't name.

And a stab off anger. Fear.

He's felt this once before. A link to the bees so strong it's impossible to control. Cobra had a name for it. *Forceful Projection.* When he feels what they feel. When he can't tell where he ends and the bees begin.

Warren whimpers as the world lurches sideways and he crumples against the wall, clutching his head. "No!" he begs. "No! Stop! Don't—"

Ignis has him by the shoulders, shaking him.

"Warren!" the other boy yells. "Warren, *what?*"

In a moment of brief clarity, Warren's normal vision returns to him. He looks into the fire boy's violet eyes, and thinks he sees concern there.

But then the bee-vision comes crashing over him again and he sees Ignis as the insects see him. Wreathed in ultra-violet, his veins standing out in pulsing blue.

Warren realizes Ignis isn't concerned for *him*. He's concern for what might be happening out there.

Because if the bees are fighting, it won't just be Warren who's punished, will it?

Ignis is scared for his own skin.

Coward.

Warren struggles to his feet as another wave of nausea threatens. He doubles over.

"The honeybees," he gasps. "They're hurting each other. They're trying to—"

But he can't finish. The projection overwhelms him again. He's nothing but panic and anger and violence.

Indigo's Workers

We are hungry.

So many empty cells that should be filled with honey. So many dead larvae. We remove the bodies, deposit them at the foul-smelling edge of the world.

But more die. There are not enough flowers.

There is only one option left.

We dance it. The hive thrums with war song. Mother presses her thorax to the comb and lets out the sharp notes that tell us she hears our dance. She agrees.

We will rob the next hive. We will take its honey. It will die but we will thrive.

A legion of us burst from the entrance, the fierce tremolo of our song filling the spring air. Our fur bristles. Poison shines on our stings. It will not be easy. They will fight us. Many of us will die. Our war song is tinged with fear. But we fly into battle anyway.

We drive towards the other nest and, with panic in their song, the bees of that nest fly to meet us. We fight them in mid-air. Jab of sting between head and thorax, bodies dropping from the sky. Bitter tang of death in the air.

We push for the entrance. We try not to sting where we can help it. If we sting, we die, and we mustn't die before we reach their comb, before we take the precious sweetness within.

Another song in the air. Deeper, more powerful. The bumblebees emerge from their nest, their huge engines thrumming against the air. They've smelled our attack. They want the honey, too.

Now, we're fighting on two fronts. The bumblebees' sharp stings can stab again and again.

It isn't the first time we've fought bumblebees. They've crowded the entrance to our hive, too. Tried to steal some sweetness. They are few and we are many. Always, we overwhelm them. Always, we leave them dead at the base of our hive.

We do the same again now. Swift jab, inject poison. The bumblebees twitch and fight as they die. They are giants. Their strongest fighters might take two or three of our strongest before they succumb to our stings. But they are hundreds where we are tens of thousands.

We fight until the bumblebees retreat, buzzing an angry song around the entrance to their nest. We fight until the other hive is overwhelmed. And then we force our way inside, surging for the precious sweetness within. Many of us die in the darkness of the foreign hive. We jab and attack, but they are desperate, now. They kill with a fury we cannot match.

And the air stinks of dying.

And the combs hum with war song.

And bee bodies litter the ground.

Thirteen

WARREN'S AWARE THAT HIS feet are moving. Someone's shoulder is wedged under his armpit. He leans against a black-clad body.

"Dammit, Warren!"

It's Ignis, puffing as he tries to hold Warren upright.

They're outside. When did that happen? Warren turns his head as the tumbledown houses rush past. The movement brings bile rushing up his throat and he doubles over, vomiting. Ignis swears and Warren barely has time to wipe his mouth before they're off again, stumbling along the path towards the glasshouses. Bee-vision pulses in his eyes. The world swims with blue and violet.

Behind him, Warren hears footfalls. People shouting, as if from a great distance. He recognises Maxen's voice.

"How the *hell* did you not see this coming?"

Warren wants to say that he *did* see it coming. He's been trying to tell Maxen for nearly a month. But bee anger stings his nostrils and it's all he can do not to throw up again.

The path splits in two. The five glasshouses stand ahead of them and, already, Warren sees the commotion.

A squad of Gatra stand outside the chemical barrier, waving their arms, shouting. One even has a pistol loaded and aimed, as if the threat of a bullet might bother a bee. Warren almost laughs, but the fury of the bees sings through his mind. His gut rolls.

Ignis throws Warren to the ground outside the chemical barrier. Dizzy and nauseous, Warren sprawls in the soil. There's dirt in his mouth. He's scraped his knee, but the disgust and pain of that remain dulled by the anger of the insects. This close, he's flooded with the butterflies' anxiety. The air stinks of warfare and the gentle, jewel-winged insects are terrified.

Warren struggles to his feet, fighting to control his limbs. Everyone is shouting but he hears it as if from underwater. Everything is—

Anger. Sting. Death.

He shakes his head. The bee-vision dies back a little. He wiggles his fingers and toes, trying to situate himself in his own body. He can't help them when he's like this. He needs his wits. He needs—

Someone grabs his shoulder, whirls him round to face them. It's Maxen, his eyes wild with panic. Spittle flies from his mouth.

"Sort them out!" he shouts.

Warren tries to speak but only manages a whimper. Maxen lets go of him and yells at his soldiers. Warren sees the five guards outside the chemical barrier try to react. But what can they do? Ilga and another soldier, on Maxen's command, rush amongst the warring insects, trying to bat them away from each other. But all that happens is the bees sense another attack. The soldiers scream as stings pepper their skin. Aldo grabs them by their collars, hauling them from harm's way.

"Idiots," Warren hears him say.

A crowd has gathered from the village. Fei and Oritch craning their necks to get a better look, ignoring the soldiers who try to bully them back to work. Some are watching the insect battle in horror, but most, Warren notices through the haze of insect anger, are staring at Maxen. At the boy-Steward losing his grip. He's yelling at everyone.

He grabs Warren, yells something in his face, then lets go before Warren has a chance to react. He moves on to Ignis, screaming while the fire boy remains stony-faced.

Vulkan materialises from somewhere and Maxen roars at him, too. But no-one can do anything. No-one except Warren. Maxen's brittle mask of control is slipping.

For a terrible moment, Warren watches Maxen fall apart and thinks that he could just stand here and do nothing. He could show Maxen how little control he really has over the insects.

But that would mean letting the honeybees slaughter each other.

It would mean watching the bodies of his precious insects carpet the grass.

At that thought, the bee-vision pulses. Warren reels as the rush of bee fear and aggression overwhelms him. The scent of their poison stings his nose. He tries to push it aside but there's so much of it.

Thousands of bees throwing anger into the air. He can't fight it. He can't get a hold of it. He can't—

He's on all fours, vomiting into the grass. Shaking. He can barely breathe.

Hands touch his shoulder. Not rough, this time. Gently, they pull him up until he's kneeling. A cool cloth cleans his mouth. Someone dabs his forehead with water. There's a face in front of him. Watery grey eyes. A network of deep wrinkles. A mouth with only a few teeth left inside it.

He knows this face. There's a name. He struggles through the haze until he finds it.

Gerta.

It's a moment before he realizes he's spoken out loud, but the old woman grins and nods. "Good," she says. "You ain't gone mad. Keep looking at my face boy. Who are you?"

Warren frowns. That's a stupid question. She knows who he is. He's about to point this out but the bee-vision overwhelms him again. Gerta grabs his shoulders.

"Who are you?" she insists. Warren fights to find his voice.

"Warren," he says.

"And who's your sister?"

"Solma. Solma's my sister."

Gerta takes him through as many names as she can. Slowly, Warren remembers who he is. The feeling in his limbs returns. The nausea subsides. He still feels the warring insects, but the projection has been pushed back.

"Good lad," Gerta says as she sees his eyes regain their focus. "Now up. We gotta stop this."

Warren realizes that everyone around him is still shouting. The soldiers have weapons drawn but stand frozen outside the chemical barrier. Maxen wrenches at his hair. He's given up yelling orders and just screams incoherently. Murmurs of fear ripple across the gathered crowd.

It's chaos. The noise is too much, but Gerta's gnarled hand cups Warren under the chin. She lifts his face so he's staring into her eyes again.

"You look at me," she says. "Keep looking at me."

She hooks him under the elbows and, with surprising strength, hauls him to his feet. She keeps her hands on his shoulders as she guides him towards the insects. Her touch grounds him, though insect anger stabs through his mind.

Gerta helps him struggle through the insect barrier. On the other side, he gets a full view of the horror unfolding between the hives.

Bee bodies litter the grass. It's mostly honeybees, but Warren sees several bumblebee corpses among them. The air is full of insects, thrumming with deep, angry war-song as they clash mid-air. The entrance to Willow's hive is clogged with bees as the defenders flood to block the entrance. The attackers sting and stab. Gerta stays behind Warren, doing her best to remain calm as bees circle them, expecting a further attack. They know Warren, can feel his kinship with them. But Gerta is another matter. Warren feels her tense as a bee lands a sting on her arm. Hurriedly, he throws out his mind.

Friend, he tells them. *Ally.*

It's enough to stop Gerta getting stung but convincing the two hives to cease their war takes him longer. There are so many workers, each dancing their aggression. It feels as if it takes him days to connect with them all. He calms their anger, convincing them that any gain cannot outweigh their loss.

At last, Indigo's bees dance of retreat and pull back from Willow's hive. The thrum of war-song dulls to the regular insect buzz and Warren's knees buckle. He sinks to the ground, gasping for breath. Gerta dabs his forehead again, then helps him out of the chemical barrier.

"Get the boy some water!" she calls. A soldier appears with a bottle. It's Aldo. He unscrews the metal cap and helps Warren drink. Gerta scowls at him but doesn't shoo him away.

Slowly, the world around Warren comes into focus and he realizes the noise around him has stopped. Utter silence. Warren feels a whisper against his skin and looks down to see a honeybee on his hand. He must have accidentally brought her through the chemical barrier with him. She looks exhausted, pumping her abdomen as she gasps for breath. He cups his other hand over her, shielding her from Maxen's view.

The boy-Steward comes to stand over him, arms folded. He's still red-faced but he's regained some of his composure. Sweat shines on his upper lip and his hair is a mess where he's dragged frantic fingers through it.

"That took you far too long," he says, loud enough for the gathered crowd to hear. "And now we've lost loads of bees. Next time—"

Warren can't help himself. Frustration gives him a courage he hasn't had in months.

"Next time?" he yells. "Ain't you learned nothing? I been saying for *ages* that this was gonna happen, but would you listen? This is your fault! You're killing them all over again and you *don't even care!"*

The honeybee on his hand takes off. Her lone song sounds mournful in his ear. Maxen's face twists with rage and he steps closer, grabbing Warren by the collar. Gerta yells a protest, but Aldo holds her back.

Maxen pulls Warren close, their noses almost touching.

"You don't get to speak to me like that," the boy-Steward says. Warren suppresses a whimper but refuses to lower his gaze. He glares at Maxen, at the way rage contorts his features into something horrifying.

How can he ever make this boy understand? Every time he tries to explain, Maxen only hears insubordination. Warren is a tool to him, like the bees are a tool.

But Maxen needs to understand, or he'll kill them all. Maxen needs to *see*—

With a sharp cry of pain, Maxen drops Warren and reels back. Warren loses his balance and falls on his backside, watching in confusion as Maxen bats the air.

A honeybee limps away from Maxen's throat, where it's left a deep, red welt. Warren feels its tiredness and knows it left its sting in Maxen's flesh. Its flying away to die—

But there's another sensation, too. A strange humming at the back of Warren's mind that has nothing to do with the bee. He feels an echo of the bee-sting stab that made Maxen cry out. He feels the bee's venom coursing through Maxen's blood. And then—

Must contain this. Can't let them see I'm weak. The boy ... the boy ... have I failed?

It takes Warren a moment to realize these aren't bee thoughts. They're not even insect thoughts. They're *Maxen's* thoughts. How is that possible? He's sent bees to sting people before but never, through the venom, has he felt what they feel, heard what they think.

As quickly as it comes, the sensation is gone. Warren is thrown back into his own mind. Maxen claps a hand to his stung throat, snarling.

"Did you make it do that?" he growls. "Did you—?"

Gerta wrenches free of Aldo and limps between Warren and Maxen. Another murmur ripples through the assembled crowd. Someone yells, "Leave the kid alone! He just saved our bees!"

Maxen blinks, as if he's just become aware of where he is. He stares around him, at his soldiers and the crowd, at Ignis and Vulkan stood a few metres behind him. No-one moves.

Then, Maxen lifts his chin. He smooths his hair, gestures to his guards and stalks back towards his house. He doesn't look back.

Warren watches him go, still struggling with what he heard through the honeybee sting. Gerta helps him to his feet.

"C'mon, kid," she says grimly. "Best get you back, eh?"

Warren looks into her face, but she's turned away, watching the Fire Makers as they come to take charge of Warren.

He's too shocked to argue. Instead, he lets Ignis take his arm and lead him away. The crowd watches him go. Warren can't bring himself to look at any of their faces.

Fourteen

Solma winces as her right knee buckles. She stumbles and Olive lets out a growl between her teeth.

"That's it," she says. "We're stopping. You gotta rest."

Mamba sighs. "We can't," he says. "We've barely made it three miles. They want us gone. That means nowhere within five miles. Sidewinder will come and check." His eyes darken. "Not all Whisperers are gentle."

Olive fixes him with a dark glare. She gestures at Solma, who now leans on her knees, trying to steady her breathing. Solma waves a hand vaguely in Olive's direction.

"I'm ok," she says. "I can keep going. I just—"

"No," Olive says. "You can't. You should'a been allowed to rest at the camp and you weren't. Ain't no point in getting to Sand's End and you're too exhausted to fight." She pulls Solma upright, wrapping her in a fierce hug. She presses a kiss to her forehead and Solma leans into the affection.

"We need you, Sol," Olive murmurs. "Rest. We're all exhausted anyway."

"Agreed," Bell says, rummaging in their packs for rations. "Ana's been carrying Krait for the last half hour and Habu ain't stopped crying all morning."

Solma sees Mamba's fists clench. Cobra puts a gentle hand on his arm.

"Ten minutes," she says. "Just enough time for Roseann to see to Solma's leg. Then we'll go."

Mamba takes one look at her face and relents. "Ten minutes," he agrees. "But we can't stay any longer. If Sidewinder finds us—" he shudders and Solma looks away. The fear in his face is unsettling.

She winces as Olive helps her onto the cart, her legs dangling over the edge. She unstraps her prosthesis and untangles the cloth wrapping. Her lucky leg, Warren used to call it. Lucky because she lost it below the knee, but she didn't lose her life.

Earth, she misses him! She misses his relentless hope. She even misses his tantrums. She misses how he always insisted she do the right thing. Without him, she wonders if she knows what the right thing is. Sometimes, it feels like the ache of his absence could drive her into a frenzy. She'd set the world on fire just to get to him.

Then she thinks of Vulkan and Ignis and shudders. She doesn't want to be that person. But what if she can't help herself?

She yelps as Roseann's fingers dig into her right knee, testing the joint. Olive stands nearby, arms folded.

"She ok?" she asks. Roseann shrugs.

"It'll be fine," she says, sighing. "But only with rest. You should stay off it for a day, really."

"Yeah," Solma drawls. "'Cos we got all the time in the world."

Roseann holds up her hands. "I'm just the messenger," she says, and wanders over to help Bell with the kids. Olive hops up beside Solma.

"It's alright, Sol," she says, wrapping an arm around Solma's waist. Solma leans against Olive's shoulder, breaths in her scent. Gunpowder. Sweat. Safety.

"It ain't alright, though," she murmurs. "What're we gonna do? We can't march on Sand's End just us. It'll never work."

She glances at Krait, who's in the process of trying to untangle his feet from a web of fungus he's accidentally grown over them. He looks helplessly at Taipan as the girl tries to help him, but when her fingers touch the fungus, it grows with new intensity. The children fall back with a cry as three enormous, bright yellow mushrooms wrap themselves around Krait's leg. Solma shakes her head.

"Look at them all," she says. "Everywhere they step, mushrooms sprout all over the place. What use is this power if they ain't got control over it? We need an army only we don't have one. Without that, we'd need a miracle."

Olive doesn't answer and Solma glances into the other girl's face. A deep frown creases Olive's brow. Hope and fear battle for dominance in Solma's gut.

"What?" she asks. "You got a plan?"

A slow grin spreads across Olive's face.

"I got a ... a thought," she says. She hops down from the cart and helps Solma down, too. She calls Mamba and Cobra over, her tone commanding enough that they don't question her. Mamba folds his arms as Ana and Bell join them, leaving Roseann to watch the kids.

"What's up?" Cobra asks. Olive grins maniacally.

"Ok," she says. "Hear me out."

Solma pinches the bridge of her nose. That isn't a good start. But if Olive notices, it doesn't dampen her enthusiasm.

"We don't need a whole army of Whisperers," she says. The others gape at her. "How many Whisperers are as powerful as Tai?" Olive continues. "As powerful as any of you, now you can connect with the mycelia?"

Cobra rolls her eyes. "We can't control that power," she points out, gesturing towards where Krait and Taipan are still wrestling with Krait's mushrooms. "We don't even know half of what it can do." Olive wafts an impatient hand in the air.

"Just answer," she insists. "How many Whisperers are as powerful as you?"

Mamba frowns. "Well ... just The Seasons and—" his eyes widen. "You cannot be serious."

Solma looks between him and Olive, sees the shine in Olive's eyes and the fear in Mamba's. Something important is happening. "What?" she demands. "What's going on?"

Olive grabs her by both shoulders. "A miracle, you said," she replies. "We seen miracles before. We seen miracles when Tai reached into the Earth and found the mycelia. When she taught the others how. When their strength and power grew giant vines from underground and made a path through the fire."

"O-kay," Solma says, slowly. She doesn't like where this is going. "So?"

"So, there's one Whisperer who knows the mycelia better than anyone. Who can teach you all the control you need. Who's been connected to it longer than anyone else and *is still alive!*"

Solma blinks at her. Bell swears. And then Solma gets it.

"Oh, Earth," she whispers. The ache behind her eyes throbs. This is a terrible idea. This is going to get them killed. "We can't just—"

"Yes. We can."

Everyone jumps and looks down. Solma is unsurprised to see that Taipan is standing between them all. The strange rings around her irises glow with a pale sheen.

"Olive's right," she says. "I said it before, didn't I? We need Python. If no-one else can help, maybe he'll be enough." She holds out her hands, palms upward. They're covered in bits mushroom and torn silver threads from where she helped Krait get himself free.

"We need to learn to control this," she points out. "And he's the only one who can teach us how. Let's go get him."

"Go *get* him?" Solma splutters. "He's locked in an underground prison with no door! His power is dampened and his mind is half gone!"

Taipan cocks her head. "We can get him out," she says.

Solma shakes her head. For once, she's grateful when Mamba says, "this is a really bad idea."

Olive's smile falters as she turns to look at him. There's apology in Mamba's eyes but he doesn't back down.

"If we go back, Sidewinder and her lot will find us. They won't be so kind next time. They might not kill the troupe, but they'll not let us go." He turns to Solma and Olive. "And I wouldn't be surprised if she *did* kill you. You're not Whisperers. You aren't bound by our laws. Things are changing."

Solma nods firmly. "And how are we planning on sneaking back into the woods, getting past those guards, opening the grass-hut and persuading Python to come with us?" she demands. "We're better off just heading to Sand's End—"

"No," Taipan says quietly. "We're not. We need Python."

"We need an army—" Solma retorts.

"And we don't have one," Taipan interrupts, impatience creeping into her voice. Solma stares. Sometimes, she forgets this kid is Warren's age. "Python is the next best thing."

"But he's *dangerous!*" Solma protests, remembering what The Seasons had said. She gestures to Mamba. "You told me yourself. He rotted a whole field with one fingertip in the soil. He might—"

Tai shakes her head. "We need help," she says. "Olive's right. He knows the mycelia better than any of us. He can teach us to be our own army."

No-one says anything. Then Bell swears again. Cobra turns to Mamba, a hand on his arm.

"Maybe Tai's right," she says. "And we—" she bites her lip. "*I*...owe him."

Mamba covers her hand with his. "You don't owe him anything," he says quickly. "He'd have done the same for any of us. It's not your fault. It's—"

Cobra shakes her head. "I owe him, Mamba," she insists. "And I think Tai has a point."

Solma frowns. This is another thing she doesn't understand.

"Okay," she says, massaging her aching temples. "I feel like there's a thing here we ought to know. Why do you owe him, Cobra?"

Cobra and Mamba turn guilty eyes on Solma. Cobra bites her lip, then says, "when Python connected to the mycelia that first time ... the reason Sidewinder took him away ... it was 'cos of me."

Solma stares. No one says anything. Even the little ones have fallen silent. Solma shakes her head. "I don't understand—"

"It wasn't 'cos of you, Co," Mamba interrupts, cupping Cobra's face in his hands. Cobra pulls free.

"I was sick," Cobra says. "Feverish. Dying, I think. He needed to find healing herbs to help me but there were none in the ground nearby. He couldn't feel any. So, he ... he connected with the mycelia so he could search wider. He didn't mean to rot that field. I don't even think he knew he'd done it. He was searching. He traveled the network and found the herbs. He saved me. And that's why they took him away."

Solma doesn't know what to say. She had no idea her friend was carrying this guilt. No wonder Cobra

was so devastated when she saw how Python was being treated.

Solma imagines, again, those four children abandoned in the wilderness, left to die by the people they
thought would protect them. But now, she imagines
Cobra, pale-faced and shining with sweat, weakened
by fever and barely able to walk. She clenches her fist
and thinks if she ever sees Sidewinder again—

"We should go back," Ana says quietly. Habu nods
agreement. Everyone looks at Mamba.

He presses his fingertips to his temples as the rest of
the group fall silent, waiting. Solma watches him, her
heart a wild thing fighting her ribcage. She hopes he'll
say no. She hopes he'll say yes. Warren's face bursts
into focus as she closes her eyes. She bites back a sob.
Those shining, meadow-green eyes. That smile.

Nearly half a year since she last saw him. He's so
close. He's so far away. What would he do if he was
here?

He'd take every chance, wouldn't he? He'd stop
at nothing. He'd fight as hard as he could, and he
wouldn't stop.

Solma opens her eyes. She and Mamba speak at the
same time.

"Alright," they both say. Solma meets Mamba's gaze and smiles. He smiles back.

"I still think this is mad," he says. "But ... maybe we don't have a choice."

Olive punches the air. "Ok," she says. "Let's go get Python."

Fifteen

WARREN COUNTS THE STEADY beats of his boot hitting the door. He's at four hundred and eighty-three now, but he had to start again a few times because he forgot where he was. He has no idea how long he's been kicking the door, but it's annoying the Gatra on the other side. So, he keeps doing it

"Kid!" the boy calls for the eighth or ninth time. "Seriously, if you don't stop, I'm gonna come in there and—"

"And *what?*" Warren snaps back. "Gonna hurt me? *Kill* me? Don't reckon Maxen'll be pleased."

The soldier grumbles. "It's annoying," he whines. Warren gives a bitter laugh.

"Not half as annoying as being locked in here," he shoots back. "Shivering and hungry and getting no sleep."

The soldier heaves a frustrated sigh. Warren keeps kicking the door, making it rattle in its frame. Kicking the door helps him think. It's been a few days since the strange incident with the bee sting and ...

And Maxen's thoughts.

Warren still doesn't understand what happened. He hasn't seen Maxen since then, and he's been too afraid to try it again. It seems impossible that the bee's venom allowed him to hear another person *thinking*, but he has no other explanation. Is his gift getting stronger?

Or is he losing it?

He's up to six hundred and thirty-six when a noise outside makes him pause. Voices. Raised.

"You can't be down here, old woman!"

Warren presses his eye to the keyhole, but the soldier is on his feet and blocking Warren's view. It doesn't matter though. The voice that comes in reply makes Warren's heart stutter.

"Steward sent me," Gerta says. "You want me to tell him I can't do my job 'cos you turned me away?"

The soldier hesitates. Warren sees his hand go to the knife at his belt, but then he thinks better of it.

"Why though?" he asks. Gerta gives an impatient grunt.

"The boy's sick," she says. "Can't afford to lose our Beekeeper, can we? I'm bringing him medicine."

Warren frowns. Is he sick? No-one's told *him*.

The soldier seems to agree. "He ain't sick," he says uncertainly. "He's fine."

Gerta's voice becomes threatening. "You suggesting you know better than the Steward?"

"No," comes the nervous reply. "But ..."

The soldier hesitates. Warren smiles to himself.

Eventually, Gerta loses patience. The guard yelps and Warren realizes Gerta's jabbed him with her cane.

"You know who I am, boy?" she barks. The guard rubs his bruised ribs.

"You're an Aldren—"

"I'm the Steward's chemical expert," she retorts. "It's my know-how keeps Blaiz alive, keeps the bees safe. I ain't just Aldren. You let me through, or you can explain to the Steward why his Beekeeper's too sick to work."

The guard grumbles but unclips a set of keys from his belt. Warren withdraws from the keyhole as the door clicks open and Gerta hobbles inside.

"Five minutes," the guard says, frowning.

Gerta limps over to Warren.

"How you feeling, boy?" she asks. She stares at him hard. Warren realizes she expects something. He forces a cough, sways on the spot.

"Not good," he says. "It's damp in here and I can't breathe right and—"

Gerta bends towards him. She holds the back of her hand against his forehead. Warren closes his eyes, relishing the unusual touch of kindness.

A sharp pain shoots through his arm. He tries to yelp, but his jaw has gone slack. His knees buckle beneath him, his eyes slide out of focus. He falls, but Gerta's there to catch him. Warren has just enough control left to glance down at his arm, where Gerta is withdrawing a thin needle. She hastily stows it out of sight.

She gives a strangled cry. "Warren!" she yells, shaking him. Of course, he can't respond. He has no control over his limbs now. He can only move his eyes, but he fixes them on Gerta and hopes she can tell he's furious.

Gerta turns to the guard. "Run to my house!" she tells him. "Third shelf from the door. A bottle labeled greenroot tincture."

The boy stares, aghast. "I—" he whimpers. "I can't read—"

Gerta growls her frustration. "It's got a black stopper and the liquid inside is dark green," she says. "Fetch it! Now!"

"But—"

"The Beekeeper will die unless you *do as you're told!*" Gerta yells. The soldier's eyes grow wide, and he disappears down the corridor. Warren hears him trip on the stairs.

When he's gone, Gerta calms. She strokes Warren's hair out of his face and props him against the wall. Warren's limbs tingle.

"Sorry 'bout that, kid," Gerta says. "It'll wear off soon. I just needed to give you a message."

She crouches in front of him, wincing as her knees protest. From the folds of her skirt, she produces a silver cannister like the one Ignis used to disperse the chemical barrier. She shakes it.

"Blink once if you know what this is."

Warren wants to swear, but although the feeling is creeping back into his fingers, he can't yet move his face. He blinks once. He'll swear at her later.

Gerta nods. "It'll be hidden by the bumblebee nest," she says. "When the time comes."

It disappears amidst her skirts again and she withdraws something else. Warren stares at it for a long time before he realizes it's a knitting needle.

"Have they already checked your room today?" she asks. Warren glares, but blinks once. *Yes.* Gerta nods approval. She shuffles to the pallet in the corner. She pulls out a wooden slat, holding it up so Warren can see. In one end is a hole, just the right size for a knitting needle. She pushes the needle inside and replaces the slat.

"Use that for the lock," she tells him.

Warren wiggles his toes and finds they move. He twitches his fingers. Pins and needles spike up his arm.

Gerta hobbles back to him. With great difficulty, she sinks to her knees and cradles his head. "Two days' time," she says. "You wait ten minutes after the sun goes down. Pick the lock. You gotta be *patient*, okay? Then you hide by the glasshouses 'til you hear the distraction."

Warren now has enough control over his face to scowl. He tries to ask what she means, but his words slur. Gerta raises an eyebrow.

"You'll know when you hear it," she says. "And then, boy, you get those insects out. You let them go and if you can, run. Far away."

Warren feels a tightness in his throat that has nothing to do with whatever Gerta's injected him with. He swallows, then nods. Frantic footsteps sound down the corridor. Gerta grins, showing her few remaining teeth.

"Let's give 'im a good performance, eh?" she says. "Close your eyes."

Dutifully, Warren lets his eyelids drift closed. The soldier-boy skids to a halt in the doorway, holding out a small, glass bottle with a black stopper. A dark-green liquid sloshes around inside.

"I found it!" he gasps. "Can you save him?"

Gerta throws up her hands in mock despair. "That's the *wrong one!*" she shrieks. "Can't you do anything right?"

She fusses and wails and makes a show of feeling Warren's forehead. She produces a bundle of herbs from her skirts and wafts them under Warren's nose.

It's all Warren can do not to sneeze. Eventually, she leans over him and mutters in his ear, "you can wake up now."

Warren lets his eyes drift open. Gerta winks at him, then throws her arm around him and apparently begins to sob.

"Oh, thank *Earth!*" she cries. "He's alive!" She casts a disdainful glance at the poor guard. "No thanks to *you!*"

The soldier looks so pale, Warren thinks he might faint. He flops against the wall, sighing with relief

"Thought he was a goner," he says. "You *saved* him!"

Warren bites down on the inside of his cheek to avoid laughing. The feeling has come back now and, although his limbs ache, he can move.

Gerta makes an impressive performance of helping him onto his pallet. She strokes his hair out of his face, wafts her herbs under his nose again, and tells him to rest. Then, she rounds on the soldier.

"You!" she roars. "You want me to tell the Steward you ain't doing your job? I got a few choice things to say to *you!*"

She marches him out of the cell, admonishing as she goes. Warren turns towards the wall and stuffs both his hands over his mouth to muffle his laughter. That was the most fun he's had in ages.

The door clicks closed. Warren hears the key grate in the lock. He rolls back over to face the ceiling. His body still aches and his head whirls. But he's smiling.

This is a long shot. Full of danger. Totally reckless. But it's all he has.

Two days' time, Gerta said.

Softly, Warren kicks his heel against the wood of his pallet and begins counting the beats.

Sixteen

THE LIGHT FADES QUICKLY in this part of Alphor. Solma's reluctant to use the torches yet. She and Olive crouch in a heap of dry ferns just inside the treeline. Solma's certain she's got every thorn on the continent embedded in her backside.

She peers into the gloom on her right and can just make out Cobra and Mamba, huddled in a similar hiding place. Ana's up a tree nearby, but Solma can't see her. Taipan's tucked away in a nest of moss and leaves.

They've left Bell and Roseann with the boys about half a day's walk away. Bell was not happy about staying behind, but Solma pointed out that she had nowhere near as much combat experience as the rest of them and she was needed with the youngsters.

Solma, Olive and the Whisperers crept around the Whisperer camp and snuck through the woodland, remaining out of sight. Now, they wait.

Taipan hasn't wanted to connect with the mycelia, fearing The Seasons might feel her from this close by. They're saving that as a last resort.

Solma watches the Whisperer camp through the trees, silhouetted against the setting sun. A voice carries through the still evening air.

"Inside, then, children. Boa, stop picking that scab—"

The sound of a child protesting, an adult scolding.

"Any minute now," Olive mutters.

The camp settles. The fires are doused, tents laced tight.

Five figures detach from the camp, heading into the woodland. Solma holds her breath. Sidewinder and her troupe march past, making no sound as they melt into the forest.

Solma watches until she can no longer see them in the darkness, then turns her attention to Mamba and Cobra. Mamba gets to his feet, watching carefully to make sure Sidewinder and her troupe are gone. When he's certain, he turns to Solma and Olive, beckoning.

They disentangle themselves from the ferns as Cobra stands. Taipan emerges and Ana swings deftly from a tree. They stand still, half-expecting Sidewinder to appear from the darkness with a cruel smirk and arrest them on the spot. But she doesn't.

"Okay," Mamba mutters. "Their patrol takes half an hour." He glances at the moon, gibbous and glowing through cloud. "It'll be harder to time at night, so we got to move fast."

Solma nods. Ana grabs Cobra's hand and they exchange brief smiles. Those two will stay here, ready to cause a distraction while the others get Python to safety. Taipan, as the one who connects best with the mycelia, is needed to reach Python.

And Solma and Olive? They're muscle. But Solma's fine with that. It's what she's good at.

Mamba pulls Cobra into a hug. "You make a racket, then get straight out," he says. "Clear?"

Cobra chuckles. "Clear," she says. She wriggles free of Mamba's grip, touching his cheek before she grabs Ana's hand. They disappear into the gloom. Mamba takes a deep breath.

"Let's go," he says.

Olive crouches so Taipan can clamber onto her back. They head deeper between the trees, wincing at every crunch of leaves or snap of dry wood. Solma's pulse thunders in her ears, no matter how hard she wills it to be quiet. She's certain every shadow is the one Sidewinder's hiding in, waiting to leap out.

They fall into single file as the woodland thickens, following Mamba's lead. Solma unsheathes her hunting knife. The wood feels too silent, as if the world is holding its breath.

The trees widen out into a small clearing and there's the silhouette of the grass-hut they'd visited yesterday. Python's prison. Mamba holds up his hand and they hunker in the shadows.

Movement outside the grass-hut draws Solma's eye. The two Whisperer guards. She looks to Mamba for confirmation.

"No killing," Mamba mouths. "Just disarm."

He stares at Solma until she feels herself redden with indignation. That's not fair. She doesn't *like* killing. It's just that people sometimes don't give her a choice. She fixes Mamba with a glare and nods. She's got no interest in spilling blood tonight.

Mamba crouches by Taipan, a hand on her shoulder. "You sure you can do this?" he asks. Taipan smiles.

"Yeah," she whispers. "But we gotta be quick."

Solma's stomach convulses. This is the bit she's most worried about. When they discussed it earlier, Taipan said she was certain The Seasons would feel as soon as Python's prison was opened. They'd know when Python was withdrawn from the mycelia. From that moment, their time will be running out. They'll have to hope Ana and Cobra provide a big enough distraction for them to get away before Sidewinder and her team return.

Mamba straightens. "Ok."

Solma glances at Olive, sheathes her knife. They won't need anything more than their fists for this. Leaving Mamba and Taipan in the shadows, they split up, creeping round the edge of the clearing. Solma sees Olive emerge from the trees behind one of the Whisperer guards. Solma approaches the other. As soon as Olive grabs her guard, Solma strikes. She wraps her arm across the Whisperer's mouth, then whacks her in the side of the head. The Whisperer's eyes go glassy, and she crumples to the ground. Solma's careful to make sure she doesn't hit her head on the way down.

She glances up to see Olive's laid out her guard, too. Olive winks and beckons to Mamba and Cobra.

Taipan scurries forward, pressing her palms against the grass-hut. She closes her eyes, Whispering furiously. The grass-hut trembles, the vines peeling back to reveal the ladder into the dark. Solma and Olive unclip and wind up their torches, leading the way. There's no time for discussion now. The Seasons will have felt Taipan opening the prison. They need to move.

Together, they race along the tunnel and into the wide, glowing chamber where Python kneels, exactly as they'd left him. Solma and Olive hang back while Taipan and Mamba rush to Python. Mamba grabs his shoulders, shakes him. He doesn't respond.

Taipan starts to cry quietly.

"Dammit," Olive mutters, staring back down the tunnel. A split second later, Solma hears it, too. Voices. Angry and impatient. She recognises Sidewinder's clipped tone and swears.

"Mamba, Tai!" she hisses. "Hurry up!"

Mamba slaps Python across the face, growling at him to wake up. Python's head lolls, but nothing draws him out of his stupor.

Solma meets Olive's gaze and sees fear there. This isn't working. And now, they'll have to fight their way out. Solma clenches her jaw and feels that familiar flood of adrenalin. The world slows down. She goes for her pistol, then changes her mind. Ammo is scarce. And she promised no killing tonight. She'll take them with her fists if she can.

Mamba stands helplessly over Python. He meets Solma's eye, shaking his head.

"I can't—"

"Move!" Taipan growls, shoving him aside. She's tiny, but she pushes him with such force he staggers back. She drops to the ground and thrusts her hands into the earth in front of Python. A gasp escapes her lips, her pupils dilate. Suddenly her eyes are nothing but endless black, shining with stars. Solma's heart stutters as she watches. Taipan's body convulses. Mamba grabs her shoulders.

"Tai!" he yells, heedless of the fact Sidewinder is heading towards them. "Tai, no! Get out! You can't—you're not strong enough—"

But if Taipan hears him, she doesn't show it. Her head tips to one side, her eyelids drift closed and her lips form words Solma can't hear. Then she convulses again, her body shaking with such force that Solma's worried she'll break a bone. Mamba drops to her side, cradling her, trying to stop her snapping her own neck.

Sidewinder's voice sounds down the tunnel, painfully close.

"Mamba!" she calls, an edge of barely contained fury in her voice. "Do you realize what you've done?"

Mamba frowns and glances at Solma, but she's none the wiser.

"Play for time!" she mouths, gesturing at Taipan.

Sweat prickles across Mamba's forehead. "I've done what's right," he says. "I'm rescuing a friend."

Sidewinder's voice echoes down the earthen corridor. "Those guards," she says. "They are the last line of defence. You're unleashing a demon!"

Solma doesn't like the sound of that. But she's come too far to back out now.

"Terrible defence!" she yells. "We took them out before they could even scream!"

"They're not there to defend *him* from *you*," Sidewinder says, her voice withering. "They're s'posed to defend *us* from *him!* You've put us all in danger. Give up! Get out!"

Still clutching Taipan, Mamba looks up desperately.

"This isn't fair!" he calls back. Solma's heart breaks at how young and frightened he sounds. A few months shy of eighteen and the fear in his eyes is that of a child. Still, Sidewinder's words send a nasty chill through her blood. Her hands tingle, desperate to hold a weapon.

"Nothing is fair," Sidewinder says, bitterly. "But you're breaking the rules."

Rules. Solma's so sick of rules that only apply to those too weak or vulnerable to question them. To hell with that.

She glances at Olive and sees the same anger in the other girl's face. Olive nods. They both raise their fists.

Mamba shakes his head. "Please," he says, and Solma hates that he's begging. Hates what Sidewinder reduces him to.

"Please what?" Sidewinder demands. She's close now, hanging back in the shadows of the tunnel. Solma suddenly realizes that Sidewinder can reach them all without stepping any closer. All she has to do is reach her hands into the earth. She doesn't need to enter the chamber and give Solma and Olive the chance to attack her.

Olive curses under her breath and Solma knows she's realized the same thing. Solma reaches for her pistol as Olive does the same. So much for no killing. But if Sidewinder attacks, they'll not have a choice.

"The Seasons commanded me to stop you releasing the traitor at any cost," Sidewinder says. "I'll kill you if I have to, Mamba. I don't want to."

And it sounds, Solma thinks, as if she *means* it. There's genuine sorrow in her voice. That sneering tone she used before is gone.

Mamba says nothing, just holds Taipan's shoulders. Tears streak his face.

"As you wish," Sidewinder says. There's resignation in her tone. Sadness. "You're not leaving me any choice, y'know."

And Solma thinks how that's utter crap. Of course, there's a choice. There's *always* a choice. Even when the options are terrible, even when no alternative will be the right one, there is still a choice.

There's a beat of silence. The earthen chamber around them trembles like the aftershock of a faraway earthquake. Clumps of soil fall from the ceiling. Solma peers at the roots protruding from earthy chamber wall. They twitch and snake outward, reaching for her.

Solma cries out, drawing her knife to slash at them. She tries to back away, but something grabs her foot. She glances down to find a thick vine twined around her flesh-and-blood ankle, a knotted root curling around her prosthesis. She hacks at both. The vines split and wither but more snake up from underground, slithering up her calf, squeezing until Solma feels her leg might break.

Voices echoes down the tunnel. Solma hears Olive cry out, the sound of a gunshot. Mamba yells and Solma looks up to see a thick root has snatched him by the wrist.

Solma growls and attacks the vines holding her. But no matter how thoroughly she slashes at them, more shoot up and take their place.

Sidewinder steps from the shadows, her face a mask of calm. Behind her are Copperhead, carrying his javelin, and Keelback and Cascabel, their bows strung. Urutu isn't here. Fear pulses in Solma's throat. If she were Sidewinder, she'd have brought Urutu. She'd have made sure her strongest warrior was at the heart of the battle—

Unless this is not going to be the heart of the battle.

Solma slashes helplessly at the grabbing vines. Where are Cobra and Ana? Are they safe? But then a root explodes from the wall behind her, grabbing her by the waist, and she can think of nothing except freeing herself.

Sidewinder's hand brushes the earth wall, sending tremors through it that shake soil from the ceiling. Either side of her, her troupe members lower their weapons, push their hands into the wall. Solma manages to free her pistol, aiming at Sidewinder.

"Stop this!" she snarls. "Stop! Or I'll—"

A vine blasts from above, curls around Solma's wrist, and squeezes until her hand goes limp. The pistol drops from her grip.

"Oi!" Olive barks, struggling against roots that now hold all her limbs. "Let her go!"

She fights like a redbear. Her pistol and knife are both on the floor and, with nothing else at her disposal, Olive uses her teeth. She bites at her bindings, tearing vines and spitting out their remains. But as quickly as she frees herself, more roots come from the ceiling, the walls, the earth, and hold her tighter.

Solma thrashes. She tries to kick out, but her foot and prosthesis are both held fast. The vine that holds her wrist squeezes so tight her fingers tingle. She claws at it with her free hand, so distracted by the pain that she doesn't feel the vine at her throat until it starts to tighten. Her eyes widen, her throat constricts.

"No!" she gasps. Olive's yells grow more frantic.

Solma kicks, rakes her nails against the vine squeezing her throat. She claws for breath, coughing. Her lungs convulse in desperation.

"Let her go!" Olive screams. Sidewinder says nothing. But something shines in her eyes. Solma thinks it might be regret. Guilt. But fog is creeping through her brain. She can't hold onto her thoughts long enough to unpick them.

Her vision darkens. Her eyes roll. In the centre of the chamber, Python still kneels, unresponsive. In front of him, Taipan is almost entirely covered in creeping roots. Only her eyes, black with a blue-white sheen, are visible through the plant matter. Behind her, Mamba fights his own battle, his hands in the earth as vines lash at him. Muscles bulge on his neck as he tries to wrestle control of the plant life from Sidewinder.

But she's older than him. Stronger. He has no chance.

They're going to die here.

Fog fills Solma's brain. Her eyes roll into her head. She feels her muscles convulse, her body fighting suffocation. Her limbs are heavy and rebellious. She can't fight anymore.

Earth, she hopes Warren never learns it ended like this. His face drifts in and out of her mind as her brain grows slow and dark.

And then the vines release her. She's on all fours, spluttering, taking deep, delicious lungfuls of breath. Olive's beside her.

"Sol? Sol, oh Earth."

Strong hands help her up. Olive's arms wrap around her waist. Solma's head lolls and her vision's still blurry. Someone's screaming. She wishes they'd stop.

Her knees give way, and she sags against Olive.

"It's ok, Sol. You're ok."

Solma blinks away the blurriness in her eyes. She frowns towards Mamba. He's on his feet, staring past

Solma and Olive to where Sidewinder stands. His eyes are wide, mouth agape. The vines have retreated from Taipan, too. She's withdrawn from the mycelia and now shivers on all fours, tears pouring down her face. Moss covers most of her shaved scalp and there's a white mushroom growing from her ankle. Mamba's beside her, pulling the plant- and fungal-matter away.

The screaming won't stop. Solma turns to tell whoever it is to shut up and realizes it's Sidewinder and her troupe.

All four of them, shrieking their heads off. Solma stares, her brain still misty, trying to work out what the hell is going on.

Sidewinder's troupe still have their hands deep in the earthen walls, but their faces are full of horror as they try to pull free. Something holds them fast and when Solma's vision clears, she sees fine silver threads crawling over their hands, across their wrists, up their arms. Mycelia. It's delicate at first, but it thickens fast. Sidewinder fights against a creeping vine snaking up her leg. She grabs it, trying to Whisper it under her command but it won't respond. As Solma watches, the vine splits, then splits again, spider-webbing across Sidewinder's body. The torchlight is weak, but Solma sees the silver threads of mycelia criss-crossing the vine's surface. The vine reaches Sidewinder's throat, wraps around it and squeezes. Sidewinder's screams cut short. Her eyes bulge. She claws at the suffocating plant as it tightens. Solma feels sick.

"Wait ..." she croaks. Her throat still feels raw. It hurts to talk but she doesn't want this. This is hell. "Don't ..."

The screams from Sidewinder's troupe intensify and Solma sees the mycelia has reached their shoulders, spreading up their necks and across their chests. Copperhead roars, managing to wrench himself free, though Solma sees from the way his arm hangs limp that he's broken it in the process. He collapses, staring in horror at Cascabel and Keelback. They're still stuck in the mycelia. Their screams reduce to gurgles and coughs. Their eyes go glassy, heads lolling. Cascabel sags to the ground as fruiting mushrooms sprout from her throat and cheekbone. Keelback fights a little but he's losing strength. His eyes roll back into his head as moss blooms out of his mouth.

Sidewinder's still choking and Solma doesn't know how to stop it. She can't watch this. But her head pounds and her throat feels bruised and swollen.

"Please ..." she rasps, but she can barely hear herself above the sound of Sidewinder dying.

Olive hears, though. She turns to Mamba and Taipan, who watch the scene with wide, frightened eyes.

"Alright," Olive barks. "That's enough. Let her go."

She's looking at Taipan, a flash of disapproval in her eyes. Taipan shakes her head.

"I can't," she protests. "It isn't ... I'm not ..."

Olive stiffens. "Stop it, Tai!" she yells. Taipan jumps and tears spring to her eyes.

"You don't understand!" she protests. "I can't—"

The sound of Sidewinder's choking stops. Solma forces herself to look up, afraid of what she might see. Relief floods her when she finds Sidewinder on all fours, gasping for breath, her face streaked with tears. The vines have retreated and she's alive. Copperhead crawls to her side but his strength gives out before he reaches her. He sags to the floor. Solma keeps her eyes fixed on the pair of them. The survivors. She can't look at Cascabel, whose eyes are now full of mushrooms. Keelback's face is covered in moss. They're both deathly still.

"Let's get outta here," Olive says grimly. She jerks her chin at Python. "What we gonna do about him?"

Mamba shakes his head and starts to speak but Taipan interrupts him.

"It's ok," she says. "We can carry him. He'll come with us."

Solma frowns, but there's no time to ask. They need to find Cobra and Ana. Olive brushes a strand of hair from Solma's face.

"Can you walk?"

Solma tests herself. She's wobbly but she can hold her own weight. The dizziness and fog are receding.

"Yeah," she says huskily. "Just don't ask me to talk for a bit."

Olive and Mamba hitch their shoulders under Python's arms, heave him to his feet. The light in his eyes go out as his hands withdraw from the mycelia. His head lolls, but he doesn't resist. He winces as he takes his own weight. Solma sees his bare feet are chapped and blistered. He leans heavily on Mamba and Taipan but his legs move as they coax him down the tunnel. Solma can't work out if he's conscious or not. Does he know what's happening, or is he still lost in the mycelia? They hurry up the ladder, persuading

Python to pull himself up. The moon is still high. It can't be that long after midnight.

And it's too quiet. Where are Ana and Cobra?

Solma massages her throat. She touches Olive's shoulder, intending to speak.

And a scream cuts the night.

Seventeen

THE SCREAM GOES ON for a beat too long, then cuts short. It's Cobra. Solma feels it as surely as she felt that vine around her throat. She draws her pistol, thrusts her torch at Mamba.

"Get them to safety," she growls. "We got this."

Taipan's orange eyes shine in the moonlight. "But—"

"Just do it!" Solma barks. She meets Olive gaze, and they bolt towards the camp. Solma's pulse drums in her ears. Her oxygen-deprived body still won't do as it's told but adrenalin drives it onward. She leaps over protruding roots, dodges trees. Even without her torch, fear and anger sharpen her senses.

She and Olive skid into the Whisperer camp, weapons raised. They fall into a defensive stance, back-to-back, teeth bared, as if their wild appearance might be enough to frighten off attackers.

But the camp is silent. There's no-one here.

Olive grunts, puzzled. "What the—"

The ground shifts. Solma's eyes widen as a wall of brambles bursts up around the camp. Three of the tents fly open and, suddenly, Olive and Solma are surrounded.

A huge figure steps from a tent, his Whisperer robes tight across his muscled chest, tattooed vines creeping up his neck and scalp. Urutu. In his arm, he holds a small, struggling figure. It's Cobra. He snarls as he throws her to the ground and Solma rushes to help. Cobra winces as she leans against Solma. She holds her arm awkwardly.

"Where's Ana?" Solma mutters. Cobra shakes her head. Her eyes are misty with pain.

"Dunno," she says. "Say nothing."

Urutu grins, and he looks so much like Vulkan that Solma's breath catches.

"You're going nowhere," he snarls.

Solma raises her pistol, then lowers it again and gestures for Olive to do the same. Something tells her a vine will be around her wrist the moment she tries to pull the trigger. She needs to be smart.

"Fine," she growls. "What do you want, then?"

Urutu shrugs. "Give the defiant back," he says. "He broke our laws. He's a traitor." Solma raises an eyebrow.

"Strikes me," she says, "that Python ain't no traitor. He could just do something The Seasons didn't want him doing."

Urutu raises an eyebrow. "That's the definition of a traitor," he points out. "He's not yours. Give him back and we might let you live."

"But you won't let us go," Cobra says. She's trying to stand but Urutu's treatment has injured her. She favours one leg, wincing. Urutu shrugs again.

"Maybe not," he says. "But you'll survive."

Solma bares her teeth. That's not good enough. Slowly, she ushers Cobra behind her. Cobra's legs buckle and Olive catches her as she crumples. Olive raises her gaze, fixes Urutu with a hateful stare.

Solma scans the faces of the Whisperers surrounding them. There are ten. Most are teenagers Solma reckons she could easily overpower, but a few are older, steadier. There's an air of strength about them.

It's Urutu that worries her the most, though. Sidewinder obviously guessed she and the others would come back for Python. She trusted Urutu enough to set a trap for them. And even if they do manage to fight their way past the Whisperers, how're they supposed to get through that wall of brambles? Her eyes dart, searching the shadows ...

And snag on something.

A small figure darting between two tents. Did she imagine that? She could have sworn she saw a bow across the figure's back. Solma looks away quickly to avoid drawing attention to Ana's presence. Her mind whirls. Ana's a good shot but she can't save them all alone. She needs help. She needs ...

Solma thinks about what happened in Python's prison. How the mycelia had burst from the earthen chamber walls, overpowering Sidewinder and her troupe members.

He rotted a whole field in seconds with one fingertip in the soil ...

She turns her attention back to Urutu. "Maybe we can do a deal," she says.

"Sol!" Olive hisses. Solma ignores her. An idea's starting to form but there's no time to explain. Urutu's eyes glitter. He's listening.

"It ain't all of us The Seasons want to keep here, is it?" Solma continues, folding her arms. "It's just two they got a problem with. The defiant, and the leader of the troupe that disobeyed you. So how about you let us go, and we leave Python and Mamba behind?"

"Solma!" Cobra and Olive bark at once. They both grip her arms. Olive looks furious but Cobra's full of desperation. She shakes her head.

"Please, Sol," she begs.

Solma feels her heart shudder. She grabs her friend's hand, hoping Cobra understands.

"We have to," she says, fixing Cobra with a hard stare. Cobra searches her face. Solma thinks she sees something like realization there. Hopes Cobra will forgive her.

Cobra's jaw tightens. She gives a tiny nod, then puts on a show. *"No!"* she shrieks, wrenching her hand free. She pushes away from Solma, covering her face with her hands.

Solma glares at Urutu. "If we do that, you'll let the rest of us go?"

Urutu chuckles. Solma watches as he pushes his bare toes under the grass. His eyes glaze over briefly and then he withdraws his foot, triumph on his face. "Agreed," he says.

Cobra shrieks, clawing at Solma's arm. "No Sol! *Please!*"

Olive says nothing, just glares at Solma. There's something in her face though, an inkling she realizes there's more to this than Solma's letting on. Solma tears her gaze away, glancing towards the bramble wall. She can just make out the crouched outline of Ana, the moonlight reflecting in her eyes. Ana meets Solma's gaze, nods once, and slinks away.

"Fine," Solma says. She turns to Cobra. "Call him."

Cobra stares, mouth agape. "What?"

"Call him, Co," Solma says again. "It's the only way."

Cobra crumples to the ground, shaking her head. "I won't." She protests. "You don't know what you're doing. You—"

Solma takes her friend's hands and presses them against the earth. Instinctively, Cobra's fingers curl into the soil. She's really going for this performance, pulling away, pretending to resist the connection. But Solma sees the sheen in her eyes intensify and knows she's in the mycelia. Blood red mushrooms burst from the earth where her fingers connect with it. Silver threads snake through the grass. Solma sees the Whisperers surrounding them shrink back, horrified. Cobra shakes her head, sobbing bitterly. Solma sees real tears pour down her friends face and knows that, though Cobra understands, she's still terrified. The sight makes Solma's heart hurt.

She lets go of Cobra's wrists. Cobra doesn't get up, just kneels and sobs while yellow fungi unfurl around her, distress making her power erratic. Olive puts a hand on Cobra's shoulder but doesn't take her eyes off Solma.

"It's done," Solma says, dusting her hands on her shirt. Urutu watches her, then turns to one of the other Whisperers and nods. Three Whisperers crouch, push their fingers into the dirt and Whisper. The bramble wall behind them peels back to reveal a small opening. Now, they have an escape.

Urutu narrows his eyes. He beckons for Solma, Cobra and Olive to accompany him as he trudges towards the opening. His Whisperers follow, surrounding them.

"They step inside," Urutu says, "then we let you leave."

Solma nods. "Fine."

Still crying, Cobra takes Solma's hand, holding it so tightly Solma thinks her fingers might break. "Sol," she chokes. "*Please!*"

Solma covers Cobra's hand with hers. "It's for the best," she says. "He'll understand."

Cobra shakes her head, weeping, and throws Solma's hand away. She meets Solma's gaze, tears shining on her cheeks. Solma sees the warning in her eyes.

I trust you, Cobra's face says. *But if you mess this up ...*

Solma bites the inside of her cheek. She glances past Cobra to where the silent figure of Ana crouches inside the bramble wall. Ana pulls an arrow from her quiver, nocks it, draws the bow. Solma shuffles closer to the opening. Urutu moves to block her, just as she'd hoped.

Now, he's directly in Ana's aim.

"Not yet," Urutu says. Solma shrugs, pretending nonchalance. She looks aside to find Olive still watching, a frown creasing her brows. Solma chews her lip. She needs Olive in on this, but how's she supposed to explain without giving everything away to Urutu? Her mind works furiously. Earth, she hopes Mamba's brought Python. This won't work without him.

"Co?"

Mamba's voice makes Solma jump. He steps inside the bramble wall, Python behind him. Relief floods Solma and she fight to keep her face neutral. Cobra keeps up her ruse. She screams, running to him. She shoves his chest.

"Get out!" she yells. "Go! Run!"

Mamba holds her shoulders, looks into her face. Solma sees the moment he realises what's happening. "It's ok," he says quietly. He kisses her forehead. "I love you."

Cobra puts her face in her hands, wailing. Mamba looks at Solma. "Your idea?" he says. Solma swallows the sour taste in her throat and nods.

"Yeah," she says. "Sorry."

Mamba shrugs. "I get it," he says, and the intense look in his eyes tells her he does. And he bloody well hopes this will work. "Just ... take care of the others, yeah?"

Solma says nothing. She doesn't trust herself to speak.

Mamba takes Python's wrist, guiding the other Whisperer into the camp. Urutu folds his arms, smirking. Solma turns so Ana can see her hand. And clenches her fist.

There's a whisper of air, a grunt of pain, and an arrow sprouts from Urutu's chest. He stares at it as if he's not sure what happens next. Blood darkens his robe. He drops.

Olive reacts without question. Weapons drawn, she barrels into the nearest Whisperer as he drives his hands into the earth. She elbows him in the face, leaves him unconscious, and barely breaks stride as she charges and disarms two more.

Solma glances at where Ana had been moments before, but the girl's already gone. A hiss of air, a shout, and two more Whisperers go down with arrows in their shoulders. Another has crawled to Urutu and crouches over him, pressing her hands against his wound. Solma whirls on Mamba, points to Python.

"Get him into the network!" she roars, throat still raw. "Now!"

Her Whisperers all react at once. Cobra knuckles tears from her eyes and pushes into the mycelia. Mamba shoves Python into a crouch. Instinctively, Python's fingers dig into the earth. Fungi burst from where his hands touch the soil, silver filaments spider-webbing outwards. Everything they touch begins to wither and die.

"Sol!" Olive yells. Solma turns to see Olive battling vines as they shoot from the earth and wrap around her wrists and ankles. Solma curses, scanning the camp. Her eyes land on two Whisperers, crouched behind a tent, their hands in the earth. Their eyes are on Olive.

"Ana!" Solma cries, pointing. An arrow thuds into one of the Whisperers. He grunts, falling. Solma charges the other, driving her blade foot into his face. She hears a sickening crunch, and he tumbles backward, blood bursting from his nose.

Olive slashes the now dormant vines with her hunting knife and kicks them off. She grabs Cobra as the bramble wall trembles. Its leaves blacken, its thick stems shrivel. A delicate, silver film spreads over it.

Solma casts a triumphant look at Mamba, but he stares at Python, aghast. She runs to Mamba's side, grips Python under one arm. "Get him up!" she yells. "Let's go!"

Mamba grabs Python's other arm and they drag him free. He lets out a whimper as his hands peel out of the soil. He sags against them. Solma throws his arm over her shoulder, and they hurry towards the opening.

The others have made it through the brambles. Cobra turns, staring at Solma and Mamba. Her eyes widen.

"Mamba!" she shrieks. The bramble wall shudders again and the opening narrows. Ferns and creeping vines burst from the earth. Solma curses, but there's no time to find the Whisperer controlling it. She lengthens her stride. Cobra and Ana drop to the ground to try and slow the growth.

Mamba cries out as the greenery thickens, but there's no way Solma's staying to face Urutu or The Seasons. With a roar, she hurls Python and Mamba towards the escape. They fall through and land heavily in the grass, widening the opening enough that Solma can dive after them. She skids on her elbows just as the bramble wall slams closed behind her. She tastes blood and realizes she's bitten her tongue, but adrenalin deadens the pain. She's on her feet in moments, seizing Python's hand. She drags him up.

"*Run!*" she bellows.

Mamba takes Cobra's hand. Olive takes Solma's. They don't stop until their lungs are burning and their legs give way.

~ A Moment ~

IT'S DARK. NOT JUST inside this grass hut, but in his mind, too. Urutu tries to turn over. Pain lances through the wound just below his collarbone and he falls back, hissing air. The healers have worked on him. By some miracle—or perhaps by design—the arrow had missed piercing anything vital. It tore muscle, though, so that arm will always be weaker. Slower. It'll ache in the cold. Urutu clenches his jaw, but not with pain this time.

With anger.

He bites down on it. He has more reason than most to know how dangerous anger can be. But he can't stop it. It rushes through him like an unleashed tide.

He's angry with Python for escaping. For how he tainted the mind of a promising young Whisperer.

He's angry with Mamba. How could the boy be so *stupid?*

He's angry with that girl with the bow and arrow. What was her name? Ana, that was it. Self-righteous little weed.

The anger scares him. It's always scared him, but the more he tries to contain it, the more forceful it becomes. The strain makes him dizzy. He needs to sleep but he doesn't want to sleep.

When he sleeps, he sees the face of that girl. The tall one with dark hair and a world of pain in her eyes. He hears her shouting. He feels waves of fury pouring off her. There's something about her that scares him. While the others were whining on about the insects coming back (which is impossible, isn't it?) she looked as if there was something deeper at play. Something *personal*. Urutu saw it in her eyes.

He saw how she'd tear the world apart for—

For who?

There was someone at the other end of this. Someone she would kill for. Die for.

Urutu remembers once having someone he felt like that about. A long time ago. Before anger and discord broke them apart. He's not spoken to that man for fifteen years. Urutu had thought he was dead until recently. Discovering him alive hurt even more than believing he was gone.

Seeing what he's become …

Even conjuring a memory of his face makes Urutu's eyes sting with tears. He wipes his hand across his face. It's cold and he pulls the rough wool blanket up under his chin. But when he touches his forehead, he realizes he's burning up. Fear grips him. A fever? Did the healers' medicine not work? He pushes the fear away. He's strong. Even with a hole under his collarbone, he can weather this.

He cries out as light spills over his face. He lifts a hand to shield his eyes. The moss-and-vine wall of the grass-hut slithers open. Someone slips inside, presses a hand to the earthen wall and Whispers it closed. Urutu drops his hand and turns away. He closes his eyes. He has no energy for this conversation.

"What do you want, Sidewinder?" he croaks. He'd meant for it to be gruff, but his voice comes out plaintiff and pathetic. There's a grunt as Sidewinder kneels beside him. A cool hand touches his forehead, then presses something bitter between his lips.

"Chew," Sidewinder says. Her voice sounds strange, raspy. Urutu chews. The root is tough and when he bites into it, bitterness bursts in his mouth. He splutters and goes to spit it out, but Sidewinder puts a hand over his mouth.

"You want to live? Chew."

Urutu glares. Sidewinder busies herself with something. There's the spark-and-hiss of a lantern being lit. A warm, orange glow fills the chamber. Sidewinder's face is lit from below and Urutu sees there's a bandage around her throat, deep, purple-and-black bruising visible above and below. Sidewinder sees him looking and raises an eyebrow.

"To stop swelling," she rasps. Urutu sees her wince and realizes that speaking hurts her. She's come here to talk, though she knows it will be painful.

And that means what she must tell him is important. He searches her face, expecting to find the same anger he's been nurturing in his own mind, but it's not there.

A frown draws grooves between her brows. She's chewing the inside of her cheek. Urutu waits, too tired and weak to be impatient. He wants Sidewinder to speak, and he doesn't want her to say a word. The look on her face unsettles him.

It's probably just the fever. He was never a good patient, hating how sickness incapacitated him. As a youngster, after Sidewinder had taken him in from his village, he remembers being struck down with a pox. Itchy and irritable, he'd wasted energy throwing tantrums until Sidewinder had bound his arms and legs to keep him from lashing out. He'd calmed down after that. Sidewinder had tended him carefully. Gently. She'd only been a teenager at the time. As surrogate mothers go, she was never all that affectionate. But she was practical. Decisive. In her presence, he'd always felt safe.

Now, though, she looks uncertain. Though he left childhood behind over two decades ago, the fear in the eyes of the woman who raised him brings a primal kind of horror.

At last, she speaks. "The healers say you'll recover in a few days."

Urutu splutters a mirthless laugh. "Do they?"

It doesn't feel like it. Pain shoots through his wound, making him wince. Sidewinder shrugs, says nothing. Eventually, Urutu looks away.

"This is pointless," he says, spluttering as the root he's chewing ejects more bitter juice. Sidewinder still says nothing. Urutu sneaks a glance at her. There's a faraway look on her face.

"You came to say something," Urutu says. "Speak."

Finally, Sidewinder meets his gaze. "Mamba," she says, and his name makes Urutu wince. "Those girls. They're saying the insects are back."

Urutu raises an eyebrow. "I heard," he says. Sidewinder doesn't answer. Urutu searches her face and a terrible understanding dawns on him. "You believe them."

"It could be true," Sidewinder says. "The Seasons don't believe it."

Urutu tries to shrug but the movement makes him growl in pain. "That's that, then," he says. "If The Seasons think—"

"Maybe they're wrong." Sidewinder says. Urutu gapes.

"*Wrong?*"

It's not possible. The Seasons are tapped into everything. They are in the network of the Earth, the veins of the world. They listen to its heartbeat, its ever-murmuring thoughts. They're never wrong.

If The Seasons are wrong, that means that what he and Sidewinder did to Python all those years ago ... it wasn't for the good of Alphor, it wasn't to preserve their precious way of life. It was evil.

Urutu shakes his head, pain lancing through his injury. That can't be true. They were acting on The Seasons' orders. The Seasons are the world. The pulsing arteries of Alphor. They weren't wrong about Python then. They're not wrong about him now. Urutu glares at Sidewinder, willing her to back down. Sidewinder's face is pale.

"They—" she says, then clamps her mouth shut and looks away. Fear chills Urutu's heart.

"They what?"

Sidewinder doesn't look at him. "They told us the defiant would break everything when he connected to the mycelia," she says. "Remember?"

"I remember he rotted a whole field," Urutu mutters. "I remember feeling those plants die before we put a stop to it."

Sidewinder shakes her head. "Maybe there's more to it than that."

Urutu scowls. "Or maybe there isn't," he says. But Sidewinder shakes her head.

"I was there, remember?" she murmurs. "When The Seasons spoke with Mamba and Cobra. They got so angry. But I felt it in the roots and the vines. They were ... afraid, too."

Urutu lifts his eyebrows. "Afraid?" he says. Sidewinder nods. She touches a hand to her bandaged throat and winces. But she goes on.

"Something's going to happen," she says. "The Seasons know it. The world is going to catch fire."

Urutu only just manages to stifle a moan of fear. Sidewinder isn't looking at him, so she doesn't see the way his skin drains of color, or how he begins to shake. Urutu, for his part, only just manages to get himself under control.

Catch fire.

Could it be ...?

No. It must be coincidence. There's no way she could know. No way the Seasons could know. He's carried his secret like a thorn in his heart for so long. He's so used to the pain of it, he's forgotten what it feels like to walk through the world without guilt. He hasn't spoken that name for such a long time. Hasn't even allowed himself to think it.

But still.

Still, the fear is enough to make him struggle into a sitting position. Enough to make him say, "What do you need?"

Sidewinder bites her lip. "You should rest," she says. "For now. When you're recovered, we'll talk again. I have an idea."

Urutu doesn't trust himself to speak. He watches as Sidewinder hands him another root to chew, then stands and Whispers the hut open. He blinks as the light of a dreary afternoon spills inside. Sidewinder glances back. She looks like she's about to say something, but then thinks better of it.

She leaves quickly, sealing the chamber behind her.

Eighteen

WARREN HUDDLES ON HIS pallet, waiting for the sound of the key in the lock. The soldier who'd come to check his cell was bored, barely casting his eyes over the room before leaving again. The knitting needle Gerta hid remains undiscovered.

A crescent moon casts dim light on the stone floor. For a wondrous moment, Warren thinks maybe the idiot soldier has forgotten to lock his cell. But then there comes the scrape of a key. Warren's heart sinks. Quietly, he lifts out the slat on his pallet and retrieves the needle. A part of him—quite a big part—is still angry with the old woman. It's her strange knowledge that's keeping the insects imprisoned. It's she who tends the comatose Blaiz. Her skills give Maxen his power. But it was also Gerta who wandered into the wilderness after Solma lost her leg, returning with an old-world prosthesis so Solma could still be a soldier.

It was Gerta who looked after both Solma and Warren when they were Yuen-caste, and it was Gerta who took care of Warren during that wonderful, awful summer when Blaiz made him control the bees.

The world isn't as simple as it was when he was seven, though he wishes, desperately, that it was.

He forces himself to wait, counting the seconds, for ten minutes. With the door locked, the squads will head out on their evening patrols. Everyone will forget about Warren until morning.

Wait ten minutes, Gerta said. He's got no idea what she's planning, but he has to trust her. Earth, he wishes his sister was here. Memories of the terrible fire in the forest behind Skyheart village burst into his mind. He pushes them away. He has to believe everyone made it out. To believe his sister is on her way. She won't abandon him.

Not unless she—

Warren clamps down on that thought before it can take hold, and clambers off his pallet.

Solma's on her way. She's bringing help. And Warren needs to do something, or Maxen will kill her.

He creeps to the door and kneels, pressing an eye to the keyhole to check the coast is clear. The corridor beyond is silent, empty. Warren slips the sharp end of the knitting needle into the lock, his tongue poking between his teeth. He jiggles the needle, ear pressed to the door, waiting for a click. Nothing happens.

Warren growls through his teeth, twisting the needle sharply. The lock scrapes but there's no click. Warren's hand slips and catches on the edge of the lock. He yelps as the needle clatters on the stone floor. A bulb of blood blooms at the end of his finger. He puts it in his mouth, wincing. Why couldn't the stupid guards just forget to lock the stupid door?

Buoyed with a new wave of frustration, Warren snatches up the needle. He shoves it back into the lock and takes a deep breath. Patience, Gerta told him. It's easy for her to say. She's not locked in a cell! Still, he closes his eyes and twists the needle, lifts, feels a little resistance. Hope bubbles in his chest. Carefully, he pushes the needle, lifts again. Pushes. Lifts.

The click of the lock opening is so sudden it makes him jump. He almost drops the needle again but catches it before it falls. He shoves it in his pocket and stands, pulse pummelling his ears.

The door handle creaks as it turns but the door opens. Warren bites his lip against a shout of joy.

Carefully, he slips out, hugging the shadows as he scurries up the corridor. There are no soldiers manning the stairs. The carpeted hallway is empty. The electric lights are off, curtains drawn. Warren makes a break for it. The carpet muffles his footfalls enough that when he reaches the front door, he's certain no-one has heard him.

The front door's closed and Warren prays Maxen is still dealing with aggrieved villagers or sergeants issuing reports. He won't lock the door until he's done with those.

The handle is stiff when Warren grabs it and his heart lurches painfully. But then the handle yields, the door opens, and Warren darts outside, scurrying up the path. He doesn't head through the village but turns south, towards the glasshouses. It'll be a matter of minutes before Maxen sends a guard to check on him. And then his time will be up. He must be done with this when they find him.

And they *will* find him. And he *will* be punished. But he has to do this. For Solma.

He follows the path towards the insects, then darts between the last two houses and hunkers down in the shadows. Maxen won't be stupid enough not to post soldiers by the insects.

Wait, Gerta said. So, he does. It feels as if he waits for a hundred years.

And at last, he hears it. A cry of outrage and frustration. He recognises Gerta's scolding voice, then other voices raised in answer. Warren holds his breath as hurried footsteps sound from beyond the glasshouses. He lifts his eyes just enough to see a squad of soldiers hurrying towards the village centre. The shouting intensifies. More voices join the commotion. Now, Warren hears guards trying to control the growing chaos. Gerta's voice raises above the others, yelling something about injustice and mistreatment. Warren whispers a quiet thanks to the old woman, then bolts from his hiding place.

The last of the sunlight glints off the glasshouse walls. There are no soldiers. Maxen might be smart enough to post guards by the insects, but they aren't clever enough to stay put. An anxious buzz sounds from the hives. Butterfly wings glimmer like jewels. Warren pushes his way through the chemical barrier, spluttering on the stench. The bees greet him, but they're distracted. The temperature is dropping for the night. The light is gone. They're tired. It's time to huddle together in their nests and sleep.

Warren pushes his mind out to them

Don't sleep yet, he begs. *I need a few to stay awake. To fly.*

The bees hover by his shoulders, their scent full of fear. They can't leave the nests now! No bee survives a night outside its nest! Warren gentles them, but it's hard to explain what he needs them to do. Instead, he drops to all fours and searches the long grass by Clover's hive.

It'll be hidden here, Gerta said. The silver cannister. The key that frees the insects. Not that they know that. As soon as they feel his presence, Clover's daughters flood from their entrance tunnel, drawing halos round his head.

What is he doing? Why is he disturbing their nest? He feels the sharp tang of their confusion and fear. He sends out a wave of what he hopes is calming scent. It's ok, he doesn't want their nest. He's looking for something else.

But they don't believe him. The sour stench of their suspicion hits him and his eyes burn. They don't trust him. *Clover* doesn't trust him.

The realisation makes him freeze. He sits back on his heels, lip quivering. A pain he can't explain beats in his chest. She doesn't trust him. He feels waves of aggression coming from her nest.

Go away. We don't need you.

The scent is dismissive. Aggressive. Warren clutches at his heart, fighting tears. He sends out another scent.

I'm sorry. I'm sorry.

But there's no time to explain. The sun dips below the horizon and the sky dims. Warren can barely see. He pushes his fingers through the grass, searching. Another shout goes up nearby. Warren tenses. He's running out of time. Frantic, he shoves both hands into the grass, ignoring the outraged scent of the bees.

What're you doing? What're you doing?

Warren grits his teeth, trying to make his scent calm.

It's ok. It's—

But Clover isn't convinced. The first sting sends such a shock through his body that he can't suppress his yelp. He jerks his hand free, and the offending bee zooms away. Her sisters circle closer. Warren sees poison glistening on their stings.

Please, he begs them. *Don't attack. I'm trying to help—*

Another sting lands on his neck and a third on his ankle. He hisses air through his teeth, bites down on a shout of pain. There's no time to calm them.

Again, he shoves his hand under the hive, groping in the dark. Pain puckers on his elbow. His forearm. There's nothing here. Where the hell did Gerta leave it?

And then his fingers brush something cold and hard. He almost cries with relief as he pulls the cannister from the grass and backs away, letting the bees settle. He rubs the soreness on his arms and neck, holds out his palm for a little buff-tail to settle there. She shivers her wing-muscles before zooming back into her nest. Warren still feels the shock-scent of Clover's dismissal, a bitter tang at the back of his throat.

We don't need you.

It's so potent, that scent, it makes him nauseous. He swallows against rising bile. There'll be time to feel sad later. Whether Clover knows it or not, she does need him now. He shakes the cannister and glances over his shoulder, hoping he's got enough time. He covers his mouth with this shirt collar and sprays the cannister in the air, on the grass, across the glasshouse walls. He's not sure how much Gerta said to use, but—

"What're you doing?"

Warren whirls round, dropping the cannister behind him. It falls soundlessly in the grass, and he hopes the evening is dark enough to keep it hidden from Ignis.

The other boy stands in front of him, arms folded. His violet eyes shine in the last of the sunlight.

"Nothing," Warren says. Which is obviously not true. His cheeks flush with heat. Ignis lets out a derisive snort.

"How'd you even get out?"

"I—" Warren doesn't want to get the guards into trouble, but he can't tell the truth. "They forgot to lock the door," he says, hating that the soldier responsible for him will be punished. His aunt's face bursts into his mind.

How would you like it, young man?

He hopes she'd understand.

Ignis raises an eyebrow. "Yeah," he says. "Well. You still ain't answered my first question. What you doing?"

Warren shoves his hands in his pockets and shrugs. He can feel the bees' excitement as the antidote breaks down the chemical barrier. Their scent changes.

Freedom! Comes their collective cry, in many insect languages. Warren thrusts out his mind and grabs hold of them.

Wait.

The bees buck against him. Even in the evening chill, they're desperate enough that they would risk the night for fresh flowers and greater space. But Warren can't let them go. Not yet. The strain of trying to contain them is exhausting and he feels something burst in his nose. He wipes his hand across his face before Ignis sees the blood.

"Warren!" Ignis barks. "*What* are you doing!"

His face flushes with anger. In the dying light, Warren sees the bee-sting scars stand out on his cheek. Warren bites his lip against a needle of guilt. Despite everything, he still can't bring himself to hate this boy.

He wants to. He has no idea why he can't.

"I—" Warren stammers. "I wanted—to make sure they were ok. I heard them calling. They were distressed."

Ignis rolls his eyes. "They're always distressed," he drawls. "It could'a waited 'til morning."

"Yeah," Warren agrees. "Look. Can you just—don't say anything. I'll go back now."

Ignis glares. "Yeah," he growls. "Bet that was always your plan. You know how much trouble you keep getting me into?"

Ignis stops, clamps his mouth closed. Warren blinks, looking closely at Ignis' face. Is that a new bruise on his chin? Is his lip split? There's a haunted look in his eyes. Warren doesn't know how Ignis keeps picking up these injuries, though he's got his suspicions. He steps forward, reaching out a hand.

"Ig—" he says. Ignis' eyes flash.

"Don't call me that!" he snarls. "That ain't my name!"

Warren tries to make his face kind. "It was, once," he says. "When we were friends. Remember?"

Ignis' lip curls. "We weren't never friends!"

Warren bites his lip and tries to pretend he doesn't feel his heart crack. He's not sure how many more fractures it can take.

"Maybe you weren't mine," he tries. "But I was yours. I wanted to be. I liked you."

Ignis lets out a barking laugh. "Yeah," he says. "'Til you found out who I really was. That's always how it works, ain't it? I can't never be myself. I'm just the fire boy. Just the one who burns the world. That's all me and Dja will ever be to people like you!"

He steps forward, sparks flashing at his fingertips. Warren instinctively steps back …

And knocks the cannister he dropped in the grass. It rattles. Warren freezes. Ignis' eyes narrow as his gaze darts to Warren's feet.

"What's that?"

"Nothing." Warren closes his eyes. "I mean, I don't know. I never seen it before, I—"

"Shut up," Ignis snaps. He grabs Warren's arm and pulls him aside. He lifts the cannister into the light and glares at Warren.

"You weren't just checking on the bees," he says. There's cruelty in his voice, but Warren thinks he detects something worse, too. Hurt. Betrayal. Ignis rounds on him, almost shouting. "You were trying to let them go! You *little—!*"

He grabs Warren by the collar and pulls him close, so angry he's practically spitting. His yell makes Warren wince.

"Oi! He's here! I got him!"

Warren struggles, but Ignis' grip is vice like. Warren whimpers.

"You're hurting me—"

"So?" Ignis snarls. "You deserve it!" He shakes Warren roughly. Warren grabs Ignis' hands, trying to pry them free. Footfalls sound behind him and he sags in Ignis' grip. He's caught. It's over.

He's only got one more thing to try. He hopes the bees will respond and Ignis won't notice.

He pushes out a final, desperate scent to the insects he knows best. The ones whose song echoes always in his mind. The buff-tails.

Go!

But nothing stirs. There's no excited tremolo of wings. They aren't listening.

Clover's vicious scent-song resonates in Warren's mind again.

We don't need you.

She meant it. She isn't listening. Warren finally succumbs to the pain of it and tears spill down his cheeks.

A squad of soldiers charges up the path, headed by Vulkan. The Fire Maker's palms burn. Warren notices with a stab of fear that two of the soldiers have Gerta restrained between them. Despite being half their size and five times their age, she fights like a redbear. She stamps on one's foot and he yells out, letting go of her.

But there's another soldier to take his place and Gerta is contained again. She meets Warren's gaze. Warren sees sadness in her eyes.

Vulkan stalks up to Warren, now subdued in Ignis' grip.

"Dja!" Ignis calls, triumphant. "I—"

Vulkan raises his burning hand and swipes it hard across Warren's face. The force sends Warren sprawling in the dirt. He cries out at the sting-burn pain, his hand flying to his cheek. He looks up and sees Ignis face, eyes wide with shock, before his father rounds on him and delivers a similar blow. Ignis joins Warren in the grass. He doesn't cry out, Warren notices. He just raises his head and glares at Warren.

"Stupid boy!" Vulkan growls, looming over Ignis. "Why weren't you watching? Thought you could make a friend of the bee kid, eh? They ain't like us, Ignis."

"I know, Dja," Ignis says sullenly. Vulkan snorts.

"Do you?" he says. "People like us don't have friends. Never forget it."

"Yes, Dja."

Vulkan grunts. "Get him up, then," he says. "Don't be gentle."

Ignis grabs Warren and pulls him to his feet. Warren doesn't struggle. He's too tired and confused to try. Instead, he lets Ignis twist his arm behind his back. Vulkan sneers.

"Take them both to Maxen," he says.

Gerta struggles the whole way, shouting and spitting and making trouble. Warren marvels at her resolve. He wishes he felt the same, but he's so tired. He can't stop himself from sobbing. Maxen will want him punished and he can already feel the rain of blows, the cold and hunger, that will come as a result.

But more than that. More than that is the echo of Clover's scent-song in his head.

We don't need you.

And the rain of stings her workers landed all over him. The most ferocious rejection. The pain of that hurts worse than any punishment. He cries harder.

"Shut up!" Ignis hisses, but Warren can't.

It's dark enough that no-one sees the buff-tail that stirs in the last of the sun. She flexes her antennae as Warren is dragged away. Inside the nest, the song has changed.

The world is wider. The world smells of flowers.

The little buff-tail powers her engine and lifts into the evening air. The humans are too far down the path, too focused on themselves, to hear her song.

As the day fades, she leaps onto an evening breeze and swoops away.

Nineteen

IGNIS KICKS A STONE along the path, watching it skitter away. A few Yuen playing nearby glance up. Their faces darken when they see him. Typical. Ignis glares. He lifts a hand and conjures flame. The Yuen scurry away. Ignis watches them go, then extinguishes his fire. He flexes his fingers, feeling the echo of that burning pain.

It's one thing Dja says never to let others see. The fire that Vulkan and Ignis conjure doesn't blister or blacken their flesh, but it still *hurts*. Every time Ignis pulls flames from within himself, it feels as if he's burning. Sometimes, it hurts so much he's afraid to look at his hands afterwards, convinced he'll see the skin puckered and glistening.

But there's never even a mark.

Ignis shoves his hands in his pockets and trudges down the path, away from Maxen's house. He's been there all night and most of the day, while Maxen interrogated the bee boy and the old woman. Warren, of course, cried and denied everything until Vulkan pressed a burning hand to Gerta's back. The old woman's made of tougher stuff than Ignis first thought. He'll give her that. She didn't scream for ages. But when she did, the sound sent a cold thrill through Ignis' body. He thought he'd never heard anything so terrible.

As soon as Gerta shrieked, Warren admitted everything. Yes, he'd tried to free the bees. It hadn't worked. None had flown. He did it because Maxen wouldn't *listen.*

Maxen dismissed Gerta after that, telling the old woman to see to her wounds and be back to tend Blaiz within the hour. Gerta, who never learned her place, spat a whole bunch of swearwords that Ignis had never heard before, until that insipid sergeant, Aldo, persuaded her out of the house. Then it was up to Ignis and Vulkan to make sure Warren was locked up, and punish the guard who'd forgotten to seal the cell. They've stationed a whole squad down in the basement to make sure the nine-year-old who'd outwitted them doesn't escape again.

Finally, there was no-one left to punish. Except one. Vulkan had turned burning, violet eyes on his son. Ignis ran. It's the only thing to do in those situations. When Vulkan looks like that, there's no point staying around.

Ignis stops round the back of the council hall, leaning against the cracked mud walls. He stares at the sky, painted flaming orange-and-pink by the sunset. Dusk makes him restless, especially when the sky is clear enough to catch fire like that. It makes him want to burn things, too. He doesn't know why. It's silly. Childish.

He kicks another loose stone.

The Fei head back from the fields. He hears their inane babble carrying on the breeze. They're tired after a day's work, talking of food supplies and whether there's enough for dinner. One older woman gently asks the man she's with if he'd like to join her family for a meal that evening. Ignis can't stand it. He claps his hands over his ears, glaring. He's so sick of *villages* and *families* all pretending everyone around them matters. All hugging each other, smiling, tucking their kids in at night. Pathetic.

Like family ever does anything except let each other down.

Ignis takes his hands from his ears, breathing a sigh as he realizes the chatter is dying away. They're heading into their houses, swapping bread or broth with their neighbours. Yuen skip home from their Aldren minders. Slowly, the village begins to settle. Now, the only footsteps are those of Gatra squads, patrolling the village.

There's little sound, now. Only the scuffle of rodents, the cry of something within the forest. Ignis leans his head against the wall and breathes deeply. He doesn't hear the crunch of stones beneath heavy feet until his father is almost upon him.

"Been looking for you, boy," Vulkan growls. Ignis whips round in time to receive the back of Vulkan's flaming hand across his face. There's a hiss of steam and smoke at the impact. Ignis sprawls in the dirt. Wincing, he lifts a hand to his cheek, feels the way his father's fire has scorched his face. He scowls.

"Din't have to leave a mark, Dja," he grumbles, getting to his feet. Vulkan raises an eyebrow. He reaches a huge hand towards Ignis, who flinches back. Vulkan pauses. He clicks his tongue, then unwinds a cloth from his belt and soaks it in water from his bottle. He crouches in front of Ignis, beckons him forward.

Ignis hesitates. Sometimes, this is kindness. Sometimes it's a trick.

But there's regret in his father's eyes today, so Ignis shuffles forward, tilts his head so Vulkan can gently press the damp cloth to his cheek. He sucks in air as the burn sears with pain again. Vulkan grunts, but he's patient and careful as he cleans the wound.

"If I never left a mark," he says sadly, "you'd never learn, eh?"

Ignis says nothing. He could draw the heat out of the burn, the way he'd drawn that fire in Warren's cell, but he knows how his father feels about that. Vulkan can't do it. Or at least, has never bothered to try. And Ignis showing off that ability will only make his father cross again.

Instead, he lets Vulkan soak both the wound and his guilt with that damp cloth. The burn throbs. He knows it'll blister, later.

Another thing Vulkan says never to mention. Their fire might not damage their own skin, but they can certainly burn each other. Or at least, Vulkan's fire can burn Ignis. He's never had the guts to try it the other way around.

Finally, Vulkan pulls the cloth away, cups Ignis' chin, and examines the wound.

"Not serious," he says, tucking the cloth back into his belt. "It'll heal."

Ignis leans back against the wall, making sure to keep more than an arm's distance between himself and his father. Vulkan settles against the wall, too. He sips water from his bottle. Ignis grimaces as some dribbles down his father's unshaven chin.

"The bee kid's secure," Vulkan reports. "Maxen's calm, for now. And the old woman won't cause more trouble in a hurry," He clips his bottle back onto his belt without offering Ignis any. Ignis dabs at his burned cheek.

"Why'd you hit me for, then?" he mutters. Vulkan's eyes flash and Ignis gets ready to run. But Vulkan only shakes his head.

"'Cos that bee kid makes you soft," he says. "We ain't soft, you and me. We don't got no-one. No family. We don't *need* no-one."

"No," Ignis says quietly. It's the response his father always expects. But, recently, Ignis has begun to wonder whether it's true. He's heard Warren ranting about his sister enough times. He remembers how they'd defended each other last year. How she'd fought to keep Warren safe, how he'd summoned his bees to save her. He raises a hand to his cheekbone and fingers the bee-sting scars. Ignis has seen Warren looking at these scars, seen the regret in his face. But he knows Warren would do it again, to save his sister.

And where was Vulkan when Ignis was under a carpet of bees? Did he come and save his son? 'Course not. He was busy, burning things elsewhere. Ignis had saved himself. As usual. And even when they finally *had* Warren and had blown up the cave entrance so they wouldn't be followed through the mountains, Vulkan had still left a stinging burn on the back of Ignis' neck.

"That's for losing the other two kids," he'd said. "We could'a used them."

Instinctively, Ignis' hand goes to his cheek, wincing as his fingers brush the damaged flesh. He turns to find Vulkan watching him.

"Don't you go soft," Vulkan warns. "You remember what happens when we go soft. You remember your mother."

Ignis' heart lurches. He doesn't really remember his mother. Not beyond what Vulkan has told him over and over. Quietly, sometimes, when Ignis can't sleep. Sometimes in rage or drunken frenzy. Sometimes in snarling tones, as if he blames Ignis for it.

Now, he says it with threat in his voice.

"If it weren't for her, we'd never be the way we are. Begging favours from rich Stewards, limping across the continent, chasing scraps. It's her. Too weak to stand up to her own stupid Dja."

"I know," Ignis says. He doesn't want to hear it. Not now. He's angry as it is, and he can't get Warren's face out of his head. Vulkan either doesn't notice or doesn't care.

"You understand she betrayed us, kid? She turned us in. She was our own. Our only family. But when it came to it, that din't mean nothing to her. Like it never meant nothing to those kids you played with."

Ignis feels sick and swallows the taste of bile. Why must his father always bring this up?

"They took you in when you came, though," he says, bitterness in his voice. "When you turned up, half-starved and all that, the village took you in. They nursed you. Ma married you. You had me. It weren't all bad."

It's the first time he's ever voiced that. It takes them both by surprise. Vulkan's face twists and he launches himself at his son. Years of practise has made Ignis quick. He darts aside before his father can catch him. Vulkan draws himself up, over six foot of terrible, raging power. Ignis readies himself to run, but Vulkan's got no interest in landing another blow. Not a physical one anyway. His eyes flash, and Ignis sees himself reflected in them, the way Vulkan sees him.

A child of rage and flame. Born to destroy. Vulkan's own past, his own pain, made flesh. Vulkan lunges forward.

"They were *weak!*" he spits. "All'a them! When your mother saw what we could do, she ran straight to her Dja. She was *with the mob* that drove us out. Remember?"

Ignis doesn't, but he nods all the same, keeping an eye on his father's fists.

"And any village we found refuge in after. Any of those Yuen boys you played with, you remember what they did when they found out what you are?"

Ignis clenches his jaw, not wanting to answer. He does remember. Those memories are seared into his mind and Vulkan never lets him forget.

"*Do you?*" Vulkan insists. Ignis skips backwards, glaring.

"Yeah," he says. "I remember."

"They chased us out!" Vulkan roars. "Again and again! First your pathetic Ma, then every village we ever tried to find safety in."

Ignis' ears ring. He feels that familiar, burning anger. The kind that ignites every muscle. Every nerve. He sucks air in through his teeth, trying to control the pain. Vulkan laughs.

"Pathetic," he sneers. "Just like her. That's what family does, kid. It makes you weak. We're lucky we ain't got none besides each other. And I'll stop you going soft if it's the last thing I do."

Ignis bares his teeth. "I hate you," he snarls. Vulkan barks a laugh. The tension goes out of him, as if he's got exactly what he wanted.

"'Course you do," he says, folding his arms. "You hate everyone. Good lad."

He stares at Ignis, a smile tugging one side of his mouth. Then he turns and disappears into the gathering gloom within looking back. Ignis scowls after him, hating him.

Eventually, the fire in his nerves dies and he sinks to the ground. Tears burn his eyes, but he blinks them away. Crying is weak. His Ma cried, Vulkan always says. She cried even as she joined the mob that chased them away. Her own husband. Her own *son*. Those stupid boys always cried when they learned the truth about Ignis. Cried, then grabbed sticks and beat him until Vulkan appeared to spirit him away.

Those ridiculous Keeper kids cried, too. And Warren summoned his bees to sting him. And—

Ignis blinks as he thinks back to the previous night. To what Warren had said.

I was your friend. I liked you.

Those words open a whole new kind of pain. Not a burning, ferocious pain, but something deeper. An ache like a long-ago broken bone. Like a callous in his heart. He clutches his chest.

Warren isn't his friend. He never was. He lied to Ignis, didn't he? Got Ignis in trouble. *Again.* Ignis might hate his Dja, but Vulkan's here, isn't he? Vulkan might goad and burn and yell, but he's never abandoned Ignis.

Not like Ma. Not like everyone else. And Warren would, too, if he got the chance. He'd run off with his stupid sister without looking back.

So Ignis buries the memory of Warren's words somewhere deep and dark. No point thinking about them again.

Instead, he trudges after his father as the sun dips below the horizon.

Twenty

A BREEZE STIRS THE grass, throwing pollen into the air. Solma sneezes. Beside her, Burdock pricks up his ears, turns to nuzzle her. She strokes his velvety muzzle.

"I'm alright," she says.

The pony returns his attention to plodding. They passed into High Savannah Province a few days ago and the land has flattened out. The grass is short and stiff, cropped by the grazing of huge herbivores. Solma's never seen anything so massive in all her life. Cobra says they're managed by the locals for game, which makes Solma balk. Hunting a giant boar is bad enough. But these things?

The animals are broad-shouldered and muscular, with short, tan hair and whipping, bristled tails. Their cloven hooves kick up dust and they toss their horned heads, snorting steam if the travellers get too close.

Their necks are long enough that they can graze at the scrubby leaves of savannah trees. Wildervores, Cobra calls them. And she warns Solma and the youngsters to steer clear. Solma doesn't need telling twice. She does catch Taipan looking at them strangely, though. The girl's been quiet since the Whisperer camp.

The pain in Solma's knee is constant, but with Python's mind still lost, the cart is needed to carry him. Solma glances at him. He's sat with his knees drawn up under his chin, rocking with the rhythm of the cart. He hasn't spoken since they rescued him. Has only eaten what's been spooned into his mouth and, whenever they stop for the night, he sinks his fingers into the soil with a sigh of relief.

Solma wonders what the point is. They risked everything to free him from that damn prison. What the hell have they got to show for it? He's an empty husk.

She'd thought, when she realized it was him—not Taipan—that had rescued them from both Sidewinder and Urutu, that he might come back to himself. But they've been travelling for weeks. Spring has lengthened and warmed into the promise of a bright, hot summer. The trees are thick with leaves.

Solma's seen baby animals scuffling about in the scrub.

But still, Python is only a shell. Perhaps his help had been nothing more than instinct. Just distress making his mind lash out. Perhaps it was mere luck that he'd attacked the Whisperers and not Solma and her friends. They're still over a fortnight away from Sand's End and Python's shown no sign of awareness. Solma sees her Whisperer friends exchanging dark looks. She knows they're talking through the mycelia.

She can guess what they're saying.

Was risking their lives at the Camp worth it?

Solma clenches her jaw. Weeks of delay, injuries, and another mouth to feed. Their rescue effort has achieved nothing but a series of disasters.

She notices Olive pause behind the cart to scan the horizon, a frown bridging her brows. Solma goes to her, touches her arm.

"You ok?" she asks.

Olive chews her lip.

"Dunno," she admits. "Keep feeling like ... ah, maybe it ain't nothing."

Solma raises an eyebrow. "Don't do that," she says. "No secrets. We promised."

Olive wraps an arm round Solma's waist. "Alright," she says, kissing Solma gently. "You win. But it probably ain't nothing."

Solma gives her a withering glare and Olive chuckles. "I keep thinking we're being followed," she admits. "Thought something tried to sneak into camp when I was on watch two nights ago. But when I stood up, it weren't nothing but shadows." She shakes her head. "I swear I'm going crazy, Sol."

Solma feels her insides curdle and rests her temple against Olive's, hugging her close.

"You ain't going crazy, my love," she says, kissing Olive's shoulder. "You should sleep properly tonight. I'll take your watch."

Olive starts to protest but Solma stares her into silence. Olive's shoulders slump. "Yeah," she says finally. "Okay."

Solma nods, satisfied, even though she, too, hasn't slept properly for days. Every time she closes her eyes, Warren's face appears. What will she find when she reaches Sand's End? Is he even alive?

She pushes that thought away as she and Olive catch up with the procession.

The sun dips towards the horizon, throwing a swathe of orange across the sky. Ana lifts Krait and Habu onto the cart beside Python. Cobra, still favouring one leg from the fight with Urutu, carries Taipan. Bell's limping and Solma winces as she sees her aunt stumble, catching herself on Roseann's arm. They're exhausted.

"We should stop for the night," she says. "I'll let Mamba know. We'll do a quick scout of the area while Bell sorts food."

Olive nods and strides ahead to call a halt. The others set up camp while Olive and Solma do a perimeter check. They return as darkness falls to find Bell cooking over a fire. They hunker down among the Whisperers and Bell hands out bowls of steaming food. No-one talks as they eat.

Solma glances at Ana as she spoons broth into Python's mouth. His lips barely open enough to receive the food and his fingers still dig into the soil.

"What're we gonna do?" she murmurs. Olive slips an arm round her waist, pulls her close.

"We'll think of something," she promises.

Solma takes first watch while the others crawl into the tents. She douses the fire and paces the camp's perimeter, pistol holstered but knife at the ready. Last year, Warren and Taipan had taught her to wild-walk—a Whisperer skill that allows them to travel unheard and unseen. Solma wildwalks now, her footfalls utterly silent.

The night is clear and the moon hangs like a great eye above, bathing the plains in a ghostly glow. Without it, Solma might have missed the flicker of movement that catches her eye.

A shadow of a shadow, twitching in the gloom. She unholsters her pistol, aims it towards the movement. The camp is silent, the grasses stirring in a soft breeze. Solma scans the gloom. Nothing stirs. The land is deathly quiet and—

A rustle. Is that a long tail flicking in the darkness? Solma swears she sees a flash of two yellow eyes. She clicks the safety off her pistol.

The point of a knife presses against her collarbone. Solma freezes, baring her teeth.

"Put the gun down," says a voice Solma recognises. Slowly, she lowers her pistol to the grass and turns to face Urutu. He towers above her—something Solma's not used to—and he holds one arm stiffly. The bulk of a bandage is visible above the collar of his robe. His face is thunderous.

"I told Sidewinder you'd never outrun me," he says.

There's an edge to his voice, a sullen uncertainty she's not heard from him before. Solma frowns but says nothing. All she can think is that he hasn't told her to drop her knife. Slowly, she tucks it against her side to keep it hidden. Urutu steps closer, his hot, angry breath spilling over Solma's face.

"Where is he?"

Solma shrugs. "Where's who?"

She needs time to think. Is Urutu alone? He snarls.

"The defiant!" he growls.

Solma glares. "You might be good at creeping, Urutu, but Olive'n I are better fighters. Foolish to come face us on your own."

Urutu scowls but doesn't respond. Solma curses quietly to herself.

"He's still lost in himself." Urutu says. "Give him back to me. Him and Mamba. I'll spare your lives. I promise."

Me, not *us,* Solma thinks. She doesn't reply. A vein in Urutu's temple twitches. He presses the knife against her collarbone a little harder. Solma sucks in air as the blade nicks her skin. The jolt of pain gives her some clarity, though. She frowns.

"He *is* lost in himself," she confirms. "All Mamba's Whisperers are joined to the mycelia, but they ain't lost. You and your lot told Mamba they'd go mad if they touched the network. So far, the only mad one I seen is Python. Only he ain't really mad, is he?"

Urutu's scowl falters a little. There's a glint of something in his eye. Something like guilt.

"You did something to him," she says. "It ain't the mycelia making him weird. What d'you do to him?"

Urutu's eyes dart to the side and Solma thinks she sees sweat beading on his upper lip.

"We had to," he says, his voice softer now. "We had no choice. The Seasons told us ..." he clamps his mouth shut as if he's already said to much. He pushes closer to Solma. "*Give him to me!*"

Solma winces as the cut on her neck lengthens. Hot blood draws tracks towards her collarbone but hope surges in her chest.

"You know how to free him," she says.

"Shut up!" Urutu snaps. "He's a defiant! He broke our laws. He deserves—"

There comes a thud from behind Urutu. His face goes slack and then he crumples in a heap on the ground, his knife falling into the grass. Solma stares at his unconscious form, then glances up.

"Dammit, Bell!" she says.

Aunt Bell rolls her shoulder. "Earth, that man has a thick head!" she says. "Hold this."

She hands Solma her rolling pin. There's a dent in it where it hit Urutu's head. Solma takes it dumbly as Roseann and Olive appear. Between them, they drag the huge Whisperer towards the remains of the fire.

It doesn't take long for everyone to wake. They huddle in the dark under blankets, unwilling to light a fire. Solma and Olive scour the perimeter for more Whisperers, but either they are well hidden or, as Solma suspects, Urutu came alone. Why would he do that? Surely, The Seasons wouldn't have left so important a mission to one Whisperer.

Solma frowns as she heads back. She keeps her knife drawn.

Olive binds Urutu's wrists and feet. She's a little too aggressive with it, Solma thinks, as Roseann cleans the nick on Solma's collarbone.

Cobra helps Python over to the group, then she and Ana crouch among the groggy kids. The boys blink blearily but Taipan is bright-eyed and alert. She sits with Python, slipping her tiny hand into his. Is it just Solma's imagination, or does she see the flicker of a smile pass across the man's lips?

Bell kneels in front of Urutu, scowling. Then she backhands him across the face. Urutu grunts and his eyelids flutter open. Solma watches as he tests his limbs, finds them bound. His eyes dart between his captors, but he doesn't seem angry. Or even surprised. There's fear in his eyes, but mostly what she sees is …

Resignation.

Solma clutches her knife tighter. Something about him has changed. The sneering, self-assured man she remembers from the Camp now seems unsure. Shame-ridden. Solma trains her pistol on him. Just in case.

"Who hit me?" Urutu asks. He's going for defiance, but his words come out slurred. Bell holds up her rolling pin so he can see it.

"And I'll do it again without a thought," she tells him. "Don't you ever threaten my family."

Urutu watches her. "What d'you want?" he murmurs. Solma leans forward.

"You know how to get Python's mind free of the mycelia," she says. It's not a question. She knows it's true.

Urutu glares, nods.

"Yes," he admits.

Solma steps closer. "I get it now," she says. "He did something The Seasons didn't like, so they locked him up and you bound his power. You pretended it was the mycelia driving him mad to scare other Whisperers. But he ain't mad. *You* trapped him."

She waits. Urutu says nothing, but his eyes shine with shame and Solma's suspicions are confirmed.

Eventually, he nods. "Me and Sidewinder," he says. "We bound his mind. The Seasons helped us. We pulled him into the roots, the network, and trapped him there."

There's silence around the camp. Taipan flushes with fury. Cobra touches Mamba's arm. He doesn't respond. Solma looks at Mamba and realizes he's shaking with rage. Urutu can't meet their gaze. He stares at the ground, his face ashen in the moon's glow.

"He nearly killed Sidewinder," Urutu protests, though Solma thinks he doesn't sound convinced of his own argument. "He *did* kill two other Whisperers. He's dangerous."

"He saved our lives," Olive counters. Her fingers twitch on the hilt of her knife. Her eyes are murderous. Solma grabs her hand, imploring her to stay calm. Olive takes a breath. She keeps hold of Solma, though. Her fingers shake. Solma imagines being woken in the middle of the night to see Olive being held at knife point by Urutu. She imagines the rage and terror she'd feel and squeezes Olive's hand hard. Olive says nothing. But, when Solma looks over, she sees angry tears spilling down Olive's cheeks.

No-one says anything. Urutu finally lifts his gaze. His eyes linger on Taipan and his frown deepens. Taipan, to her credit, holds his stare unflinchingly. It's Cobra who finally speaks.

"Urutu," she says, and Solma hears the effort it takes to keep her voice gentle. "We came to you for help. Our brother has been taken."

Our brother, Solma thinks. A year ago, she'd have objected to that, but looking Cobra's face now, she sees how Warren's absence weighs on them all.

"He's being held captive," Cobra continues, "for a power he has to communicate with insects—"

Urutu snorts, but there's that tell-tale gleam of fear in his eyes again. "I heard these stories," he says. "Insects returning to Alphor. A few Whisperer troupes have come through the camp saying that." He shakes his head. "It ain't true. It can't be—"

"It is," Cobra says. "And it's also true that there's a small group of children who can communicate with them. A new kind of Whispering. But the Stewards have discovered it and they want to use it to make themselves rich. You and I both know it'll start another war. The insects can't survive if they're controlled like that. We'll lose them all over again. We need to save our brother. We need to stop Maxen."

"Maxen?"

Solma's gaze snaps towards Urutu. His voice suddenly sounds small and scared.

"Maxen Camber of Sand's End?"

Solma frowns. "Yeah," she says. "Know him?"

Urutu turns frightened eyes on her. "I know who he's working with," he says. His tongue flicks over his lips. "I know he has a man at his side ... a man who ..." He slumps forward. At first, Solma thinks he's lost consciousness. She lowers her pistol as Bell rushes forward, but then Urutu lets out a low, agonised cry, as if he wants to scream but can't find the breath to do so. There's a wild terror in his eyes when he raises them. "A man who can make fire with his bare hands," he says.

Everyone stares at him.

"How—" Solma narrows her eyes and peers at Urutu. Again, she sees the shadow of Vulkan in his face. The dark hair, the flashes of arrogance. She guesses a split second before he says it.

"Vulkan's my brother," he murmurs. The words come out strained and broken. As if he's never dared to speak them before now.

Solma feels Olive's hand tighten around her own. She doesn't move. Barely breathes.

"That's—" Cobra says, then trails off. Urutu nods, glaring at the ground.

"Yeah," he says. "It is."

Solma watches him as he struggles to contain his emotions. Fear. Shock. Anger. Feelings she knows well. And then another. An old friend of Solma's. It makes her heart hurt to see it on Urutu's face. Guilt.

"Sidewinder was right," he says, shaking his head. Solma frowns again but Urutu doesn't seem to be talking to them. With great effort, he lifts his head.

"We discovered our power around the same time," he says. "I was five. He was four. When the Whisperers came for me, my parents kept Vulkan hidden. They knew the Whisperers would likely harm him. But when Vulkan lost control of his power as a teenager, the village—including our parents—drove him out. He turned up at the Whisperer camp and I looked after him for a time. We worked hard to keep his power hidden, but Vulkan's just ... so *angry*. I never knew why, but it's like the fire he had inside him was too much for him to bear. We argued and he left. Just disappeared one night. That was fifteen years ago. I've not spoken to him since. I thought he was dead, 'til—" he pauses and Solma sees how much it hurts him to tell this truth.

"'Til we heard what happened in Skyheart," Urutu continues. "I knew it was him, even before I left camp to go and find out for certain. I followed him for days. I knew he had two kids with him. Never realised one was—" he meets Solma's gaze. Anger flares in Solma's gut.

"Yeah," she says. "Warren is special. But he ain't just special 'cos he can talk to insects. He's special 'cos he's Warren. Hear me? And you knew he was with Vulkan, and you did nothing."

She stops. The rage is too great. It clogs her throat, tightens every muscle like she's going to burst. Only Olive's fingers, entwined with hers, keep her grounded.

Urutu stares at the ground. He doesn't argue. "I been keeping an eye on him since Skyheart," he says. "Tracking him, trying to work out how to stop him. How to save him." He shakes his head. "I went back to the village he lived at for a time, looking for some way I could help him. Met the woman he was once married to." Tears shine in his eyes. "I never knew he had a son."

"Hmm," Bell says, leaning forward. She's still holding her rolling pin. "The boy's as dangerous as his father, too. We got to stop them."

Urutu stares at her, a single tear trickles down his cheek. A long, unbearable silence yawns. Krait whimpers and Habu puts an arm round him. Finally, Urutu sighs.

"Sidewinder was *right*," he says again. He meets Solma's eye and nods. "I'll help you," he says. "I'll release Python and I'll go back to the Whisperers and try and persuade them to help, but—" he shakes his head. "The Seasons won't like it."

Solma raises an eyebrow. "Do they know about your brother?"

Urutu's silence is heavy with guilt. "No," he admits. "No one does. But ... it's time they did. I'll tell them the truth," he promises. "I'll try. But it might not work. I could end up with my own head locked in the fungus, never seeing the sun again."

The thought sends a shudder through him, but Solma sees the resolve in his eyes.

"Ok," she says. She leans down and cuts his bonds. "Help us, then."

Twenty-One

THE SUN CREEPS ABOVE the horizon. Warm dawn light washes over the camp. Solma hears the distant call of wildervores as they wake. Is it her imagination, or do Python's eyelids flutter as the beasts roar? Does he hear them?

No-one moves as Urutu guides Python to kneel. Unbidden, Python digs his fingers into the earth. Urutu kneels in front of him. Solma notices his hands are trembling. She tightens her grip on her hunting knife. If he makes one wrong move—

She needn't worry, though. Bell's watching him with the fierce, flashing focus of a darkcat. She holds her rolling pin ready. But, since the revelation about his brother, Urutu's been in a daze. Fear shines in his eyes. Solma doesn't blame him. None of the Whisperers are sure if Python knows it was Urutu who trapped his mind. If he'll recognise Urutu and lash out.

None of them are sure what Python is capable of.

Solma glances at Ana and Roseann, telling stories to the kids. The boys are rapt, roaring with laughter at all the right moments, but Taipan seems distracted. She keeps looking over to where Urutu's kneeling, a frown creasing her brow.

Solma returns her attention to Urutu as he finds the courage to push his own fingers into the soil.

"Without The Seasons," he says, "I'll have to ... connect directly with the mycelia." He stares at his shaking fingers. "I don't know if this'll work," he admits. "Python's been under for ... a long time."

Solma looks at Cobra and sees her friend's eyes darken.

"And whose fault is that?" Cobra growls. Urutu doesn't answer, just stares at the ground for a long time.

"There's no coming back from this, is there?" he says. Cobra and Mamba shake their heads.

"No," Cobra admits. Golden mushrooms sprout around where she's kneeling. She strokes them absently. "But I'm not sure that's a bad thing."

Urutu takes a breath. He closes his eyes and starts to Whisper. His eyebrows twitch into a frown as he searches, trying to forge his own connection with the fungal network. Solma's seen all her Whisperer friends go through this, so she knows the exact moment when Urutu makes contact.

His lips part in a gasp. His eyes flutter open, pupils dilated. He gleams with a strange light as dark rings forms around his irises. The sign of a Whisperer who can talk to the mycelia.

"Wow ..." he breathes.

"Yeah," Olive drawls. "They all say that."

Cobra and Mamba look at her. Olive shrugs. "You do," she insists.

Urutu doesn't hear. His eyes search, sightlessly. His mind digs into the mycelia, shooting along those silver threads, learning the language of every tree, every plant, every seed, for miles. A look of pain passes across his face.

"Dying tree," he murmurs, then, "dormant seed," and a series of mutters that Solma can't make out. A few grey mushrooms burst from the ground around his fingers. He winces and seems as if he might pull back.

"Focus, man!" Bell barks. "Find Python."

Urutu twitches. "Yeah …" he says distantly, pushing his hands deeper into the soil. A vein spasms in his neck. Solma focuses on Python, chewing her lip. She's got no idea why, but her heart batters against her ribcage. What if they can't reach him? What if they *can* and he doesn't want to help? What if his help isn't enough? She reaches for Olive's hand and feels that familiar jolt of electricity as their fingers interlace. They grip each other tight.

Urutu's body jerks, his face contorting with pain. "He's …" he starts, breaking off into a whimper. He twitches again, as if trying to pull free. Solma and Olive let go of each other, hands flying to their pistols. But what is there to shoot? Whatever's going on, it's happening underground, in Urutu's mind.

Helplessly, they watch as the spasms intensify into violent convulsions, as the whimpers grow into an animal howl that cleaves the air. Tears burst from Urutu's eyes. Over by Roseann, Taipan stands, fists clenched. She's staring at Python.

"Please …!" Urutu begs. Hands still deep in the soil. His body shudders. His back arches, then hunches. The veins in his neck stand out. Blood pours from his nose. Cobra rushes forward.

"Get him out!" she yells, grabbing his massive shoulders. "It'll kill him!"

Mamba goes to grab his other shoulder but Bell steps in, glaring. "Wait!" she says. Cobra and Mamba stare at her, aghast. "*Wait!*" Bell insists again. She points towards Python and everyone turns to look.

His eyes are open and, for the first time, Solma thinks she sees a spark of consciousness there. He's watching Urutu, mouth set in a grim line. There's still the blue-white sheen of mycelial connection shining in his pupils, but he's fighting it. Solma can see he wants to pull back into his own body. But it's been so long ...

Urutu's head snaps back, jaw stretching wide. He's run out of breath and his scream is a silent picture of agony. Blood from his nose pours into his mouth, down his chin, mixing with his tears.

"Please!" he begs again, and Solma wonders if it's the mycelia doing this—if he's not strong enough to handle it—or if Python is exacting a kind of revenge.

Krait starts to wail. Solma hears Ana trying to shush him, but his distress sets King off and Solma glances back to see poor Habu standing between them, his lower lip wobbling. The ground around them is awash with mushrooms. Solma turns back to Python, gripping her hunting knife.

"What's happening?" she says. "What's taking so long?"

Her blood bellows in her ears, her body aflame with adrenalin. They're making too much noise. They're going to startle the wildervores. Attract enemies. This needs to end. Now.

A hideous animal shriek cuts the air. Solma turns, frowning at the horizon, where the silhouettes of a wildervore herd stand out against the pale sky. Has the herd turned towards them? Are they gathering speed?

Urutu's back arches and blood dribbles from his ears now, too. From his eyes.

"*Please!*" he cries, but the word is lost in the endless pain of his scream.

Python's eyes are wide. Staring. His irises pulse with a strange light. His lips move, forming words Solma can't hear. Urutu spasms. He tries to pull his hands free, but some force holds him fast. He sobs bitterly.

"I'm sorry," he moans. "I'm sorry. Please ..."

So, it *is* Python. Python's tortured mind exacting revenge. Horror claws at Solma's throat. Is this who they want fighting at their side? A man capable of vengeance like this?

"'Liv," she says, grabbing Olive's hand. "Olive, look!" she points back towards the horizon, where the herd of wildervore kicks up a cloud of red dust, hurtling over the plains. "Are they coming towards u s?"

Olive stares dumbly, then slowly nods her head.

"We need to move," Solma says. "Now. Stop this. Get everyone up."

The wildervore draw closer. A dozen or more of them. Their long, muscular necks stretch forward as they pick up speed. They toss their heads, snorting steam, and lower their horns. They're charging.

"Everyone up!" Solma yells, running towards Bell. " *Now!*"

Movement behind draws Solma's attention and she whips round. It's Taipan, scurrying out from under Ana's gaze. She rushes between Python and Urutu.

"Tai!" Cobra yells, lunging to grab her. Taipan ducks under Cobra's arm and drops to a crouch. She grabs Python's face with both hands. Her little fingers press into the sallow flesh of Python's cheeks. He gasps.

"Stop this," Taipan tells him firmly. "He isn't the enemy."

Python frowns. His lips form words but, instead of speech, the ground beneath them all pulses. The grasses tremble. There's a low groan, as if the Earth itself is yawning. Taipan scowls.

"He says Urutu is *his* enemy," she reports. "He says he wants them to know how it feels." She shakes her head, digging her fingers deeper against his face. "You don't want to be this person," she tells him. "You're not a murderer. You're not a torturer."

The frown falls from Python's face and a look of sadness replaces it. But there are bigger things to worry about. A herd of a dozen giant, angry wildervore is *charging straight for them.*

Solma grabs Bell's arm and drags her towards the cart, where both Burdock and Poppy paw the ground. Roseann swings Krait onto her hip and runs after them with the other two boys on her heels. Mamba and Cobra haven't moved. Python's still in the mycelia. Taipan's still clutching his face. Urutu writhes on the ground. The herd is almost on them. This is—

Urutu slumps forward, yanking his hands from underground. Solma sees the flesh of his fingers is blackened, almost necrotic. He lays in the soil and sobs bitterly.

"I'm sorry," he whimpers.

Roseann rushes forward, gestures for Bell and Mamba to help her. Between them, they get Urutu up and guide him to the cart, where Roseann's medical supplies are.

"Sol," Olive breathes. "Look!"

Solma turns. The wildervore, now only a few dozen feet from them, have skidded to a halt. They paw the ground and snort steam. But they've stopped charging. They watch the little group of travellers with liquid brown eyes. Then, they toss their heads again and wander off to the west. Solma watches them, open-mouthed, then looks towards Taipan. The girl is still kneeling in front of Python. She's taken her hands from his face and Solma winces when she sees the fingernail-shaped dents in his cheeks. Some of the marks are bleeding. Python blinks. He pulls his hands from the earth. The strange, blue-white sheen hasn't quite gone from his eyes but, for the first time, he looks ... present.

He focuses on Taipan, frowning.

"I ..." he says. His voice is quiet, barely a whisper. He hasn't used it in five years, after all. "I know you."

Taipan smiles. "You met me in there," she says, pointing to the ground. "You been there a long time. But now you're out."

Python gazes around him, eyes lingering on each face. His stare is full of pain and fear, guilt, and relief. Finally, he sees Urutu. The huge Whisperer lies, unconscious, in the grass while Bell dabs his head with a wet cloth. Roseann works furiously to save his fingers. Python's face crumples.

"I ..." he croaks. "Did I do that?"

Taipan hesitates, then nods. "Yeah," she says. "You were angry."

Python frowns, his eyes darting as if he's searching his memories. He nods grimly. "Yes," he says. "I remember. It's been ... I've had such a long time to feel such hatred. To wish them all dead. All the ones that did this to me." His eyes lift towards where the wildervore graze in the distance. Solma sees his eyes narrow. She frowns. Was there more to those animals charging than just the noise Urutu was making? Could it be that Python—

No, that's impossible. That's *mad*. Solma pushes that notion away.

Taipan touches Python's hand and Solma sees the way that simple connection sends a jolt through him. He gasps, staring at Taipan's fingers. Then he turns his own palm upward, so they can hold each other. Suddenly, he's sobbing.

"I don't want to hurt him anymore," he says. "I never ... it's so hard to remember who you are down there. When you're ... when you're not just you, but you're *everything*. And that prison ... It didn't just hold my body, it held my mind, too. I could feel the mycelia, feel the power it held, but never influence it. Never make it feel *me*, beyond those awful, earthen walls. I couldn't call for help. Couldn't—"

He stops, lowering his head. It's a long time before he speaks again.

"What they did to me," he murmurs. "The cruelty."

He lifts his eyes towards Urutu and there is both guilt and resentment there. An anger kept chained and impotent for so long, it'll be with him for a while. He tears his gaze from Urutu and back to Taipan. Solma goes to approach, but Olive holds her back.

Taipan wipes the tears from Python's face. "But now, you're you again," she points out. Cobra and Mamba move slowly to his side. Tears streak their cheeks.

"Py ..." Cobra whispers.

Python's eyes widen as he takes in those two faces. Five years older than he remembers them. Five years of struggle and pain. Five years of believing them dead.

"I know you," Python says, reaching towards them. "You're here. You're—"

And then they're all crying, all hugging. Ana rushes over and falls to her knees beside Python, her arms around him. Habu runs from behind Bell and barrels into them, wriggling into the hug and sobbing heartily. They stay in a tangle of limbs and grief and memories for a while, trying to convince themselves this is real. Finally, they settle in a circle. Python holds Taipan's hand.

Solma steps forward and, this time, Olive doesn't stop her. Together, they kneel amongst the gathered Whisperers.

Hey," Solma says. She tries to smile and realizes, after everything, that she's shaking. "You're you again," she affirms. "I'm glad. But we need your help."

Python looks between each of their faces. Solma has no idea what he sees there. The desperation. The hope. His sobs subside immediately. He wipes his face clean.

"Help me up," he says. Cobra and Solma pull him to his feet. They guide him over to where Bell is nurturing a small fire, preparing some food. Urutu still lays unconscious, his hands bandaged. Roseann leaves him sleeping to join Bell by the fire. Everyone gathers and Python sighs as Cobra and Solma ease him to the ground. "Let me eat," he says. "Then tell me what's going on."

Someone presses a bowl into Python's hands and in stumbling, halting words, they explain.

When they're done, Python is gaping at them, a spoonful of food frozen halfway to his mouth.

"You can't be serious," he says. Solma swallows a brief flash of anger.

"We are," she says. "And the Keeper Maxen took? He's my brother. I can't abandon him. We have to get him back."

Python watches her intently. The silence stretches long enough that Solma struggles to hold his gaze. After a while, he sighs.

"I've been lost a long time," he says. "What makes you think I'll be of use?"

Taipan wriggles beside him, but it's Mamba who speaks. "We know The Seasons have been lying to us about the mycelia," he says. "We all connected with it last year, and none of us faced the same madness you did. It's powerful, but we don't really understand it. Taipan's the best at it. But ..."

He gestures to the ground around them. Python looks, his eyes widening.

"I see," he says.

From beneath every one of the Whisperers, mushrooms sprout and bloom. They're a multitude of colors, like strange, bulbous flowers. Silver threads lace the ground between them. Where Krait is, some of the grass wilts and yellows, covered with a strange, white fuzz. Ana wraps an arm around the youngest boy, but his anxiety won't be quelled. He whimpers and the white fuzz around him grows thicker. Python frowns.

"How long have you been like this?" he asks. Cobra and Mamba exchange glances.

"Since we connected," Cobra says. "The connection is strong, but we think it's linked to our feelings.

Whenever we are angry or frightened, the fungi react. We can't control it."

"We've tried!" Habu pipes up, and everyone nods.

"We can't fight Maxen like this," Mamba says. Solma feels a lump forming in her throat. Her hands ball into fists. Olive touches her arm gently.

"We need to understand the mycelia," Cobra says. "If The Seasons won't give us an army, we need to learn to control what strength we have. We don't understand half of what the mycelia can do. Half of what *we* can do."

"You need a teacher," Python says. Everyone nods. "Do you have time for that?" Python asks. "Don't you want to get to Sand's End as soon as possible?"

"Yeah," Solma says, hating the desperation in her voice. "But we tried asking The Seasons for help and they sent us packing. This is all we got."

Python finishes his soup and thanks Bell profusely. Bell's cheeks flush with pleasure and she's quick to ladle another portion for him. Solma raises an eyebrow. Bell frowns at her.

"Poor man ain't eaten a proper meal in half a decade, girl!" she protests.

The corners of Solma's mouth quirk into a smile as Bell turns away, beckoning the little ones over for their breakfast. Solma jiggles her foot, impatience curdling to anxiety in her belly. He's going to say no. They'll have risked everything for nothing. She can't stand it.

Olive's hand touches her back, rubbing gentle circles, but Solma's lungs feel as if they're fighting to draw breath.

At last, Python opens his mouth to speak.

And freezes.

His mouth falls open. The color drains from his face as he stares over Solma's shoulder.

Solma and Olive are instantly alert, hands flying to their pistols. But Python's expression is not one of fear. It's one of awe. He stares towards the vast, flat plains where the sun still hangs low over the horizon.

And from which Solma hears bee song.

She turns so sharply, she jars a nerve in her neck. "Ouch!"

The kids are on their feet in seconds, but it's Taipan who lifts her little hand so the tired bumblebee can land. Taipan brings her over and Solma sees how the creature's wings droop with exhaustion. Her abdomen pumps, gasping for air.

"Quick!" Solma cries, waving a frantic hand at Bell. "Sugar! Water!"

She remembers how Warren had fed Blume when they'd first found her, a spoonful of water mixed with sugar to replenish her energy. She hopes the same thing will work now.

Bell hurries a pot of sugary water over to Taipan. Everyone crowds around the little bee while she drinks. Everyone except Python, who holds back. Solma glances over to see him sobbing. His face, weathered by years underground, is flushed with a mixture of joy and despair. He staggers a little, his legs unused to holding his weight, and grabs the side of the cart to steady himself.

Solma turns to the little bee. After a long drink, she buzzes her wings. Solma doesn't speak bee, but she likes to think that note was a thank you.

"You're welcome, little one," she murmurs. Gently, she scoops the bee from Taipan's hand and carries her to Python.

"Look," she says. Python stares, tears shining on his cheeks.

"This is ..." he stutters. "Impossible."

Solma grins. "I know," she says. "That's why we got to save them."

Python nods. "Yes," he agrees.

And that's when the little bee lifts her wings and buzzes frantically. She's not a honeybee, so she doesn't dance, but there's no doubt in Solma's mind that the way she dashes madly across Solma's palm is some sort of message.

As far as she remembers, none of the other Keeper children from Skyheart can communicate with buff-tailed bumblebees. She only knows one person who can.

This message must have come from him.

Buff-Tailed Bumblebee Worker

I HAVE FLOWN SO far. Endless stretches of flowerless deserts zooming past beneath me, and all We can think is that I must find the Sister. The not-bee-boy's scent was overpowering. We felt the tremor in his heart as the enemies dragged him away. It made us afraid. It made us angry.

We buzzed and rushed in circles, sending heady scent messages.

We spent so long distrusting him. What was he to us anyway? A little drone. A male. Lazy. Mother stank of suspicion whenever he came near.

But then ...

Then he opened the world. And as he was carried away, he threw a frantic scent back to us. A plea.

Find my sister! Tell her to stay away!

Sister. That is a thing we understand. Sisters are life. Industry. Growth. The *future*.

We knew we must help, that our future was linked to his. So, I flew free.

I flew free. A single worker bee.

I spend a night outside the nest, convinced I will die. No bee survives outside the nest. Perhaps it's the not-bee-boy's lingering scent on my antennae that keeps me alive. I burrow under loose soil and huddle there until dawn. I'm weak with thirst, but I must keep flying.

I must find the Sister. The not-bee-boy has left the scent that tells me how to recognise her. I fly as far as I'm able, sense her nearby. My wings seize by the time I reach her. My antennae droop.

I land on an outstretched palm, so thirsty I can barely push my tongue out to drink the offered sweetness. I drink and drink as my wing muscles shiver with fatigue. I wait for the sweetness to replenish me. Because I have a message.

I won't make it back to the nest. I'll die here, on this palm. But I must give the message.

I have seen the strange, hypnotic language of the honeybees. Their stench taints our nest, and my sisters are agitated by it. But we don't speak in dance. Instead, I shiver my wing muscles, making my engine hum. I rush left and then right. I throw my scent into the air. These humans aren't like the not-bee-boy. Not as subtle. They can't detect the nuanced language of b ee.

But I keep trying. Throwing the last of my energy into it.

I say, *the Sister must not come.*

This message must be a cry in the silence. I deliver it as if I have the whole nest behind me, every sister I've ever had and all those yet to hatch. As if every generation of my kind is here with me. The not-bee-boy was clear.

His sister must not come.

I buzz and tap, rush back and forth, bumping into fleshy fingers as they move.

His sister must not come. They will kill her. She must stay safe. She cannot come for him. He forbids it.

I do not understand this. The not-bee is a male. A drone. Drones do not speak for the nest.

But I do understand sisters. Sisterhood is life. I understand how, though we are one, great organism made of many bees, a single sister can save a nest. A single sister might find the flowers that strengthen eggs or find the cure to a disease.

And this sister is special. The not-bee-boy insists.

So, I buzz and tap until my legs give out and my wings droop and my vision darkens. I speak my message until my heart gives out.

His sister must not come. She must not come for him. She must not—

Twenty-Two

IT HAPPENS SO QUICKLY that, at first, Solma doesn't understand. She's still watching the bee when it spasms. It gives a last, frantic buzz, and its body tips to one side, legs curled beneath it. She stares, waiting for it to sort itself out. It doesn't. Huddled around Solma's outstretched palm, the others exchange sad glances. Solma knows what they're thinking, but they must be wrong. The bee can't be dead. With one, shaking fingertip, she prods it gently. No response.

She's not sure why the tears come, but they do.

"No!" she chokes. "No! You can't—"

Several arms wrap around her. Olive on one side, Bell on the other, Cobra behind her, rubbing her back. Small hands—probably Taipan's—scoop the dead bee from her palm so that she can weep into someone's shoulder.

"Warren," she gasps. She doesn't know why. She knows the bee isn't him. But he *sent* it. He must have. Even though Solma doesn't speak bee, she's in no doubt of what the creature was trying to say.

Warren needs her. He's suffering. He's desperate. He needs her to save him.

She pulls away from the many arms that enclose her, wiping tears from her face.

"We have to go," she says. "Now. Warren needs us."

Bell's hand is still on her shoulder. "We know, girl," she says. "Let's just—"

Solma pushes her off. "It's been *months!*" she snaps. "*Months* he's been under Maxen's power. We don't even know if he's ok. We can't wait anymore. He sent that bee, right? And it *died* to get its message to us! No more waiting. We leave now."

For once, Bell doesn't bristle. She watches her niece, waiting. No-one moves. Solma swears and marches to her tent. She begins tearing the canvas from the wooden poles. The fabric snags. Solma swears again, kicking at the poles.

"Sol," Olive's voice is gentle in her ear. "Sol, stop—"

"Don't tell me to stop!" Solma screams, pushing Olive back. "You all keep telling me to wait. *Let's go get a Whisperer army. Let's rescue Python from the fungus.* None of it's worked! It ain't helping him! No more waiting, I'm gonna—"

Olive grabs her wrist. She squeezes, enough to show Solma she's here, she's listening. Her green eyes are fierce.

"I ain't telling you not to go, Sol," she says. "I'm telling you to stop panicking. Go sort the ponies."

"But—"

"Go sort the ponies!" Olive insists.

Solma glares but does as she's told. Carefully, Olive starts packing down their tent. The Whisperers follow her lead and suddenly the camp is a flurry of activity. Bell packs their supplies. Roseann kneels to wake Urutu.

Burdock lifts his head as Solma approaches. He pushes his velvety muzzle against her hand, stands quietly while she runs her fingers down his nose.

"Hey, buddy," she says. Fresh tears warm her cheeks, but Burdock's steadfast presence soothes her. She presses her forehead against his. He lets her cry against him.

Ana appears, gives Solma a small smile, and coaxes Poppy towards the cart. Solma knows she needs to bring Burdock, too. They need to go, but the plucky pony's calm presence is a balm for her raw heart. She breathes in his scent of hay and sweat, letting herself c ry.

Burdock nudges her softly, blowing hot air against her face. She smiles and strokes him between the eyes.

"Thanks," she tells him. She's not sure what else to say, but Burdock doesn't seem to need anything else. He just waits, ever-patient.

A whisper of movement behind her. Solma turns to see Python. He hovers, nervously, until Solma motions for him to come over.

"He won't hurt you," she says, as Python draws closer. "He's gentle. Smart, too. He saved us last year, when Vulkan set the forest on fire."

Python steps forward and runs his hand along Burdock's muscular neck. He's silent for a bit before he turns to Solma. The shock still hasn't gone from his eyes. Solma can't blame him. She thinks that waking after half a decade trapped in the fungal network, to find the future of your species hanging between bee song and fire would come as a shock to her, too.

"Tell me about your brother," Python says, which Solma isn't expecting. She strokes Burdock's muzzle in silence for a bit.

"He's brave," she says. She's not sure why that comes to her first. "And he's kind." She smiles wryly. "He can be a little pain sometimes. He gets frustrated. He don't always understand that things ain't as simple as he wants them to be. But he's learning. At least, he was when I last saw him."

Python says nothing, just runs his hand along Burdock's neck.

Ana calls for Solma to tack up Burdock. Solma clips a rope to the pony's harness, leads him towards the cart. Python follows.

"And this Maxen," he says. "He's not a good man?"

Solma breathes against the maelstrom in her gut. She hates that Maxen's name still makes her insides roil. Not with anything like love. That has been dead a long time. But there's a series of other complicated things that come after. Perhaps anger. Perhaps sadness. She's not entirely sure.

"No," she says.

Python helps her harness Burdock to the cart. Beside him, Poppy paws the ground. The tents are rolled away and Bell barks instructions at the youngsters. There's nothing left of the camp but a little circle of blackened tinder where the fire had been.

Urutu's awake, now, but Roseann's reluctant to leave him alone with his hands in the state they are. He agrees to travel with them for the day, but he's not happy about it. He keeps casting fearful looks towards Python. Solma reckons there's more to those glances than simple dislike. After everything, Urutu no longer seems like the burly, self-confident man he'd been before. His shoulders hunch, as if trying not to be noticed. He cradles his hands to his chest and stares at his feet, saying nothing. Roseann stays beside him.

Ana takes her customary position beside Poppy and the procession heads off.

Python walks beside Solma and Burdock for a while. Neither of them speaks. Then he glances up and smiles.

"You said you need an army," he says. "I can raise one."

Solma stares at him. "What?"

Python turns his gaze in the direction of the Whisperer children. "I said I can raise you an army," he repeats.

"*What* army?" Solma demands. "Every Whisperer hates us now."

Python stares at the horizon, where the wildervore graze. "Not an army of Whisperers," he says. "An army of the Earth."

Solma frowns. "What does *that* mean?"

Python's eyes are glazed, as if he's back in the mycelia. "I can't do it on my own," he says. Solma can't help noticing how that doesn't answer her question. Python nods at the other Whisperers. "I'll need to teach them all I learned while I was trapped in the mycelia. Do you trust me?"

Solma gapes. "I've only just *met* you!" she protests. Python doesn't answer. Finally, Solma growls in frustration. "Ain't got no choice but to trust you, do I?" she mutters. "You're our only hope."

Python smiles. "I'll start with Taipan," he says. "She shows the most promise."

Solma raises an eyebrow. Python shrugs.

"We're only a couple of weeks from your village, right?"

Solma nods agreement.

"Well, then," Python continues, "You want your army. I'd better get started."

He smiles, clasping her arm. Despite the five years he's spent imprisoned underground, his grip is strong.

"There's more to the mycelia than even The Seasons know," he says. "You can allow yourself to hope, Sergeant."

Solma starts at the sound of her former title and wonders how he knows. The insignia on her Gatra uniform is gone, now. But when she looks at him, she sees that faint sheen in his eyes. Even now, he's connected to the mycelia and, as with the other Whisperers, it *tells* him things. That power ought to be terrifying. But Solma realises she isn't afraid.

Python nods, then falls back to find Taipan. Solma hears them talking quietly.

Olive jogs to catch up with her, slips her arm through Solma's. She plants a kiss on her shoulder. "You ok?"

Solma nods, then shakes her head, then nods again. "Dunno," she admits. Olive shrugs.

"Ain't surprising," she says. They fall silent, walking together. No-one talks, and the pace is relentless. They've found a new urgency.

Solma keeps her eyes on the horizon, on the miles still stretching between her and her brother. Whatever's happening in Sand's End, he needs to hold on until she gets there. He can do that. He must.

Twenty-Three

Warren sags against the wooden fence around orchard four. A group of honeybees, sensing his exhaustion makes a break for it. Frantically, they power toward the edge of the orchard. Warren clenches his jaw and throws his mind after them. His vision blurs. He grips the fence post to avoid collapsing.

He's cleared waves and waves of dead insects from the hives today. He's stopped burying them—he'd be digging, constantly. And he's seen the red *Varroa* mites—the ones that decimated Orchid's hive in Skyheart village last year—on the workers of one hive. He pleaded with Maxen over it, explained what it could do. Maxen had waved an impatient hand.

"Are they still working?" he'd asked. Warren threw up his hands in frustration.

"For now, but—"

"Then there is no problem. They can live with a few parasites."

And Warren had been dismissed.

That was over a week ago.

Now, the pear blossoms are almost finished. Maxen has instructed Warren to see to the herbs in the glasshouses next. But Warren's worn to the bone and the insects fight his control. Wrestling them back under his influence often leaves him with a nosebleed. Once, he had a seizure.

He's tried reasoning with them—with Clover's buff-tails in particular—but the bees see things simply. They need food. Food is out there. Why is Warren insisting they stay within these boundaries? And despite their capacity for collective decision-making, it's become clear to Warren that bees don't do *politics*.

Warren takes slow breaths and pulls himself up, leaning against the fence. He throws out his mind, checking on the bees. For now, they're happy with the last of the pear blossoms. He blinks away the bee-vision, scans the orchard for Ignis. A squad of Gatra—mostly teenagers—are stationed around the orchard to oversee the work. The Oritch keep their heads down. They work relentlessly, but Warren's convinced most of them don't know what they're doing. He caught a team of them spraying some foul-smelling chemical on the roots two days ago. He yelled at them, but they just stared until he ran out of breath. Kallo, the new orchard-master, is barely older than Warren's sister and thinks Maxen is a kind of god. Maxen says spray the trees, so he sprays the trees.

Never mind that Warren's bee-linked mind can feel what those awful substances are doing to the insects. Warren's seen Gatra head out of the village, returning weeks later with unmarked cannisters that they've scavenged from the distant ruins of old-world cities. Maxen's promised the chemicals will help crop grow, keep disease away.

Warren thought of trying to connect with Kallo the way he did with Maxen that day. He sent a bumblebee to sting, but Kallo saw it coming. He smacked it out of the air and crushed it beneath his boot, glaring at Warren. Warren wonders if Maxen warned the Gatra somehow, if he *knew* Warren was in his mind. Warren didn't try again.

Thankfully, no-one's spraying the trees today.

Warren spots Ignis lurking by the orchard entrance. The older boy scowls at the ground as his father looms over him, issuing orders. Ignis huffs a sigh and Vulkan cuffs him across the ear. Ignis yelps, clutching his head. Vulkan reaches out again, as if to gently touch Ignis' face, but Ignis flinches back. Vulkan frowns and stalks away.

Warren watches as the fire boy wanders over, violet eyes scanning the orchard. He's chewing his lip, lost in thought. A honeybee zooms over to him and Ignis stops, surprised. There's fear in his eyes and he jerks back a little. The sun catches the bee-sting scars on his cheekbone. But the bee only hovers, curious. It doesn't want to hurt him. Warren stiffens as Ignis lifts a hand, afraid that a flame will spring from those fingers. But nothing happens. Ignis stands very still as the bee lands on his knuckle to rest. The frown clears from Ignis' face and Warren sees his lips quirk into a half smile.

The bee flies off and Ignis watches it go. A breeze wafts his mop of black hair, pushing his fringe aside to reveal the flame tattoo above his eyebrow. His frown returns as he shoves his hands back in his pockets, heading for Warren.

"You done then?" he asks. Warren shrugs.

"Yeah," he says meekly.

"Good," Ignis says. "We gotta go to the glasshouses."

He marches towards the gate, pausing when he realizes Warren isn't following. "Do I gotta drag you?" he calls back, "or are you gonna move your own two feet?"

Warren sighs. He calls the bees, and they gather round in a swarm. Warren looks up to see Ignis flinch at the sight of them and feels a kick of guilt. One bee, Ignis can obviously deal with. Many bees together conjure the memory of being stung last year. Warren feels bad about that. But he'd do it again. He'd do it a thousand times to save his sister.

They leave the orchards and skirt around the main village. Maxen doesn't want the bees amongst the village folk for some reason, so they have to strike out into the unmanaged grassland to the south before meeting the path again. The bees tug and buck at Warren's scent-hold. Warren winces with every assault. He wishes he could just let them go. But Ignis is watching him carefully.

The glasshouses glimmer in the afternoon sun. Warren delivers the honeybees back to their hives, reaching instead for the buff-tails.

Their minds brush his and he feels them trying to buck his control already. Instinctively, he reaches for Clover.

Hungry, her scent says. *Tired.*

I know, Warren tells her. *I'm trying.*

But Clover's sharp-scented reply leaves him in no doubt of her feelings about that. Bees don't believe in trying. You either do or you don't. Trying is not an excuse for failing, for a bee. Warren winces at the bitterness of her scent and withdraws. He carries the bumblebees through the opening in the chemical barrier, watching as Ignis sprays the barrier closed behind them.

"Ok," he says. "Glasshouses. Go on."

Warren hesitates, staring at Ignis. There's a small cut under his eye and it looks like he's trying to hold back tears. Warren almost reaches for him, then thinks better of it.

"You alright?" he asks. Ignis glares.

"Yeah," he snaps. "Why wouldn't I be?"

Warren shrugs. "You keep getting cuts and bruises and stuff," he says. Ignis' mask of sullenness slips. Warren thinks he sees the other boy's lip wobbling. For a moment, he looks like he did when Warren met him last year. A clumsy urchin. Lost. Uncertain. He blinks furiously, and then the mask is back. He glares.

"So?" he snarls. "Like you'd care. You set a bunch of bees on me last year, remember?"

Warren stares at the ground. "Yeah," he says. "I didn't want to, y'know. But you went after my sister and my friends and I—"

He stops, biting his lip. "I'm sorry," he admits. "I never wanted to. But you hurt my sister."

Ignis rolls his eyes. "Whatever," he growls. "S'alright for you. Got a whole future, ain't you? Got everything."

Warren stares. He's said something like this before and it felt like a confession. A cry for help. Warren steps closer. Ignis steps back.

"Ignis," Warren says. He takes a breath. "Ig."

Ignis' eyes snap up. He opens his mouth to berate Warren, then seems to change his mind. Warren hopes maybe he's remembering the friendship they had back when Ignis was Ig. Back before he stole Warren away and attacked his sister and burned the insects.

"What?" he says in the end. Warren steps closer again. This time, Ignis doesn't move. Warren reaches out. When his fingertips touch the back of Ignis' hand, the other boy flinches. As if he's been burned. As if human touch means nothing but pain. When it doesn't hurt, he looks surprised.

"Help me," Warren pleads. "We gotta get the insects out. You gotta let me go."

Ignis stares. Not angrily. Instead, he looks at Warren as if he's seeing him for the first time. He starts to shake his head. Warren grips his hand.

"You can come with me," he says. "We can go together. I'll look after you."

Ignis looks down at their hands, touching.

"If we save the insects, there can be a place for everyone," Warren pushes. "Your powers ain't all bad. You can make fire, but you can take it back, too. That's a *good* thing. I can talk to Solma. She'll—"

Ignis rips his hand free and shoves his clenched fists in his pockets. "Shut up," he says. "Don't talk about that."

Warren stares. "Why not?"

Ignis' eyes narrow. "'Cos taking the fire back ain't power," he growls. "That's *weakness*. That's what you do when you ain't strong enough to see things through."

Warren blinks, nonplussed. "But you saved me," he says. "My sleeve was on fire and ..."

"Should'a let you burn," Ignis snarls. "It's what Dja would'a done."

That stings. Warren's not sure why. He reaches for Ignis again but the other boy backs away. Warren sees resentment in Ignis' face.

"You don't got to be like your Dja," Warren says quietly. "There's other ways."

"Stop it," Ignis says quietly. "I ain't an idiot. There ain't no family. No friends. No-one but me and Dja. You're trying to trick me. Like everyone. Like my Ma."

Warren frowns. "Like your—?" he's never heard Ignis mention his mother before. But Ignis reddens and clamps his mouth shut.

Warren bites his lip. He steps closer again, but Ignis draws his hand from his pocket like he's drawing a weapon. Fire bursts along his fingers.

"Don't!" he snarls. Flames reflect in his eyes. Warren freezes.

"Kids like you," Ignis sneers. "You'll never get kids like me. Just do as you're told, yeah? I might not be as scary as my Dja, but I can still burn your stupid bees to a crisp."

Warren says nothing, just watches as that slow, cruel grin he's so used to creeps across Ignis' face. He pulls his bees close, glaring. He reminds himself he should hate Ignis. He hates him as hard as he can. He hates him as much as—

But it doesn't matter how deeply he tries, the hate won't rise. He doesn't hate Ignis, even though he should.

"Fine," he murmurs. He turns towards the glasshouses, bees drawing lazy halos around his head. That kid is a lost cause.

There's a commotion to the west, beyond the glasshouses. Both Warren and Ignis look up. A patrol of Gatra shout and wave. Someone hurries past the boys, into the village. Ignoring Ignis' cries of protest, Warren rushes past the glasshouses—bees in tow—to see what's going on.

He skids to a halt beyond the watchtower that marks the village perimeter. His mouth falls open. Ignis almost barrels into him. "Warren, you can't just—"

He stops when he sees the astonishment on Warren's face. He follows Warren's line of sight, and his own mouth falls open, too.

A caravan stands at the edge of the village. Five wagons, pulled by powerful horses that paw the ground. In the wagons are workers dressed in Fei grey and Oritch blue. They're varied in race and stature. The squads of Gatra that protect them hail from many provinces. The soldiers are fierce-eyed, solemn, and their captain argues animatedly with one of Sand's End's Sergeants.

Warren turns to see Maxen and a squad of soldiers sweep past. It's Aldo's squad, and the older boy gives Warren a smile as he passes. Warren almost smiles back, but then he notices Vulkan is among them. Of course, he is. Warren scowls.

Maxen calls a greeting, and the foreign captain comes to meet him. They clasp hands. Warren notices the way the captain's jaw tenses as he looks into Maxen's eyes.

"They're here to trade," Ignis murmurs. When Warren looks at him, he's frowning. The bottom drops out of Warren's stomach. He turns his attention back to Maxen and the foreign captain, sees the tension in both men as they size each other up.

The caravan might have come under the guise of trade, but Warren feels the agitation in his bees. They sense it, too. The aggression in the air. This is a struggle for domination.

The beginning of another Hive War.

Twenty-Four

Ignis tugs Warren's wrist.

"C'mon," he mutters. "We got work to do."

But Warren's damned if he's going back to the glasshouses now. He snatches his hand away, bolts for Maxen and the foreign captain. Bumblebees draw frantic orbits around his head. Ignis' cry of frustration carries to him on the still air, but he ignores it.

He skids to a halt beside Maxen, who looks down in surprise. Vulkan's lip curls in disdain. He glares towards where his son is running to catch up.

"Sorry, sir," Ignis puffs as he draws close. "I'll take him back now. We still got the glasshouses to do."

He casts a nervous glance towards his father. Though no words are exchanged, Warren sees Ignis flinch under Vulkan's gaze. He frowns, jerking his arm away when Ignis tries to grab it. Ignis stares at him dangerously but to Warren's surprise, a hand lands on his shoulder. It's Maxen's.

"No need," Maxen says, smiling. "I'm sure the traders would be very happy to meet our Beekeeper."

Warren blinks, unsure what to say. Maxen's eyes crinkle at the corners, his smile widening. He almost looks like he used to. Kind. Honest.

Maxen turns to the foreign captain and Warren finally gets a good look at the man. He's white-skinned, but with a deep tan that has left his cheeks and forehead raw and peeling. His grizzled hair falls into his eyes, and he pushes it aside. Days on the road mean he's got the best part of a beard. His blue eyes are ice-cold. He's wearing Gatra black, patched up here and there with leftover material from old uniforms. He's muscular but wiry and holds himself like a fighter. His hand twitches ever-closer to his pistol.

"Where might you be from, Captain?" Maxen asks smoothly. He sounds so much like Blaiz. The captain doesn't look at Maxen. He's watching Warren, watching the way the bumblebees buzz around him. Warren creeps further into Maxen's shadow.

"Westwater Province, mostly," the captain says, still staring at Warren. "But we bring goods from Last River Province and Hallow Island, too."

Maxen raises his eyebrow. Warren sees a gleam in his eye. Something like triumph. But then Warren blinks, and the gleam looks more like desperation. Longing.

"How many villages?" Maxen asks.

The captain scowls. "Five," he admits. "In total. I must say, Steward, it is ... *impressive* that a humble village in this barren corner of Alphor can command such power across the continent."

Warren hears the growl in the captain's voice, realizes there are many words he'd rather have chosen than *impressive*. The captain's fingers brush his pistol. His gaze is hard. Distrustful. Warren sneaks a glance at the other travellers. While many busy themselves with unloading cargo, the Gatra stand stock still, hands on their weapons, staring as if they'd like nothing more than to shoot him where he stands.

Only they aren't looking at Maxen.

They're looking at *him*. Warren's gut tightens, and he senses the way his bees respond to the atmosphere.

Danger, their scent sings. *Threat.*

I know, Warren says. He tries to send out a calming fragrance, but the bees aren't having it. Poison gleams on their stings.

Maxen gestures behind him. Aldo steps forward, presenting the young Steward with a wax tablet. Maxen studies it.

"Ten kilos of cured fish and meat, twenty of root vegetables, ten of cheeses, five of scavenged old-world material, five of herbal medicines, and the promise of beaten sheet metal and twenty rounds of ammo from your own village, Captain?" Maxen says. The captain nods.

"We have less of the fish and meat," he admits. "Despite the curing, some of it spoiled on the way."

Maxen frowns. "Less food means we can spare less ourselves," he says. "Perhaps I was wrong to assume I could trust you with our Beekeeper."

His hand returns to Warren's shoulder, gripping it hard. Warren feels the color leeching from his cheeks. What does he mean? Is Maxen making deals about *him?* Trading his powers as if he's no more than a pollenbot? He starts to shake his head, but Maxen's fingernails dig into his shoulder. He bites his lip, forcing himself to stay silent.

The captain's eyes flash. "We've risked a great deal to get these goods across Alphor, Steward," he growls. "Raiding parties, wild animals, threats from other villages. You would do well to keep your word on this."

Maxen stares at him for a long while, and Warren feels the way the older boy struggles to keep his composure. His fingernails bite into Warren's shoulder. His knuckles are white. He's afraid. Warren scowls. Not nearly afraid enough.

Maybe Maxen hasn't noticed, but Warren sees the way the Gatra soldiers stare at him. Almost *hungrily*. They know what a Beekeeper, especially one with Warren's unique abilities, could mean for their own villages.

And Warren begins to see his future unrolling before him. Captured first by one village, then another. Fought over. Threatened. Killed eventually, probably. Just like the bees in the last Hive War. He's an asset to whoever owns him and a danger to whoever doesn't.

Tears burn his eyes. He lowers his head quickly. His hands tremble. He balls them into fists.

Maxen hands the tablet back to Aldo. "We'll see," he says.

He turns away, but the captain grabs his arm. Immediately, Aldo's squad are on alert. Pistols drawn and trained on the captain. The foreign Gatra respond, and now everyone's pointing weapons at everyone else. No-one moves. Vulkan raises his hand and fire bursts along his palm. Cries of horror go up among the foreign workers. A few dive for cover beneath the wagons. The horses toss their heads. Warren reaches for his bees, feeling how their agitation turns to anger. They're ready to fight.

No! He begs them. *Don't!*

They settle under the calming scent he sends out, but they're still on edge. Their buzzing has the threat of war song underneath it. Warren can only just hold them steady.

But the captain doesn't look as if he means to hurt Maxen. He releases the Steward's arm.

"Perhaps," he says gruffly, "you might be more inclined to generosity in exchange for ... information."

Maxen stares at him. "Go on."

"Weeks ago," the captain says, "we came across a band of Whisperers. Seven of them. They weren't travelling alone." Warren's heart lifts so suddenly it's almost painful.

Maxen's eyes darken. "What do you mean?" he demands. The captain shrugs.

"There were four women travelling with them. Two older, two barely more than teens. The younger ones were in Gatra black. One had dark hair and wore a prosthetic leg. They mentioned you. They said they had a message for you—"

Warren doesn't hear what else the captain says. His ears roar, panic clawing at his chest. His sister. His sister is coming. But she mustn't. She mustn't! Maxen will kill her. He'll—

Calm hands take his shoulders and draw him away. Warren, through a haze of panic, sees Maxen and the foreign soldier talking earnestly. Then Maxen clasps the captain's arm as if they're friends. The captain smiles. He turns, issuing commands to the civilians in his caravan. The activity resumes.

Warren falls to his knees, barely hearing the voice that tries to calm him.

"Breathe, Warren. Breathe. That's it."

It's Aldo. Warren looks up and the older boy's face swims into view. Ignis hovers over his shoulder, watching. Warren shakes his head.

"I can't—" he says. "I—"

Aldo rubs his back. "It's ok," he says. He turns to Ignis. "I think the glasshouses might need to wait until tomorrow. Warren's tired."

Ignis starts to protest but Aldo shakes his head. "I'll explain to Maxen," he says. He helps Warren to his feet. Warren fights against the tears, but he's losing. They stream down his cheeks, splash onto his clenched fists.

Remarkably, Ignis doesn't scuff him or grab him, just says, "C'mon then," and leads Warren away. Warren, too stunned to do anything but follow, trudges after Ignis. He casts one last look over his shoulder.

Maxen waits, arms folded, as the goods are unloaded from the caravan. But the Gatra, even as they direct the civilians, keep their eyes trained on Warren. There's greed and hope and pain in their faces.

Aldo watches Warren disappear behind the glasshouses and there's a feeling in his gut that he can't explain. A voice in his head says, *this isn't right,* but Aldo's not sure what *this* is, or how he's supposed to judge right and wrong anymore. He made his choice two years ago when he chose Blaiz over Solma. His Steward over his Sergeant.

It felt right at the time, but Aldo remembers how he and Ilga had talked themselves round in circles in the days following Solma's exile.

For the good of the village, they'd said. Can't save the whole world, they'd said. She was a dreamer. Her and that stupid brother.

Now, though ...

Someone calls and Aldo glances back. Maxen beckons to him. He lowers his head and trudges over. A vein twitches in Maxen's temple. So much like his father.

But up close, Aldo sees the sweat prickling on Maxen's forehead, the way his eyes dart.

"She's after me, isn't she?" he says. "I knew she'd never leave it alone."

He drags his fingers through his hair. Aldo watches him, frowning.

"If my Dja was awake—" Maxen says, through gritted teeth. He says that a lot. He says it like a threat. Like a reckoning. Aldo's frown deepens. A year ago, perhaps, he'd have felt that Blaiz waking was the best the village could hope for. Now, he's not so sure.

And he hates that.

He pushes the thought aside. "What do you need, Sir?"

Maxen draws him close, a gleam in his eye. "Take four of your most trusted soldiers," he says. "Only four. There's a village to the west, beyond the Earth-root Mountains, and a Steward there who might be friendly to our traitor."

Aldo nods, not understanding.

"Go there," Maxen says. "Take the solar trucks."

Aldo raises both eyebrows before he can stop himself. The two old-world trucks—hidden away in the storehouse and a secret only he and a few other Gatra know of—were expensive to trade for, both in supplies and status. Maxen argued hard with a Northtip village and ended up relinquishing a beehive for them. He'd been in a terrible mood for days after that, angry that he'd had to part with something so precious.

But then Vulkan and Ignis returned with Warren, and Maxen was reassured. He might have lost a beehive, but now he had the Beekeeper. The one child in Alphor who could control all insects. Finally, the trade for the trucks seemed worth it. He's kept them hidden under canvas cloth at the back of the storehouse, unwilling to let anyone know he has them.

The fact he's giving Aldo charge of them now ...

Aldo's stomach twists. "What message should I take there?" he asks.

Maxen shakes his head. "No message," he says. "Just make sure the Steward is ... unable to send help."

Aldo blinks. He opens his mouth to protest, then thinks better of it. "Yes, sir." He says, quietly.

"And Aldo?" Maxen says. "There are some precious children in that village. They could help us, or they could ... prove a problem. Bring them to safety if you can. And if not ..." he shrugs, and lets the silence hang in the air.

Aldo tries to keep his face passive. Slowly, he salutes.

"Yes sir," he repeats.

Maxen stares at him, searchingly. Aldo stares back, trying to keep his face impassive, though his heart thunders like a galloping horse. Finally, Maxen seems satisfied. He reaches under his shirt collar and draws out a set of keys hanging from leather string. He hands it to Aldo.

"For the trucks," he says. "Leave tonight. Wait 'til dark."

Aldo turns to go. He tries to keep his head high as he heads towards the village to gather his chosen soldiers. He tries to dismiss the dark thoughts swirling in his head.

It's too late. He's made his choice. He's a Gatra of Sand's End, and that's all there is to it.

Twenty-Five

Solma jumps at the movement behind her. She grips her hunting knife but immediately recognises the shape emerging from the moonlit camp. She'd expected Olive, but it's Bell who sits beside her.

"'Liv told me you ain't sleeping," she says. Solma snorts.

"'Course she did."

Bell gives her a sharp look. "That girl loves you," she says. "More'n you—"

"Than I deserve?" Solma asks bitterly. "I know."

A wry smile plays on Bell's lips. "I was gonna says she loves you more'n you know," she says. "You deserve that love, girl. You always have. I thought you quit punishing yourself about that?"

Solma shrugs. She thought she had, too. Maybe that's a lie.

Bell sighs. She places her rolling pin on her lap and flexes her shoulders. The wound Vulkan inflicted on her last year never fully healed and it causes her pain sometimes. Solma risks a sideways glance.

"You hurting?" she asks. Bell shakes her head. Solma doesn't believe her.

"I can go get some of that poultice Roseann made," Solma says, getting to her feet. Bell grabs her arm and pulls her back down.

"I'm fine," she growls. Solma's still not convinced, but she doesn't push it. They sit in silence for a bit.

"So," Bell says after a while. "Nightmares, eh?"

Solma frowns. "'Liv told you that, too?"

Bell snorts a laugh. "Your nightmares? Been hearing you have 'em since we left Sand's End. Olive might'a mentioned it, too. She's worried about you."

Solma's jaw clenches. "I know," she says. "She's really trying. She's so patient—" she stops as her throat clenches, and glances towards her tent, where Olive waits. She doesn't deserve that girl. Not really.

"You wanna talk about it," Bell says. It's not a question. Solma balls her hand into a fist to stop it shaking. She doesn't really want to talk about it. Ever. But she needs to. Because if everything goes wrong in Sand's

End, she needs Bell to know she's trying to make the right choice. The hard choice, like Bell wanted her too.

"Ok," she says. "It's like this ..." She tells Bell her dream. Her voice cracks when she talks about how she aimed the pistol between Maxen's eyes but couldn't pull the trigger, how she let him get too close. She talks about looking down to see the knife embedded in her gut, how Maxen had turned into Blaiz and then into Warren. When she's finished, Bell sits for a while, looking out over the darkened landscape. Then, she pulls Solma close and hugs her.

"I'm sorry, Sol," she says. "I'm sorry this has fallen on you. It shouldn't have." Her voice is thick and Solma worries that if she pulls away, she'll find Bell crying. She can't handle that. Instead, she wraps her arms round her aunt, holds her close.

"S'ok," Solma says. "It's made me realize ... oh, it don't matter."

Bell pulls back, frowning. "What?" she says, in that tone that Solma can't refuse. She needs to say it. She *has* to, no matter how painful. She must make it real.

Solma bites her lip. She imagines the look on Warren's face, remembers how he's held her back from that terrible choice so many times.

Don't, Sol! He'd said, when she'd almost slit Vulkan's throat.

They ain't worth it, when she'd almost shot the Gatra that attacked them in the mountain caves.

He's kept her good. She's killed before, but it's always been to defend her home, her brother, herself. It's always been reactive. To save lives. Now, she's planning a death. And there's no going back from that. But what else can she do? What else does she *know?* It's them or him.

Bell grasps her shoulder. "Sol?" she says. "Spit it out."

Solma closes her eyes. She hates how the truth has this way of creeping up on her.

"I got ..." she starts, stops when her voice cracks, take a breath. "I got to kill Maxen."

Bell stares.

For a moment, Solma doesn't understand what she sees in her aunt's face. Pride? Disgust?

Bell looks away. She flexes her shoulder again.

"You know," she says quietly. "Your Ma always said to me that killing should only be done when it's necessary."

"I remember," Solma says. She pictures her mother's face, stern but loving, as she's said those words. But if ever it's necessary, surely it's now?

"I told you last year," Bell continues, "that you weren't alone. You still ain't, you know that?"

Solma nods. Her throat tightens. She doesn't trust herself to speak.

"Ain't none of us an island," Bell says. "But some things ... some things we can't help you with. Some choices you gotta make alone. I think this might be one of them."

Solma frowns. What's that supposed to mean? She opens her mouth to ask, but Bell hasn't finished.

"Thing is," she says, clasping her niece's hand. "When it comes to it, d'you think you *can?*"

Solma shrugs. She's thought about this, too. A boy she grew up with, has known all her life. She kissed this boy. Loved this boy. And, yes, his face haunts her most nights, but can she pull the trigger when her pistol's pointed between his eyes?

Can she drive the knife in?

She opens her mouth to insist that she can. She must. But a sound in the camp disturbs her. She and Bell turn to see a tent opening and Urutu's huge frame emerge. Dawn makes the eastern sky grey and Urutu's silhouette stands still against the light for a moment. He looks around, then creeps to where Burdock and Poppy are tethered, dozing. He pats Burdock's nose, then turns to Poppy, untying her lead-rope. Solma feels Bell stiffen beside her.

"Bastard," Bell hisses. "I knew he was bad news. C'mon."

They get to their feet. Solma unsheathes her hunting knife and Bell's got her rolling pin ready. By her tent, Solma spots Olive, who clearly hasn't been asleep. She glares at the silhouette of Urutu, then catches Solma's eye. Solma signals and the three of them split up, stalking round the outskirts of the camp until they reach Urutu. He sees Solma first, swears as she aims her pistol at him. He flings Poppy's lead-rope away and turns to run, but Olive blocks his path. Bell appears in front of him, slapping her rolling pin against her open palm with a menacing *thwack* that echoes through the camp. Urutu's shoulders sag. He lifts his hands in surrender.

"Planning on leaving, eh?" Olive says. She and Solma guide him back into camp and sit him by the remains of the fire. They keep their weapons trained on him. Urutu sits without complaint. He glares at them in turn. Bell raises an eyebrow.

"Well?" she barks. Urutu lowers his gaze.

"Yeah," he says. "But not for the reasons you think."

Solma hisses air through her teeth. "Go on, then," she says. "What's your reason?"

Urutu flinches but meets Solma's eyes.

"S'my fault," he says. "All of it. I have to make it right. I was going back to speak to The Seasons again. I reckon there're Whisperers who'd want to fight for you. We can stop Vulkan. We can—"

His voice cracks and he stops. The frown on Solma's face falls away as she watches Urutu trying not to weep. Solma and Olive exchange glances. Olive raises an eyebrow. Urutu finally succumbs to his grief. Tears draw shining tracks down his cheeks. He takes a shuddering breath.

"That kid," Urutu murmurs. "That boy. My *nephew.*" He wipes angry tears from his eyes. "I should've done something when I realised. I should've taken him from Vulkan. Taken both him and your brother. I should've—"

Tentatively, Solma puts a hand on his shoulder. She sheathes her knife.

"I get it," she tells him. And it's true. Guilt has been her constant friend for years now. It throbs in her like a second heartbeat, lines her gut like sickness.

Urutu stares at her through his tears. He shakes his head. "I'm sorry," he says. "We should've listened."

Solma shrugs. "Yeah," she agrees. "There's still time, though."

Urutu looks from Olive to Bell and, finally, back to Solma. "I gotta head back to the camp," he says. "My brother, he's ... he won't stop. If he's working for Maxen ..." he trails off. Solma glances at Olive and neither of them say anything.

"Can Burdock pull the cart on his own?" Urutu asks. Solma hesitates. There's no doubt Burdock is as strong as he is clever and brave. He can not only pull the cart on his own, he'll pull it through roiling flames to rescue those he considers his friends. But he and Poppy are close. Solma hates the idea of separating them. She reckons Burdock would understand, though. The flighty little mare might not have Burdock's guts, but she's quick and clever, too.

Solma nods. "Yeah, he can," she says. "But ... you gotta give them a chance to say goodbye, ok?"

Something stirs and Solma looks up to see Mamba and Cobra emerging, little Taipan behind them. Ana appears with the boys in tow. Cobra meets Solma's eye and smiles.

"We can spare a few supplies," she says. "Even on horseback, it's a long journey."

Solma suppresses a grin. Of course, they were all awake and listening.

"I'll get Poppy ready," Ana says.

Solma claps Urutu on the back as the big man gets to his feet. He picks at the bandages on his fingers and Solma thinks that riding such a long way, gripping Poppy's reins, is going to hurt. She wonders if he knows that. He likely believes he deserves it. She opens her mouth to tell him he doesn't have to do this. He should take more time to heal.

But the truth is, they don't have time. And they *do* need help.

"I'll wake Roseann, then," Bell says, throwing more tinder on the fire and searching her skirts for a matchbox. She nods at Urutu's bandaged hands. "She'll look at those fingers before you head out."

Urutu starts to protest but closes his mouth at the look on Bell's face. "Ok," he says. "Thanks."

Solma feels that familiar twist of her gut as she watches the camp bustling. Maxen's smiling-then-snarling face flashes in her mind every time she blinks. How easily he'd lied to her. How he'd held a gun to her brother's head.

She realizes Urutu is watching her as Roseann re-bandages his hand. Solma holds his gaze, thinks the guilt he carries is a lot like her own. Will Urutu kill Vulkan if he needs to? Perhaps, for people like them, this was always going to be the only choice.

A warm hand slips into Solma's, fingers intertwined. Olive. Solma feels that familiar electric-touch and sighs.

"Did you talk with Bell?" Olive asks. Solma nods.

"Yeah."

"Did it help?"

"I ..." Solma bites her lip. "I don't know."

Olive casts her a sideways glance but doesn't pry further. Solma's grateful for that. She's not sure she can explain how she feels. In a way, she's more confused than she was before.

As the others pack saddlebags, Ana leads a tacked-up Poppy over to Urutu.

"She's said goodbye to Burdock," Ana says. Her voice is thick and she turns her back on everyone to stroke Poppy's nose. Solma goes to her, puts a hand on her shoulder.

"You'll see her again," she says. "This ain't forever."

Bell looks around, frowning. "Well," she says. "Nobody's going nowhere without having a decent breakfast."

Solma meets Olive's eye and the pair of them look away quickly, suppressing giggles. Bell gets a fire going and organises a hot breakfast. The boys clamour for her attention and she indulges and scolds them in equal measure. They don't seem to mind. Solma thinks they quite like having someone to parent them, even if that parenting often involves being told off. Solma realizes suddenly that she can't see Taipan. She stands, looks frantically around, but it doesn't take her long to spot the Whisperer girl kneeling in the grass with Python. She hangs off his every word as he talks to her in hushed tones.

Solma relaxes and kneels by the fire again. Olive sits beside her. Neither of them speaks, but Olive puts an arm round her and draws her close, kissing the top of her head. Solma leans into the embrace and tries not to think about Maxen. Tries not to wonder how it might feel to slide her knife between his ribs. Tries not to imagine the look on his face as she kills him. What might he feel?

Some choices you got to make alone.

Surprise? Rage? Fear?

I think this might be one of them.

Solma has no idea what Bell meant by that.

In the end, it doesn't matter. All that matters is she keeps Warren safe.

Blaiz's face flashes, unbidden, in her mind. Half of it is puckered with bee-sting scars. Warren had done that; set his bees on Blaiz to stop him. He'd almost killed him. He *could* have killed him.

And if anything, that floods Solma's heart with terrible strength. Because if Warren can do it, so can she. She can thrust the knife in. Pull the trigger.

Even if it means killing a boy she once thought she loved. Even if it means her brother might never forgive her. Even if it means she'll never forgive herself.

Twenty-Six

TAIPAN PULLS HER HANDS from the earth with a frustrated huff.

"It isn't working!" she protests. Python smiles.

"I'd argue otherwise," he says, indicating the small colony of mushrooms sprouting around her. Taipan glares.

"I could do that *before,*" she points out. "Without even trying. You're s'posed to be teaching me to control it!"

Python shrugs. "Control is an illusion," he says. "What you want is connection. Proper connection. And that comes with time. And patience."

Taipan reddens. Sometimes, Python's lessons are a painful reminder of a few years before, when she'd first discovered her power.

She'd been a strong Whisperer. Too strong. She shudders at the memory, at the cry of a boy—a friend—she'd almost trapped in the roots of a tree. She'd given in to her fear during her first, accidental, terrified Whispering and he had almost died.

Back then, control was the answer. Discipline. A tight hold on this desperate, wilful magic inside her.

And now this man she barely knows is telling her to *let go?* Does he have any idea what that means?

She risks a glance back towards camp to see if anyone heard. But Bell is still fussing over a fire. The boys are squabbling. Roseann's lost patience with trying to manage them and stalked into a tent. Ana's with Burdock, still pining for Poppy, though it's been two days since Urutu left. Taipan's got no idea where Solma and Olive are. Patrolling, probably. Like always.

"Let's try again, shall we?" Python suggests. Taipan looks at the sky. Clear, pale blue. Wisps of cloud drifting across a faint, evening moon. The rolling landscape is dotted with trees and Taipan hears the distant calls of wildervore as they settle for the evening. Ignoring Python for a moment, Taipan turns and shields her eyes, trying to spot the creatures on the horizon. The wildervore fascinate her. These are a smaller species than the huge, tan beasts that roamed High Savannah province. They're dark brown—almost black—with pale stripes on their flanks. Their herds are smaller and currently calving. Yesterday, Taipan was delighted to see a herd of four cows, each with a spindly-legged calf. She's hoped to catch another glimpse of them since, but wherever the herd are now, she can't spot them.

"Taipan?" Python says. Taipan drags her eyes away from the horizon, frowns as she pushes her hands into the soil.

"I still don't get it," she says. Python's eyes twinkle.

"That might be half the problem," he says. "What don't you get?"

Taipan wriggles. One of her feet is going numb where she's been sitting on it for half an hour. "How you want me to *reach out* through the mycelia. I can do that already. I can speak to the others through the fungus. We been doing that since last year."

Python smiles, which makes Taipan's frustration spike.

"Well," he says. "If you can talk to your fellow Whisperers, what's to stop you talking to other life forms?"

Taipan looks at him quizzically. "You mean Solma and Olive?" she suggests. "But they can't—"

Python shakes his head. "I mean," he says, "other *non-human* life forms?"

Taipan gapes. "*What?*"

Python winks. "Fungus of all species will create fruits," he says. Taipan chews her lip and nods.

"That's what mushrooms are," she says. "Fungus fruit."

Python inclines his head. "Exactly," he agrees. "And some of those fungal fruits will create spores. Spores are everywhere. We breathe them in and breathe them out. And so does every other creature."

Taipan frowns. "So?"

Python laughs softly. "So, we can use those spores to send messages, like you use the mycelia to send messages."

Taipan wriggles again. She's not sure about this. She's not sure Mamba would approve.

But, says a mischievous little voice at the back of her mind, Mamba's not here. He's in camp, helping Cobra count supplies. He's not even *looking*.

"You mean like ... mind control?" she asks in a whisper. Python shakes his head.

"No," he says. "There are some fungi that will allow Whisperers to do that, but that's not the sort of Whispering we want in the world, is it?"

Taipan shakes her head, bites her lip.

"All we want," Python continues, "is to use the spores to pass a message. What the animals do with that message is up to them."

"So …" Taipan says, wrinkling her nose. "We're not controlling anything. Not really."

"No," Python agrees. "We're reaching a hand in the dark. Offering friendship. We're hoping someone—or something—is willing to reach back."

Taipain shuffles her numb foot out from under her bottom. Hope. That's the thing Warren always has. Endless, boundless supplies of it. But you can't control hope. It's wriggly and confusing and never does as it's told.

Still, Taipan feels a tingle in her fingers at the thought of what Python's suggesting. She leans forward.

"Show me," she says. Python pushes his fingers into the earth up to his knuckles. Immediately, that strange, white sheen covers his irises. His eyes slide out of focus.

"Watch the horizon," he says. The grass rustles as he speaks. Despite herself, Taipan shuffles back. He's frightening when he's like this. He's spent so long controlled by his prison that now he trembles with all that pent up potential. Taipan doesn't entirely trust he can control it.

But she swallows down her fear and does as she's told, turning her attention to the horizon. The orange sun hangs low in the sky, making her squint. If she looks hard enough, she can just make out a herd of wildervore streaking across the land. There are three adults and a single, awkward-legged calf. Taipan smiles, delighted.

And then the wildervore turn in a neat arc, veering south. Taipan leans forward to get a better look as they disappear into a trough in the undulating landscape. They reappear a moment later, much closer.

The smile disappears from Taipan's face.

"Py ..." she murmurs, but Python isn't listening. He's locked in the mycelia. The wildervore kick up dust, their cloven hooves tearing the ground. They might be smaller than their High Savannah cousins, but they're still huge, could easily trample a little Whisperer girl.

"Python ..."

He still hasn't heard her. The wildervore leading the charge tosses her head, snorts steam. Her eyes are wild. Taipan can see the whites of them. She scrambles back. The wildervore are metres from them, snorting and stamping. There's a shout from the camp. Someone screams Taipan's name. Taipan yells.

"Python, they're gonna—"

And then the wildervore stop, less than ten metres away. The lead female detaches herself from the herd, trots over to Python and, to Taipan's astonishment, *lies down* next to him. Taipan's mouth falls open. Python withdraws from the mycelia, wipes his soil-caked hands on his robes, and then gives the enormous creature a tickle under its chin. It closes its eyes in appreciation.

Taipan stares.

"How—?" she says. "What—?"

The sound of footsteps startles the wildervore. It's on its feet in moments, ears pricked, head lifted high. Solma and Olive skid to a halt beside Taipan, their weapons raised. The herd charges off into the distance, leaving Solma and Olive looking very confused.

Python smiles. "We're fine," he says. "They just came over to say hello."

Solma shoots him a dark glance, mutters something under her breath. She and Olive move back to a respectful distance but, Taipan notices, they don't go far. Python chuckles.

"They don't trust me," he says. Taipan scowls.

"I'm not sure I trust you anymore," she points out. "That was scary."

Python's eyes soften. "It's scary because you don't feel in control," he says. "But the natural world—the mycelia—isn't about control. It's about harmony. Talking to a wildervore is a big ask. Even The Seasons would struggle to call more than that small number. Smaller creatures can sometimes be a little easier."

Taipan brightens. "Like bees?"

Python winks at her. "Bees could work," he says. "You won't be able to communicate with them like your friend, Warren, does. It'll be a little clumsier, and you'll only be able to speak *to* the bees, not hear their language. Do you understand?"

Taipan frowns. "So, they can't talk back to me?"

"Not in a sense you'd understand," Python admits. "And I don't know of any bee colonies nearby."

"There's one at Skyheart!" Taipan says, sitting up. "We could try there!"

Python looks at her critically. "It's a long way away," he says. Taipan shrugs.

"I can reach their fungus tree from here," she says. The fungus tree in the forest behind Skyheart had provided the answer to the sick beehives last summer. When they'd discovered the cure, it had been Taipan who first linked with the mycelia and managed to grow those same fungus in the glade. The glade is burned now, but the fungus tree, near the river, survived. If she concentrates hard enough, Taipan feels the pulsing energy from that tree, even at this distance.

Python shrugs. "Alright," he says. "There's no harm in trying."

His uncertainty makes Taipan's insides tighten. But she's said it now. And there's another reason to talk with the Skyheart bees. The girl she met last year—Yennevieve—is there. A girl with a power, like Warren's, to talk to bees. Unlike Warren, she had only been able to understand one species of bee. The honeybee. But Taipan remembers how intricate the language of those insects had been.

And perhaps, if she can reach the Skyheart bees, she can reach Yenn. She can reach help.

She might not be an army of Whisperers, but Yenn and her bees are better than nothing.

Taipan digs her fingers into the soil. She lets her mind elasticate, stretching down into the mycelia. It's still a shock to connect, and a gasp escapes her. The fungal network is a haphazard web of messages. Pulses, thoughts, and nutrients whizzing along these silver filaments, racing from plant to plant.

Water needed!

Can give extra food.

Parasites! Under attack!

Tree, dying.

Tree, being born.

It's a tangle of feelings and impressions, pulling her deeper. Taipan's mind wants to pursue it in every direction, but she knows that's dangerous. Instead, she forces herself to focus on just one path, feeling her way along the mycelia. The intensity of the messages lessens the further she gets from herself. By the time she reaches the fungus tree, it's no more than a faint muttering in the back of her mind.

Perhaps she *is* too far away?

She bites her lip hard, determined to try.

She can't *see* the fungus tree from underground. Fungi have no eyes. But she pictures it the way she remembers it: a hollow, blackened, lightning-struck tree, long dead, stood amongst the green of living trees. Fungus of all colors bloom over its trunk. Silver filaments coat its dead bark.

And at its base—

She can't see them, but she can feel them. The vibration of wingbeats. Their tiny feet against the skin of each mushroom. Bees.

Through the haze of her connection, Taipan hears Python's voice.

"The spores. Put your message in the spores," he says. *"Release control. Let the bees define the message."*

What's that supposed to mean? Taipan frowns, her eyes moving under closed lids. She travels up the silver filaments, finding a fruiting fungus filled with white spores. She pushes her mind into them, feeling the way the fungus bulges, ready to burst. A bee wanders across its surface.

I need to speak to you! Taipan says into the spores, thickening them with her message. She tries to reach beyond them, to grab hold of the bee. She feels the way the spores blacken and congeal, sticking together. No! This isn't how it's supposed to work! The fungus is dying. It's—

Listen! Taipan insists, grappling for control. Control is the answer. She feels that chaotic pull of her power, its endless possibilities. It terrifies her. She clasps the fungus tighter in her mind, squeezing it. The fungus withers. The spores inside are no more than a liquid mess. The bee takes off, zooming away. It hadn't even heard Taipan calling.

Shaking, Taipan pulls herself free of the mycelia. She takes three, gulping breaths and then is thoroughly sick into the grass.

"Tai?" calls a frantic voice. Olive and Solma are beside her. Olive fixes Python with an accusing glare.

"What did you *do?*"

Taipan tries to shake her head, but the movement just makes her nausea spike. "It's not him," she says. "I just—"

She doubles over and is sick again.

"Right," Solma says, helping Taipan to her feet. "Lessons over for today."

Python doesn't object. He follows quietly as the soldier-girls help Taipan back to camp. They sit her by the fire and Bell fusses over her, wiping her mouth and offering her water. She casts Python a dark look.

Taipan stares into the flames, waiting for the nausea to subside. But it's not the sickness keeping her quiet. Her fist opens and closes, and she keeps thinking of that fungus she'd killed.

She hadn't meant to. Really, she hadn't.

Just like that first time. Just like the tree roots. The boy. His screaming.

She sneaks a glance at Python, who's watching her intently. Had he felt what she did?

Release control, he'd said, and she hadn't been able to.

Because there's too much at stake to relinquish control, isn't there? Warren under Maxen's power, vicious traders moving across Alphor. A Hive War on the horizon.

And Vulkan and his son, ready to set everything on fire.

Tears burn her eyes. Python puts a hand on her shoulder. "It's ok, Tai," he says. "It takes practice. It's—"

Taipan shoves his hand off. It's not ok. She can't do it. She's not strong like Python or brave like Warren or clever like Yenn.

She's just Taipan. Plain, little Whisperer, Tai.

And she can't be what everyone wants to her be.

"Teach someone else, tomorrow," she says sullenly. Then, she buries her face in her knees and cries.

Twenty-Seven

Solma stares at the stationary cart as Bell and Roseann unpack it. She and Olive did a final count of their ammo that morning. The rifles pellets are gone. The rifles themselves are only useful as blunt instruments now. There is a single pistol magazine each.

Solma checks and rechecks her pistol. There's a bullet in the chamber. She hopes she'll only need to pull the trigger once.

The sun hangs low against the horizon and the sky is a riot of evening color. Spring is nudging into summer and a comfortable warmth lingers in the air.

Mamba and Cobra erect the tents, camouflaging them with grasses and knotted vines, before joining Python and the others. For the last few days, Python's been including all the Whisperers in his lessons. He no longer talks out loud. Instead, the Whisperers plunge their hands into the soil and communicate through the mycelia. Solma hopes she'll get used to the sight, but it still makes her uneasy.

Taipan's been quiet for days, reluctant to join the lessons. Python is patient with her, but Solma sees worry in his eyes. When she asked him about it a few days ago, he did his best to smile and said, "The training's just taken a little longer than we'd hoped."

He wouldn't say any more.

Olive returns from her perimeter check, holstering her pistol. She catches Solma's eye and shrugs.

"Looks clear," she says. Solma nods and pats the grass beside her. Olive sits and Bell brings them both a meal of slightly stale bread and some hard, yellow substance that looks like cheese but definitely isn't. Solma eyes it suspiciously. Bell raises an eyebrow.

"It's that or nothing," she says. "And nothing ain't an option, girl."

Solma sighs and takes a tentative bite of the yellow stuff. It's surprisingly ok. Not a patch on Bell's cooking, obviously. She says as much, and Bell's cheeks flush. She turns away, calling the others for dinner.

Solma nudges Olive gently. "You sure no-one saw you?"

Olive's lips quirk with an indulgent smile. "I never went close enough to draw attention," she says. "Kept my hair tucked under my bandanna. Stop worrying."

Solma frowns. "Can't," she says, and Olive laughs, kissing her. Her face becomes serious again.

"You gonna come with me tomorrow to scout it out?"

Solma's stomach twists and she no longer wants to eat. The idea of viewing the village she grew up in as if she's an outsider—a raider—makes her lungs constrict so much she can barely breathe.

For the last week or so, they've skirted the edge of Southtip Province, staying out of sight of the villages, and working their way south. They've made camp a mile from Sand's End, camouflaging themselves with the help of the Whisperers' powers. But it's only a matter of time before a Gatra patrol finds them. They need to act soon.

Solma has a plan, but it's reckless and brutal and she's afraid to action it. She'll have to, though. There's no choice.

She forces herself to take a bite of bread and nods. "Yeah," she says. Olive wraps an arm round her waist.

"It's hard for me, too," she murmurs. Solma leans her head on Olive's shoulder.

"I know."

They sit in silence. Eventually, Python's lesson ends, and he ushers Ana and the children over to Bell for food. He sits quietly beside Solma and Olive. Solma notices he still winces as he lowers himself to the grass. There's a tremor in his hands when he's lost in contemplation. Solma's tried to imagine what it would be like to live underground for years, mind lost, power strangled. If she thinks about it too much, she gets breathless with panic. She hasn't decided whether it makes her respect Python or fear him. Either way, she offers him a smile when he kneels beside her. He returns it.

"Are you ready?" he asks. Solma's smile falters. She shrugs.

"Dunno," she admits. "As I'll ever be, I s'pose."

She nods towards the Whisperer children, eating quietly. "How d'you think they're doing?"

Python casts an appraising glance over his young students. "They've learned a lot," he says. "But ... I'm not sure it's enough. What I'm trying to teach them is new. Dangerous." He fixes her with a stare so intense

Solma finds she can't look away. "But you said you needed an army ... I think this is the only way."

"Right," Solma says, finally tearing her gaze away.

She's still not sure about this *army* Python says he can raise. Animals of all kinds—called through the mycelia—coming to defend the future? It's mad. She'd dismiss it entirely if she hadn't seen him call that herd of wildervore. But four wildervore is hardly an army, is it? And not even Taipan has managed to master this strange new power yet.

She feels Olive's arm around her waist, squeezing her close. She nestles her face into Olive's neck, breathing that gunpowder-musk scent.

The sun dips below the horizon and Bell ushers the little ones to bed. Olive stands and offers Solma a hand. They head to their tent together and snuggle into a single sleeping bag. Solma clings to Olive and their limbs entwine.

"What if—?" Solma whispers. Olive kisses her. Mainly, Solma suspects, to shut her up.

"Don't think it," Olive says.

"But—"

"Don't," Olive says, a fierce edge to her voice. "We go in together. We come out of it together. Don't think it. Don't say it. Just sleep, yeah?"

Solma nestles closer. "Yeah," she says.

But she doesn't sleep. And she doesn't think Olive does, either.

Solma peers through the trees, out across the grasslands. The village is a smudgy silhouette on the moonlit horizon. The land around Sand's End is mostly flat, with little cover. But Solma hopes the darkness will give them a chance.

"Hold still," Cobra tells Solma as she kneels in front of her. "It won't hurt,"

Solma jiggles her leg. It's not pain she's worried about. It's just these are the only clothes she has. They're already stiff with grime.

Cobra presses one palm against the Earth and touches the leg of Solma's pants with the other. Moss and lichen branch out from beneath her fingers, coating Solma's clothes in a fuzzy mass. As agreed, Cobra leaves Solma's prosthesis clear of growth. Instead, they've painted it with mud and some dye Roseann made from Earth-knows-what. It's now striped green and brown and shouldn't draw any wandering eyes.

Cobra withdraws her hand. "All done," she says. Solma tests the moss doesn't restrict her movement. It doesn't seem to. Still feels weird, though.

She glances around to find Olive similarly camouflaged, red hair tucked under a green bandanna. Like Solma, Olive has striped her face with mud and dye. She catches Solma's eye and winks. Bell and Roseann are similarly prepared, though Bell looks severely put out at the moss growing on her dress.

Ana, Mamba and the youngsters are nowhere to be seen. Python sent them into the forest to grow mushrooms. Solma raised her eyebrows when he told her this, but Python had only shrugged.

"You wanted an army," he said. "We need spores."

Solma said nothing. It hasn't escaped her notice that in the two weeks since they freed Python, no miracle army of Alphorian wildlife has appeared, no matter how much the Whisperers trained.

"Trust me, Sergeant," Python said. "That's all I ask."

Solma assured him she did. Which is a lie. But it seemed pointless to argue.

Cobra squeezes Solma's arm. "Say hi to Warren for me," she says. Solma smiles.

"You can tell him yourself," she replies. "I'll be bringing him back, soon."

Cobra's eyes sparkle. "Good luck," she murmurs. "And ... once Warren's safe, I'll see you on the battlefield."

Solma's heart kicks. The battlefield. Because, of course, this isn't just a rescue mission. It's also a robbery. They intend to release the insects that Maxen has laid false claims over. Free the future of the world. Once Warren's safe, she and the older Whisperers will face Maxen's Gatra. Python had better come good on his promise to raise an army.

In most of her recent nightmares, he hasn't.

She stands at the tree line with the others, meets Olive's gaze. "Ready?"

Olive nods. "Ready."

Roseann beckons Python over. Bell tucks her rolling pin into her belt and puts a hand on Solma's shoulder. "We're with you, girl," she says. Solma covers Bell's hand with her own.

"I know," she says. "C'mon."

They hug the tree line as they move round the outskirts of the managed forest. Solma draws everyone to a halt as the forest tapers and the path to the village comes into view, lit by the moon. Two Gatra soldiers loiter on the path, their wind-up torches illuminating grass and gravel. Their rifles are ready, but they look relaxed, chatting quietly. Solma narrows her eyes as she tries to make out who they are. She recognises Ilga. They'd been in the same squad, once. Ilga had been a sorry thing back then, terrified of her own shadow. But two years have seen her grow tall and strong. There was another boy in their squad, too. Allergy-ridden, jumpy. What was his name?

Aldo. That was it. Solma wonders where he is now.

He's not with Ilga. Solma doesn't recognise the other soldier. She's certain she could easily take both Ilga and her companion. But that isn't the plan. She looks at Olive.

"On it," Olive says. She melts into the forest. A few minutes later, a shot echoes across the sky. The patrolling Gatra jump and swing their torches towards the forest, eyes scanning the tree line. Ilga says something and they charge into the forest.

Olive reappears shortly after. "Idiots," she mutters. Solma suppresses a laugh.

They wait until it's clear the two soldiers aren't coming back.

"Let's go," Solma says. They spread out, avoiding the path. It's slow going. There are two watchtowers on this side of the village. The darkness gives some protection but, every so often, a yellow light sweeps across the open land as the watchtower guards scan the area. Solma and the others dodge out of the light, or flatten themselves to the grass, their camouflage meaning they look like no more than grass-and-moss.

They make it to the outskirts of the village and hunker down behind the mud-and-stone walls of a house. Solma waits, counting under her breath. The gunshot has obviously set the Gatra on edge, as they suspected it would. A group of five scurries past, heading towards the forest. Candlelight glows in a few windows. The door of one house opens.

"What's going on?" says a hushed voice. "Was that a gunshot?"

"It's nothing," a soldier answers. "Go back inside."

The door closes. The candles go out. Solma turns to the others and sees moonlight glowing in their eyes.

"Bell, Roseann, go carefully," she says. Bell touches her cheek.

"Proud of you, girl," she says. "Remember that."

Then she and Roseann disappear. They'll head to Maxen's house, where Olive says Warren is being held. It'll be heavily guarded, which is why Solma, Olive and Python are heading to the middle of the village, where the storehouse is. They'll cause chaos and draw the Gatra—and hopefully Maxen—away from the house.

They won't have long.

Solma crouches, creeping round the other side of the house. She waits.

Three ... two ... one ...

Three Gatra hurry along the path. They stop on a corner, and one gestures to the other two. They split up, each heading in different directions.

"Guess that shot really spooked them," Olive mutters. Solma doesn't reply. She watches the soldiers head away.

"I dunno," she says. "That looked ..."

But she's not sure how to describe it. It didn't look like the frantic reaction of a squad caught off guard. It looked purposeful.

"We need to be quick," Solma says.

Silently, they head towards the centre of the village. They cut across the path by the council hall and sneak between the houses. The storehouse will be guarded. There's no way Maxen will station any less than two squads there.

But Solma's not interested in stealing anything yet.

The huge, arched form of the storehouse comes into view, moonlight glancing off the corrugated tin. Solma sees the silhouettes of at least eight Gatra wandering up and down its length. They're alert, torches lit and scanning the area. Solma shrinks into the shadows as one shines his torch towards her. She holds up a hand to halt the others, gestures to Python to head round the back of the storehouse. He clasps her arm briefly.

"You'll only have a few minutes," he mutters. Solma nods, not trusting herself to speak.

If anything goes wrong here, if Python is caught or killed, the other Whisperers will have to fulfil the promise to raise his mystery army without him. And she's not sure they can.

Python withdraws. Solma sees him dart beyond the storehouse and melt into the shadows. She clasps Olive's hand.

"Hold steady," Olive says. They draw their knives. The plan is not to kill. They'll leave cuts and bruises but nothing worse. And from now on, they won't fire a gun until they absolutely must. They need to create the illusion there are more than just two of them. A whole raiding party if they can manage it. They need to frighten Maxen out, draw the Gatra away from the house.

"Sol," Olive says, voice muffled by a thick scarf she's wrapped around her mouth and nose. "Cover your face."

Solma wraps her own scarf across her face. She breathes experimentally. The air feels hot through the fabric, but it's exactly what she needs.

She won't want to be breathing in too much when Python's assault starts.

In the dark, she doesn't see the fungi he's growing. But she knows when spores explode into the air because the Gatra start coughing. It's a splutter at first, then a prolonged fit, then they're clawing at their throats, eyes bulging. Their rifles and torches fall, and they crumple on the floor. Two of them have enough sense to duck low and wrap cloths over their faces. The rest collapse, kicking and choking.

Solma stares, eyes wide with alarm. "He said he wouldn't kill them!" she hisses. Olive squeezes her shoulder.

"Then we gotta trust him," she says. "Let's go!"

They split up.

The spores don't last long, and the cloud doesn't carry far, so the Gatra that reacted quickly escape the onslaught. Already, they're alert. Their voices raise, cutting the night.

Solma smacks the butt of her pistol into the side of the storehouse, creating a report like a gunshot that reverberates along the metal wall. Someone yells, fires an answering shot. Solma dodges a torch beam and comes up behind a soldier. She clamps a hand over his mouth then elbows him sharply in the temple. He crumples at her feet. She charges away.

Another shot and a strangled cry of pain. Something hits Solma in the back and she staggers forward, leaping aside as a huge soldier appears out of the darkness. She jerks her foot out as he shoots past and catches his ankle. He sprawls in the dirt, and she clubs him in the head with the butt of her pistol. He falls still. She bends to check his pulse. It's steady. She leaves him and moves on. Round the front of the storehouse,

Olive's laid out two guards. The noise of gunshots should be drawing more, but Solma hears no sound of running feet, no yelled commands.

There's a cut across Olive's forehead. Blood drips from her eyebrow. The last of Python's spore cloud has dissipated and Olive pulls the scarf off her face.

She beckons Solma over. "Where's Python?" she demands. Solma shrugs, gesturing towards the darkness.

"Over there, he's—"

"He ain't there," Olive growls. "I went to check after I took these two out. He's gone. The spores have stopped."

Solma pulls down her scarf and takes an experimental sniff of the air. A few strange particles tickle the back of her throat, but it's not enough to make her splutter like the Gatra did. Python promised he'd return to them as soon as he'd grown the spores. But he's not here.

"Where'd he go?" Olive asks again. "Something ain't right ..."

They stand back-to-back, scanning the darkness. Python's got to be there somewhere. He wouldn't just have run off—

Then the shadows shift. For a moment, Solma thinks she sees someone. Pale blue eyes reflecting torchlight. Bee-sting scars. A cruel smirk.

She's sure she sees that mouth move, the lips forming her name. Like they once did, when she thought he loved her. Like they did when he exiled her.

The face she's saving this bullet in her pistol chamber for.

She turns and fires, the gunshot cracking against the still night. But Maxen's face is gone. Solma blinks. Had she imagined that?

Olive grabs her arm. "Hold still," she says. "Keep calm. We're—"

Torchlight blinds Solma and she throws a hand up in front of her face. Olive lets out a grunt of pain beside her. There's a shuffle, a thud. Something grabs Solma's wrist, twisting it sharply behind her back. Something smacks her in the gut, and she doubles over, dropping her weapons. More hands grab her. She's forced to her knees. There are three rifles pointed at her face. Olive kneels beside her, fighting furiously. It's taking at least five Gatra to keep her down. Then a rifle is trained on her, and she falls still, glaring.

A silhouette steps into the light and Solma looks up to see Maxen. Whole and alive. She *had* seen him. She'd had a shot. She'd missed.

She glares, hating him. He hasn't changed much. Those bee sting scars look livid on his face and one eye doesn't open properly. But his hair is still that same blonde, his eyes that pale blue. Solma almost sees the ghost of the boy she grew up with. Then he smirks and that boy is gone. He holds a pistol loosely at his side, flanked by soldiers. He looks almost like a copy of Blaiz. A young tyrant in the making. Except, Solma sees the manic gleam in his eye, the sweat beading on his upper lip.

"Knew you'd come back," he says. "You always were stupid, Sol."

Solma's jaw clenches. "You took my brother," she growls. "What d'you expect?"

Maxen doesn't answer. He gestures behind him and two Gatra step forward, carrying a limp figure between them. They throw the figure down and he rolls into the light. It's Python. A deep bruise swells on his head. He's unconscious but his face is twisted with pain. His fingertips are black. Maxen smiles at Solma.

"I got a room made up," he says. "Just for you."

Twenty-Eight

Olive fights her captors all the way to Maxen's house. Solma hasn't got the energy. Not anymore. The sun's coming up and a fine mist hangs at ankle height. At Maxen's order, two soldiers dragged Python off. Solma's got no idea where they've gone. She hopes they don't realize how powerful he is—that it was him who created the disabling spores—or his doom might be sealed. And if he dies, any hope they have of raising this army probably dies with him.

Outside the house, Maxen calls a halt. He stands aside so Solma can see Roseann and Aunt Bell kneeling in the dirt, hands on the backs of their heads. A dozen rifles are trained on them. Bell looks thunderous. Solma notices a couple of the Gatra have significant bruising to the sides of their faces. Bell has been relieved of her rolling pin.

"Might be a little cosy," Maxen says. "But aren't you glad you're home?"

Solma fixes him with a hateful stare. "This ain't been home for a long time," she growls. Maxen shrugs and gestures for his Gatra to escort his prisoners inside.

He turns. "Vulkan!"

Solm feels her gut clench and twists in the guards' grip. Vulkan's massive form lumbers up the path, Ignis scurrying at his side. Solma's eyes narrow as they meet Vulkan's. He smirks, lifts a hand, palm upwards. Fire bursts along his fingers.

"Hello, little soldier-girl," he rumbles.

Solma considers spitting at him. She wants to claw his eyes out with her bare hands. But none of that feels like it'll be punishment enough for what he's done. She stands, glaring silently. Vulkan puts a hand on Ignis' shoulder and Solma notices the boy flinch. That's interesting.

"My son's been taking care of your brother," Vulkan says. "Doing a good job, too."

Solma's breath catches in her throat. "If you've hurt him—" she growls. But then she catches sight of Ignis' face and falls silent again. Is that regret she sees there?

Vulkan looks down at his boy and the strange expression falls from Ignis' face. He looks just as mean and mercenary as Solma remembers. His violet eyes gleam.

"Will you two stop playing with your prey?" Maxen says. "Some of us have business to attend to." He turns to his guards. "Get them inside and keep them quiet 'til I can make an example of them."

He starts to head down the path towards the village centre, then stops and looks back over his shoulder. "And let Dja know," he says.

Solma notices how the Fire Makers and the Gatra stiffen at that command. Her gut rolls as she meets Olive's gaze.

"Blaiz is awake?" she says. "He's *alive?*"

Olive says nothing, just watches the Gatra as they look darkly at each other. Maxen beckons Vulkan and Ignis to follow him and heads away. Someone shoves Solma between the shoulder blades and she stumbles forward. She glowers behind her. The offending Gatra glares back.

"Steward's Dja's been asleep for years," he growls. "Thanks to *you.* The Steward just ... likes to keep him notified."

Solma hears the edge in the guard's voice and realizes none of Maxen's Gatra know what to make of this. She meets Olive's gaze again. Neither of them says anything. Solma thinks she hears Bell mutter, "mad as a moonbadger," under her breath. Thankfully, none of the Gatra seem to hear.

That, or perhaps some of them agree.

The electric lights are off, the hallway dim. The prisoners are manhandled through a smaller door, down some stone steps and into another corridor. Here, the walls are bare brick and a dank stench hangs in the air. There's a thick, wooden door at the end of the corridor with a tiny, barred window.

A little face peers out. Solma's heart leaps.

"Sol!" Warren clasps the bars, eyes glistening with tears. "Sol! What're you *doing*? I told you to—"

One of the Gatra hammers on the door, making Warren jump. "Move back!" the Gatra yells. Warren glares but does as he's told. The Gatra makes a show of taking a heavy chain of keys from his belt and unlocking the door. Two more soldiers keep their weapons trained on the door as it swings open.

Warren stands in the middle of the dark, stone-walled room, arms folded, glaring murderously as Solma and the others are shoved into his cell. The door slams closed behind them. Solma barely registers the sound of the key in the lock. She closes the gap between her and Warren and thrown her arms round him.

"You're ok," she says. Her voice cracks and she can't stop herself from sobbing. "You're ok."

There's a rush of air behind her and Bell's arms are around them both. She's crying, too, kissing the tops of their heads in turn.

Warren mumbles something.

"What?" Solma says.

"Too tight," Warren gasps. Solma and Bell release him and Solma gets a good look at her brother for the first time. He's taller. Thinner, too. His face is pale and gaunt. His hands are cold. He's grown too much for his clothes and his sleeves end halfway up his forearms. There's a hole in the knee of his pants. Solma has no idea where he got those boots but they're far too big and have holes in the bottom. His hair is lank, plastered to his forehead. There's grime all over his face and under his fingernails. And he's staring at her furiously, hands on hips.

"I told you not to come!" he says. "I can handle it. I told you—"

Solma holds up a hand. "Wait," she says. "We got your message. The bee you sent—"

"Then *why'd you come?*" Warren demands, tears spilling down his face. Solma stares at him. She glances at Bell, who seems equally perplexed, and then at Olive and Roseann, who are both frowning, nonplussed.

"Warren, we came to get you. We—"

Warren covers his face with his hand. "No, no, no!" he moans. "You were s'posed to stay away. I can sort it myself. Maxen's gonna—he said he'd—"

Whatever Warren was about to say is lost as he gives in to sobs. Solma kneels and pulls him close. "It's ok, Warren," she says. Warren struggles free.

"It ain't," he says, wiping his face with his arm. "Maxen said he'd kill you. And I tried to warn you and you still came and now—"

Solma lifts his chin until he's looking at her. "Warren," she says, and she's pleased to hear how steady her voice is, though her blood is roaring in her ears. "We'll figure it out, okay?"

Warren's eyes shine. His lower lip wobbles but Solma sees how he rallies himself, pushing back his tears. He's got so tall. He's had to deal with so much. She pulls him close again and, this time, he wraps his arms round her.

"Missed you," he says, pushing his face into her shoulder. She kisses his head.

"Missed you, too."

Olive wanders around the cell. She kicks the wall experimentally, reaches up to test the bars in the high window, then sits on the single pallet in the corner.

"Well, ain't this the picture of luxury," she grumbles. Despite everything, Solma lets out a laugh.

"Yeah," she agrees. "Maxen's outdone himself."

Solma goes to sit beside Olive while Bell fusses over Warren. Roseann hovers by the door, muttering. Solma thinks she hears the names of their Whisperer friends on the doctor's lips. Tears shine in Roseann's eyes.

Solma looks away. She hopes the Whisperers had the sense to run when they realized Solma and the others weren't coming back. She hopes they aren't planning anything stupid.

She wraps an arm round Olive's waist. "What do we do now?"

Olive shrugs and hugs her back. "Dunno," she says. She sounds tired. That, more than anything, makes Solma's heart tighten with fear. Solma squeezes her close, afraid that if she lets go, it might be forever. She battles a sudden panic and feels tears sting her eyes. Olive seems to sense it.

"Hey," she says, cupping Solma's chin and kissing her softly. "We'll think of something," she says. "I ain't going down without a fight. Neither are you."

Solma manages a small smile and nods. "Yeah," she says, though it sounds hollow.

Warren clambers onto the pallet between them. He snuggles into Solma's side, and she hugs him close. Roseann and Bell perch beside Olive. The five of them sit silently, huddled together for warmth.

Olive laces her fingers through Solma's. "Let's get some rest," she suggests. "At least we've got shelter for now."

Warren slips from the pallet. "You two should sleep first," he says. "Then Bell and Roseann."

Solma looks at him and smiles. How brave he's grown. How thoughtful and kind. She's so proud of who he's becoming. It makes the guilt in her gut fester more.

"I should've shot Maxen in the face when I had the chance," she says bitterly. Everyone stares at her. Olive frowns.

"You tried," she says. "I saw you." She lays down on the pallet and beckons Solma to join her. "You'll get him next time," she says. "I know you. You won't miss again."

Solma gives a tight smile. "Yeah," she says. "I won't miss again."

Olive grips her hand, but when Solma glances up, she catches her aunt's eye. Bell's brows are drawn together in a frown. She says nothing, but Solma feels heat flooding her face. She turns away, quickly. Bell's has a knack for detecting her guilt. Her lies.

"You alright, girl?" Bell says eventually. Solma shrugs, afraid to meet her aunt's gaze again.

"Yeah," she lies. "Fine."

Bell gives a dissatisfied grunt, but pries no further, for which Solma is grateful. She's not sure she has the strength to explain herself.

She lays down and Olive hugs her tightly. She smells of gunpowder and sweat, of months on the road. Of safety. Love. Solma relishes her warmth. She closes her eyes but knows she won't sleep.

All she can think is that, when she'd seen Maxen's face in the darkness, she had a clear shot. She could have hit him, but she didn't. With that single bullet in the chamber, with only one magazine left, she'd aimed wide. She knew she'd miss because she'd fired to miss.

She hadn't been able to kill him, even after everything he's done. And now, despite Olive's confidence, she doesn't reckon she'll get another chance.

Long after Olive starts snoring softly, and everyone in the cell falls quiet with either despair or exhaustion, Solma opens her eyes to find Bell watching. There's a tell-tale gleam in her aunt's eyes, that suggests it doesn't matter how hard Solma tries to lie. Bell knows something's wrong.

~ A Moment ~

THE GRASS-HUT IS MUGGY, packed with bodies. The Whisperers cluster together. Only those over the age of fourteen were summoned for this meeting. Some-one is outside watching the younger ones. Clearly, Urutu thinks, the meeting is expected to get tense.

The pulsating, fungal lights of The Seasons' home cast an eerie glow across the sea of concerned faces. In their strange, floral bindings, The Seasons are restless, eyes moving under closed lids. They're talking to each other, but not yet ready to share their thoughts. Urutu waits, rigid with tension. He's doing everything he can to avoid looking at Sidewinder, who leans heavily on a cane beside The Seasons.

She, though, stares at Urutu as if she both wants to throttle him and hug him close. Her throat is still bandaged and, in the two days Urutu has been back at camp, he has yet to hear her speak. He's wondered, in his darkest moments, if she hates him. If he's let her down. Which hurts. But he watches her now and sees a flicker of uncertainty in her eyes. She's subdued. Not the powerful, dedicated Whisperer he's always known. Something's changed in her. In him, too. He's not sure what, yet, but it scares and exhilarates him.

The Seasons, though, are furious. Urutu feels it pulsing through the earth. His newfound connection to the mycelia amplifies their rage, despite his efforts to keep the link hidden. He'll be lucky if he leaves here with his hide intact.

He forces himself to stand tall, squaring his shoulders. If he looks ashamed, the other Whisperers will see it. He must look assertive, confident. Not as if he's come crawling back to plead Solma's case because he's afraid of his brother.

He remembers when they fought. How Vulkan was angry enough to set the world on fire. And Urutu had let him walk away, knowing how full of hate he was. Knowing he was like an old-world bomb waiting to detonate.

My brother. My fault.

The Seasons shift in their swathes of foliage. Urutu feels the way everyone in the grass-hut takes a collective breath. Then, the moment passes. The Seasons go back to their ceaseless muttering. Urutu feels his gut tighten.

And still, Sidewinder *stares* at him. He avoids looking back, resolutely watching The Seasons. His palms sweat. He hides his hands behind his back.

On some signal only they can perceive, The Seasons fall still. The glow of the fungal lights dims and then ...

Oh, and *then* The Seasons open their eyes.

Urutu's only seen any of them do this once before and the memory still makes him shudder. Their eyes open and there is nothing in them but a pulsing, blue-white light. He knows The Seasons—at least, their human bodies—are little more than husks, now. Filled with fungal spores, creeping roots and vines. The Seasons only keep them around to communicate. The Seasons themselves are everywhere. Racing through the silver filaments that connect the Earth, feeling each footfall on a grass blade, each axe blow on a tree.

Except, now, they're back here, looking through long-dead eyes. Looking at *him*.

They speak all at once, their collective voices ringing round the chamber, and it takes all Urutu's self-control not to shudder.

"*You have failed,*" they say, their voices like the splintering of tree roots, the crack of thunder, the scuttle of long-dead insect feet. Urutu forces himself to meet their sightless gazes.

"I made a judgement," he replies, and is relieved that his voice holds steady. "I know Mamba and his company ... damaged us."

Winter raises an eyebrow. It's the most human gesture Urutu has ever seen a Season make. It catches him off-guard. He clenches a fist behind his back and avoids looking at Sidewinder. She's lowered her head, her face hidden in shadow.

"They were desperate," Urutu says. "I have seen with my own eyes what they speak of. The return of the insects. I also know ... who it is they intend to fight." He pauses. Because here is the truth in all its festering ugliness, a confession he's spoken only in his dreams. Always it has come out broken and twisted, as if he's holding a corpse to the light.

He's never told anyone what his brother is capable of. The brother this camp once sheltered and kept safe, with no knowledge of the simmering, violent power inside. Not until he told Solma.

But now he must speak it again.

He stares straight into Winter's glowing eyes.

"They fight my brother," he says. "And his son. And we need to fight them, too. They are dangerous." He looks around, meeting the eyes of many he's known all his life. "Some of you will remember Vulkan. He was a boy back then, on the verge of manhood. He was sullen. Quiet. You took him in. Cared for him. And then he disappeared and no-one asked what happened to him. Because he made you all afraid. It was easier not to ask questions."

The gathered Whisperers mutter guiltily. Urutu pushes on.

"But none of you knew the truth. And I should have told you. Like we can grow with our hands, like the children Mamba speaks of can touch the minds of insects, Vulkan and his boy have a power. But theirs is destruction. Fire."

The congregation of Whisperers falls silent as he explains what Vulkan can do. From the corner of his eye, he sees Sidewinder lift her head. She meets his gaze briefly but whatever she's feeling, he can't read. Her jaw tightens. She looks away. The fungal lights stutter as even The Seasons are unable to contain their fear.

Fire, conjured from human fingertips. Destruction in its most primal form. He sees them imagine how it will attack the mycelia, blistering the silver filaments, blackening trees, erasing swathes of grassland.

Despite the gasps and cries of horror from the gathered crowd, Urutu keeps going. He doesn't know much about Maxen, or Solma's brother. But he understands greed. And anger. He remembers, years ago, when he was a boy, how his grandmother described the Hive Wars she remembered from her childhood.

He conjures those images, now. Fire and death. A carpet of insect bodies littering the plains. Vast cities toppling as their inhabitants fell upon each other, reduced to the base need to survive. Already, he tells them, villages are sending caravans south. Some will want to trade with Maxen. Others will want to take what he has. It's beginning, this second war. And there is only one way to stop it.

He weaves the story of destruction. Hears the doom in his own words. But he needs The Seasons to understand. He needs them to look beyond the secretive, possessive way they've been leading the Whisperers for too long. He needs them to recognise that they are human, too. Or they were, once.

And they must act.

He finishes in a rush of breath, surprising himself with the force of his speech. He blinks, realising that everyone around him has fallen utterly silent. He stares at each of The Seasons in turn, the hope in his chest hurts.

"Well?" he says. "What's your decision?"

He doesn't mean to look at Sidewinder, but his eyes meet hers. A jolt goes through him. Tears streak her cheeks. And there's the ghost of a smile on her lips.

The Whisperers behind Urutu mutter again. Urutu does his best to ignore them. He drags his gaze away from Sidewinder and fixes it on The Seasons. Hoping. Dreading.

His fists clench so tight, his ragged nails cut his palms. The fungal lights flare and dim.

Winter lifts his chin.

"*We have not changed our minds,*" he says. His voice resonates through the earth and Urutu feels how the roots shift and tremble. "*We are not soldiers. We are Whisperers. Let the village folk settle their scores. We will endure.*"

Urutu's temper flares.

"Solma's right, though," he says. Shocked gasps sweep through the crowd. "It's our world, too. We're part of it. If it falls, so do we. We have to help. We *must*."

He hears how pathetic his final plea sounds. Blood heats his cheeks but he holds Winter's gaze. He's not backing down.

"*We do not have to,*" Winter says, and Urutu detects an edge in the Season's voice. "*And we do not wish to. This is our law. You have disobeyed us and we must decide your punishment. Leave us be.*"

The roots and vines of the grass-hut creak open. Daylight pours in. The assembled Whisperers shuffle out, quiet and subdued. But Urutu can't move. He stares, open-mouthed at The Seasons as their bodies fall limp, minds seeping back into the mycelia. They've gone. Urutu's left staring at their empty, moss-and-fungus covered husks.

He stands there so long that the other Whisperers have all disappeared by the time he realizes he hasn't moved. But he can't leave it like this. How can that be their decision? How can they separate themselves from the world and its problems without so much as a shred of a remorse?

He's beginning to see why Python defied them. Why Mamba did, too. Why the village folk are growing more hostile towards Whispering troupes.

This isn't right.

And Vulkan is out there, burning and breaking and killing.

Urutu lowers his gaze, glaring at the earthen floor of the hut. A hand touches his shoulder, and he turns to find Sidewinder stood behind him. She looks older. Deep grooves line her face. Urutu sees the shadows of bruising at her throat. It's healing, but slowly. She gestures for him to follow and leads him outside.

He blinks against the daylight, though the sky is white with clouds. The air is muggy and sweat prickles on his forehead.

"I know you think I should do as I'm told," he says gruffly. "I know you side with them, but—"

Sidewinder gestures for him to hush. He scowls at her, intending to disobey, but the look she gives him stuns him into silence. There's something in her eyes. As if she—

—As if she *agrees* with him.

She takes his hand and pulls him towards the woodland. When they're a safe distance away, and enough trees and foliage obscure the camp from view, Sidewinder kneels in the earth and signals Urutu to do the same. She fixes him with a thoughtful stare.

"You didn't tell me," she says. It's not an accusation. Her voice is soft. But Urutu flinches.

"No," he acknowledges. "I told no-one."

Sidewinder blinks. "Why?"

"*Why?*" Urutu tries to laugh but the only sound he manages is like a moan of pain. He rocks forward and Sidewinder reaches out, steadying him.

"Why?" she asks again. "After how long we've known each other. After everything we've been through. You could have told me."

He shakes his head. "I couldn't," he said. "Your loyalty to The Seasons ... you'd have despised me."

His voice cracks. He hates how vulnerable he sounds. How *weak*.

Sidewinder says nothing. When Urutu looks up again, he sees sorrow burning in her eyes. She knows he's right. However patient she was as a surrogate mother, her loyalty was always to her beloved Seasons.

If he'd told her before, she'd have gone straight to them.

But something's different now. There's a hesitancy to her he's never seen before. She's afraid.

That thought alone sends needles of fear through him, as well. He's never seen Sidewinder scared.

She looks away and digs her fingers into the soil. Urutu hesitates, but she frowns and grabs his hand, pulling it towards the ground.

"What?" Urutu says, shaking her off. Sidewinder's glare is withering.

"You know what," she says. He half-smiles. There's the fierce woman he's always known. Still in there. Just ... growing. *Evolving.*

He presses his palms against the soil and digs his fingers in. He meets Sidewinder's gaze.

"Connect," she says. Urutu gapes at her.

"What?"

He can't believe what he's hearing. The withering look she gives him is enough to convince him he hasn't misunderstood. This is happening.

"Connect," she says again. "I know you can. I can see it in your eyes and ... there's a message for you."

Urutu stares at her. "A message ..." he says. "How would you know—"

His mouth falls open. The realisation is almost too much for him. "*You?*" he splutters. "*You* connected? You broke Whisperer law?"

Sidewinder shrugs, which only makes Urutu's jaw slacken further.

"I needed to know," she says. "For myself. If they were telling the truth. If we really would go mad if we plugged ourselves into the world like this. What was I supposed to do? Ask someone else to try? Cascabel and Keelback are dead. Copperhead's still gibbering like a baby. I could risk no-one but myself. But I'm glad I did." She fixes him with a hard stare. "Mamba was right. Python was right. The Seasons might be plugged into the world, but there's still a very human part of them in there. The part that wants to stay in charge. Wants power."

She covers his hands with her own. "Things need to change," she says. "They've needed to change for ages."

Urutu chews his lip, peering at his hands. They look pale against the dark earth. Fear coils in his gut. This is wrong. It's against everything he's ever known.

But Sidewinder watches him, determination written into her face.

"Connect," she says,

So Urutu closes his eyes, reaches his mind down into the earth.

His consciousness brushes the silver filaments of the mycelia and his first reaction is revulsion. Fear. It feels so alien, still. He remembers how easily Python had used it to hurt him. The seething mass of life beneath the soil had twisted his mind, started to unspool him. It *hurt*. And the memory of it hurts, too. He pulls back, his mind reeling. But he feels Sidewinder's hand touch his own. He clenches his jaw and pushes back down, trying not to give in to the memory.

Once he relaxes, he slips right into it, his mind running freely along the silver filaments. His eyes fly open and he knows his pupils are dilating. Light flushes into his eyes. Everything is too bright. He can barely see. He is—

He is everything. And this time there is no pain. No assault. It's as if he has eyes within eyes that have opened for the first time. He'd never realized plants had *thoughts* before. He'd known they lived, needed, hunted and grew. But he had not known they were aware, developed friendships and conflicts, fought and reconciled. He hadn't known that trees could be generous. That brambles tended towards greed. That grasses were sneaky.

And under it all is the constant whisper of something other. Something deeper, older, endlessly sentient. He balks at the earthy darkness swimming through his thoughts. Is this the beginnings of madness? But it doesn't feel like madness. It feels ...

It feels like home.

And then something else cuts through his mind, urgent and frantic and—

And he recognises it.

It's a message from someone he knows. Not communicated in words but in images and impressions that his human mind forms into a meaning.

And the meaning is.

Help!

It's Taipan. That clever little Whisperer girl from Mamba's troupe. His fingers tighten in the earth. His teeth grind together as he clings to the impression she's sending.

It's gone wrong! They've been taken!

He doesn't know what that means.

We need help!

His eyes dart as he sends his own message back, trying to calm her down so he can understand her. He tries to tell her the Whisperers won't come. That The Seasons have refused. He tries to say he's sorry. She cuts him off.

Skyheart, she says. He frowns.

What?

She says it again. *Skyheart. The Keepers. They will help.*

And then she withdraws. In a sudden panic, he shoots free of the mycelia and throws up all over the mossy ground.

He glances up and finds Sidewinder watching him. She raises and eyebrow, then hands him a waterskin. He drinks. Washes out his mouth. Drinks again. He hands the waterskin back.

"What's Skyheart?" he asks. Sidewinder stares. Urutu tries not to think about the vile taste in the back of his throat. "Taipan said the Keepers will help us," he says. "What are they? She mentioned—"

Sidewinder holds up a hand. "I heard," she says. "It's a village. West. Where Mamba and his troupe found the insect children."

Urutu's eyes widen. He remembers what Solma had said about children who could speak with insects. Others like her brother.

"I have to get there," Urutu says. He doesn't know why, but he thinks suddenly of his nephew. The boy with dark hair and fire in his hands that he'd seen from afar. He can't get the child's face out of his mind. The boy whose name he doesn't even know.

He stands, brushing down his robes. Sidewinder stands, too. She clasps his arm and, when he looks into her face, there's no trace of anger. It's as if the Sidewinder he'd known all these years has gone, except—

She's not gone. She's still there, that ferocious woman who believes fiercely in what's right.

He sees a new shine in her eyes. "I'll go with you," she says.

Twenty-Nine

TAIPAN PULLS HER HANDS free of the earth and brushes away the loose soil. She leans forward, hands on her knees, and breathes deeply.

That was *hard.*

It was hard to reach so far, to push into someone else's mind and speak. Hard to Whisper on the edge of control. But she had to. Something has gone horribly wrong. Above, the moon is a blind eye, staring through the gaps in the leaves. She watches it for a bit, waiting for her vision to stop swimming, Then, she gazes at the three boys. They're gathered around her, chewing their lips.

"Did you find him?" Krait asks in a breathy whisper.

Taipan nods. "Yeah," she says.

She doesn't know why, but she thinks again of her friend. The boy she'd almost trapped in the tree root. She'd almost killed him. But she'd managed to stop before it went too far. Even sick with fear, she'd pulled her power back. He'd been ok. For the first time, picturing his face doesn't come with that stab of guilt.

Habu glances back to the two drooping tents they're supposed to be tucked up in. There's a nervous gleam in his eye. Taipan doubts anyone else is sleeping, but no-one has noticed the four of them have sneaking out. Behind the tents, Burdock pricks his ears but makes no sound. He watches them intently.

"We should get back to bed," Habu says. "Mamba said to wait."

Taipan scowls. "We can't *wait!*" she insists. "Something's gone wrong! Can't you feel it?"

Habu shrugs. "Yeah, but—"

King wriggles unhappily. Taipan takes a breath and tries to stay calm. She loves these boys, but they're *idiots* sometimes. Scared of their own shadows. What would they do without her? Run around in chaotic circles getting mud on their faces, probably.

Mamba *did* say to wait. Even though Solma and the others should be back by now. With Warren. They should be planning how they're going to raise the army. They *need* Python because—

Well, never mind that. Just *because.*

But Cobra ushered them to bed, telling them not to worry, even though she was clearly worried, herself. Ana said they shouldn't go charging in until they know what's happened. Which is stupid. Taipan knows what happened. She can feel it.

It's not her fault none of the others have bothered to spend as much time in the mycelia as she has, that they haven't learned it properly.

But she *has*. She's explored every inch of it, afraid this new strength will overwhelm her, that she'll hurt someone else. She hasn't. Instead, she's learned and grown. The mycelia has soothed that old wound. *It wasn't your fault*, it tells her over and over. *We are here. The Earth is here.*

And she's let herself join with it. Become one with it. She knows it better than any of the others. But, because she's a child, they won't listen.

Which is annoying.

So now, she must take matters into her own hands. Only her hands are small, still frightened of their own strength. She still doesn't quite trust herself. Which is where the boys come in.

Taipan leans forward, glaring. "We *got* to do this," she says. "You *know* we do."

The boys exchange glances. Finally, Habu sighs.

"Fine," he says. "Let's just ... do it."

He pushes his fingers into the soil. King and Krait follow suit. They close their eyes, plug into the mycelia. Tentatively, she reaches her own fingers into the earth. She looks at each of the boys to make sure their eyes are closed, that they can't see the fear in her face.

Because she's not completely sure she can do this. Though she's tried and tried. Python has been so patient, so kind. But it hasn't worked. She hasn't been able to loosen control.

And she needs to. She needs to get a message to Skyheart. To the hazel-eyed Beekeeper girl, Yennevieve. Yenn can't read the mycelia like Urutu can. The message can't be delivered directly.

Taipan needs to try the thing she's failed at over and over. The thing Python is convinced she's capable of.

She reaches into the soil, feeling the minds of the three boys brush hers as she plugs into the mycelia.

Let's go, she tells them. And, leaving only a small portion of themselves behind, they race along the mycelial network. They travel the breadth of Alphor, until they reach a tree near a river beyond the mountains.

A dead tree, struck through the core by lightning, festooned with fungal growth.

A tree that, in the morning, will be alive with the song of honeybees.

Thirty

A VOICE BREAKS INTO Yennevieve's consciousness.

"Yenn!"

She jumps, eyes flying open. The bees on her up-turned palms shoot into the air. In front of her, the single beehive is awash with activity. Bees zoom back and forth from the narrow opening at its base, unconcerned by the bustling village around them. They're happy. Healthy. They hurry from their hive, across the village square. Flowers of all types have been planted for them under windows and alongside pathways. The square is awash with color. A few villagers pause, watching, as a bee wanders past them. Their eyes shine with delight. Yenn smiles.

It's taken so much to get them to this strength. So many nights laying sleepless and worried. But they're ok now.

This is the hive of a queen she named Orchid. She and Warren had worked to rescue these bees last year, from the threat of a parasite that sapped their life force.

Warren.

His name makes her ache.

"Yennevieve!" the voice says again. "Earth's *sake*, would you pay attention?"

Yenn glances up, shielding her eyes against the sun. Above her, hands on hips, stands another girl. She's wearing the same iridescent purple robes as Yenn. Her hair is dark, her eyes still a little sunken and hollow, though there's more life in her now than there was a year ago, when she was found half-starved in a mountain cave.

"What, Addie?" Yenn sighs.

Addie scowls. "The bees are being weird," Addie says. Yenn gets to her feet.

"No, they're not," she says. "They're fine. Look."

She gestures towards the hive, where the bees are behaving exactly as bees should. Addie rolls her eyes.

"Not *those*," she says. "The ones by the fungus. Come look."

Yenn huffs. There's nothing *wrong* with the bees. Addie's just interfering because she hasn't found her own insects since the fire last summer. Yenn feels sorry for her. The other Keeper children at least managed to find a few of their insects scattered through the remaining forest, but Addie's peacock butterflies are nowhere to be found.

It's still *annoying* that she's interfering.

Addie beckons impatiently, then sets off through the village square. It's midday, and a few Fei and Oritch have returned from the fields to eat, swap stories and get things mended. Yenn ducks under arms and squeezes past hips as crowds gather.

The scent of fresh bread makes her pause. She turns towards the edge of the square, where an Aldren woman stands on the porch of her squat house, offering steaming slices to the workers. Earth, it smells good!

"Yenn!" Addie's voice sounds sharply up ahead. "Come *on!*"

Yenn scowls and follows. At the edge of the square, a heap of logs and rotting wood has been piled to waist height. To any outsider, it would look like a rubbish heap. Strange, in the otherwise pristine square where the cobbles are swept, debris quickly cleared.

But every Skyheart villager knows this is no rubbish heap. This pile of apparently useless wood is precious because it houses the most spectacular fungal growths. Oranges and yellows, white and pale greens, with silver filaments criss-crossing through the wood. Bees cluster around it.

This is what Yenn discovered last year, along with the Whisperer girl, Taipan. Orchid and her hive were saved by this miraculous discovery; that a fungus could cure bees of parasites.

When the glade was destroyed, Taipan managed to draw some of the fungi into the village centre, so the bees would have some close by. Many still prefer to zoom into the unburned section of the forest, where a huge, dead tree stands, covered in fungi.

Yenn joins Addie beside the wood heap, folding her arms.

"They look fine," she says again, casting a cursory glance at her bees. "You're just being annoying. They—"

She stops. Several bees scuttle across the wood, antennae probing the mycelial threads. They clamber over each other, buzzing excitedly, and then start to dance. Addie gives a look of triumph.

"See?" she says, smirking. Yenn shoots her a mean look. She kneels and scoops up a handful of bees, closes her eyes and pushes out her mind. She feels the whisper-step of bee feet on her palm. Their scent hits her like a poison sting. She reels.

Message! They cry. *Message! Fly! Fly!*

They take off in a fit of excitement. Yenn's on her feet in moments. Message? What message?

"C'mon!" she says. Addie doesn't need telling twice.

The girls fight their way through the crowds in the square, straining to keep an eye on the disappearing bees. They follow between the haphazard houses, down narrow streets where Aldren on rickety chairs yell at them not to go too far.

The girls ignore the warning. They come to the edge of the village, where an electrified fence marks the perimeter. The bees, of course, buzz straight past the wire restraints. The girls skid to a halt, watching in dismay.

"The forest," Yenn says. She and the other Keeper children are forbidden from entering it unaccompanied now. After what happened last year, when a boy called Ig managed to trick them into believing he was a friend. Since then, the village Steward, Norsen, has been protective over the Keepers. Yenn finds it suffocating. It's worse for her, because Norsen's her Dja, and terrified of losing her. Today is one of the few days he hasn't posted an entire squad of Gatra to follow her around. It's difficult to commit yourself to a make-believe game, or even talk to your bees, when seven black-clad soldiers watch your every move.

Yenn glances along the wire fence, where a watchtower looms at one corner of the village. A new watch will be heading there soon.

"What now?" she says. Addie gives a triumphant smile.

"The dead bit of the fence," she says. Yenn rolls her eyes.

"They fixed that," she says. "Ages ago."

Addie's grin widens. "Yeah," she says. "And then Auntie Reya and I *un*fixed it so I could search for my butterflies."

Yenn gapes. She knows Reya is a maverick. Reya is captain of the Gatra and, last year, she and Norsen had suspected each other of being responsible for

Addie's disappearance. Reya's got a rebellious streak. But, even by her standards, this is bad.

"Your Auntie Reya is gonna get in so much trouble," she says. Addie laughs.

"She's always in trouble," she shoots back. "Come on, before we lose them!"

Yenn darts after Addie as the other girl charges behind the houses, heading for the northern perimeter. Here, a year ago, Norsen kept a section of the fence electricity-free, so the Keeper children could sneak into the forest glade. That glade has long-since burned, and the Keeper children no longer live there. Norsen ordered the dead section electrified as soon as the Whisperers left last year.

But when Addie reaches out to tap that same section of fence now, Yenn sees the other girl is right. There's no electricity in these wires. She frowns.

"This is dangerous," she points out. "I should tell Dja—"

"No!" Addie cries, grabbing her wrist. For the first time, she looks scared. "*Please,* Yenn! My butterflies ..."

Her lower lip quivers and Yenn's resolve crumbles. She remembers what it was like all winter when her bees were hibernating. The ache of their silence, a physical pain in her heart. She knows what Addie's going through.

"Norsen's got patrols out," Addie insists. "No-one's gonna break into the village. *Please,* Yenn!"

Yenn chews her lip, still uncertain. Addie looks so desperate. She's the only one of the Keeper kids who hasn't found her insects. Guilt overrides Yenn's sense of duty.

"Fine," she says. "But we need to be quick."

They crawl under the wire and scurry into the forest. The bees have disappeared, their song lost on the breeze, but Yenn's got a good idea where they're going. They follow a path beside the river, where the trees are still green and growing, until they find the fungus tree.

The children stand and stare for a long time, unsure what to do. The tree is always an incredible sight, it's blackened trunk festooned with fungus.

But it's not the tree itself that makes the children stare.

"I don't—" says Yenn.

Addie smirks. "Told you," she says.

The tree is awash with bees, carpeting every inch of the fungal growths. They clamber over each other, buzzing frantically.

"Are they sick again?" Yenn asks. Addie shakes her head.

"Ain't sickness," she says. "It's ... something else."

Yenn gulps. She doesn't like the sound of that. When she glances at Addie, the other girl is twisting her robes between her hands.

A little worker detaches from the tree and zooms to Yenn. She circles Yenn's head, then fires her engine and powers back towards the tree.

"She wants you to follow," Addie says. Yenn shoots her a look.

"I *know* that," she says. "*I'm* the honeybee Keeper, aren't I?"

Addie rolls her eyes. Yenn steps closer and holds out her hands. Bees swarm over her fingers. She gasps as they flood her with scent. They're dancing in a tangle of excitement.

A message! A message!

Yenn closes her eyes as her vision throbs purple. She concentrates on the scent of the bees.

From who? she asks. The scent feels strange. Thicker, somehow, more earthy. She cracks one eye open, peering at the bees on her palm, and is alarmed to see white particles coating their fur. Paler than the yellow of pollen. She balks. *What's on you?* she demands. *Are you sick?*

The bees dance a negative. No, they're not sick. The particles are safe. *Spores,* they tell her. *A message.*

Right, a message. Yenn's still confused about that. *From who?* She asks again.

From the fungus, the bees say. *From the Earth. From the future.*

Yenn has no idea what that means. Fear roils in her belly.

Listen, the bees insist. *Connect. Let go.*

Yenn shakes her head, resisting. This isn't right. It's not—

Addie's hand lands on her shoulder. Yenn looks at her and the other girl smiles.

"It's ok," she says. Gentle. Encouraging. "Whatever they want, do it."

Yenn doesn't point out that Addie can't hear the bees, doesn't know *what* they're asking. She takes a breath, forces herself to relax.

And opens her mind.

Immediately, it's flooded. Scent. Song. Dance. She's hauled out of her body and, suddenly, she *is* the bees. Tens of thousands of individuals in perfect, chemical harmony. A many-bodied entity. Yenn wants to scream. Wants to laugh. But she can't find her mouth, her voice.

She's in the air. Crawling across the tree with her sisters. Tapping and stamping and buzzing with that *urgency.*

Let go, the bees say.

What does that mean? Yenn has no control anymore. She has no idea where she ends and the bees begin. She can't find herself, can't—

It doesn't matter, the bees say. *Trust us.*

Yes. Trust. That's how bees work. In honesty.

Yenn lets go.

The message surges through her. It's in her blood, her bones. In the gaps between her breaths. A message spoken through the fungi, delivered to her bees who, in turn, pass it to her.

A message from a friend.

Taipan's voice thunders in Yenn's consciousness. Vibrates between the wingbeats of the bees.

Help! Taipan says. *We need you! Help us!*

Yenn's eyes fly open. The bees explode upwards, swarming in a great tornado around her as she thuds back into herself. Finding her lungs, she takes a great gasp of air, yelps as she remembers what it's like for her heart to beat. For a moment, she's dizzy and lurches sideways, trying to find her balance.

"Addie!" she slurs, reclaiming her voice. "Addie, it's amazing! It's Taipan! We got to—"

She stops.

Addie is turned away, frozen with fear. She's shaking. "Addie?"

Addie says nothing.

And then Yenn looks past Addie, and fear freezes her in place, too.

Blocking their path home are ten Gatra. Not Skyheart Gatra. She's no idea where they're from, but there's a hunger in their eyes that suggests they're not friendly.

"Get behind me, Addie," Yenn growls. She opens her palms, reaching out to her bees. She has twenty thousand tiny fighters at her command. These Gatra won't take her and Addie without a fight.

One of the soldiers steps forward.

"I wouldn't do that, if I were you," he says. Yenn doesn't let go of her bees. She looks him up and down. There's a Sergeant's insignia on his uniform. He's tall, well-built. A seasoned soldier. But his gun is holstered and his rifle is slung across his back. He holds his hands up.

"Who are you?" Yenn demands.

"My name is Aldo," the soldier says. "I'm a Sergeant from Sand's End."

Yenn feels as if the breath has been punched from her body. Sand's End. Warren's home. The village that cast him out, then kidnapped him when they realized his power. The village who hired the Fire Makers. Burned the glade to the ground.

Yenn lifts her hands, and the bees rise from their tree. They blacken the air, their war-song thrumming with such intensity that Yenn barely hears what Aldo says next.

"Stand down, girl," he tells her. Now, he's reaching for his weapon. Not quite so peaceful, is he?

"Why should I?" Yenn yells. Aldo gestures to the fungus tree.

Yenn looks, and her heart stutters.

While she's been gathering her bees, another soldier has crept behind her and Addie. He's dressed differently to the others, with a thick, black suit over his uniform, a netted helmet covering his face to protect him from bee stings. He stands next to the fungus tree, a flaming torch in his hands.

"Stand down, girl," Aldo says again. "I've got orders to burn it if you don't do as I say."

Yenn's eyes fill with tears. She lets out a frustrated scream.

But she can't sacrifice the fungus tree. Not when it's so important to her bees. She pulls her mind back from the swarm and drops to her knees, reaching for Addie's hand.

"I'm sorry," she sobs.

"It's ok," Addie says.

The children huddle together, crying quietly, as Aldo and his soldiers surround them.

Thirty-One

GREY DAWN LIGHT FILTERS through the window. Solma hugs her knees, listening to the breathing of her friends and family. Olive's asleep on the pallet, Warren curled against her. Roseann and Bell are propped against the wall, snoring softly. Solma notices their fingers are loosely intertwined. Her eyes burn with tears.

She's failed.

Again.

She replays the memory of Maxen's face appearing in the dark. Lifting the pistol, aiming wide. Wasting that precious bullet. She tries to imagine shooting him, but every time she does, a chill washes through her and she can't stay inside the thought.

She's weak. And now, they're trapped in this basement. Python is Earth-knows-where and her Whisperer friends are stranded in the woods. She's let her family down. Maxen will kill them all.

But perhaps there's still a way to fix this. Perhaps Maxen will accept Solma's life in return for the others' freedom. Perhaps she might, at least, persuade him to let them live ...

Something stirs. Solma glances up to see her aunt watching her.

"Did you sleep?" Bell asks. Solma shakes her head.

Slowly, so as not to wake Roseann, Bell gets to her feet and hobbles over to sit beside Solma.

"Are you hurt?" Solma asks, noticing how Bell grimaces when her knees bend. Bell gives a wry grin.

"No, girl," she says. "Just getting old. I should count myself lucky. This pain is a triumph. Means I beat the odds, lived longer than most other people I know."

"Right," Solma says, drily.

Bell rests her head against the wall. Neither of them speaks for a moment. Solma leans her chin on her knees again.

"I'm sorry," she whispers. "I really am."

Bell looks at her, a strange light in her eyes. "For what?" she demands. Solma shrugs.

"All of it," she says. "For getting it so wrong. For …
for not shooting Maxen when I should'a done. I …"
she bites her lip as her voice cracks. "I thought I was
strong enough to do it, but I ain't. I'm sorry."

For the longest time, Bell says nothing. Solma buries
her face in her knees and breathes deeply to avoid
weeping.

Then there's a rustle of skirts and Bell's arms are
around her.

"You remember," Bell says, "how I told you I had
faith in you?"

"Yeah," Solma says, her voice wavering. "Now you
know it was misplaced."

"No, girl," Bell says fiercely. "I know I was *right*."

Solma glances up. What? Have hunger and stress
addled her aunt's brain? But Bell's expression is ferocious. She grabs Solma's hand, holds it tight.

"The world has been full of violence for too long,"
she says. "But it don't have to be that way. That's the
world built by men like Blaiz and Maxen. We don't
got to live in that world, girl. We can build something
better."

Solma throws her arms up. "How?" she demands.
"We're stuck in a cell, waiting to die."

Bell shrugs. "True," she says. "But we got outta worse scrapes than this before. All I know is, I'd rather die trying to build a world I believe in, than live fearfully in one built for me. Maybe that's just me. We all gotta make our own choices. Our own peace."

Solma chews her lip, thinking. Maybe that's true. But she's not sure she's as brave as her aunt. When she looks at Olive, looks at her brother, she thinks there's nothing she wouldn't do to keep them alive.

Bell squeezes her hand. "Sometimes, Sol," she says, "there are other ways of winning. Other ways of fighting. Sometimes, death ain't the answer. Your Ma knew that."

"But Ma's dead," Solma points out. She sees color rise in her aunt's cheeks and regrets her words. "I'm sorry, Bell, I—"

"No," Bell says. "You're right. She's dead. But she lived long enough to make you, din't she? And Warren. She made two people who're fighting for a new world. Keep that in mind, girl. Keep in mind that the world lives beyond us."

Finally, Solma feels the tears come. "I don't know what that means," she says. Bell pulls her close, holding her while she cries.

"It don't matter," Bell says softly. "Not right now. What matters is you know I love you. And I couldn't be prouder of you and your brother. Whatever happens, you remember that."

Raised voices sound from outside. Immediately, everyone's awake.

Solma stands, shielding her family. She reaches instinctively for her knife, but of course, it isn't there. She catches Olive's gaze and sees the same ferocity she feels in her own heart. They have nothing but their fists to fight with if there's any trouble.

And from the sounds of things, there's going to be trouble.

Roseann rubs her eyes blearily. Bell goes to Warren and tries to usher him behind her but he's not having any of it. He's been on his own, dealing with this, for months. He doesn't need to be babied. He stands beside her, watching the door. Solma and Olive position themselves on either side of it, fists raised.

There's an urgency to the voices outside, but also uncertainty. Solma hears one of the Gatra say, "Is it true?"

She doesn't hear a response. She frowns at Olive, who shrugs back. Then, Maxen's voice sounds down the corridor. Halting and concerned. Solma listens and finds herself lowering her fists. Is that ... *fear* in his voice?

Then he comes close enough for her to hear what he's saying, and the fear is in her as well.

"I had it under control. We'll put them on trial. I'll sentence them. It'll show the villagers we're fair. *Dja, wait ...*"

And then a voice that haunts Solma's nightmares.

"Fair is a matter of perspective, Maxen," Blaiz says. His voice is raspy, an edge of pain to it, but Solma would recognise it anywhere. "Is it fair that they get fed precious resources for sitting in a cell?"

Solma has just enough time to catch Olive's eye, to register the alarm and horror there, and then someone's banging on the cell door.

"Stand where I can see you!" someone yells.

Reluctantly, Solma and Olive shuffle alongside the others. A face peers through the metal bars. The lock clicks, the door opens slowly.

And there he is.

He's hunched, leaning heavily on a cane. He wears a cowskin waistcoat over a simple shirt and cotton pants. What little hair he has left is stubble and most of his face is puckered with scars. One eye is pale as moonlight, the pupil utterly gone. His lips are mis-shapen, swollen with sores and scars. Solma begins to regret what she and Warren did to him. Then he smiles, and there's that cruel gleam to his eyes, that wicked twist to his mouth, that reminds her he's monstrous.

"I wondered when you'd show up again," he sneers.

Behind him, Maxen shuffles into view. His eyes dart and he licks his lips, hiding in his father's shadow. He sees Solma watching and tries to square his shoulders, but his father's gravity is too much. He bends towards it. Solma almost feels sorry for him.

Almost.

Behind Maxen is Vulkan with a hand on Ignis' shoulder. A squad of five Gatra flank him. Solma examines their faces, finds one she recognises.

Ilga. The girl's grown since she was a weedy recruit in Solma's squad. Her hair, no longer lank with grease, is swept off her face and tied in a red-blonde braid down her back. Like the others, she has her weapon trained on Solma and Olive, but Solma sees she's shaking.

Blaiz shifts his weight until he takes up the whole door frame. Solma glares and makes a show of raising her fists. Beside her, Olive does the same. And so does Warren. Solma tries not to look at him. Tries not to let this break her heart too much.

Blaiz looks Solma up and down. His lip curls.

"I believe we exiled you, Solma," he says. "And, with regret, you know what happens to exiles who return from the wilderness?"

Solma says nothing. She does know. But she isn't giving Blaiz the satisfaction of acknowledging it. He's enjoying himself too much already.

"Doctor Roseann has skills that, I'm sure, she'd be happy to share with the village. Warren has already shown his worth and, I have no doubt, will continue to do so. The rest of you have broken your exile. I'm sure you understand the village cannot afford to keep prisoners indefinitely."

He doesn't wait for an answer, just turns and hobbles out of the door.

For a moment, Solma fears the Gatra might open fire here. Now. She grabs Olive's and Warren's hand, preparing to throw herself in front of them.

But Blaiz has a streak of showmanship in him, too.

"I see there's been a little dissent in the village," he says. "That's unfortunate, but not surprising given a certain ... lack of leadership."

Maxen opens his mouth to speak, then thinks better of it and hangs his head. Blaiz strokes the stubble on his chin. "A public execution should quell that nonsense." He waves a dismissive arm towards Vulkan. "After a trial, of course. We aren't animals."

"A trial?" Solma blurts out. "With who as judge?"

Blaiz raises an eyebrow. "Me, of course," he says. "The only one who knows your true colors. The only one qualified to do so."

Solma risks a glance at Maxen, but he's staring resolutely at the floor.

"That ain't a trial," Solma growls. "It's a trick. You know it. I know it. The villagers will know it, too. You ain't the smooth talker you think you are, Blaiz. People know. Everyone knows ..."

She trails off. Blaiz is smiling so wide he barely looks human. He shakes his head, a gleam in his eye. "The rightenousness of youth," he says. "It's quite astonishing, really." He waves a hand at Vulkan. "Arrange the trial," he says. "Tomorrow evening."

He turns, leaving his words hanging in the air. Solma sees the shock on Ilga's face, sees how even Ignis is drained of color.

"*No!*"

Warren's voice rings out, stronger and more forceful than Solma's ever heard it. Blaiz freezes, half turns back.

"No?" he repeats, amused. "I don't really think you're in a position to negotiate, Warren El Yuen."

"That's 'cos you ain't as clever as you think you are," Warren says.

Blaiz turns back, fixing Warren with an appraising stare. The amusement is gone from his face. He's angry now. Solma raises her fists again. But Warren is using a weapon even she hadn't considered.

"You hurt my family," he says, "I'll make sure the bees never do anything you want."

Blaiz stands utterly still. Beside him, Maxen starts to shake.

"It seems," Blaiz says coolly, "that you have failed to instil a sense of duty in our Beekeeper."

He's talking to Maxen, Solma realizes. Maxen begins babbling, his face flushed.

"No, Dja, I did everything you wanted. I—"

"Quiet," Blaiz says. Maxen clamps his mouth closed, glares at Warren. But Warren's isn't backing down. Solma lowers her fists, watches her brother as he speaks.

"You want my help?" he says. "You let my family be. You let them go. Otherwise, I'll fight you with everything I got. I'll sneak bees out wherever I can. I'll tell them not to pollinate your food."

"They'll die," Blaiz points out, raising an eyebrow.

A tear draws a track down Warren's cheek. "Better than belonging to you," he says.

Blaiz watches Warren for a moment, thinking. "There are plenty of others in the village I believe need punishment, Warren," he points out. "That old Gerta, for example. Some of the neglectful soldiers that failed to keep you in your cell. I could pardon them in exchange for your co-operation. Or I could ... not?"

He leaves the threat hanging, but Warren's tear-streaked face is set with determination. "You think I'll care about any of that if you murder my family?" he asks. "You think I'll care if *I* live after that?"

Solma grabs his shoulder. "Warren—" she says, her heart tightening. But Warren pushes her away.

"Spare my family," he says. "Let them live. Or I swear, I'll fight you. For the rest'a my life."

Blaiz's jaw tightens. His gaze flickers from Warren to each member of his family. There's a long, agonised pause. Solma sees Warren as he's been for the last year. An island in a storm-tossed sea. Weathered. Beaten. But still *here*.

"I want your full co-operation," Blaiz says at last. "No more of these little … *defiances* I've been hearing about. You do as you're told without question."

Warren makes no move to agree. "My family," he says.

Blaiz smiles cruelly. "You seem to have forgotten," he says, "who has the upper hand here. I will hold off executing your traitorous family *for now*, but they will not be released, boy. They broke Sand's End law and were exiled. They will stand trial."

Warren says nothing. His fists are clenched at his sides. The smile falls from Blaiz's face. He turns to Maxen. "We'll take the prisoners through the village tomorrow," he says, "so I can show myself, and our people can see we have overcome the traitors who threatened our safety."

He turns, fixes Solma with a cold stare. "Then, they will be confined here. I will decide what to do with them after the harvest. But," and here, he turns to Warren. "Their lives are dependent on the behaviour of our Beekeeper. Understand?"

Solma feels Olive's hand grip hers. Warren trembles, but he holds Blaiz's eye, nods an affirmative.

"Good," Blaiz says. He turns to Solma. "Welcome home. Such as it is."

And then he's away, limping down the corridor. Maxen scurries in his wake like a kicked dog. The Gatra hover, weapons trained on the prisoners. Solma sees Ilga lean towards the guard next to her and mutter something, her eyes flick towards Solma. Vulkan hands Ignis a key.

"Lock it," he says.

Ignis stares at the key, then at Solma. His expression is hard, full of hate. But as he swings the door closed, Solma sees him look at Warren.

And perhaps it's only the last vestiges of hope, but she thinks that, as Ignis meets her brother's gaze, the hate falls from his face.

Thirty-Two

Urutu pulls on Poppy's rein. The mare slows, tossing her head in protest. Urutu jumps down and runs a hand along the mare's neck. It's slick with sweat.

"She ok?" Sidewinder asks, swinging down beside him. Urutu shrugs.

"She's tired," he says. "We should rest her for a bit. She'll run into the ground if we keep going like this"

He glances at the horizon. The sun has set behind the mountains now, and the foothills are in gloom. They've been making their way alongside a river, hoping to avoid the forest terrain. But it's hard going. Urutu's lost count of the days. Poppy's exhausted. Sidewinder's eyelids droop with tiredness. They've travelled relentlessly, barely stopping to eat or sleep. Every so often, both Whisperers dip their hands into the soil to see if there's any more news. But Taipan's message is always the same.

They're hiding in the forests nearby. Their friends aren't dead. They're certain of that. But something is happening in Sand's End. They've tried to plan a rescue, but the village is well-guarded. They don't know what to do. And every day that passes is another day they might be caught.

Please help, Taipan pleads, her fear and sorrow making the mycelia ache.

Several times, Urutu has even tried to reach Python, despite nearly losing his mind—and his life—the last time he connected with that Whisperer. He's beginning to understand how powerful Python is. If what Taipan tells him is true, the fungal network gives Whisperers a power beyond comprehension. A deep connection to all life. To the heart of the world itself.

But Python can't be found. He's not in the mycelia. It's as if he's been erased. Not dead, Urutu is almost certain. If Python was dead, at least part of his essence would have found its way back into the Earth. Urutu would feel fragments of him. But there's nothing. He's completely cut off. Urutu finds that disturbing.

"We need to keep going," Sidewinder says, her words slurring from exhaustion. "We can't stop ..."

Too tired to reply, Urutu takes Poppy's reins. They plod towards the mountains, the pace frustratingly slow. But Sidewinder's right. Every step, however small, is a step closer.

Urutu feels Vulkan's flames at his back. The thought of his brother's destructive power drives him through hunger and tiredness. Through fear and guilt.

The moon lifts above the mountains. The river gurgles. A small animal calls ...

And then there's another sound. A deep rumbling, like the guttural growl of some huge beast. Poppy snorts and paws the ground. Urutu tries to calm her, but in her agitation, she kicks out.

"Sidewinder," Urutu says through gritted teeth. "What's—?"

"Get off the track," Sidewinder says. "Now."

She grabs the end of Poppy's rein and, together, the Whisperers haul the horse into the surrounding trees.

Now hidden, Poppy calms. The Whisperers peer through the foliage at the most startling sight.

Two, massive vehicles, the like of which neither Urutu nor Sidewinder have ever seen. Painted black, with glaring lights at their front and a set of solar panels mounted at the rear. Their huge wheels churn the ground. Great engines roar like beasts. The vehicles move slowly, lurching over difficult terrain. Marching alongside them are black-clad soldiers. Lots of them. The vehicles are open-topped, so Urutu and Sidewinder can see the passengers.

Urutu feels his heart grow heavy.

Inside each vehicle are civilian children. They aren't dressed like typical Yuen, but clad in robes like those of a Whisperer. Except, where a Whisperer's robes would be green, these children wear iridescent purple.

Keeper children.

With them is a man, balding, stubble shadowing his chin. He's too old to be wearing the haphazard clothing of Yuen, and yet he's not wearing caste colors. He's dressed in simple black slacks with a linen shirt and a black cowskin waistcoat. Only one adult caste have no clothing color. This man is a Steward.

And he doesn't look happy.

"What's happened?" Sidewinder says. "Where are they going?"

"I don't know," Urutu says. There's something about the way the children look at the soldiers that makes his skin prickle with unease. Children know the soldiers of their own village as protectors. They're often brothers and sisters, friends and family members. They aren't people to be feared. But these children look at the Gatra with terror in their eyes.

The Keeper children, Urutu knows, are from Skyheart. But something tells him the Gatra don't hail from the same place.

Some instinct suggests they're from elsewhere, sent by their Steward on a mission. And not a friendly one.

"I think the soldiers are from Sand's End," he says.

Sidewinder says nothing, but Urutu feels her tense. Her hand brushes the trunk of a birch tree beside them. Silver filaments spider-web from beneath her fingers. Urutu's jaw tightens. He reaches back and clasps her hand. He hasn't held her hand in a long time. Not since he was a frightened boy, taken from his village and she, a softly spoken pre-teen.

There's a moment when her hand hangs limp in his, then he feels her fingers tighten.

"The Gatra at the front," Urutu says. "I think he's in charge."

He indicates a young man—barely out of boy-hood—leading the procession. Occasionally, he stops to direct the drivers around a difficult patch of terrain, or glance back to check the passengers are behaving.

"What about the woman at the back?" Sidewinder asks. Urutu follows her line of sight and sees an older woman bringing up the rear. She's tall and wiry with narrowed eyes, watching the man-boy at the front as if she doesn't trust him. Her hair is midnight black, fading to red at the tips.

"She looks like a captain," Urutu agrees. He shields his eyes and peers at her. "And the children in the trucks keep looking at her like ... like they *trust* her."

Sidewinder gives a frustrated grunt. "What does that mean?" she asks.

Urutu shrugs. "Something weird's going on," he says.

"What do we do?" Sidewinder asks. Urutu's heart gives a nervous kick. It's the first time she's deferred to him. Normally, she's the one giving orders. But now, there's a vulnerability to her that makes him afraid. She's been his adoptive older sister for as long as he can remember. Now, she's the fragile child.

"Wait here," he says.

"Wait—what?" Sidewinder splutters. "You can't just—"

But he already has.

Despite Sidewinder's hissed protests, Urutu lets go of her hands and steps out from among the trees. He calls to the convoy, raises his hands to show he means no harm.

Immediately, the trucks rumble to a halt. Every weapon is trained on him.

He doesn't dare glance back at the trees, where Sidewinder and Poppy are concealed. Instead, he stands still while the boy-soldier and the woman with red-tipped hair stride towards him.

There's nothing he can do but hope he's made the right call.

Thirty-Three

A LOW-HANGING CLOUD MAKES the summer evening muggy. Ignis and Vulkan had a hard job keeping the workers on task, today. The heat was distracting, and more trade delegations arrived. The newcomers are inquisitive, and keep wandering up to the fields, demanding to know how the crop is doing. As far as they're concerned, most of it is theirs already. It's making the Sand's End natives twitchy. A few scuffles broke out today, which Ignis failed to contain before they became nasty. He's received several smacks around the head from his father for his negligence.

Ignis tries not to think about this as he checks the lock on Warren's cell, ignoring the curses Olive and Solma shout. For weeks, they've been hurling insults at him and, to Ignis' surprise, some of them hurt. He gets more worried, though, when they're quiet. Two nights ago, they tried to jump him as he entered the cell. Idiots. He left a nasty burn across Olive's shoulder and Solma backed down quickly. On Vulkan's orders, Ignis left them for two days without food.

But on the second day, Warren looked so tired and hungry that Ignis sneaked the boy half a bread roll.

Vulkan would've given him two black eyes if he'd found out. Ignis pushes that thought away and checks the guard schedule. Ilga's on duty at midnight. Then a couple of new recruits, barely out of boyhood. Ignis sighs. So many of Maxen's guards are idiots.

Blaiz's guards now, he supposes. Now the true Steward is awake. Why does that fill Ignis with such dread? He shakes himself and heads up the steps and along the corridor.

Outside, Vulkan waits with arms folded, watching the workers scurry home for the night. Ignis pauses out of sight, noticing how villagers lower their eyes as they see Vulkan, hurrying their children past. He gives a grim nod. Good. They *should* be afraid.

But there's something a bit different in how a few of the Aldren look at Vulkan now. That old woman—Gerta—is the worst. Even escorted by two soldiers, she doesn't look away as she limps by. Her watery eyes fix on the Fire Maker and her jaw clenches.

Vulkan sneers but instead of blanching and hurrying by, she stops, fixes him with a glare.

"You're a disgrace," she mutters. "You *and* your boy."

The soldiers prod her, and she moves on without looking back. Vulkan makes to go after her, teach her a lesson, but two burly Fei workers step in his way.

"Evening, sir," they say, all fake smiles. Vulkan glares but they don't move until Gerta turns the corner, out of sight. Then, they touch their heads respectfully and move off. Vulkan growls and Ignis hangs back, waiting for his father to calm down.

It's been like this for weeks. Ever since they've had Solma and her mob locked up. Defiance from the workers, villagers a bit too slow to follow orders. Even some of the soldiers are acting strangely. Ignis couldn't get his head round it until he overheard a couple of the Aldren gossiping.

"It's bad enough they've kept the boy locked up," one said. "But the others, too? Those're our people."

And then, something that made Ignis frown with concern.

"He's just like his father."

Ignis couldn't work out if they'd been talking about him or Maxen. But either way, it sounded like an insult. He'd shaken his head, dismissed it as the deranged mutterings of Aldren. They're always the most troublesome caste. Too many opportunities to talk and scheme.

Now, he watches from the shadows until he sees the tension ease from his father's shoulders. He steps into the evening light.

"Hey, Dja," he says. Vulkan grunts but doesn't look round. "I checked on that Whisperer," Ignis continues. "He's heavily drugged. How'd your search in the woods go?"

He knows, immediately, it was the wrong thing to ask. Vulkan's face darkens and Ignis takes a step out of his father's reach.

"Bloody Whisperers," Vulkan growls. "I know they're in there. I'll find 'em. Kill 'em, too."

Ignis says nothing. He wonders if Vulkan's right, and the Whisperers really are hiding in the woods. Vulkan's searched relentlessly since they caught Solma and the others. But either the Whisperers are well hidden, or they're not there.

Ignis casts his father a sideways glance. Dark circles round the eyes. Hollowness in the cheeks. He's twitchy. Sparks dance at his fingertips. Ignis keeps his distance.

"Got guards posted for Warren and the traitors all night," he says. He folds his arms, mirroring his father's stance. He chews his lip before asking his next question. "Any idea what Maxen's gonna do with them?"

Vulkan doesn't answer immediately. When Ignis risks a glance at him, he sees those piercing eyes scan the horizon like a wildwolf tracking prey. Finally, Vulkan shrugs.

"He ain't gonna do anything," he says. "Ain't his choice no more."

Ignis turns aside to hide the fact he's rolling his eyes. "Fine, what's Blaiz gonna do with them?"

Vulkan grunts. "Kill them eventually," he says. "He's biding his time." He spits on the ground, making Ignis jump. "He's an arrogant showman at heart. Still—" Now he frowns at Ignis. "Don't think it's the best idea. Better to get rid of 'em now. Quietly."

Ignis blinks. "Why?"

Vulkan rolls his eyes, delivers a lazy smack to Ignis' shoulder. Ignis staggers. "'Cos the villagers like the Gatra girl," he growls. "No idea why. Longer she's alive, more trouble we'll have."

"Why?" Ignis says again. He receives a second smack. He scowls as he steps further away from his father, rubbing his arm where's he's sure another bruise is forming. Still, he knows his Dja's not angry yet. Just hungry and tired. He's grown up knowing his father communicates through violence. It's just how he is. Violence and anger are currencies they've both traded in for a long time.

Only ...

Ignis hasn't forgotten what Warren did last year when Ignis finally overpowered him. How he'd yelled out for his sister, not to call her to save him, but to plead with her to go and save their friends. To abandon him, at least for the time being. The only time he's ever seen Warren use violence is when the kid was trying to save his sister.

Ignis fingers the scars on his cheek and winces with remembered pain.

He thought he'd understood Warren, then. But this summer, watching that ridiculous kid with his bees and butterflies, Ignis reckons he's got no idea about Warren at all.

"Why don't Blaiz just kill them now, then?" he asks sullenly.

"'Cos he's an idiot," Vulkan rumbles. Ignis doesn't reply and, eventually, Vulkan elaborates. "He wants the villagers to respect him," he says. "To love him." He lets out a derisive snort. "Fool. He don't need respect. He needs fear."

Ignis frowns. "Ain't that the same thing?"

This time, he dodges aside before Vulkan lands another smack. Vulkan bares his teeth. His eyes flash.

"Ain't you been listening to a word I said for the last decade?" he snarls. "People like you and me, kid, we make others fear us. Blaiz 'n Maxen reckon they're a better class of person. They ain't. Fear's all we got and that's the truth."

Ignis frowns at the passing villagers. A few Aldren have set up a cowskin awning, offering to mend broken equipment as Fei and Oritch workers wander past. Some take them up on the offer. Ignis shields his eyes and squints towards the gathering of people. Gerta hobbles under the awning to join the menders, her guards loitering nearby. She smiles as she takes a pair of broken secateurs from an Oritch. Ignis watches her work. Sinking into a rickety old chair, her smile alarmingly devoid of teeth, she turns her attention to mending the secateurs. Ignis stares. The old woman has been such a pain this summer, her defiance has emboldened the other villagers since Maxen captured Solma.

And that's the thing, isn't it? The villagers don't fear Maxen or Ignis or even Vulkan as much as they love Solma and Olive and Bell. As much as they love Warren.

"Dja," he says tentatively, "I don't reckon keeping the villagers scared is working. Maybe there's another way—"

His father moves so swiftly even Ignis' reflexes don't save him. Vulkan grabs a fistful of Ignis' black hair and yanks his head back, drawing a yelp from the boy's throat. Ignis struggles, then falls still, blinking back tears. He knows how his Dja hates tears. Vulkan shoves his face close. Ignis feels his father's spittle fleck his face.

"You going soft, kid?" he growls. Ignis tries to shake his head but Vulkan's holding his hair tightly. Instead, he chokes out, "No."

Vulkan flings him aside and Ignis staggers. He presses his fingers to the back of his head where his father's roughness has left his scalp tender. Vulkan watches him. He steps forward, reaching out, as if to undo the violence. But Ignis shrinks away. Vulkan scowls. He folds his arms and glares at the villagers. The queue to the Aldren's mending tent is growing long.

"Your Ma was soft," Vulkan mutters. Ignis feels his cheeks flush.

"I know," he says. He's got no wish to hear this again.

"Never had the strength to resist her family, did she?" Vulkan continues.

Ignis shuts his eyes against a rising tide of anger. He knows this. His father has yelled it at him in anger, slurred it in a drunken frenzy, spoken it softly in the wilderness.

"It weren't like she didn't try, Dja," Ignis says, his teeth gritted. "She did, but you ... you got *angry* that time like—" he stops himself before he can say it. *Like you always do.* Because Vulkan won't take that. He won't take the idea that it might have been him that drove away his wife.

Vulkan's lip curls. There's threat in his eyes.

"She could've stuck by us," he says. "If she'd had any strength, she would, too. But she was weak. Had to go tell her family, din't she? Went crying straight to her Dja like the snake she was."

Ignis says nothing. What's the point? What good would come of mentioning that maybe his mother told because *she was afraid*?

"She betrayed us, Ignis," Vulkan snarls. "She told them what we were, even though she knew what they'd do."

Ignis clenches his teeth. "I know," he says again. He hates the way his voice wavers. He barely remembers that day. He can't have been more than five or six years old. He remembers his father scooping him up, the fear in the eyes of the man he'd always thought above fear. He remembers running for their lives as the village had come for them. He'd remembered how terrifying and wild the fire had seemed when it was being used against him. The rest, though, Vulkan has filled in for him since. Their family turned on them as if they were beasts, he'd said. Driven them out. Ma sobbed as she chased them, cowardly fool.

Vulkan fought his way through the mob, scorching, blistering, burning. He'd carried Ignis over his shoulder as he ran. Ignis is only alive because of his father. He's never allowed to forget it.

Ignis feels a heavy hand on his shoulder and flinches. But his father's touch isn't violent, this time. He lifts his face to meet Vulkan's gaze.

"Family makes us weak," he says. "You'n me, we're better off the way we are. Alone. No-one but each other. We keep everyone else scared. If people fear us, it keeps 'em in check."

"I know, Dja," Ignis says. His voice holds steady, though he's not sure he believes his own words anymore. He thinks of Warren, sneaking out that night to release his insects. He remembers what Warren had said.

You could come with me.

Had that been true? Ignis thought it was a trick. But he's seen how Warren quakes under Maxen's gaze, how he can't even look at Vulkan without trembling.

But he still snuck out to try and save the insects. He still held out a hand to Ignis and offered him a place in a new world. In the future Vulkan has always said is closed to them.

Some commotion from the village centre draws both the Fire Makers' attention. Vulkan frowns. "Reckon we're needed, kid," he says.

A young Gatra runs up the path, face pale. He sees Vulkan and gestures hurriedly.

"It's the Fei," the Gatra pants. "They're starting fights with the trade folk. Quick!"

He scurries back down the path, drawing his gun.

Ignis feels his father's huge hand squeeze his shoulder, then Vulkan trudges after the soldier. Ignis hesitates, hating himself. He's being weak, like his Ma. But his Ma's been gone a long time and, like Vulkan says, it's just the two of them. Always has been.

Always the punch and remorse. Always the fist and the flame. That deep, infernal rage Ignis sees whenever his father looks at him, mixed with such terrible, jealous love.

Is it love, though? Is it love like Warren has for Solma? Like those soft-spined idiots all have for each other? Love that drove them across half the world. Love that means they save each other over and over. Love that leaves scars, yes, but scars they're proud of. Scars that show they survived.

Ignis opens a palm, watching the flame that flickers to life across his skin.

For so long, this flame, this heat and rage, has been his whole self. But the thing about fire—the thing his Dja never wants to talk about—is that it's transformative. It changes.

And Ignis pauses just long enough to feel the way it's changing inside him. The way the ash around his heart falls away, leaving something bright and tough and glittering underneath.

He follows his father just like he always has. But a part of him—a faint glimmer of something new—tells him it might not be this way forever.

Clover

I wake. The night-torpor still slows my body. It's dark and the heat of my daughters warms me. What has woken me if not the sun? I clamber over daughters, shivering my engine-muscles to make heat. Something energises me. I edge towards the entrance-tunnel, close enough that I can sense the air outside.

And there it is, a sharp scent.

I think *predator*, and poison shines on my sting. But there is no fear-stench in the air. No tang of hungry things.

I think *flowers* but I can't sense anything beyond the foul-smelling walls of the world.

And then I think *message*.

I sense someone. Someone that is not a bee, but that *speaks* bee. At first, I think it might be the bee-speak-boy. I shiver my wings, waiting to sense his footsteps. But this scent is different. Not his sadness, his desperation. There's a shimmer to the scent. An energy. I creep down the tunnel, stretching my antennae.

This is not the bee-speak-boy. This is something new.

In the soft, cold light filtering through our tunnel, I see white particles floating in the air. They drift towards me, cling to my fur. I try to kick them off, but they stick. Some get onto my tongue. Taste of earth and decay. But not unpleasantly so. Not poison.

Suddenly, the message-scent intensifies. I feel it resonate through my body, burning the tips of my antennae.

I flick my tongue in agitation. In excitement. The scent grows stronger. Around me, my daughters' wings rustle. Pre-dawn greyness stains the cold sky outside. We are waking.

Hundreds of questing antennae lift to the morning. Wing-engines shiver to life. We stamp and bluster. We taste the air. We are listening.

And slowly, the distant speaker's scent begins to make sense. A message. A promise.

We're coming, it says. *We're on our way.*

Thirty-Four

THE SNAP OF A key in the lock sounds like a gunshot. Solma whirls to face the door, fists raised. For weeks it's been like this. Every time someone comes through that door, she fears Blaiz has changed his mind. That he'll march in with a pistol raised, firing before she can even scream.

Olive is by her side, Roseann and Bell on the other. Warren, dear Warren, refuses to be sheltered. He takes his place in their ranks, little fists raised.

The door opens and adrenalin floods Solma's exhausted body. It's almost dawn. Solma expects soldiers to enter and drag her brother away, set him to work controlling the insects. She glances at Warren, at the sunken craters around his eyes and the hollows of his cheeks, the ashen pallor of his skin. He's exhausted. Broken. He's kept his word. Of course, he has. His co-operation for the lives of his family. But Solma hears him sobbing at night, knows how much it hurts him to treat his precious bees like this.

Anger flares in her gut. She bares her teeth.

Warren might've made a promise, but she bloody-well hasn't. She'll fight the guards who come for her brother, as she does every day. She'll lose, of course, but she'll leave a couple with bloody noses. She's going to make them dread the sight of her. She's going to—

A small face peers round the open door and Solma's fists drop.

"What do *you* want?"

Ignis scowls, pushing his hair out of his face. He slips inside the cell and closes the door. He's got a bag over his shoulder, bulging with something heavy. Solma folds her arms.

"Come to kill us here, have you?" she drawls.

"Sol," Warren says, touching her arm. She places a hand on his shoulder.

"It's ok, Warren," she says.

"I know it is, Sol, I think—"

"I won't let him hurt you," Solma insists.

"Sol, I don't think he—"

Ignis opens his bag, rummaging inside it. He pulls out a pistol. Everything happens at once. Roseann yells. Solma and Olive leap for Ignis, slamming him into the door. Warren's screaming something. Bell grabs the pistol, aiming at Ignis' head.

And instead of struggling or yelling for help, Ignis is imploring them to *shut the hell up* before they alert the Gatra.

Solma frowns. That's not what's supposed to happen. Her grip slackens but Olive, still flooded with battle rage, grabs his collar and shakes him.

"Thought you could take us out on your own, eh?" she snarls. "Playing hero for your precious Dja? You little—"

"Olive," Solma says, touching the other girl's wrist. Because the scowl has fallen from Ignis' face. He doesn't look angry or scared. Instead, he looks—

He looks ashamed.

Lost.

"Let him go, Liv," Solma murmurs. Olive gapes.

"What?"

"Sol's right," Warren says. "He ain't here to hurt us. He's come to help."

Everyone stares at him.

Ignis wriggles feebly in Solma's and Olive's grip. Olive rounds on him, glaring. But she releases her hold. Ignis straightens his rumpled shirt. He points at the pistol in Bell's hand.

"Think this one's Solma's," he mumbles. Solma stares at it, convinced it's a trick, but Warren takes the pistol from Bell and places it in his sister's hand. He smiles at Ignis.

"Knew you'd come round," he says.

Olive rolls her eyes. Solma's about to berate her brother, when she sees the quirk of a smile at the corners of Ignis' mouth. Not the smirk of the trickster, but a small, grateful gesture. A look that says he understands he doesn't deserve forgiveness.

But he sees that Warren is offering it, nonetheless.

She tightens her hold on Ignis. "If you're lying—" she says.

"He's not," Warren insists as Ignis hands him the bag. Warren produces Olive's pistol, the hunting knives. There are knives with which he, Ignis and Roseann arm themselves. And Bell's trusty rolling pin, which makes Solma bite back a laugh.

"She's lethal with that thing," Ignis grumbles. Bell raises an eyebrow.

"And don't you forget it," she says. There's a sparkle in her eye.

Olive's still glaring, eyes narrowed. "I don't get it," she says. "You tricked us, burned the glade, kidnapped Warren and held him captive for months. Now you wanna be on our side?"

She folds her arms, waiting. Beside her, Solma feels Warren bristle and she puts a gentle hand on his shoulder. She looks at him, and a silent understanding passes between them. Warren might be right about Ignis. But the kid's got to tell his own truth.

Ignis takes a deep breath. "Look," he says. "I know I done some bad stuff—"

"Understatement of the century," Olive grumbles. Roseann nudges her into silence. Solma gestures for Ignis to go on.

"I ..." he flattens his fringe over his forehead—a gesture Solma remembers from when he'd been pretending to be the orphaned urchin, Ig. Then, it was to cover his flame tattoo and hide the color of his eyes. Now, Solma thinks, it's something different. She feels a strange tug at her heart, like it's pulling in two directions. How can she hate this boy and want to save him at the same time? She clenches her jaw, glaring. He reddens under her stare.

"I ..." he tries again. "I don't want ... to be the one who destroys things. I wanna be part of your new world. I don't wanna be a monster no more. My Dja, he's so angry. All the damn time. Just burn this and break that, like it's all we're good for. He's told me, my whole life, it's all I'll ever do. Destroy. Like making people afraid was the only way we'd survive. He said it about my Ma, too. But ..."

And now he looks at Warren, and tears fill his eyes. Solma thinks they're swimming with shameful secrets. He twists his fingers and stares at the ground.

"Warren ain't scared of me," he says, voice small. "Or, maybe he was, but that weren't why he was nice to me. Even after I burned the glade and ... and made him attack me with those bees. He was nice to me 'cos ... he reckoned I was more than fire and destruction. Ain't no one thought that about me before. Not even my Ma or Dja. And I want ... I want to be better."

He stares at them each in turn, chewing his lower lip until the skin is raw. Olive's still glaring, arms folded, as if she fears this might be a trick.

But he's handed them their knives and pistols. He's returned Bell's weaponised rolling pin. And he hasn't yelled for help. Blaiz has them cornered, ready die at his leisure. There's no reason for Ignis to trick them.

And even if there is, what's their choice? Trust this boy? Or wait here to die?

Solma decides, then. It's worth the risk.

"Ok," she says, checking her magazine and flicking the safety off her pistol. "What's the plan?"

Another grateful smile quirks Ignis' lips. A smile that says he didn't believe they'd trust him. His eyes sparkle.

"I know where they're keeping that Whisperer you came with," he says. "Python, is it? We should go get him."

He jangles the keys, grinning. "I sent the Gatra on a made-up errand. We got about ten minutes before they realized I fibbed."

Solma catches Olive's gaze, searching for signs of doubt. Olive's still frowning, but there's a shine in her eyes Solma knows well. The thrill of a fight to come. The hunger of hope. She wants this to be true. Solma does, too.

She reaches for her brother and feels his hand slip into hers, exactly where it should be. This isn't over yet.

"Alright," she says, fixing Ignis with a frown. "But I swear on the Earth and everything on it that if you're lying to us, I'll end you. Understand?"

Ignis meets her eye. "Yeah," he says. "That's fair."

Solma gestures to the door. "Lead on, then, Ig."

Ignis grins. Solma notices he doesn't correct her when she calls him Ig, as if a part of him—a big part—wants to be that kid, again. As if, maybe, he was that kid all along. He just needed permission to admit i t.

She's not sure she's ready to believe that yet. But she follows him anyway.

Thirty-Five

IGNIS LEAVES THE GROUP of escapees in the shadows and darts upstairs to distract the Gatra.

Solma watches as he disappears. She hears him making urgent suggestions and the guards, mindless, frightened kids, rush out of the house at once. Their boots crunch on the gravel outside. Ignis' face appears around the door, grinning.

"All clear," he says. "But be quick!"

Solma herds her family after the fire boy, hoping it won't turn out she's just as gullible as those Gatra kids. Hell, she's *been* one of those kids, desperate to believe her Steward, proud of her uniform, her station.

She hopes she's not doing the same thing now. But, despite her misgivings, Ignis leads them true. He slips along the hall, silent as butterfly wings. He directs them out of the house and down the path where they hide in the dusky gloom. Ignis' eyes gleam in the dying sunlight, but Solma sees no cruelty in them.

He's tricked you once before, says a mean voice at the back of her mind. It's not wrong. She glares at the back of Ignis' head. If he tries anything …

Warren, though, follows Ignis without question. He smiles warmly when he meets the other boy's eye. Ignis beams back. They fall into step and, watching them, Solma could forget they're fugitives on the run. It's as if she's just watching two Yuen, young and playful as it's possible to be in this broken world. Relishing the last dregs of their childhood.

She jumps as someone touches her hand, but it's only Olive. They smile at each other and Olive nods towards Warren and Ignis.

"Through all this," Olive murmurs, "guess we forgot he's just a kid, too. Prob'ly ain't never had no one to play with before."

Solma doesn't know why that thought makes her eyes sting, but it does. She squeezes Olive's hand. "When this is over," she says, "I'm gonna make sure my brother can play again."

Saying it loosens the tightness in her throat. Olive grabs her face and kisses her fiercely. "We gotta get outta here, first," she says. She releases Solma's face and lifts her pistol. "I got a bullet in this chamber with Blaiz's name on it. I hope you got one for Maxen."

Solma opens her mouth to say she does. Oh, she *does*. And this time, she won't miss. But Bell shoulders her way between them, an arm wrapped around her niece.

"Oh no you don't," she growls. "Not before I've knocked both their teeth out."

Solma suppresses a laugh and meets Bell's eye. Her aunt winks, touching her fingertips to Solma's face. Solma remembers Bell's words.

The world has been full of violence for too long.

It's true. But can they win this without killing the two men who tricked and exiled them? Earth knows, Solma feels sick at the thought of putting a bullet in Maxen's head. If there's another way ...

She searches her aunt's face for any trace of that sentiment. Bell just plants a gentle kiss on her forehead. "Proud'a you, girl," she says. "And don't you forget it."

"I won't," Solma mumbles. Her gut tightens and she's not sure why.

Ignis hurries them between houses and across the path. Curfew means the villagers will be inside now, settling down to sleep or tending to household chores. Only the Gatra will be out after dark.

The Gatra and Vulkan.

Ignis sneaks them towards the council hall. They melt into the shadows as soldiers dart by in pairs or threes. Solma frowns after the fourth such group has hurried past. She catches up with Ignis.

"What's going on?" she mutters as they crouch behind a house, waiting. Ignis frowns.

"What d'you mean?"

"Something's happening," Solma says. "Look."

She points as another pair of Gatra run past, rifles ready. They're heading in the same direction as the others.

"I dunno," Ignis admits. "But I don't wanna stick around to find out."

Solma gives Ignis a hard stare. "I really hope you ain't lying, kid," she says. Ignis looks away.

"I ain't," he says. "Not that you'd believe me. Not that you even *should,* I just ..." he shrugs. "Guess I'll have to prove it to you."

Solma searches the fire boy's face, wondering why she's not scared. This is the closest she's ever been to this kid, crouched next to him in the shadows with their shoulders pressed together. She realizes she expected his touch to set her on fire. She'd never thought about it before, but she wonders if Ignis remembers the last time anyone except his father came near him without flinching. When someone last hugged him.

She wonders about his mother. Without thinking, she grabs his shoulder and squeezes.

Ignis jumps, stares at her hand, then into her face.

"I don't trust you," she admits. "Not yet. But ... I hope I can. I'm done fighting everyone. I wanna win a different way. Together. I hope you're telling the truth."

Ignis' flushes. "I am," he mutters, flattening his fringe. "But I get it." He shrugs her hand away and turns to watch the darkening path. "We ain't got long, so ..."

"Right," Solma says. She unsheathes her hunting knife. "What next?"

"Python's in the council hall," Ignis says. "Reckon they're keeping him drugged. Ain't seen no guards, though."

Solma nods. "Right," she says. "We get him out. Then we get you to safety, Warren."

Warren shakes his head. "No," he says. "Then we go to the glasshouses. Free the bees."

Solma touches his shoulder. "I ain't forgotten the bees, War," she says. "We got a plan. But we need you safe. The Whisperers said they can ..." she frowns. "Well, *Python* says he can raise an army. We need to get you—"

"No," Warren says again. There's no petulance in his voice. He looks at her steadily. "The insects might get harmed if you all start fighting. They need me. We rescue Python, then I'm coming to help with the bees."

Solma sighs. Her heart hurts. It aches with old wounds and stings with fresh ones. She can't let her brother onto a battlefield.

But what's this for, after all, if they fight Maxen and destroy the insects in the process? Warren asked her to abandon him last year so she could save their friends, stop the insects burning.

Stop another Hive War.

He's right. She hates that he's right.

She looks at him earnestly. "I hear you," she tells him. "We'll talk about it when we're back together, ok? But whatever happens, we *need* Python."

Warren hesitates, then nods. "Okay."

"And," Olive points out, "you told us Maxen's using chemicals to keep the bees in."

Warren nods. They've had plenty of time to talk over the last few weeks. Warren has explained how Maxen has been keeping both him and the insects prisoner.

Olive raises an eyebrow. "We need to find a way to break that barrier," she says. "Or all this is for nothing."

Warren looks at Ignis. The fire boy sighs. He reaches into his bag and produces a silver cannister. "If Dja finds out I gave this to you, he's gonna kill me," he says. Solma smiles.

"I reckon you've already done stuff he'll think is way worse."

Ignis shrugs. "Guess I'm all in then, eh?" he says, handing the cannister to Warren.

Solma gathers them closer. "Everyone, stay alert." she says. "Olive and I will get Python. Bell? You keep watch, take out any Gatra that approach. Roseann?" she fixes Ignis with a hard stare. "Watch the kids."

Roseann scowls but there's no time to argue. Instead, she nods and beckons the two boys to her. Solma notices that she takes a firm hold of the back of Ignis' collar. Ignis' lips tighten, but he doesn't protest.

Bell brandishes her rolling pin. Olive laces her fingers through Solma's.

"Let's get this done," she says.

More Gatra scurry past. Everyone shrinks into the shadows. That must be nearly three squads' worth of soldiers that have run past, all in the same direction. Solma's gut constricts. Something's going on. She watches the council hall intently, searching for a way in.

Maxen has installed steel shutters over the windows at what Solma reckons is great expense. He's clearly afraid of raiders. Solma looks at Ignis, who holds out a set of keys and grins triumphantly. Solma takes them with a nod of thanks.

They wait while another three Gatra stalk past. Solma thinks she hears one of them say something like, "reckon he set them loose," and she knows they're running out of time.

Solma and Olive edge towards the council hall. Solma fumbles for the right key, wincing as the others jangle against each other. She pushes it into the lock, drops it, curses, picks it up again. She feels a phantom itch in her missing leg.

"Hurry up," Olive growls. Solma finally manages to turn the key in the lock. Olive shoulders the shutters open and slips inside. Solma follows. But once inside, they both pause, stunned.

The council chamber is being used as spill-over for the storehouse. Solma sees crates of bulbous tomatoes, herbs hanging from the ceiling, juicy peppers, cucumbers, and myriad types of beans all stacked in boxes or tied with string. There's fruit, too. Apples, bigger than any Solma's ever seen. Peaches. Berries of many kinds. Solma and Olive—when they regain their composure—navigate around the crates piled high against one wall.

"This is ..." Olive says, but she can't finish. Solma nods, knowing what she means.

"Imagine if everyone in Alphor could have this," she murmurs. "Imagine if ... we had enough food that we could build cities again. We could build schools. Teach. We could learn to invent stuff again."

Olive clasps her hand. "We'd have to do it better this time," she says. Solma smiles.

"We will," she says. "But first …"

They tiptoe past the crates to the far end of the hall. Cushions and blankets are arranged around an old wooden chair and a few wax tablets—scraped clean of any notes—are heaped in the centre. In the gloom, a figure lies prone on the floor, his head propped on a folded blanket. Unconscious, his robes rucked up to his knees. Moonlight falls between the shutter seams, illuminating a cruel bruise across the back of a shaved head. Python.

Solma curses.

"He breathing?" she asks.

Olive crouches over him, feeling for a pulse. She nods.

"We gotta wake him up," she says.

Solma frowns. "Wait," she says. Olive makes a frustrated noise.

"We don't got time to—"

"Why ain't he guarded?" Solma asks. "They kept him unconscious. They know he's powerful. We've just seen three squads of Gatra running about. Something's going on."

Olive stares at her, eyes shining in the moonlight. Then, she stares past Solma. Her eyes widen, mouth falling open in horror.

"Sol—" she breathes.

"He *is* guarded," Maxen says. Solma feels the barrel of his pistol press against the nape of her neck.

Thirty-Six

SOLMA'S PULSE BEATS IN her ears. She can barely hear what Maxen says. She feels strangely calm, as if it's no surprise he's engineered this trap.

Except, *he* didn't engineer it, did he? This has Blaiz written all over it.

And Solma hears the tremble in Maxen's voice, even through the rush of blood in her ears.

"Get up," he says, a little too harshly. "No! Drop your weapons, *then* get up."

Slowly, Solma lowers her pistol to the ground. Maxen kicks it away.

"You too, Dri Gatra," Maxen snaps. Olive glares.

"Ain't Gatra no more," she says, lowering her own pistol. "Remember?"

Maxen says nothing, but Solma feels him press his gun harder against the nape of her neck. She winces and a splinter of fear spikes through her. She won't give into it. She keeps her voice steady when she speaks.

"Don't reckon Blaiz'd want you to kill me here," she says. "He'll want the village to see."

"Shut up!" Maxen says. Solma hears the edge to his voice. He's shaking. Terrified. Barely under control. She meets Olive's gaze and they both raise their hands at the same time.

"What do *you* want, Maxen?" Solma asks quietly. "Want to kill me?"

There's a pause. Maxen makes a muffled noise. Solma raises her eyebrows. Is Maxen crying?

"I never wanted to hurt you, Sol," he says quietly. "I hope you believe that. You never gave me a choice. I'm the Steward—I mean, I will be, one day. I got to make tough decisions. Protect my people."

Solma says nothing. What is there to say? Maxen sniffs, seems to recompose himself.

"I want you to know," he says. "When we were … y'know. I meant it. I did."

Solma looks at Olive, studies her face in the moonlight. The constellation of freckles. The gleam in her eyes. The way she's bunched like a darkcat, ready to jump. The way she hasn't given up. Not even now.

"Did you?" Solma says. "Could'a sworn you were only doing it 'cos your Dja told you to."

Maxen shuffles behind her. She imagines him running a hand through his hair, blinking against tears. The pressure on the nape of her neck lessens.

"I wasn't," he says. "I really … it's just … you don't *get* it, Sol! You don't get what it's like! Even when he was in a coma, it was like … his shadow was still longer than mine. Since the bees came, it's been him and then Vulkan. It's … you don't get it."

"We do get it," Olive growls. "We get that you're a coward."

The pressure against the nape of Solma's neck intensifies again. She shoots Olive a warning look. Olive clamps her mouth closed, but Solma can almost hear the curses lined up behind her gritted teeth.

"You got no idea!" Maxen snaps. "Earth, it's …" he makes a strangled noise, halfway between a sob and a scream.

In a thin shaft of moonlight, Solma thinks she sees Python's finger twitch. She says nothing, just stares at Olive, then glances towards Python. Olive's eyes flick towards the Whisperer, then back to Maxen. She gives no sign she's seen anything.

"You ain't answered my question, Maxen," Solma says quietly. "What do *you* want?"

She hears his breath catch. "I want ..." Maxen says. "I mean, I think I want ... I don't *know!*"

His boot strikes her between the shoulder blades and she falls onto all fours. His gun presses against her skull again, forcing her head down.

"I want him to be proud of me," he says through gritted teeth. "And he was, once. He used to be. Except *you,* Sol, you had to interfere, didn't you? You had to find those *stupid* bees as if the whole of Alphor would come together and hold hands now they're back. Like that's how it's *ever* worked. But it's not. People don't share. We didn't share a hundred years ago and we don't share now. You grab what you can and you shoot anyone who tries to take it. He was doing it *for the village,* Sol. Why can't you see that?"

Olive opens her mouth to say something scathing but catches Solma's eye and stops. Solma takes a breath against all the insults she wants to snarl. He's the one pressing a gun to her head, after all. She needs to stay alive for a bit longer. Python's foot moves. His eyelids flicker.

"The thing is, Maxen," she says. "What d'you reckon's gonna happen if we do things like we did before the cities fell? You reckon it'll work out different this time? Men like Blaiz take what they can. They say it's for other people, but it ain't. It's always for them."

"Shut up!" Maxen cries. "You don't know him! You don't understand!"

Solma shuts up. He's losing it. She can hear how ragged his breathing is. She glances at Python. His eyes are open, watching her. He's almost perfectly still but, slowly, his hand moves across the floor, towards a cracked, wooden board a little darker than the rest. A little ... *rotten*. Solma says nothing. Olive says nothing. Maxen makes furious, frustrated noises. He pushes the barrel of his gun harder against Solma's head.

"He wants me to shoot you, Sol," he growls. "To prove I'm loyal to him."

"Yeah," Solma says. She's barely listening. She sees Python's hand slip between the wooden slats, sees him curl his fingers in the dark. She just needs Maxen not to shoot her for a few more, precious seconds.

"Thing is, Maxen," she says. "I don't want you to shoot me. I wanna live."

She hears his breath catch, feels how his grip on the pistol slackens. He steps back.

Then everything happens at once.

Vines, laced with silver threads, burst from the floor, wrapping around Maxen's neck. He drops the pistol, eyes wide, clawing at his restraints. Solma whirls round. She grabs both Maxen's pistol and her own, aiming them at him. Olive's rearmed herself too, a pistol pointed at Maxen while she kneels by Python.

Maxen flails, choking. "Please!" he rasps. "Please, I ..."

The vines tighten and his eyes roll back as he scrabbles against his restraints. His nails leave bloody lines down his throat.

"Get Python up," Solma yells. "We gotta go!"

"I'm trying!" Olive growls. "Earth, Sol, just shoot him! *Shoot Maxen!*"

She should. It would be so easy. Just squeeze the trigger and the bullet does the rest. She imagines Maxen's body going slack, a smoking hole between his eyes, the life oozing out of him. She imagines seeing the pain and anger drain from his face as he goes wherever people go when they die. Into the sky. Into the earth.

Away.

Bell's face bursts into her mind. *The world has been full of violence for too long.* And is one more dead boy going to change that? There must be another way ...

"I ..." Solma says, hating herself. "I can't, I ..."

Olive grabs Solma's wrist and pulls her away. She's got Python up, slumped over her shoulder. Withdrawn from the mycelia, Python's no longer controlling the vines and they're already falling from Maxen's throat. He falls to his knees, gasping for air.

"Let's *go, Sol!*" Olive says. They rush for the open shutter and into the light of dawn.

Silence.

Python groans and slumps forward, his face grey with nausea. Solma and Olive lower him to the ground and step away just in time. Python throws up heartily.

"Urgh," he says, wiping his mouth. "Help me up. We've got to go. They're—"

"It's too late," Olive says quietly. Solma looks up and fear punches in her gut.

Three squads of Gatra have their rifles trained on Solma and Olive. Another squad waits nearby, Bell, Roseann and Warren restrained between them. Warren struggles, Bell glares. Roseann is stony-faced, resigned to whatever awaits them. Probably death.

Behind the Gatra stands Vulkan, holding Ignis by his collar. There's a fresh split in the boy's lip. And behind them ...

Blaiz.

Solma meets his gaze and everything inside her goes quiet. His face twists in triumph. He holds a pistol at his side.

Solma glares at Ignis. "*You!*" she growls, but Ignis raises his hands.

"It wasn't me, Sol!" he insists. "I swear, I ..."

His father rams a fist into his jaw. Blood sprays from his mouth. Solma's heart clenches as Ignis groans, eyes losing focus.

Footsteps sound behind them and Maxen staggers out of the council hall. He's still rubbing his throat and glares at Solma as he limps past, taking his place by his father. Blaiz doesn't look at him.

"You failed, then," Blaiz says. "What a surprise."

Maxen frowns. "Dja, I tried. She—"

"Quiet."

Maxen falls silent.

Olive raises her pistol, aiming it at Blaiz. "Could shoot you here and now," she says. A dozen rifles train on her. Blaiz smirks. Solma grips Olive's arm.

"No," she says. "Please, Liv. It ain't worth it."

But Olive's shaking, tears streaking her face. She bares her teeth, eyes shining.

"He's gonna kill us anyway, Sol," She says. "It *is* worth it. It's worth taking him with me."

Solma tightens her hold, imploring. "Don't," she begs. "Please. I can't—I can't watch that."

Olive turns towards her.

"I can't watch you die," Solma says, hating the catch in her voice.

Olive drops her pistol and hugs Solma fiercely, kissing her forehead, her eyelids, her mouth. "I know," she says. "I'm sorry. I'm sorry."

They hold each other. Blaiz raises an eyebrow.

"Touching," he says. "But you've had your chance, and you've shown yourselves to be every bit the conniving traitors I've always known you to be." He turns to his guards. "Disarm them. Get them ready."

Beside him, Maxen's eyes widen. He turns to his father. "Dja, no—"

Blaiz rounds on him. "I told you to be *quiet!*"

Solma feels ice in her gut. "Ready for what?" she asks.

Warren bursts into tears, struggling against his captors. Screaming. "You *promised!*" he shrieks. "I'll fight you! Every day for the rest of my life! You *promised!*"

"So did you," Blaiz says smoothly. "But you broke your word."

And suddenly Solma understands.

Soldiers form a line in front of the fugitives, rifles at the ready. A firing squad. Bell and Roseann are wrestled into position beside their niece and daughter. Two guards step forward, disarming the captives. They holster the pistols and pocket the knives, relieving Bell of her rolling pin. Solma doesn't try to stop them. Numbness sweeps her body. She can't move. Instead, she watches Blaiz and his son.

Maxen doesn't speak but, Solma notices, he holds Blaiz's eye this time. They glare at each other, each refusing to back down. Blaiz's hand, holding the pistol, even twitches towards Maxen. Towards his *son.* Still holding Olive close, Solma looks between them, between the mirror-images of their faces. Her eyes flick to Ignis, struggling against Vulkan's grip despite the blows his father rains on him. He still fights. Fights the hold of his father's fist, both now and for every time before.

"Those're my *friends*, Dja!" he yells as Vulkan hits him again and again.

"You ain't got no friends, boy!" Vulkan says.

Solma watches. Numb. Fascinated. Maxen and Blaiz. Ignis and Vulkan. Reflections staring at their originals and realising perhaps they don't like what they see. After everything, she's got only a few moments left. What is there to lose?

"He *does* have friends," she calls. Everyone looks towards her. "And now he has a ..." she struggles to say the word, struggles to believe he can be anything other than that vengeful boy on fire. But if Warren can forgive Ignis, then she must try, too. She has to believe he can be better. "He has a family," she says. "A proper one ... if he wants it." Blaiz rolls his eyes. Maxen blinks, nonplussed. Vulkan scowls.

But Ignis. Ignis looks as if sunlight has fallen across his face for the first time. He beams through the blood on his lip, his violet eyes shining as he stares at Solma. She meets his gaze, smiling.

Smiling like she knows her brother has smiled at this broken kid, smiling because she loves her brother and Ignis is her brother's friend. Even if he's half the reason they're in this mess. Even if he still has a long way to go to prove he's changed.

Blaiz rolls his eyes. "Enough!" he snaps. "Can we get this done?"

Vulkan shakes Ignis into submission, then looks to Blaiz. "The Whisperer, too?" he rumbles. Blaiz shakes his head.

"No, we need him."

Vulkan signals and two soldiers shoulder their rifles, dragging Python away. Solma notices how they're careful to avoid letting his hands touch the soil.

Warren renews his struggles, yelling, *screaming* so loud that Solma feels his pain echo through her. He'll be fine, of course. Blaiz won't risk shooting him. They need him. At least, Solma thinks, at least her brother will live.

And for herself? She will die holding her aunt in one hand and the girl she loves in the other. Staring straight into Blaiz's eyes so he knows he hasn't broken her.

That he never will.

Noises from beyond the council hall draw Solma's attention and she glances over to see a crowd gathering. Of course. It's dawn and the villagers are emerging. They probably wondered where the regular Gatra patrols were and came to investigate. Now they gather around the circle of soldiers. A murmur sweeps through them. A few look approving but, Solma notices, many glare at Blaiz, shake their heads.

No-one says anything. Of course, they don't. Not while Blaiz has three squads' worth of guns trained on these so-called traitors. Not while anyone from the village could easily be added to the line-up.

Behind Blaiz and his soldiers, there's more movement. The traders from foreign villagers have also heard the commotion. They come running from their camps and skid to a halt, staring at the scene before them. Their Gatra cluster around them, weapons ready. They look to Blaiz, then to the gathered crowd. Their faces blanche.

"I love you," Olive murmurs in Solma's ear. Solma feels her heart squeeze, her eyes sting.

"I love you too," she says.

Blaiz grins. He looks almost manic. Enjoying himself. He's won. Men like him always do.

Solma turns to Bell, ready to tell her aunt that she's sorry. That she tried. That she knows she's not been the easiest girl to raise and she loves her aunt with everything she has.

But the look on Bell's face stops her. Bell isn't looking at her. She's looking towards Roseann. As Solma turns, she sees Roseann meet Bell's gaze. Something passes between them. A fierce, mad light in both their eyes.

"Bell," she says. Then she realizes what her aunt is about to do. "Bell," Solma says, frantically. Bell doesn't respond.

"Ready," Blaiz says. The Gatra raise their rifles. Solma dimly registers that she recognises one of the soldiers taking aim at her. Ilga. Is she crying?

"Bell," Solma pleads. But there's no time.

"I love you, girl," Bell says. "Always. Remember what I told you."

"What?" Solma says. "No, please. I—"

"Fire!" Blaiz yells.

Solma closes her eyes as gunshots crack the dawn air, as cries of despair rise from the crowd. She expects a brief stab of heat. Sharp pain.

But there's nothing. Then Solma hears what sounds a lot like bodies crumpling to the ground. She opens her eyes, already knowing what she'll see.

Bell and Roseann collapsed on the packed earth in front of her, riddled with bullet holes. Their eyes are wide and staring. They're holding hands. Of course, they are. Of course, they agreed they'd take Blaiz's bullets, even if it meant only giving their girls a few more seconds of life.

And then the air is full of screaming and Solma realizes most of it is hers. She's fallen to her knees in front of Bell. Blood pools beneath her aunt. The light goes out of Bell's eyes.

"Bell!" she screams. "*Bell!*"

She tries to hold the blood inside her aunt but there's so much of it. And Bell's already dead. *Dead.* No. Solma can't accept it. Blood roars in her ears and no amount of screaming stops this terrible ache, like the horror is a great maw opening inside her, trying to swallow her whole.

Beside her, Olive holds her mother's face in her hands, her forearms stained red. Roseann is alive but barely, and not for long.

"Ma!" Olive roars. "Ma, don't die. Don't—"

But Roseann's head slumps sideways. The pain leaves her face. Solma's pulse thunders in her ears. Bell's blood covers her hands, her arms. And she's *shrieking,* her throat raw. She can't stop. Warren's screaming too. And Ignis. And half the crowd. They raise fists, surging forward, yelling at the Gatra trying to hold them back. Solma can't hear them. She can't hear anything. She's still trying to hold the blood in her aunt's body, and she knows there's no point but she can't let go.

"Bell ..." she begs, half-expecting her aunt to sit up and start admonishing Blaiz for his recklessness. She doesn't. She never will. She's gone.

Died to build a world she believed in.

Through the haze of tears, Solma sees the traders and their soldiers exchange horrified glances. Some back away. A few raise weapons, coming to Blaiz's aid. The crowd jostles. A gun goes off and Solma tenses. Everyone's shouting and Solma looks up to see Maxen's face, slack with shock as he stares at his father. His mouth forms words Solma can't hear. His father rounds on him. The firing squad have lowered their rifles. Ilga stares, open-mouthed, at the bodies on the ground.

Bodies. Not Bell and Roseann, anymore. Just collateral damage. Those who caught the sharp end of Blaiz's temper so their children wouldn't have to.

Something tightens in Solma's gut. Her lip curls into a snarl. She glares at Blaiz, finally relinquishing her aunt's body. Her blood-smeared hand finds Olive's blood-smeared hand. They hold each other. Solma feels Olive shaking and knows it's for the same reason Solma herself is shaking.

Utter, obliterating rage.

She will kill this man. She swears it.

"We haven't finished!" Blaiz booms. "Raise your weapons!"

No one moves. Ilga swears under her breath and meets Solma's gaze, eyes full of shame.

"I'm—" she stutters. "I'm so sorry—"

Solma can't speak but she nods acknowledgement. It isn't Ilga she blames. But Blaiz is oblivious to the waves of hate pulsing off her, to the fact the jostling crowd are getting louder. The Gatra aren't really trying to hold them back anymore. They're looking at their leader, too. Their faces dark with shock.

Blaiz hasn't noticed. He grips Ilga's shoulder so tightly the girl winces.

"Raise your weapon!" he growls. "And *shoot* the traitors! Or you can join them!"

Shaking Ilga raises her rifle. Tears streak her face. She says something under her breath. Something Solma thinks might be, "This isn't right."

The others hesitate before following suit, but Solma can't blame them. She knows which end of a gun she'd rather be on, too.

She gives Ilga a small smile as the girl aims at her. She aims between her eyes. She'll at least try to make it quick.

"You lower your weapon, girl!" comes a croaky voice from the crowd. Solma turns to see Gerta hobbling past the soldiers. They don't try to stop her. She limps past Solma and Olive, past the bodies of Bell and Roseann, and stands in front of the firing squad, shielding the two girls who played in her house a lifetime ago.

She leans heavily on her cane, glaring.

"I ain't moving, Blaiz Camber," she says, not even bothering to look at him. "Not one inch. You'll either need to arrest me or shoot me. Take your pick."

The noise from the crowd intensifies. They're fighting each other now. Solma hears someone yell, "shoot her!"

And someone else shouts, "Leave 'em be!"

"Dja," Maxen says quietly, reaching out to touch his father's arm. "She kept you alive all this time. She—"

Blaiz shoves him off, his face twisted with hate.

Solma makes to go and stand beside Gerta, but the old woman waves at her to stay back. "No, Sol," she croaks. "You give an old woman the chance to do her bit. Do it right, this time. I should'a done this years ago."

"Done what?" Blaiz demands. His face is so contorted he barely looks human. Some of his guards step away from him, exchanging nervous glances. The firing squad lower their weapons. Behind Solma, the crowd gathers momentum. Something crashes and Solma jumps, realising a stone's been thrown at the council hall. One of the shutters is dented. The yelling gets louder. Some of the soldiers plunge in, taking sides as the crowd split into factions. Some for Blaiz but many, Solma notices with a stab of hope, many not for Blaiz.

Many for her. And Olive. And Warren.

For Bell and Roseann.

Solma turns back to Blaiz, squeezing Olive's hand so tight she can barely feel the tips of her fingers. Olive squeezes back, equally fierce. Their skin is slick with blood. Warren has fallen still between his captors. His eyes are closed. He's muttering. The soldiers restraining Python let go of him and he slumps to the ground. Solma sees him dig his fingers into the soil. Blaiz's eyes are frantic. When he speaks, spittle flies from his mouth.

"Shoot her!" he screams, thrusting a finger towards Gerta. "Shoot them all!"

Nobody moves. A frantic light shines in Blaiz's eyes. "Burn them!" he yells.

Vulkan raises a hand.

"*No*, Dja!" Ignis cries, twisting from his father's grip. Vulkan shoves him aside and Ignis sprawls in the dirt. He's up again in moments, ready to wrestle his father. Ready to fight for his friends.

Only someone else has got their first.

Solma's mouth falls open as a vine shoots from the earth beneath Vulkan, thick and corded as a muscle. It wraps around Vulkan's wrist.

And then. *Then*, everything changes.

Thirty-Seven

THE VINE HOLDING VULKAN'S wrist wrenches him down. He drops to his knees, clawing at the restraints. Sparks crackle from his fingertips and the vine blisters, but more burst from the ground. They wrap around the soldiers' guns, sprouting leaves in the trigger-guard, flowers in the barrel. Many of the soldiers struggle. Others, Solma notices, simply relinquish their weapons and step away.

Python is in the mycelia now, eyes glowing. Solma sees mushrooms bloom from the earth around him, swell and then burst, shooting spores into the air. Soldiers cough and splutter. Solma throws an arm across her mouth and gestures frantically at Warren to do the same. He kicks his captor in the ankle and drops to the ground as the soldier lets go. He clamps his hands over his mouth and nose.

The spores dissipate quickly, but give Solma, Olive and Warren time to break away from Blaiz's soldiers. Solma and Olive turn to Gerta. The old woman has tied a handkerchief over her face. She looks for all the world like some ancient vigilante. Spores collect in her hair.

There are more shouts from behind. A series of gunshots. Screams. A child crying.

"Right!" Gerta growls as the crowd becomes violent. The soldiers break into factions, too. Some remain loyal to Blaiz and Maxen, but others have defected, joining the dissenting villagers. Gerta meets Solma's gaze. "Give 'im hell, girl," she says, then marches away joins the fight, walloping someone smartly around the head with her cane.

Solma and Olive glance at each other. Olive's eyes are aflame. She nods. Solma grips her hand and they charge forward.

Solma races at Ilga, expecting to have to grapple with her, but the other girl holds up her hands. Tears stand in her eyes. Solma sees the glint of sunlight off a pistol at her hip. She looks up to meet Ilga's gaze.

Ilga shakes her head. "I'm sorry," she says. She draws her pistol. Solma tenses, ready to fight, but Ilga doesn't raise it to shoot. Instead, she offers it to Solma.

"I chose wrong," she murmurs. "Take it."

Solma doesn't need telling twice. She grabs the pistol from Ilga's hand and takes the girl's hunting knife, too. She darts past Ilga to see that Olive has left two of the firing squad on the ground. One lays still, a bruise at her temple. The other has followed Ilga's lead and simply surrendered his weapons. He kneels with his hands up.

Armed, Solma and Olive race through the wall of confused soldiers. Some put up resistance but they're young and poorly trained, easy to disarm. Vines keep shooting from the ground, grabbing ankles, wrists, the barrels of guns. Solma risks a glance at Python and sees him almost elbow-deep in the soil, Whispering furiously.

She drops to the ground beside him. "Python?" she hisses. "Py?"

He twitches at the sound of her voice, a little color coming back into his eyes. "*Need ... the others*," he says. His voice sounds strange, splintered, as if it isn't just him talking but the threads of the Earth, too.

"The other what?" Solma demands. A vein in Python's neck stands out.

"*Whisperers,*" he says. "*Can't ... raise your army alone.*"

Solma glances past him to where the villagers and soldiers grapple amongst themselves. The visiting traders are picking sides, too. Some join the Gatra still loyal to Blaiz, others have slipped away in the chaos. Solma sees a couple sneak into the council hall and has no doubt they'll steal as much as they can. Still more head west, towards the glasshouses. The bees.

Solma watches villagers with hatchets and kitchen implements fight Gatra with rifles and pistols. And Vulkan. They still need their army, whatever form it might take. They still need to send a message to Blaiz and Maxen and every leader like them: the Earth is not for taking anymore.

"Liv!" Solma yells through the rising din. "Protect Python!"

"Got it," Olive growls, elbowing a guard in the throat as she heads towards the Whisperer. Solma leaps to her feet and ducks under a swinging arm. She has to find the other Whisperers. After that, she has no weapon in her arsenal but hope.

She dodges another punch, puts a bullet in a leg and winces at the resulting cry. Half these soldiers don't look older than fifteen. Most would've still been Yuen before she was exiled. Just kids. Kids that Blaiz and Maxen are using for rifle fodder.

Anger burns inside her and her lip curls in a snarl. She turns to where Blaiz and Maxen have backed away from the fighting. Letting others take the bullets for them. A squad of soldiers have rushed to the Steward's side, and now set up a bristling perimeter around Blaiz and his son. Solma doesn't care. She'll rip through that squad if she has to. She fixes Blaiz with a hateful glare. She'll kill him. Kill them both. A deep, blistering pain drives her forward. A fierce ache in her heart where her aunt used to be.

She takes a step forward.

And Bell's voice sounds in her mind. Bright and scolding.

The world has been a violent place for far too long.

Solma blinks. Blaiz catches her eye. His mouth twists with hate. He points towards her, yelling orders. Two of the soldiers detach from his squad, heading for her. Solma's fist tightens around her pistol. But there will be time for Blaiz later. Now, she needs to get to her brother. She turns, glances at where Warren ought to be, where he escaped his captors and threw himself to the ground. He isn't there.

Panic rakes Solma's throat. She whirls on the spot, desperate to catch a glimpse of her brother's silhouette. She needs to keep him safe. She promised her Ma and Dja.

She promised Bell.

Only—

"Solma!" someone yells. It sounds like Warren. Solma blinks, trying to find the source of the voice. Is that smoke she sees drifting at eye-height? She hears the crackle of fire nearby. The crowd splutters as smoke clogs the air. Solma can no longer see Blaiz through the smog, but his two soldiers reach her, charging her with knives raised. She tackles them both with a ferocity born of desperation. They go down with cries of pain and lay still. Flames catch the grass, spreading with brutal speed.

"Warren!" Solma yells, spluttering on smoke. "Warren, *where are you?*"

But the sound of her own voice is lost and what she hears instead is the furious shriek of—

Is that a horse?

She snaps round in time to see two ponies charging through the smoke, a rider on each. Burdock tosses his head as he blasts through a wall of soldiers, scattering them. On his back, Taipan whoops a war cry. Behind them comes Poppy, carrying Urutu.

And behind *them* ...

Solma's mouth drops open.

Two enormous vehicles roar into the village, churning up earth and gravel, their headlights blinding the crowd. Figures leap from the trucks and Solma's heart tightens with horror. She recognises one of them. He's older, taller, wiry with muscle. Aldo. She grips her knife as he comes towards her, expecting a fight. But he smiles.

"Sorry it took me so long," he says. "Sorry for ... all of it, really. But I brought help."

He signals to his squad and is off, leaping to the defence of Aldren and Yuen. Solma's too shocked to speak. She turns back to the vehicles, wondering what on Earth Aldo was talking about.

And then they come out of the smoke. Whisperers. Dozens of them. Solma sees several fall to their knees and thrust their hands into the soil, vines and roots crawling from the earth around them. Ana darts past, shrieking as she buries an arrow in someone's shoulder. The three Whisperer boys scurry amongst the warring crowd. Solma sees Krait kneel and tie someone's shoelaces together. He catches her eye and gives her a thumbs up, then disappears into the fray.

It takes Solma a split second before she remembers what she's supposed to do. She needs her Whisperer friends together. They need to raise an army. But Taipan and Burdock have disappeared and she can't see Cobra or Mamba anywhere.

And she needs to get to Warren.

Smoke chokes the air. It's impossible to see, but Solma can guess where her brother might be headed. She turns in what she hopes is the direction of the glasshouses.

"*Warren!*" she shrieks, throat raw with fear and smoke. There's no answer.

From somewhere, Vulkan's hurling fireballs. They streak through the clogged air, leaving trails of black smoke and sparks in their wake. Solma dives aside in time to avoid being incinerated by one. She rolls beneath the blistering flames, then leaps to her feet, dashing between groups of villagers grappling with soldiers. She squints through the smoke and sees ... is that Sidewinder? What's *she* doing here? The warrior Whisperer conjures a root from underground, which she uses to swipe the feet out from under several soldiers. Solma grins.

And then there are bees everywhere. The bulbous bodies of bumblebees with their deep, relentless engines. The shooting stars of honeybees darting in and out of the light. Bees Solma doesn't recognise, but which have poison glinting on the tips of their stings. Where have they all come from?

"Warren!" yells a voice that Solma recognises. A sweet voice from a precious girl they met in Skyheart village last summer.

Yenn. Yenn's here.

Other voices join hers. Familiar voices.

"Warren, where are you?" comes Addie's fierce little growl.

"Warren?" call two voices together. Solma spots the two boys, Jonah and Tobias. Jonah's oil beetles swarm around his head.

"Answer us, you big pain!" That's from Nessa. Solma grins. She remembers that girl's ferocious temper.

"Warren!" calls the last voice. Leiff. Gentle, sweet-natured Leiff.

They're all here. All the Keeper children Solma remembers.

Which means—

Solma shields her eyes as she peers past Blaiz with his incredulous snarl, past Maxen, who's holding the sides of his head as he watches the madness unfold. Beyond them, a small army advances. And at their head is a tall, lean man—a Steward Solma recognises—leading a squad of soldiers. Beside him, a powerful, sinewy woman, her black hair tipped with red, leaps into battle with a roar. Solma grins. She remembers Reya, captain of the Skyheart Gatra, and Addie's aunt. The fact that she's here, means—

Solma shields her eyes. She catches sight of the tall, Steward again and sees now that his squad of soldiers are protecting many small children. Children with insects of all kinds buzzing around them, responding to their power. Many more than the five Solma remembers from the glade.

The tall Steward catches Solma's eye through the smog. He lifts his chin and smiles. Solma smiles back.

Norsen has come from Skyheart. And he's brought an army of Alphor's Keeper children.

The Insects

HONEYBEE COLONY

We are a hurricane, throwing our angry scent through the smoke. Our not-bee-girl thrusts her rage through us like a poison-tipped sting.

And now it is our rage.

The species-old anger of the besieged hive. Home under threat.

How dare they?

And we charge. A hundred thousand bodies drive out from our not-bee-girl as if she is the epicentre of a quake. The eye of our storm. Our song is the rumbling vibrato of war. We sing of vengeance against split eggs, butchered larvae, murdered sisters. We are a reckoning. Our scent mixes with that of flames. We know the world is burning.

The tips of our stings swell with venom. We are ready.

The scent leads us out and we fly, wings glittering in the firelight. The smoke stings our antennae but we fight the lethargy.

Because we will not burn.

We will not give in.

Our stings bite flesh. One of us is flattened against the palm of a hand. Another meets her death under a boot. A third, a fourth, a fifth die. And then we are dying in our dozens. Still, we keep charging.

We drive poison into necks. Arms. Faces. We swarm across skin, finding tender places to stab. We leave our stings embedded in that flesh as we pull free, limping away to die.

We know the survival of the hive can only be sustained through death.

We fly and we rage and we sting and we die.

We are angry. We are a hurricane.

Bombardier Beetle

The ground scorches. Burns. My antennae sting, but I am *angry*. The anger of the prey-thing cornered in the predator's shadow. The kind of anger that means,

Fight
Escape
Live

I ready my caustic acid. The ancient weaponry of my kind.

I don't stop to think how strange it is that I am one of many swarming across the scorched earth. Usually, we only huddle together when we sleep. I don't wonder why I am driven out in daylight instead of by the glow of the moon.

All I know is I am angry. There is threat. I must fight. The wild, furious scent of my not-beetle-boy tells me so.

I, and the thousands of others of my kind, march between the grasses until we find bare skin to burn. A mighty infantry. And our ballistics are noxious.

We stand our ground while the giants scream and flee. We take aim.

And we discharge.

Streams of caustic spray leap from our bodies. We do not stop to watch the flesh of our enemies blister. We do not hear the screams of our thwarted predators.

We crunch underfoot. We are crushed. Beaten. Sliced in half.

But there are many of us. We march on.

And we fire our furious acid like the world is ending. Like the Earth is on fire and smoke clogs the sky and insect song is drowning under the roar of flames.

Which it is.

Clover's bees

We are many. Riding the air currents thrown up by fire. Our fur is scorched. We feel our sisters caught in flames, swatted by angry hands.

But our war song holds true above the roar of the flames. We sing as we fight.

We see honeybees shudder in their death-curl as they sting. One, violent sacrifice.

Not so for us.

Our dagger-like stings jab and jab again. We swarm over faces, finding the soft flesh of mouths, noses, eyes. And we stab. A dozen deep wounds, poison driven beneath skin.

We sting though one of us is caught in the flames. Though another gets lost in the smoke and, delirious, is caught and crushed. Though many of us are grabbed and squashed.

We fight because the scent of our boy tells us this is how we will live.

His scent says, *threat*. His scent says, *no escape.*

And a deep, instinctive part of us understands that this has happened before. That now, the world is our nest and there is nowhere else to fly. We aren't just fighting for our own nest, but for the nests of our future nieces, our virgin queen sisters, our grand-nieces and great-grand nieces in a string of future genetics we can neither see nor imagine.

But none of us can explain this in either scent or song. And it doesn't matter anyway.

Because all we know is that we are bees. And when threatened, we fight.

Thirty-Eight

SOLMA YELLS WARREN'S NAME. Her brother is nowhere. Panic grips her throat. Everything is on fire. Gunshots crack the air. Screaming mixes with the sound of insect song.

"Warren!" Solma screams.

A horse whinnies. Solma turns to see Burdock appear through the smoke. He skids to a halt, and Taipan jumps from his back.

No sooner have her feet touched the ground than Solma pulls her into a fierce hug.

"You're ok," she says. Taipan struggles free.

"Where's Python?" she demands. Solma points through the smoke towards where Python kneels, Olive fighting fiercely beside him. Taipan nods.

"Get the others," she says. "We need to get south of the village, close to the forest. All of us."

Solma raises an eyebrow. "You can't fight, Tai," she says. "You and the boys. It ain't safe—"

Taipan fixes her with a fierce glare. "We bloody can!" she says. "Py promised an army. We need all of us to raise it. Together."

She darts away, towards Python, before Solma can protest further. Solma just makes out the shape of her squatting in front of him, cupping his face in her hands, before the smoke obscures them completely.

The sounds of battle, made eerie by the smoke, come from all directions. Solma's body tingles with fearful, angry energy. She must find the other Whisperers. She *must* find Warren.

Olive appears at her side. There's blood on her face that isn't hers. "What now?"

"Now," Solma says, grimly. "We take Blaiz down."

She turns to where Taipain left Burdock. The pony paws the ground. He prances from side to side, but his ears are forward. He's ready to fight.

Solma take his rein, pressing her forehead to his long nose.

"Hey buddy," she says. He blows air into her face, and she smiles, swinging onto his back. She grabs Olive's hand and pulls the other girl up behind her.

They watch as Norsen's forces march forward. A squad stays behind to surround the Keeper children. Norsen unholsters a pistol and heads into the fight alongside his soldiers. He catches Solma's eye and there's a fierceness in his gaze. She nods a greeting, which he returns. It seems a lifetime since last summer when Solma, still stung by Blaiz and Maxen's betrayal, had assumed Norsen was another greedy Steward. Now, as he roars commands at his small army, Solma's glad she was wrong. She watches him elbow an enemy soldier and winces.

Enemy soldier.

These are her villagers. Teenagers she grew up with. She'd been one of them once. Now, Blaiz sends them against Norsen's older, better trained soldiers, not caring when the first few get gunned down.

Solma steers Burdock round.

"We need to find the other Whisperers," she says. "And Warren."

Olive's arm encircles her waist. "He'll have gone for the bees," she says.

Solma squeezes her heels into Burdock's sides, but it only takes the lightest touch before he's off, streaking across the battlefield. The fighting is already fierce. Solma can barely tell friend from foe.

Bees are everywhere, filling the air with the righteous tremolo of their war song. They dart in and out of battle, landing stings before they uncouple and zoom away. Is it Solma's imagination, or are the bees covered in tiny white spores?

Beneath her, Solma feels Burdock tense, prancing sideways. She glances down and her mouth falls open. The ground is carpeted in beetles, also dotted with spores. Solma watches, wide-eyed, as a few of them take up position around one young Gatra. The soldier fires her pistol into the ground once, twice. Beetle bodies burst into the air, but there are too many of them. They lift their abdomens and the Gatra girl shrieks, clawing at her ankles as *steam* pours off her skin.

The beetles are spraying something caustic. She kicks and stamps, crushing a few, but there are so many, she has to retreat. The beetles advance.

"Sol!" Olive roars. "Pay attention!"

Solma tugs Burdock's reins as a soldier leaps out of the mist, a hatchet raised above his head. Burdock kicks out, catching the soldier in the gut. He grunts, but lands nimbly and springs forward for another attack.

Olive fires a shot, yelling curses that burn just as deeply. The soldier gives a muffled cry and falls, disappearing in the smoke.

Solma loosens Burdock's rein, letting the pony take charge.

"Careful," she says to Olive. "These are ..."

But she doesn't need to say it. *These are our people.* Olive gives her a withering look. "I ain't missing on purpose," she says, pointing to the line of Gatra behind her, downed or nursing wounds but all definitely still alive. "I ain't Blaiz," Olive growls. And then, "I ain't *Maxen.*"

Solma reaches back and squeezes her hand. She wants to kiss her. To tell her she knows, and it's why she loves Olive so fiercely. But it'll have to wait.

She splutters, smoke burning her throat. She and Olive wrap bandannas over their faces to keep out the worst off it, but Solma's eyes stream. Her lungs rattle. The villagers and Gatra have scattered. Solma hears many battles, but she can't see them. Houses loom out of the fog and Burdock skips across a gravel path. With a jolt, Solma realizes they're passing the house she used to live in with Warren.

And Bell.

Her stomach lurches.

"Warren!" she yells. "*Where are you?*"

No answer. The smoke both seems to muffle sound and make everything louder. How is that possible? Gunshots make Solma and Olive tense. Someone screams, and then Solma hears Gerta's voice yell, "*Charge!*"

A war cry goes up. There's the sound of metal on metal, knuckles meeting flesh. Someone shouts, "*Fall back!*" and Solma thinks it might be Maxen.

Burdock charges between two houses, heading towards the glasshouses. A fireball arcs out of the smoke, heading straight for them. Burdock prances aside, but another appears, hissing through the air. Burdock shrieks. He can't turn quickly enough. Solma's eyes widen as she feels the heat prickle her skin. It's going to hit them—

And then a little figure is standing in front of them, hand outstretched. The fireball arcs, as if drawn to that outstretched hand. It grows smaller and smaller, leaving a stream of black smoke in its wake, until finally it's no bigger than a fist. The figure draws it in, shuddering as the fireball hits the skin of their palm and disappears. Absorbed.

Burdock screams to a halt. Solma stares, open-mouthed, as the figure turns. It's Ignis. Sparks stutter from his fingertips. Solma sees his hand is still glowing. He flexes his fingers.

"Sorry," he says. "Would'a got here sooner. Fell over."

Solma looks him up and down.

"Neat trick," she says. "Never knew you could do that."

Ignis shrugs. "Warren said the same."

Warren. Solma grips Burdock's reins. She casts Ignis one last, grateful glance over her shoulder.

"Thanks, kid," she says. "Go keep safe with Norsen's Gatra, yeah?"

Ignis reddens and shakes his head. Solma remembers too late how Ignis had tricked Norsen, pretending to be a harmless, clumsy orphan while he secretly helped his father steal the village children.

"Nah," Ignis says. "I'm more help here. I gotta ... find my Dja."

Solma frowns. Something about the way he says that makes her think Ignis won't be giving his father a forgiving hug. There's a score he needs to settle. She hesitates. Treacherous and violent as he's been, Ignis is only a child after all. Despite everything he's done, part of her wants to get him to safety. But she can tell from the look in his eyes he won't accept that. She nods.

"Do what you gotta do," she says.

Ignis shrugs and disappears into the smog. Solma squeezes her heels into Burdock's side, but the pony is already charging off. His ears press forward. He's heard something.

Solma hears it, too. A bright little voice that makes Solma's heart lift like the wings of an insect.

"Sol!" her brother calls. "Sol! I'm over here!"

Solma twitches Burdock's rein, but the pony needs no instruction. He turns so quickly, Solma has to grab Olive to stop her toppling off.

The smoke parts and Solma sees her brother, a diminutive figure standing his ground in a ring of advancing soldiers. They aren't trying to shoot him. Solma knows Blaiz will have told the soldiers to take Warren alive. His small fists are raised, and he swings mercilessly whenever a soldier gets too close. They leap away as he goes for them, but Solma sees it's not his fists they're worried about.

Drawing protective orbits around Warren's head and shoulders, moving out in attacking clouds when he throws a punch, is a swarm of every type of bee Solma's ever seen, and a few she hasn't. Their furry bodies dart in and out, delivering vicious stings that leave the soldiers screaming.

Olive fires her pistol into one soldier's leg. The others turn as Burdock comes roaring into their mist. He rears, screaming, and jabs his front hooves into a soldier's chest. She flies backwards and disappears into the smog.

"Sol!" Warren yells, bees zooming around him. Solma kicks her prosthesis into a guard's face. She grabs Warren's outstretched hands, pulling him up between her and Olive.

"We have to get to the glasshouses!" Warren yells as soon as he's aboard.

Solma wraps his little arms round her, holding him tightly. "We can't!" she yells. "We need the Whisperers. They're—"

Warren shakes his head, eyes desperate.

"No, Sol!" he begs. "The bees! The traders are trying to burn them! Please!"

Solma stares at him, horrified. It's starting again. The second Hive War. In the chaos, the traders have decided they don't want to bow to Blaiz. They'll destroy the insects rather than become lesser players in a game of power.

Rage tightens Solma's throat. They need the Whisperers. But if the traders burn the bees, it's all for nothing.

Houses loom out of the fog, flames dancing from windows. There's the sound of brutal fighting somewhere ahead and Solma turns Burdock towards the noise. He tosses his head and is off. With three on his back, the going is slower, but he still comes barrelling into the midst of a full-blown battle with enough speed to make both sides dive apart. The glasshouses are ahead, silhouetted through the cloying smoke. Warren slides from Burdock's back before Solma can stop him. He hares into the fray, his bees zooming after him.

"Warren!" Solma yells, but he doesn't look back. Cursing, Solma dismounts and hands Burdock's reins to Olive. "Find Cobra and Mamba if you can," she says. "Take them south." Olive grabs Solma and kisses her.

"And you," she says fiercely, "stay alive. Y'hear?"

Solma touches Olive's cheek, and then they're apart. Olive wrestles Burdock under control—the stubborn little pony is determined to follow Solma—and steers him away. Solma watches Olive go, then delves after her brother.

The battle is in full force. Solma realizes most of the soldiers have sided with Blaiz and Maxen. Many Oritch, whose crop rely on bee pollination, have also fallen in with Blaiz's forces. They carry secateurs, hatchets. A few have rifles but little idea what to do with them. Still, they're driven by fear and desperation.

On the other side, Solma sees most of the Fei and Aldren fighting. A few soldiers have defected and fight among their ranks, but not enough to make a difference. Their force is determined, righteous, but full of the elderly and untrained. Solma's heart sinks as she sees how quickly Maxen's trained Gatra push the gaggle of villagers back.

She catches sight of Warren's shape flitting between legs and under arms. She darts after him, snatching at his shirt, but he's too quick.

"Come *on*, Sol!" he yells. He throws out an arm, sending bees to sort out a pair of Gatra who've cornered a young Fei. The soldiers flails under a storm of bee stings. With the Gatra distracted, the Fei worker jabs her elbow into one soldier's gut before stabbing the second above the collarbone. Solma flinches as the soldier's hand flies to the stab wound. He opens his mouth to scream but no sound comes out.

He barely looks older than Warren or Ignis. Another kid with a rifle. More collateral damage. Solma tears her eyes away and follows her brother. She catches up to him just as a roaring sound draws her attention. She glances up to see a huge fireball arcing towards them, trailing thick, black smoke.

"Warren!" she cries, diving on him and throwing them both aside. The fireball bursts against empty ground, catching on the grass.

Vulkan is nearby. Solma ushers Warren away from the flames but he bats her away.

"No time!" he insists.

He dashes off again. Growling with frustration, Solma follows. She sees figures moving among the glasshouses now. Some carry flaming torches. One raises his arms and gives a sharp cry of triumph.

The traders. They've found the nests.

Solma fights through the chaos, throwing punches, jabbing her knife. She splutters on smoke. She can barely see.

"Come *on,* Sol!" Warren yells over his shoulder. "We got to hurry. It's—"

His voice cuts off with a strangled yell. Solma's body floods with a cold dread. "Warren?" she shouts. "*Warren!*"

She wrestles through the fighting, flinching at the sound of gunshots, and staggers to a halt.

Standing before her, gripping her struggling brother by his collar, is Vulkan. His violet eyes reflect the fire, the flame tattoo above his eyebrow glows.

"Found you," he says. He lowers his arm, palm held outward. Solma sees his skin burst into flame as he conjures a fireball to hurl at her. She aims her pistol, but he pulls Warren in front of him, lifting him off the ground so Solma can't get a clear shot.

Vulkan launches the fireball. It hurtles towards her, distorting the air, so hot she feels it blistering her skin from metres away. She dives aside but the fireball ... the fireball *follows* her. She turns, aims at it. But what good will a bullet do? She trips, sprawls on the ground. The huge fireball closes on her. As if from very far away, Solma hears Warren screaming.

She closes her eyes.

And ... nothing.

There's a blinding flash of light, a hiss of energy. Solma opens her eyes to see the fireball has just ... gone. The earth around her steams and smokes. A few dry blades of grass have caught fire. Standing in front of her, flames dancing up his arms, is Ignis, glaring at his father.

"Let them *go*, Dja!" the boy says. His voice is small, but it doesn't waver. Solma gets to her feet, standing at Ignis' side with her pistol aimed. Vulkan grins.

"Make me," he says. Ignis shrugs.

"Fine," he says, and charges.

Thirty-Nine

THERE'S FIRE IN HIS hands before he can stop himself. And all that *rage*. Ignis had never thought to throw it at his father before. Towards the man who filled him with hate as if he was nothing more than a cup to deliver poison to the world.

There's smoke everywhere, billowing from houses and crops. Everything is on fire. His father's fire. Because that's all Vulkan knows how to do, isn't it? It's all he taught Ignis to do.

Set things on fire.

Never mind that their power can also absorb flames. Vulkan never cared for that. No, they were born to make the world burn.

Ignis grins. This is what he's good at, then. Burning.

Vulkan only looks surprised for a moment, but it's long enough. Ignis calls his fire, feels that familiar, blistering heat rippling through his veins, igniting his skin. It *hurts.* The kind of addictive pain that leaves his heart pounding. But this time, the pain feels purposeful. Like he deserves it. He feels the fire form a smoldering ball in his palm. And he throws.

Warren hurls himself to the ground. Vulkan turns at the last moment, so the fire strikes his back. He grunts, throwing out a hand to catch himself. Ignis fires again. This time, a stream of scarlet flame that catches Vulkan's clothes. Vulkan roars.

"Stop it, boy!" he yells. "Or you know what's coming!"

Ignis does, and that's why he mustn't stop. No matter how that voice pummels the core of everything he is. But he resists.

He resists because another voice calls to him. "Ig, be careful!"

It's Warren, peering out from under Vulkan's arm with fear in his eyes. Not fear for himself, but for the boy he sees as his friend. Even after every hurt Ignis inflicted, Warren still yells at him to be careful.

Ignis clenches his jaw, determined to deserve that forgiveness, though he knows he doesn't yet. He strengthens his fire, until Vulkan's growl becomes a roar, and he releases Warren.

"Go!" Ignis yells, grabbing Warren's arm. "Run!"

Warren hesitates. "But—"

Ignis thrusts a finger towards the glasshouses, where fire now licks greedily at the edges of the honeybee hives. The traders cheer, and disappear into the smoke.

"*Go!*" Ignis screams. His eyes flare with heat, fire bursts along his arms. Warren lets out a whimper and obeys, charging towards his sister. Ignis waits long enough to see Solma grab Warren's hand. Then they're gone, hurtling towards the burning hives.

Ignis turns to face his father again. He conjures his fire, letting it ignite every nerve in his body. He feels the flame tattoo above his eyebrow burn, knows it's gleaming white-hot. He feels that strange, new core in himself. Tough and glittering. Full of something powerful. Something *better*.

And still, Vulkan stares at him, a twisted, derisive smirk on his face.

"That all you're capable of, boy?" he demands, lifting his hands. Fire bursts along his muscular arms. When he speaks, smoke pours from his mouth. "You're gonna get the beating of your life—"

But Ignis doesn't hear the rest. He doesn't care. All he knows is that he is burning. So full of blistering heat, he can't contain it. And however much his fire hurts *him,* he can make his father hurt twice as much.

He can burn until Vulkan is a pile of ash and smoking bones. And that thought feels *good*. He pushes aside the voice in his head that tells him this isn't the way. That there's more to him than burning things. The voice that sounds like Warren.

Vulkan throws out his hands, and tendrils of flame shoot towards Ignis, lashing like striking snakes. Ignis ducks, rolling beneath the fire-ropes. He sends two fireballs hurtling towards his father, then darts aside as the fire-ropes lash at him again. Vulkan bats the fireballs aside with a grunt. He grabs the flaming ropes shooting from his hands and cracks them like whips. Ignis dives aside but he's not quick enough. A searing pain bursts along his cheek.

He will not scream. He will not cry. He concentrates, absorbing that pain. Letting it burn along his cheekbone, feeling the way his skin blisters. Feeling every ounce of pain his father ever visited on him. He pulls that heat inside him. He lets it *burn.*

And then he roars, thrusting both hands towards his father. Rivers of flame pour from his palms.

"I'll kill you!" he shrieks. "I'll kill you, I'll—"

Vulkan is laughing. *Laughing* like he always laughed when Ignis told his Dja he'd made a friend, or that maybe they'd be safe in this village, this time. Maybe no one would find out and, maybe, if they *did* find out, it would be ok.

And always, Vulkan laughed.

And then, days later, they would be chased away by a furious mob.

Now that Ignis thinks about it, it was always Vulkan who sabotaged their safety. Burned an orchard. Threatened a Steward, told Ignis' new friends what he was capable of, so they looked at him with terror in their eyes.

It was after Vulkan had burned his Ma that she turned on them. After he left a smoking blister along her arm.

It was always Vulkan, snatching happiness away, laughing as it burned to nothing.

The sound of that laugh is like oil in Ignis' blood. A detonator.

He charges.

Someone screams. A terrible, lung-wrenching roar that splits the air. Ignis realizes the hideous sound is coming from him. Fire bursts along his arms, down his spine, courses through his marrow until he glows from within.

And still, Vulkan laughs.

Ignis barrels into him. There's a blast like a bomb going off. A shockwave flies outwards, knocking back anyone within twenty feet of them. Beneath their feet, the grass turns to ash. Everything is smoke and rage. Ignis can't see. But he feels Vulkan's flesh beneath his fingernails and so he digs, channelling every ounce of heat into that touch. Vulkan roars, twists away. Ignis falls forward with a grunt. Before he can get to his feet, he feels a boot on his back, pressing down. He struggles, but the pressure only intensifies. Suddenly he's on his belly in the dirt, wriggling like one of Warren's insect grubs. He whimpers. He can't help it. He knows whose boot is on his back. He knows what's coming next, but he still lets out a yelp as Vulkan's hands tighten around his throat.

"Idiot boy!" Vulkan growls. He's kneeling on Ignis now, almost with his full weight. Ignis hears the smile in Vulkan's voice. As if he's been proved right.

Because, of course, Ignis is weak and sentimental. Just like his mother.

All he knows is that he doesn't want to die. But he can't move.

He can't move.

Forty

SOLMA GRIPS WARREN'S HAND too tightly but, for once, he bites his tongue. His sister's here, beside him. He feels the pull of insects around him.

A honeybee driving in her sting.

Bumblebees boiling across bare skin.

Beetles firing caustic acid.

But in all this, there is pain and fear. Fire flickers between the glasshouses. The bumblebees panic. When Warren plugs into them, he senses the workers pushing Clover to the entrance, trying to save her.

Let us out! Let us out!

"Sol!" Warren says, as they draw up to the hives. The flames dance around them, blackening the wood. Bees swarm from the entrance. "How do we put it out?"

He feels the insects he's cared for all year as they struggle against the chemical confines, even as smoke clogs the air and they suffocate.

Solma whirls in a circle, eyes wide. "I don't know!" she yells. She reaches for her pistol, then for her knife, but neither of them will be any use against the flames. "I don't know, Warren!" she screams, her voice edged with panic.

Warren covers his ears. He feels the tug-and-fight of the insects. It sets his skin tingling. Poison gleams on bee stings. Butterfly wings bloom with fire. They're terrified. And there's no water. No way to douse the flames. What do they *do?*

The fear of the insects reaches a crescendo in Warren's head. Color bursts in his eyes. He can't see anything. He can't—

Behind him, there's a shriek. A cry like the world being torn apart and Warren freezes. He knows exactly who's screaming.

"Ig ..." he breathes.

His friend. The boy who betrayed him because that's all he's ever known. The boy who makes fire.

And the boy who helped him. Saved him.

Who can also absorb the flames.

Warren darts under Solma's arm, ignoring his sister's shrieks of protest.

"Warren, what are you *doing?*"

But there's no time to explain. Ignis is the key. Maybe he always was.

He charges through the smoke, spluttering as it claws his throat. Behind him, his sister's cry drifts through the clogged air. She's running after him, but he's got a head start now. Vulkan's huge figure looms through the fog. Warren sees Ignis in the older man's grip, mouth stretched in a silent scream as his father tortures him. Warren clenches his jaw. When this is done, he wants Vulkan to pay. And Blaiz. And—

Maxen.

He appears through the smoke like a spectre of death. He holds a pistol in one hand and a knife in the other. He's flanked by three Gatra, each aiming a rifle straight at Warren.

Warren stumbles. He skins his knee as he goes down but he's too shocked to care. Maxen flicks his hand. In unison, the Gatra advance.

Solma skids to a halt beside Warren.

"Get behind me," she growls, her eyes flashing. Warren doesn't argue. Solma lifts her knife, aims her pistol—

And hesitates. Warren frowns, not understanding. Why is she waiting? Why is she *shaking?*

He puts a gentle hand on her arm. They don't have time for her to be afraid.

Solma takes a breath, swears, and flicks the safety off her pistol. She aims at Maxen, straight between his eyes. Warren sees uncertainty flicker across Maxen's face.

"I wouldn't do that, if I were you," says Blaiz's voice. He appears beside them, a pistol in his own hand, though it's lowered. There's an arrogant swagger in his step. He believes he's won. Warren squeezes Solma's wrist, hoping she knows what he means. He doesn't like it, but it's ok for her to do what she must.

Solma tenses, turning her face a fraction so she can see both Blaiz and Maxen.

"Why's that, then?" she growls. Blaiz laughs.

"Give me the boy, Sergeant."

Solma doesn't move. "I ain't your Sergeant, no more," she reminds him. "And my brother has a name."

Warren blinks at her. She's stalling. He suppresses the stab of fear. They don't have time for this, but he can tell Solma's realized something he hasn't seen yet. He's always asking her to trust him, to give him a chance.

Now he's got to do the same for her. He forces himself to wait.

Blaiz is losing patience. The smirk falls from his face, and he bares his teeth, raises his pistol.

"Now, Sergeant," he says. Solma rolls her eyes at him.

"You're gonna shoot me anyway," she says. "Why d'you think I'd make it easy for you?"

Blaiz's face twists. "Because I want you shot *in front* of my village," he snarls. "Where everyone can see you for the traitor you are. *Give me the boy!*"

Solma moves so she's shielding Warren fully. She glares at Blaiz. The Steward aims his pistol between Solma's eyes.

And that's when Burdock charges in, screaming. Olive's on his back, yelling her head off and firing her pistol. The Gatra flanking Maxen stumble back. Olive, roaring like some warrior of old, puts a bullet in each of them. One crumples like an empty sack. The other two clutch bloodied knees or shoulders and fall to the ground. Burdock rears, drives his front hoof into Maxen's chest, hurling him backwards.

In the chaos, Solma moves like lightning. She side-steps Blaiz, grabbed his wrist and snapped it in seconds. He roars with pain. His pistol falls from his hand.

"Go, Warren!" she screams as Blaiz throws a punch with his good arm. Solma ducks.

Warren doesn't need telling twice. Olive dismounts Burdock as Warren darts behind Blaiz and scurries towards Vulkan and Ignis. He has enough time to see Burdock rear again. To see Olive and Blaiz locked in a furious fist fight—pistols knocked to the ground. Maxen stumbles from the smoke, a gun in his hand, and limps towards them. Solma's there, knife drawn. Ready for him.

Warren's heart clenches, but there's no time. His bees are burning. He must trust his sister. He must get to Ignis.

He turns, tears stinging his eyes, and struggles through the smoke towards his friend.

Battles rage all around. Friend fighting friend. Brother fighting sister. Warren can't tell who's on whose side.

Finally, he draws level with Vulkan. The huge man looms above him, a vengeful giant, holding his own son prisoner in a wreath of flames. He hasn't noticed Warren. He's laughing, his eyes burning. Warren stares, despair spreading through him as he watches Vulkan wring the life from his son. How can he stop it? He's not strong enough for this.

Bee song sounds beside him, and he glances to his left. A bumblebee lands on his shoulder. Her fur is blackened with char, one wing a little damaged. She's big. Strong. A survivor.

Warren realizes with a jolt that it's Clover. The queen. That's all wrong. She should be safe in her nest. She's old now. She shouldn't be flying.

But she is. She's out here because her legacy is under threat. Because she sensed Warren's fear. Because she's Blume's granddaughter and, even though the old queen is long dead, that bond still means something.

"What do I do?" he asks the bee, staring in horror as Ignis' eyes bulge. Vulkan laughs. *Laughs,* as he murders his son. Warren can't stand it.

"*What do I do?*"

Clover twitches her antennae, paddles her feet against Warren's shoulder. He feels her tiredness. She'll die soon, as is the way of her species. A single, glorious summer to fill the skies with song, and then they're gone, the hope of their future slumbering all winter, deep underground. Warren feels Clover's scent. Feels the two generations that have come before her and those yet to come speaking together. A war song, not just of the bees, but of the world. Of the wild. Of Alphor.

Fight, it says. *Survive.*

A hand touches Warren's arm. He turns.

The girl behind him smiles. Her hair is clogged with ash, but he'd recognise that oak-brown shade anywhere. He'd recognise the green streak in her dark eyes. The way honeybees converge on her iridescent purple robes. Keeper robes.

"Yenn!" he yells, hugging her. Yenn pushes him off as other children in purple robes appear behind her. Bees and butterflies and beetles crawl all over them.

"No time for that," Yenn says, pointing towards Ignis and Vulkan. "We gotta stop him."

Warren grabs his friend's hand. She's right. He clenches his fists, he reaches around him, to the insects fighting to survive. And he calls them in a vast, immeasurable swarm. He feels their hum deep in his bones. He hears cries of awe and horror as the huge, black cloud of wings and stripes and stings gathers around him.

Vulkan looks up. His eyes widen, fingers loosening around Ignis' throat. Ignis draws a deep, desperate breath.

Warren fills the insects with his own fury.

Sting, he tells them. *Fight.*

Behind him, Yenn and the other Keeper children raise their hands, reinforcing his message.

Clover fires her engine, calling her daughters to the fight.

And the cloud of wings and stripes and stings charges towards Vulkan's horrified face.

Forty-One

Maxen is quick with a knife. Solma's known it since they trained together a lifetime ago. But, until now, she's never had cause to *face* him and his knife.

Their pistols have fallen in the grass. Solma can't see anything in the smoke. She shuffles her flesh-and-blood foot in the earth, hoping to feel where the weapon dropped. But there's nothing.

Olive's engaged in a furious fist-fight with Blaiz. She jabs relentlessly and she has two good arms, where he only has one. He cradles his broken wrist against his chest. But he's bigger and bulkier. When his punches land, they send Olive flying. And he drives her towards Maxen.

Maxen charges at Solma, knife glinting in the firelight.

Solma darts aside, but the smoke is thick, and Maxen's arm is a blur. She stumbles and hot pain streaks across her right cheek. She bites back a yell, jabs twice with her own knife, aiming for Maxen's belly. He sidesteps, grabbing her wrist and slicing at her arm. Solma snarls, snatching Maxen's wrist as his hand comes down. She gives a sharp pull, destabilising him. She twists in his grip, elbows him in the collarbone. He yells in pain and releases her. Solma skips away and they circle each other like wildwolf alphas.

In the smoky gloom, Solma studies Maxen's face. The bee sting scars across his cheekbone and jaw. The hateful sneer. The way that, in the last two years, he's grown to look like his father.

But underneath it all—somewhere—there's still the boy she knew. Those eyes gleaming like fresh frost. The determined set to his jaw, that frown that creases his brow.

She'd almost loved this boy once.

And she hates that, even after he's betrayed her, kidnapped her brother, stood by while her aunt was *shot,* she still holds back. Why is she holding back? Every time she lunges, she thinks of Bell lying lifeless before her, life flowing red into the thirsty earth. Pain squeezes her lungs, seizes her heart. But she still can't take the shot.

Why?

She screams in frustration, wills herself to charge at him, but even her full-on offensive is half-hearted. It's like there's a haze around him. A mist of what-ifs, shrouding him so she can't see properly.

She remembers what he'd said. That confession he'd made.

I want him to be proud of me.

Like a pup desperate for attention. Solma sees that same fear, that same hope, glinting in his eyes now. The way he pleads her, silently, to let him win. To be the traitor so that he can be the hero.

And Solma's so tired. *So tired.*

But when she feels her grip on her knife loosen, her brother's face bursts into her mind. And Olive's.

And Bell's.

Oh, Bell.

Bell whose voice echoes in the recesses of her mind. Whose pride makes Solma want to weep. Bell who told her …

There are other ways of fighting. Other ways of winning.

But like *what?*

Maxen's blade swipes at her gut. She leaps back in time to avoid it. His fist jabs for her head. She dodges aside. What other way is there to beat this aggression? This greed?

She keeps fighting. Just.

Fighting him, but also fighting herself. Because *why can't she just end it?* Why does she keep lifting her eyes to meet his, searching for some glimmer of the boy she'd once thought he was?

Someone worth sparing.

"Sol!" Olive yells. Solma tenses but doesn't take her eyes of Maxen.

"Sol! Where's the gun?"

"I don't know!" Solma yells back. Something in Olive's voice makes her gut tighten. She ducks as Maxen drives towards her. He raises his knife above his head but he's a terrible bluff. Solma sees he's intending to swing it down and drive it up under her ribcage. She raises her knife, pretending to fall for the feint, then grabs his wrist when he does as she'd predicted. She headbutts him in the nose.

He grunts, clutching his face, and staggers back, giving Solma time to whirl and catch sight of Olive.

She's now fighting on two fronts. A pair of Gatra have come to Blaiz's aid. Solma doesn't recognise them. The insignias on their black uniforms tell her they're from one of the trade caravans, still fighting for Blaiz. Even though the insects ...

Oh Earth, the insects are *on fire!*

Solma dives away from Maxen's knife, snatching another glance at Olive and her attackers. The soldiers look young and inexperienced. One carries a hunting knife and the other, a hatchet. They're wary of Olive. She's keeping them at bay, but Blaiz drives her back faster now, hoping to hem her in with Solma and finish them both. His eyes gleam, a manic grin on his face.

Solma turns at the sound of Maxen's war cry and sidesteps him as he barrels towards her. She raises an eyebrow as he goes stumbling past.

He sprawls in the dirt, his knife flying from his hand. Solma turns from him and races towards Olive. The other girl has floored one soldier and now grapples with the other. Behind her, Blaiz has picked up the fallen Gatra's hatchet. He inches forward, a nasty gleam in his eye.

Solma yells as Blaiz raises the hatchet. She rushes between Blaiz and Olive, lifting her knife in time to catch the axe as it falls. The force of Blaiz's blow sends a jolt down her arm. He roars, swinging for her. She blocks him again, aiming a solid kick at his knee.

Blaiz isn't a fighter. He always found a way to put others between himself and the danger, but Solma is surprised when he throws the hatchet aside and catches her ankle with his good hand. He throws her leg up and she loses her balance, crashing into the dirt. Her knife flies out of her hand. Blaiz laughs.

Solma scrambles to get up, but a boot lands in the small of her back, pinning her. Behind her, Olive lets out a strangled cry. *"Sol!"*

And then there's a pained yelp. Olive falls silent, and Solma's fighting for all she's worth, the boot still pressing down on her back.

Forty-Two

WARREN IS A SWARM of honeybees engulfing Vulkan's face. He's the bumblebee worker attacking Vulkan's hand. The ashy mining bees buzzing angry circles around the Fire Maker.

He's forgotten how to be a boy. He is fear and survival. His vision is awash with ultra-violet.

Far away, in a dream, someone shouts his name. That's not important right now. What's important is—

Sting! Bite! Attack!

His mind is a hive, firing instinct. He can't remember who he is. Where he is. *What* he is.

Sting! Bite! Attack!

He is the wasp driving poison into Vulkan's neck. He is the beetle firing acid. He is ...

Warren!

Someone slaps him across the face. The pain pulls him back to himself. He falls back, clutching his cheek, then looks up at the girl who hit him. She offers him a hand.

"What d'you do that for?" Warren asks, rubbing his cheek.

Yenn rolls her eyes and pulls him upright. A bumblebee hovers anxiously by his head. It's Clover. She hasn't left him. Once he's standing, she settles back onto his shoulder, paddling her feet against his skin. He feels her fear. Her anger. The scent stings his nostrils. Bee-colors taint the edge of his vision ...

Yenn shakes him hard. "Focus," she says. "We got this. You help Ig." Her face darkens. "Not that he deserves it."

Warren bites his lip. Of course, Yenn's still angry with Ig. The boy kidnapped her friends, burned the glade, and destroyed all but one of Yenn's precious honeybee hives.

But she's here, despite all that, helping.

She hugs him, smiles. Warren sees the glow in her eyes as reconnects with her honeybees. She moves forward, surrounded by her village Gatra, leading her regiment of Keepers and their insects into battle. Warren recognises some of them. Little Jonah, the youngest and Keeper of false oil beetles, waves at Warren as he passes. Leiff smiles, ashy mining bees clustering on her shoulder. Nessa punches his arm and winks. She hangs back, though, guarded by Sky-heart soldiers. Her hoverflies aren't much use in battle. Tobias has shot up like a bean vine. He stands beside Nessa, watching. He nods as he meets Warren's eye. A blue butterfly perches on his shoulder

With those two is Addie, wild-eyed and shaking. Her arms are adorned with peacock butterflies. They aren't fighting insects, but Warren feels how much she *wishes* they were. His heart kicks. Addie spent months caged in a mountain cave last year, cut off from her insects, at the mercy of the Fire Makers. Warren doesn't blame her for wanting to fight.

Besides these familiar faces are many that Warren doesn't recognise. A girl, older than Warren, with dark skin and whirls of black hair, kneels. One of the acid-spitting beetles crawls onto her hand, waggles its antennae in question, then turns and marches off with its fellows.

Twin boys with wild, blonde hair direct a stream of fluffy, red-rumped bumblebees into battle. There are others, too, frowning in concentration. Fighting. Some of them cast Warren sideways glances. Warren sees one of the twin boys nudge the other, pointing.

Warren grabs Yenn's hand.

"Thank you," he says. "For fighting."

Yenn's mouth twitches. "Don't thank us," she says. "Thank Tai. She called us."

Warren frowns. "Called—?" he doesn't understand. How could Yenn, who isn't a Whisperer, have heard a call through the mycelia? He wants to ask, but a roar of pain draws his attention back to the Fire Makers.

Vulkan, now under a cloud of insects, releases Ignis. He claws his face, tries to shoo the creatures away. But they dart and duck, stinging him again. Ignis gasps for breath as he crawls away from his father. Warren rushes to him, helps him limp away, and lets him flop on the ashy grass behind the Keeper kids.

"You ok?" Warren asks, rubbing Ignis' back. Ignis sits with his head between his knees, struggling for breath.

"Yeah," he rasps. Tears stream down his face. "Sorry."

Warren doesn't know what to say to that. He almost says, *don't apologize,* but Ignis has a lot to make up for. He almost says, *it's ok,* but it's not. Instead, he just says, "I know."

A Keeper kid hurries over to them, tugging at Warren's shirt. Warren turns to see one of the twins standing behind him. "We gotta go," he says breathlessly. "The insects! The nests are on fire!"

Warren gets to his feet. "Ig," he says. "We need you. It's this way. We should—"

A roar from behind makes them both whirl round. Several Keeper children scream, clutching their heads. One of the twins shudders, eyes rolling back as he faints. His brother shouts and rushes to his side, only to collapse halfway there.

Ignis tries to stand, but he's too weak. "What's happening?" he croaks.

But Warren already knows. He can feel it like fire in his mind. The chemical shriek of a hundred thousand tiny beings as they burn. They fall from the air as Vulkan stands, his body aflame, eyes and tattoo glowing. He throws out his hands, casting fire through the cloud of attacking insects.

It takes all Warren's courage not to succumb to the pain in his mind. The Forceful Projection. He reels. Someone's calling his name. A hand grabs his, but his skin is on fire, he's burning from the inside out. Everything is heat and panic. A chemical scream that echoes through his blood.

And then there's blackness. Warren isn't unconscious but he's lost control of his body. He feels it thrashing as his brain fires with horror.

"Warren! Warren!"

Hands grab his shoulders, rolling him over in time for him to vomit in the grass. The pain keeps going. He's lost. He's dying. He's—

"Warren, listen to me."

A different voice. Familiar. His mind clings to it. "You're ok. Come back to yourself."

Warren tries. He grits his teeth, closing his mind to the pain. Gradually, a face swims into view. A constellation of red freckles across pale skin. A gentle smile, blue-green eyes. An emerald robe.

"Cobra ..." Warren sobs. She nods, smile broadening.

"That's right," she says, offering him a hand. "Come on. Stand up."

She helps Warren to his feet. Mamba stands beside her, a look of desperation on his face.

"Co," he says. "We need to—"

Cobra waves at him to be quiet. Mamba clenches his jaw.

"You ok?" Cobra asks. Warren touches his head. The pain of the insects has dulled. Warren looks to Ignis. The fire boy has his hands outstretched, his teeth gritted, as he tries to absorb his father's fire. Bees zoom away trailing plumes of smoke like little comets. Ignis pulls the flames from their bodies, drawing it into his hands.

"Warren," Cobra says, cupping his face. "Where's Python?"

Warren shakes his head, tearing his gaze away from her. "I don't know," he says. Panic seizes his throat. One honeybee hive is completely engulfed in flames. Ignis is still struggling for breath. He can do nothing to stop it. "He went south, I—"

Cobra glances at Mamba. He nods, disappearing into the smoke. Cobra wipes sweat from Warren's brow. "It's ok," she says, gesturing behind her. "We're here, now. We'll help."

Warren blinks. Around him, Whisperers, both familiar and unfamiliar, help the other Keepers.

Two Whisperers Warren's never seen before stand in front of the terrified children, arms outstretched, faces full of fury. They're a bulky man, rippling with muscle, and a diminutive woman with flashing eyes. Their robes are mud-stained at the hems, as if they've spent a long time travelling. As Warren watches, they kick off their boots and dig their bare toes into the soil, wincing as the hot ash sears their soles.

And then, they Whisper.

From beneath their feet, long, slender roots burst from the soil, whip-lashing towards Vulkan. He staggers back and shoots fire from his palms. One of the roots goes up in flames. But more are coming. And now, they don't just come from beneath the Whisperers. They shoot up all around Vulkan, grabbing his arms, his wrists, his legs. He roars, thrashing in the bindings. Fire explodes from his shoulders, along his collarbone, down his arms. He's a living inferno, burning with fury.

But now, other things creep from the ground around his feet. Warren's eyes widen as silver filaments snake over his toes, creating a fine mesh. They slither up his legs, slowly mummifying him.

Cobra squeezes Warren's hand, then kneels and pushes her hands into the soil. At her cue, the others do the same. Warren turns to see Taipan behind him. She grins and winks, her orange eyes sparkling, as she Whispers. The three boys cluster behind her, fingers thrust into the ground. Ana's here, too. And some young Whisperers Warren doesn't recognise. All with their toes and fingers in the Earth. All Whispering. Calling greenery from its dormancy and sending it forward to attack Vulkan and his fire.

Warren stares as roots burst from the ground, binding Vulkan ever tighter. A slender vine climbs the Fire Maker's body and wraps around his throat. Vulkan hisses in pain as the vine presses nodules into his skin, plugging into his bloodstream. His eyes go glassy. Though he struggles and his fingertips crackle with fire, his movements seem less sure.

"Surrender, Vulkan!" says the burly Whisperer man in front of Warren. His voice is deep and rumbling, but full of pain. Warren frowns. It's difficult to see through the smoke, but he could swear the Whisperer looks a bit like—

"Please," the Whisperer says, cutting through Warren's thoughts. "For your son's sake."

Beside him, Warren feels Ignis go utterly still.

Vulkan bares his teeth. "To you?" he growls at the Whisperer. "Ha!"

He struggles against the restraints. Warren feels the Whisperers around him shift, concentrating as they hold him fast. The Whisperer man's shoulders slump. Vulkan gives a nasty grin.

"Should'a known you'd come for me one day," he drawls. "Just like my wife. Just like my *kid*, in the end. You're a traitor, *Urutu*."

Warren frowns. What's he talking about? Ignis gets to his feet.

"Who is that?" he asks, his voice trembling. "Dja! Who is that?"

"Shut up, boy," Vulkan says, not even looking at his son. Ignis bristles. Warren sees fire flicker at his fingertips. He grips Ignis' shoulder.

"Ig," he begs. "We gotta go. The nests ..."

But the other boy shrugs him off, glaring at his father. He marches forward.

The burly Whisperer shakes his head, sadly. "I never wanted to hurt you, brother," he says.

Ignis freezes mid-stride. Warren feels the other boy's shock like a splinter through his heart. A vein in Vulkan's temple twitches.

"Ain't got no brother," he growls. "Not since you turned me away. *Betrayed me!*"

The Whisperer shakes his head. "You know that's not true. You see treachery everywhere. After I learned you were still alive, I went to the village where your son was born. I know what happened. I know you burned your wife."

Warren reaches for Ignis' hand. The other boy snatches it away. He's staring at his father, a mad light in his eyes. Vulkan struggles fiercely.

"Shut up!" he growls. "You shut up!"

But he's not looking at Urutu. He's looking at Ignis. At his child. And the look he gives is not one of hate or violence. It's pleading. Desperate. *Don't leave me.*

"I know," Urutu continues, "that it was you they wanted gone. Not the boy. Not my nephew. They'd have kept him. Loved him. Been his family. *I'd* have been his family."

Warren tries to grab Ignis' shoulder, but Ignis is too quick. He rushes forward. As he runs, flames burst from his clenched fists. Smoke pours from him, his violet eyes glow. He opens his mouth and a terrible shriek erupts from him. He charges past the two Whisperers. The woman tries to grab him, but he twists away, heading for his father.

"Ig!" Warren yells. "No!"

But Ig doesn't hear him. He thrusts his burning hands against Vulkan. Everything goes up in flames. Vulkan roars, thrashing as his son's fire blisters his skin.

"You said I had no family!" Ignis screams. "You said they drove us out! You lied to me my whole life! I'm gonna—"

But whatever he swears he's going to do, Warren doesn't hear. All he hears is the roar of flames, the sound of Vulkan's pain. Urutu yells, too. He rushes towards Ignis, but the boy's fire is so hot that Urutu can't get near.

"Hey!" he calls. "Stop!"

But Ignis won't stop. Warren watches as his friend and enemy is consumed by the fire he's been fighting his whole life. The fire his father gave him. Both the flames and the rage.

And he thinks, if Ignis doesn't stop now, he'll be lost forever.

Warren feels his bees send alarm scents through the air, the fear of the beetles at his feet.

"Warren ..." Cobra says, her voice a warning. He looks at her. She's still got her hands pressed into the earth, that ring around her irises glowing as her mind travels the fungal network. But she's wrestling herself out of the mycelia. She knows what he's going to do. She'll try and stop him.

He's got to move fast.

He takes off, slipping on the layer of ash, spluttering as smoke billows in his face. He passes Urutu and the woman, both Whispering roots to try and pull Ignis back. But Ignis' fire is so powerful, anything that touches him bursts into flames.

The Whisperers cry out as Warren barrels past them. He hears his friends—Keepers and Whisperers alike—screaming his name. But he can't stop. Not now.

When he gets within a few metres of Ignis, a wall of brutal heat hits him. Warren feels his skin blister. He splutters as the heat burns his throat. He throws up his hands, tries to push through, but Ignis is so angry. His fire so strong.

"You're a liar!" Ignis screams, as Vulkan twists and writhes. There's no anger in the man now. No bravado. He's feeling the force of his son's fury. Every blow he dealt a child too small to defend himself. Every cruel word and deed.

Warren's eyes widen in horror. He sees Ignis' skin begin to pucker and blister. His fire is so furious that even he can't withstand it anymore. He's going to kill them both, but he barely seems to notice.

"I hate you!" he screams. "*I hate you!*"

Warren struggles against the heat, but it's no use. If he gets any closer, he's going to burn.

"Ig!" he yells, his voice lost in the inferno. "Ig, please! We need you! I need you to—"

But the flames are too much. Ignis can't hear him. Warren whimpers as the skin peels from Ignis' arms, his clothes catch fire. He knows Ignis' is crying—bitter, relentless sobs—but the tears evaporate from his eyes before they get a chance to fall.

Everyone is screaming but Warren can hardly hear them. Hands try to grab him. He pushes them away.

The nests are burning. His friend is burning. And the only person who can stop it is Ignis.

But Ignis can't hear him.

In the panic, Warren hears a voice at the back of his mind. It sounds like Aunt Bell.

You just gonna stand there, boy? The voice—his aunt—says. *After everything we been through. After I died saving you and your sister, you just gonna give up?*

Warren clenches his fists. No. He isn't giving up. Far from it. He pushes back against the hands trying to restrain him. In desperation, he closes his eyes and throws out his mind.

He has an idea. A terrible one. He doesn't even know if it'll work.

But he remembers that day when the bees fought each other, remembers how Maxen had been stung.

And how, in the aftermath of that sting, he'd heard something Maxen didn't intend him to hear. Something he never said aloud.

Maybe Warren can use this, now. If he can find a way to make it happen again. Warren focuses. And in that focus, there's a pin-prick of consciousness.

It's Clover. All this time, she's been perched on his shoulder, buzzing her wings, directing her daughters. She shouldn't be out here. Should be tucked away in her nest. But her nest is burning and if Warren does nothing, everything she's worked for will burn, too. Her future. Her legacy.

He lifts a hand to his shoulder and lets the elderly queen clamber onto his fingers. He holds her up to his eyes.

"Hi, Clover," he says. Tears well in his eyes as he thinks of Blume. The first bee he ever saw, the first bee he ever felt. His friend. Long gone, now.

But alive, in a way, in Clover.

The bee waggles her antennae. Ash clings to her fur but she's alert, eager. Warren pushes his mind towards her.

Can you do this? He asks. The bee flickers her wings, pushing an answer into his mind. It's just one word.

Yes, she says.

And that's good enough for Warren. In scent and vibration, he tells her what he needs her to do. He hopes she's strong enough. Hopes it won't kill her.

But if she's afraid, she doesn't show it. She powers towards the wall of heat. Heading straight for Ignis.

Clover

Smoke stings my antennae. But my engine is strong, and his scent is incessant.

Help him!

I don't understand. Why?

For the Hive, he says.

This is not my colony. Not my hive. But the way he speaks it makes my antennae prickle.

Because he did not say *hive.* He said *Hive.*

Connection. Network. Survival. The Hive of the world. My mind stretches into the smoke and can't imagine what he's saying. But it doesn't scare me. Because he includes us in that Hive. My sisters, my daughters. And the sisters and mother of that bee hovering by another human. And the legions of beetles marching below me. And the flashing butterflies. And more and more. More than the six-legged. The Hive includes the big four-legs, the predators, the prey. The two-legs that stand like trees. The flowers from which we feed, the ground in which we nest. Everything.

For the Hive.

I fly.

The heat buffets me. My old muscles ache, but I weather the wild heat emanating from what I now see is a human larva. Young and hungry for he-doesn't-know-what. But he's on fire. Flames crackle from every inch him. And it's destroying him. I feel the way his flesh sizzles, fire creeping up the back of his neck, burning his hair. His mouth is stretched open. The air vibrates with pain.

I can't help him. I can't save him.

But the not-bee-boy sends his scent in heady waves until my antennae sting.

Get to him. Please. Or the Hive will die.

The Hive is everything.

I battle through the heat and smoke again, though it deadens my senses, dulls my mind. My flight muscles feel heavy. I must find a patch of bare flesh. Somewhere he isn't burning yet. Somewhere I can—

There!

A pale space above his heart. It glows, but doesn't burn. Flames bursts around it, but that small field of flesh is free of fire. I dive for it. Smoke chokes my antennae. I pump my abdomen, trying to find clean air, but there is none. My vision dims. I'm free-falling. The heat is unbearable.

I'm suffocating. I know I'll burn here, but my feet find that bare patch of flesh. They cling tight. And, as the fire singes my fur, I jab my sting into that pale skin.

Forty-Three

IGNIS GASPS AT THE sudden pain above his heart. A heat that is nothing to do with fire spreads through him. He's brought back to himself. He's not an inferno. He's a boy in a column of flame, burning himself and his father. He's created a fire so intense that even his own skin—usually impervious to his flame—is blackening.

He panics.

And in his panic, his fire flares hotter. He yells, hears his cry of pain echoed by his father.

His father.

The red haze of anger clears. He sees Vulkan, bound in roots and vines. The huge Fire Maker twists and bucks in his restraints. His skin blisters, his clothes smoke. His mouth is stretched open in a scream but there's no sound. Ignis looks from his father's face, down to his own hands. The hands driving fire against Vulkan's body.

He's burning him.

Earth, he's going to kill him!

He fights to get himself free, but his own fire is so hot, it's fused his palms to the roots beneath. He struggles, crying out. His fire flares, sending a fresh wave of heat through them both.

"No!" Ignis yells. "No, I can't stop! I can't—"

That pain over his heart comes again and he lets out a strangled cry. It's not the pain of burning, but a sharp pain, coursing through his blood. Like a splinter.

Like a *sting*.

And with that thought, comes the voice in his head.

Ig!

Puzzlement dims his panic. His fire settles a little. His father slumps, held upright only by his restraints.

Ig! The voice says again.

Funny how familiar it sounds. And that name. It feels like a comfort. It feels ...

Like his friend, talking.

Pulling his focus away from the fire, he crushes his eyes closed, grits his teeth.

Warren? He thinks. Then, *how?*

My bee, Warren's voice says. Ignis opens his eyes and looks down to see a plump bee, her antennae and abdomen trailing smoke. She fires her engine and limps away. She's missing a leg, he notices, and one wing looks damaged, but she's alive. A small miracle. He examines his burnt clothes, his charred skin, the flames dancing along his arms. There's a needle-prick of pain over his heart that doesn't feel like a burn. It feels like a—

Oh, of course. She'd stung him. For a moment, Ignis is annoyed. Warren's always sending bees to sting him!

Only, this time, he knows it's different. He feels the bee's venom coursing through him, sending Warren's scent-message with it.

Please let go, Warren says. *Please don't do this. Don't be like him.*

Ignis bares his teeth, realising a moment later this is something Vulkan does when he's angry. He closes his mouth, tries to push past the panic and find himself. Who is he?

A fire boy. A thing of flame and fury. A traitor.

A murderer?

No. Calm washes through Ignis. He realizes that none of this is true anymore. Or, at least, he doesn't want it to be true. He wants to be a part of that future Warren keeps going on about. A small, treacherous part of him still wonders whether that's even possible.

It is, Warren insists, as if he's heard Ignis' turmoil. *It's not certain. And it ain't gonna be easy. But it's possible. And that's all it's gotta be, for now. Something to work for.*

Ignis feels the corners of his mouth twitch into a smile. Something to work *together* for. And he can be a part of it, not just a frightened, angry figure on the periphery.

The sound of Warren's voice in his head, and the ache of the bee venom in his blood, settles his fire. He doesn't want to burn his father. He doesn't want to *be* his father. Let the Whisperers take him.

Please, Warren says. *Let go. We need you.*

Ignis feels very tired. It's a good kind of tired. The kind of bone-deep soreness that says he's fought hard today and, despite the smoke around him, the gunshots and the screams, he feels a pulse of triumph.

Slowly, wincing, he peels his hands away from his father, calms his fire. He's about to turn back to Warren—to his friend—when Vulkan stirs.

"Couldn't do it, eh?" he snarls. Ignis looks back at him, at the smoking remains of the man he'd once feared. He shakes it head.

"Could," he says. "Don't want to."

Vulkan sneers. "Same thing," he rasps. "You're weak. Just like them. Just like *her.*"

Ignis surprises himself when the mention of his mother elicits nothing but a shrug from him. No anger. Not anymore. He turns and catches Urutu's eye. His uncle. His *family.* Urutu gives a small nod of encouragement and Ignis unclenches his fists, turns back to his father.

"I'd rather be like her than like you," he says.

At that, Vulkan lifts his head, his face a twisted mess of pain and fury.

"You're *weak,* boy! You're useless! You're *nothing!*"

Ignis stares as flames flicker to life along Vulkan's restraints. But they're not Ignis' flames. This is Vulkan's anger setting him alight. Ignis steps back, mouth falling open as the flames grow. They spread along the roots, flashing down Vulkan's body. His flesh bubbles and peels.

Ignis lifts his hands, hoping to absorb his father's fire, but Vulkan pulses a heat so furious that Ignis is blown backwards. The fire is too intense. Ignis feels the danger in it. If he tries to absorb it, he'll be burned alive.

"Dja!" Ignis yells. "Dja! *Stop!*"

"Stop?" Vulkan roars. He thrashes against his restraints. Behind Ignis, some of the Whisperers cry out in pain. More vines shoot from the ground to reinforce those now struggling to hold Vulkan. Ignis throws his hands out but doesn't know what to do.

"Warren!" he cries. And his friend's voice speaks softly into his mind.

Walk away, Warren says. *Come to us. It's ok.*

But it's not ok. Ignis stands, frozen, as Vulkan's fury sets him alight. As the man who's been his tyrant and his home becomes an inferno.

"Face me, boy!" Vulkan screams, his voice almost lost in the roar of the flames. "You're a coward! Weakling! *Just like her!*"

The vines holding him disintegrate. A shockwave pulses outwards with Vulkan at the epicentre, a flash of heat and light.

"Down!" Ignis yells, throwing himself against the ground as the wave rolls over him. He hears yelps of pain as the Whisperers and Keepers behind him duck down, too.

And then nothing. The sounds of battle rush on around them. Ignis keeps his face pressed into the dirt, unwilling to look up.

A hand touches his back. It's Warren, his eyes full of urgency.

"Quick!" he says. "The bees! We need you!"

Ignis coughs as he struggles to his feet, not daring to look behind him. To where his father ...

No. He won't think about it.

Warren points and Ignis follows the line of his friend's finger, to the insect nests. The smoke is thick, but Ignis sees the hives are alight. Burning. One is already a blackened husk.

And after all the time he's spent setting things on fire, Ignis doesn't even think before he throws his hands out. Because this time, every one of the Keeper children—those he's hurt and betrayed—looks at him with hope in their eyes. A plea for him to be the hero, for a change.

His own skin, blistered and smoking, sears with pain. He roars against it, spreading his fingers wide. He couldn't draw the fire out of his father. Couldn't absorb the anger and grief. There's still a festering nub of it inside him somewhere. It's enough to make tears pucker in his eyes as he reaches through the smoke, feeling the heat of the hives as they burn.

He sinks his mind into the flames. And *pulls*.

The air around him quickens, growing taut with heat. He feels his hair stir against his forehead. And then the fire licking the hives is drawn towards him, a rope of flame into towards his open palms. He screams as the fire sinks into his damaged skin, but he doesn't let go. He pulls at the fire until it's coming to him from all directions, from burning rooftops and smoldering door frames. Ignis throws his head back, shrieking with the pain of all the fires his father ever set. He feels it burning in his core, all its relentless heat as it roars through his veins. The pain is so vivid he can barely see. He smells himself burning ...

And then it's over.

He collapses onto all fours, shaking violently. Tears streak his face.

A breeze drifts past, beginning to clear the smoke. The fire is out. It's out across the village.

And someone kneels beside him.

"I'm sorry, Ig," Warren says. Ignis looks into the other boy's face and sees the pity there. No, not pity. *Love.* The way Warren shares his hurt. What is it with this boy? Doesn't seem to matter what terror anyone throws at him, he just keeps going. Fighting with kindness and hope. Things Ignis' father would have called *weakness,* but with which Warren has managed to rally people around him. Ignis meets his friend's gaze and thinks, in another life, perhaps one where he'd been allowed to stay with his mother, he could have been more like Warren.

And maybe he can be more like Warren in *this* life, too.

He whimpers as Warren helps him to his feet. Ignis takes a breath and forces himself to turn, to look at the blackened ground where his father had stood. There's nothing there. A few smoking splinters and the tortured remains of what could be—if Ignis thinks about it too much—a human being.

He looks away and Warren throws his arms around him. He hugs Ignis tight and, after a while, Ignis hugs him back.

"You did it," Warren says softly. "I knew you could."

Ignis hears sadness in the other boy's voice and knows that, though the fire is out, there have been a great many losses. Both insect and human. And some of that ... some of that is on him.

"I'm sorry," Ignis whispers. "Thank you."

Warren pulls away from him, smiling. "Don't mention it," he says.

Ignis smiles, but his smile falters when he hears an anguished cry behind him. Urutu rushes to Vulkan's remains and falls to his knees, staring in agony at the blackened ground. Ignis looks away. He feels Warren's hand touch his.

"I know," he says, his voice wavering. "I lost someone today, too. But we gotta be strong. We gotta keep fighting, ok?"

Ignis stares at him, wonders how this boy can only be nine years old. Warren squeezes his hand.

"C'mon!" he says. "It ain't over yet."

Cobra appears beside them. "Go to your sister," she says. "We'll find Python."

She and the Whisperers dart away. Warren and Ignis cajole the Keeper kids and, together, rush through the dregs of smoke towards the insect nests.

"Nearly there!" Warren says. "We—"

He stops, his words cut off by a strangled cry. Ignis' gut curl with fear. Behind him, the Keeper children gasp with dismay.

Blaiz blocks their path, a line of Gatra behind him. There are too many for them all to be from Sand's End, which means Blaiz's allies have stuck with him after all. The Gatra raise their rifles, aimed at Warren, Ignis and the Whisperers.

But that's not the worst bit. The worst bit, Ignis sees, is that Blaiz has Solma. He twists her arm painfully behind her back. Two of his Gatra have Olive, struggling furiously between them.

Maxen stands by his father, his face ashen.

Blaiz looks at Warren and Ignis.

And smiles.

Forty-Four

Blaiz tucks Solma's gun into his belt. He takes her knife, too, then turns her so she sees her brother.

Warren stands, stricken, next to Ignis. Behind him are the Keeper children, also frozen, their insects buzzing about their heads. Solma tries to look brave as Blaiz pushes her to her knees, grabs a fistful of her hair.

The smoke starts to clear. Somehow, the fires across the village are out. Through gaps in the smog, Solma sees a clear sky with wisps of white cloud drifting across it. Then her eyes fall on Ignis. His face is burned, his hands shake.

And she knows, without having to ask, who put out the fire.

She turns to her brother. He was right. He always has been.

Blaiz jerks her arm higher behind her back. She winces against the pain.

Warren whimpers, but Solma sees how his fists open and close. He hasn't given up. She tries to shake her head at him. He needs to run! Get away! Escape with the Whisperers, where Blaiz and Maxen will never find him.

It doesn't matter about her. It doesn't matter.

But she can see on his face that it does. That *she* matters. At least, to him.

"Come here, Warren," Blaiz says. Solma struggles and Blaiz kicks her, harder this time. Warren starts to trudge forward.

"No!" Solma cries. "Warren, don't! You've gotta—"

Blaiz drives his elbow into the side of her skull. Pain blasts through her head. Her ears ring as dizziness rolls through her. Olive yells expletives, bucking against her captors. They can barely hold her. Another two Gatra rush from their line to contain her. Even with four of them holding her, Solma sees the strain on their faces. Olive isn't having any of it. She manages to get an arm free and drives her fist into the first face she can find. The soldier yells as blood bursts from his nose. Olive kicks a second Gatra and bites a third, leaving bloody marks on his arm. None of them let go, but another Gatra steps from the line. He grabs a handful of Olive's hair and jerks her head back, pressing a knife to her throat.

"Stop fighting," he growls, "or I swear, I *will* kill you."

Olive stops struggling, her face murderous, and spits heartily in his face.

The soldier grimaces, wiping muck from his eyes. Blaiz laughs.

"Last stand of the traitors," he drawls. "Well, that was tedious. Now let's end this. Come *here*, Warren!"

Frantically, Solma casts her gaze around. She looks for a knife dropped in the grass. A discarded hatchet. Anything. But as the last wisps of smoke disappear on the summer breeze, she sees there's little chance.

Blaiz's forces, joined with those from the trade caravans, have corralled the villagers of Sand's End between the glasshouses. A few Fei and Oritch hurl stones at their attackers, but it has little effect. Bodies dot the charred earth. With a jolt, Solma notices that some of them are Yuen. Children. Blaiz has spared no one. Amidst the fray, Solma hears Gerta hurl insults at the soldiers.

They laugh.

And now there is a line of men and women stood behind Blaiz. They aren't soldiers. Far from it. Some are in the same, plain flax clothes that Blaiz and Maxen wear. Others are dressed with more opulence. But there's no mistaking them. The Stewards of Alphor. Ten of them. Stood behind the Camber men, training their weapons on Solma and her family.

She falls limp in Blaiz's hold. This is it. They've lost.

Warren resumes his shuffle towards the Steward. Solma, ears still ringing, begs him to turn around. To *run!* But the blow to her head has made her faint. Her words come out a garbled slur.

Warren sniffs, a tear rolling down his cheek. He meets Solma's gaze, those meadow-green eyes shining with anger. With determination. With—

A little shape darts in circles around Warren's head.

Solma tenses for a moment, then struggles in earnest. Somehow, she gets to her feet and bucks against Blaiz, striking him in the collarbone. He grunts and steps back, calling two of his soldiers forward. He throws her at them in disgust.

"Contain her," he sneers.

Solma kicks and fights as the soldiers try to subdue her.

"Hey," says a voice in her ear. It's Aldo. He speaks quietly. "Trust me."

She scowls. Why the hell should she do that? But when she turns to look at him, there's honesty in his eyes.

She looks towards the second soldier holding her and is unsurprised to see it's Ilga. She looks different. There's regret in her eyes.

"Struggle, then," Ilga growls. "Hard as you can."

Solma doesn't need telling again. She fights and spits and curses, making as much noise as she can. Because it's not about escaping, anymore. It's about distraction.

She sees the way Warren's eyes slide out of focus, the way his pupils dilate, his lips tremble. She knows what that means.

His mind is thrown wide, into insects scattered across the battlefield.

He's calling them to him, the few that are left.

And Blaiz, in his arrogance, hasn't noticed.

He turns to face Solma, scowling, and aims the pistol at her head.

"I've had enough of this," he says. "You being alive is an inconvenience."

Olive screams. A deep, primal roar that cuts the air, making Solma wince.

Movement out of the corner of her eye. Something is happening.

Whisperers, dozens of them, appear in a great circle, surrounding Solma, Olive, her brother, the Stewards and the army. They kneel, pushing their hands into the soil. Solma sees Taipan and Python. Something in the back of her mind tells her that's wrong. They should be by the forest to the south. Why are they here? But fear makes her head fuzzy. She can't think beyond that gun, pointing at her.

Blaiz pulls the trigger.

It takes all Solma's strength to keep her eyes open, but she manages it. So, she sees the vine shoot from the ground at Blaiz's feet, grabbing his wrist and jerking it away. The shot goes wide. She sees the root lift from the earth and sweep Blaiz's feet out from beneath him. She hears Python shouting.

"Reach!" he yells, which she doesn't understand. And, "Send your power to me!" which she understands even less.

She sees Olive duck beneath the soldiers holding her. She winds one with a kick and disarms those remaining with a blur of violence.

Maxen yells orders. Some of the Gatra detach from where they're holding the villagers, run to their Steward's aid. The foreign Stewards raise weapons of all varieties. Bullets fly.

Solma cries out as she sees one strike Cobra in the shoulder. Her friend lets out a grunt of surprise as she goes down.

And then the ground rumbles. It's a sound so deep and powerful that it makes the air shiver. A sound that penetrates Solma's bones. It takes her a moment to realize what it is at first. Then, her eyes widen.

Bee song.

A battle cry like none she's ever heard. Her eyes fall on the great, black cloud of insects powering through the last of the smoke. Alive, despite the burning. Despite the chaos.

But it's not *just* bee song. Beetles swarm past her, turning to shoot their caustic ballistics. Insects that look like bees but aren't. *Wasps* says a distant part of Solma's mind, remembering Bell's books.

And then it isn't just insects. The ground trembles, then shakes, then *quakes.* Solma's eyes widen. This can't be happening. It isn't possible.

But there's no denying what she sees.

Herds of wild boar charging through the village. They shriek with primal rage as they barrel towards Blaiz's Gatra. The memory of a huge boar charging towards her flashes through Solma's mind. The pain of her leg being trampled beneath it. She falls to the ground, covering her head with her hands. Something soft brushes past, startling her. She peers out from under her arm to see dozens of moonbadgers scurrying alongside the boar. The normally shy creatures bare needle-like fangs as they follow the boar into battle.

And then there are wildervore. Solma yells in fear as one of the enormous animals thunders past, snorting steam and tossing its huge, horned head. Swarming under the drumming hooves are snakes of all kinds. Huge, muscular constrictors and tiny, darting vipers. Every animal and insect, Solma notices, is dotted with white spores. The animals run and slither amongst the Keepers and Whisperers without a second glance. Their attention is fixed on Blaiz and Maxen, on the foreign Stewards. On the Gatra.

And the earth roars with the sound of their cries. Their shrieks and bellows, yelps and squeaks. A war song of the whole world. Of every wild thing. Solma turns, dumbfounded, to search the crowd of Whisperers. She spots Python amongst them. He looks straight at her.

He smiles, then says something. Over the thunder of hooves and trotters and paws, Solma can't hear what it is, but his mouth makes a shape like, "*I told you.*"

Next to him, Taipan grins, her cheeks flushed with joy. Solma gapes at the chaotic mass of animals charging past her, overcoming Blaiz's allies. A redbear lumbers amongst them. Huge and muscled, its russet fur bristling. It bellows, rearing up to take a mighty swipe at a soldier, who dives aside to avoid being dismembered. There are darkcats, too, their lithe, black bodies slinking between wildervore legs, hissing as they pounce. And wildwolves, working together to chase the Gatra away.

"Quickly!" Blaiz yells, throwing Maxen in front of him as he turns to run. "Shoot. *Shoot them!*"

The remaining Gatra ready their rifles, aiming at Solma and the Whisperers, but Aldo moves so his body shields Solma from the guns. She looks at him and he smiles, winks at her.

"You were right," he says. "We should've listened."

The cloud of insects draws closer and Solma sees the Keeper children—all of them—raise their hands. Their eyes slide out of focus, brows drawn together in concentration. Boar and wildervore charge past, and Solma curls up, pressing her hands against the ground as it shakes. Aldo and Ilga crouch beside her, throwing their bodies over hers.

Solma sees Ilga grit her teeth.

"You're trouble, El Gatra," the other girl says. "You always have been. You know that?"

Solma clings to her. Clings to Aldo. Clings to the Earth. "Ain't Gatra no more," she says.

The insects fill the air with war song. The wildervore throw back their heads and bellow. The boars shriek. Moonbadgers squeal and hiss.

Solma peers between Aldo and Ilga. She sees the Stewards drop their weapons, turn and run. The Gatra hold firm a little longer. They fire into the mass of wild animals and Solma sees a wildervore crumple. Hears a moonbadger scream in pain. But there are too many for the Gatra to fight. Clouds of bees carpet faces. Wildervore hooves kick at guts and shoulders. Snake fangs sink into flesh.

The Gatra turn and flee.

Ahead, Solma sees Blaiz trip and fall. No-one stops to help him. Maxen cries out and throws himself over his father, shielding them both. Solma watches, fascinated, as the animals charge round the two men cowering on the ground. They're intent on chasing away the soldiers.

The herds and packs and swarms barrel between the glasshouses, now. They scatter the Gatra who've been holding the villagers. Goring and kicking and biting. The villagers huddle together, wide-eyed with terror, as the soldiers are driven back. Then, Solma sees a Yuen step forward. A girl, no more than five. Her mother shrieks her name. But the child steps right up to a wildervore. A huge bull with horns as long as she is. It snorts air, flicks its bristly tail, then lowers its head and sniffs. The girl giggles and touches its velvety snout. The animal stands utterly still.

After that, the villagers lose their fear. Solma watches them take up arms again, chasing the retreating Gatra and Stewards. They add their war cries to those of every wild creature in Alphor.

She wriggles out from under Aldo and Ilga, calling for Warren. Yelling Cobra's name. Screaming.

Aldo and Ilga move aside to let her stand. Solma barely spares them a glance. She races towards her brother, just as Olive does the same. They gather Warren between them and bundle him back towards the Whisperers. Solma watches long enough to see her brother scuttle to Cobra's side, where Mamba is trying to stem the bleeding from her bullet wound. She's alive, groaning with pain. Ana is with her, too, frantically bandaging the wound. Solma sees how they both tremble, both wipe blood from their noses. Calling the army of wildlife has taken its toll. They're exhausted. Spent. Solma wants to go to them, to help, but Olive grabs her hand.

"Not yet," the other girl says, eyes fierce. "We got a war to finish, first."

Solma nods. It's time to deal with Blaiz and his son. Solma meets Olive's eye and sees ferocity there. Olive, as always, is ready to fight. But when they turn to face the man that exiled them, the boy that betrayed them, Solma feels a terrible cold course through her veins.

Blaiz is standing, a knife in his hand, leaning awkwardly to protect a swollen ankle. He's smirking, his eyes glinting with triumph. A little in front of him stands Maxen, red-faced and teary-eyed, his jaw clenched. He has Solma's pistol, and it's aimed between her eyes.

Solma freezes.

She meets Olive's gaze and the other girl's face is ashen. Neither of them are armed.

The Stewards and the Gatra are long gone, chased north by the army of animals. The enraged villagers have chased after them. The Whisperers and Keepers are deep in the Earth or in the minds of their insects, directing the battle at the edge of the village. Ilga and Aldo both yell. Ilga is unarmed. She stares, helplessly, at Maxen, shaking her head. Aldo has nothing but a knife. He brandishes it, but Blaiz just laughs. Mamba, wholly focused on Cobra, hasn't noticed. Ana does. She lets out a cry, but the moment she pushes her fingers into the earth, she faints. Ignis, exhausted, barely manages to conjure a flicker of fire across his palm.

There is no-one, nothing, that can stop Maxen pulling that trigger.

Blaiz's laughter sounds manic. His eyes bulge, a vein pulsing in his temple. He's lost. It's obvious. But a mad gleam in his eye tells Solma he's got no intention of letting her live.

Solma looks at Maxen now. At the boy she once thought she loved. He's shaking. Tears streak his face. He can barely hold the pistol straight, but he bares his teeth in a terrible snarl.

Solma remembers Bell, crumpled in a dead heap. How she'd thrown herself in front of her niece because she'd believed in something better.

And ...

And Solma doesn't want to live in this violence anymore. She aches everywhere. She's fought so hard. Fought her whole life. Maybe, there's another way.

Solma walks slowly towards Maxen. Olive makes to grab her, pull her back, but Solma brushes her off. Movement behind and Solma realizes Aldo is heading towards them. Warren's little voice calls from behind Cobra.

"Sol! I'll help, I'll—"

Solma holds up a hand. "Nobody move," she says. "It's ok, Warren."

She feels the air shimmer as Warren calls his bees, feels the ground around her feet heat as Ignis summons the dregs of his fire. Mamba finally realises what's happening. Frantically, he tries to Whisper, but he's spent. He manages to pull himself free of the earth before he loses consciousness, then collapses in a heap beside Ana.

Solma meets Maxen's eye.

"Stop!" she says again. "Do nothing!"

Warren frowns, but Solma smiles at him.

"Trust me," she says. "Trust me like you used to."

She looks at Maxen, the uncertainty in his face, the way his eyes shine with the ghost of a boy she once knew. His eyes meet hers. He holds her gaze.

Blaiz has lost patience. "Shoot her, then!" he snaps, shoving Maxen in the shoulder. "End it!"

Solma keeps walking. "It's over, Blaiz," she says softly. "You know that. Your village has turned against you."

Blaiz growls. Maxen tenses, but he doesn't pull the trigger. He shifts his weight, eyes darting. It's like he's searching for help. And Solma notices how his gaze keeps drifting back to Ignis. To a boy who chose different.

Chose better.

"You don't got to shoot anyone, Maxen," Solma says. "You can be your own man. You don't gotta be like him—"

Too far. Maxen tightens his hold on the gun. "I *want* to be like him."

Solma keeps her face calm, keeps walking. She's only a few feet from him now. "Don't think you do," she says quietly. "Not really."

"What would you know?" Maxen yells, his voice a piteous whine. Solma shrugs.

"I know you watched the Earth struggle to make food for us every year as long as we lived," she says. "I know you fought raiders and redbears beside me. I know you got it in you to be kind. I saw that person—"

"That wasn't real!" Maxen snaps, eyes darting towards his father. "I was tricking you! I was pretending!"

Solma smiles. "Maybe some of it," she admits. "Not all."

"I've had enough," Blaiz growls. He moves to take the gun. Maxen steps away.

"I can do this, Dja!"

"Do it, then!" Blaiz snarls. "Stop wasting my time with your *weakness!* No wonder the village was in a state when I woke. You couldn't *keep them in line!*"

A vessel under Maxen's eye twitches and he casts his father a sideways glance. Solma opens her arms wide, shielding Olive from Maxen's aim. Olive cries out.

"*No, Sol!*"

Solma smiles. "It'll be ok."

She doesn't know if that's true. But she has hope. It's the last weapon in her arsenal. The one Warren's always used. And though it won't shield her from a flying bullet, she wraps herself in it. In Bell's hope. In her brother's hope.

"I'm gonna shoot you!" Maxen yells. "And then I'll shoot Olive! And Warren!" He's holding the gun too tight, his arms rigid. Solma holds his gaze.

"I don't reckon you will," she says. "I reckon there's some of that boy I knew left in you. I reckon you don't got to be what other people make you. I reckon you can make yourself however you want. You just gotta be brave."

Maxen's eyes widen and Solma sees his shoulders relax a little. The same hope that she feels gleams in his pale eyes. A chance this might end a different way. A chance they could both be better people.

He starts to lower his gun.

"Earth's *sake!*" Blaiz yells, and suddenly he's charging at Solma, knife raised. He shoves Maxen aside and Solma braces for impact. Her fingers twitch, missing her pistol. She raises her fists, but she knows it's pointless. Sunlight glances off the blade.

Olive screams and rushes forward. Other people are running too. Solma hears Aldo shout, but only Olive is close enough and there's no way Solma's letting Blaiz anywhere near her. She grabs Olive round the waist and twists so that her back is facing Blaiz, Olive shielded by her body. Olive swears.

"Let me go, Sol!"

Solma does no such thing. Instead, she squeezes her eyes closed, expected the hot stab of Blaiz's knife. Hoping blood loss carries her off quickly so she doesn't have to see Olive's terrified face. or Cobra's. or Warren's.

See you soon, Bell.

A gunshot cracks the air, making both Solma and Olive jump. Solma tenses, waiting for that white-hot pain, but it never comes. Slowly, she lets go of Olive.

They both turn towards Maxen. He's not standing anymore. He's dropped the gun—still smoking—and rushed to his father's side.

"Dja? *Dja!*"

Blaiz lies in the grass, blood bubbling from a hole in his chest. His eyes are wide, full of disbelief. His face is twisted and he's trying to speak but no words come out. Maxen covers the wound with his hands, presses down.

"I'm sorry, Dja," he says quietly. "I had to. I *had* to."

For both the briefest and the longest time, nobody moves. The gunshot has startled everyone. The Keepers and Whisperers come back to themselves, their hold on the creatures released. They stand, open-mouthed, watching as Blaiz clings as tightly to life as he does to everything, whether it was his or not. Bees and beetles drone lazily at eye-level. A lone wildervore lumbers by, tossing its head. It casts the nearby humans a cursory glance and, apparently satisfied its role is done, it lowers its head to graze.

Solma stares. She reaches for and grabs Olive's hand, wanting to know Olive is still there. Still close.

Olive catches her eye. "Go," she mouths.

Solma's reluctant, but she knows the other girl is right. With great effort, she releases Olive's hand and kneels beside Maxen, placing her hands over his. When she adds pressure to Blaiz's wound, she can tell he's fading. And, as she watches that gleam dull in Blaiz's eye, some small, secret corner of herself is glad when she finally feels his heart stop.

This man took her home. Her family. Nearly destroyed her whole world. She holds Blaiz's wound—her hands awash with blood—and watches Maxen sob over his father's body. This doesn't feel like a victory. Solma doesn't feel much of anything, actually. Just immensely, desperately tired.

She looks up and finds Maxen watching her, tears streaming down his face. He looks so young. Like the years have fallen from him and he's a Yuen again, discovering the injustice of the world for the first time.

"I never wanted this," he says. "I never—"

Solma can think of a lot of things to say to that. She'd never wanted this either. She didn't want to leave her home, to face enemy after enemy. She didn't want her brother to be the unique, powerful Beekeeper that he is. She didn't want a war.

But most of that, he made happen.

Still, there doesn't seem much point in saying that now. So instead, she keeps pressing down on Blaiz's wound, even though he's stopped breathing. Even though his eyes have drifted closed, that arrogant snarl still twisting his lips.

"I know," she says quietly. "I know."

Forty-Five

"Sol?"

Warren's voice is quiet, but still makes Solma jump. She turns to see him with Taipan, Yenn and Addie. The kids pick their way through the long grass, careful not to step on the last summer flowers. The Keepers are dressed in purple robes. Solma still feels a stab in her gut when she sees that color on Warren. It suits him, and that's hard to stomach. He doesn't belong to her anymore. If he ever really did. And he looks happy, like he fits. Solma smiles. The expression feels so alien, she realizes she hasn't smiled in days.

Warren slips his hand into Taipan's, grinning at his friend. They've once again been inseparable since the battle, and Solma's heart warms to see how the Keeper children have mingled with the Whisperer kids. These four have rarely been apart in the last week.

Solma turns back to the cluster of trees where bees and butterflies dart in and out of the dappled sunlight. The distant noise of the village keeps her grounded, but she needs the peace of this place today. This little haven, just outside Sand's End.

Warren steps away from his friends and presses his hand into his sister's. He points towards a huge ash, towering above the birches that flank it. There's an old burrow tucked between its roots.

"Blume's nest," Warren says. "Remember?"

Solma nods. How could she forget?

As they watch, a fluffy bee emerges from the burrow. She shivers her wings and takes off, mingling with the other insects.

"Look, Sol!"

"I see her," Solma says. "Is it Clover?"

Warren's little face falls. "No ..." he says, and Solma feels her heart clench. The bumblebee nests will be coming to an end now. The elderly queens will succumb to old age while the new queens head out on mating flights. From the tremble in Warren's voice, Solma suspects Clover's song has fallen quiet now. Warren sighs, rallying himself. "But it could be one of her daughters," he says. "They flew before the nest burned. I felt them."

Solma nods. She watches the bee buzzing gently against a flower head, then drags her gaze away to the other side of the ash tree. Here, the earth has been freshly dug. A few dozen wooden markers protrude from the ground. Warren follows his sister's gaze. His face grows serious.

"I reckon she's happy here, Sol," he says. "They both are."

Solma can't think of anything to say. She swallows the bitterness in her throat and nods. It's been nearly a week since they buried Bell and Roseann. Solma still can't bring herself to write her aunt's name on the stake that marks her grave. Bell and Roseann were the first of many casualties, and for the past few days, families from all castes have wandered out here to kneel by the graves of loved ones. To cry. To grieve. Today is the first day Solma's had this haven to herself.

Two days ago, Gerta hobbled over to the Whisperer tents, where Solma and Olive are staying. Wordlessly, she handed Solma bundles of seed. She'd patted Solma's shoulder and limped away. Solma didn't need to be told what to do with the bundles. She's stashed them away, ready to plant over the graves next spring. Bell's endless slumber will be lulled by bee song.

Solma turns at the sound of Yenn and Addie muttering. She smiles at them. Yenn shuffles forward.

"Warren?" she says, casting Solma an apologetic glance. "We gotta go."

Warren looks at his sister. She kisses the top of his head. "It's ok," she says. "Go be a hero."

Warren blushes, beaming. "We're gonna relocate the butterflies today," he says. Solma winks at him.

"That's great," she says. "You all going?"

After the battle, when things had finally calmed down, Solma got a chance to talk with Norsen. After giving him a piece of her mind about bringing twenty *children* to a battlefield, she learned how, over the last year, Skyheart has been a beacon, drawing Keeper kids from across Alphor. Reya, his captain, was finding more every day, all around Warren's age or younger. A generation of gifted kids, ready to remake the world. It makes Solma both happy and sad in a way she can't explain.

The Keeper kids had, with Gerta and Ignis' help, broken the chemical barrier that held in the insects. There was unspoken agreement among Solma, Olive and the Whisperers that the children would know what was best for the precious creatures. The Keepers had decreed the nests would be moved, placed in suitable but secret locations. Some would remain near Sand's End, others would be carefully transported across Alphor, where they could benefit other villages across the continent. No-one would own them. No-one would control them. They would be the responsibility and privilege of those children with that remarkable gift. Just how those kids—still so young—would carry out these duties, is yet to be determined.

That's where Olive's been for the last few days; she and a few trusted Gatra, including Ilga and Aldo, are escorting some of the Keeper kids and their insects to the edge of Southtip Province to establish insect colonies there. She'll be back soon, but Solma aches for her return.

Warren shakes his head, bringing Solma back into the moment. "Nah," he says. "Most of us are staying here. Just me, Taipan and the butterfly Keepers are going. We need Tai to grow some flowers, so the butterflies don't get hungry."

Taipan stands taller, swelling with pride. "I could do it from here," she boasts. "And I could tell the rodents not to eat the butterflies if I wanted."

Solma smiles. She understands the Whisperers' newfound gift—the miraculous conjuring of the animal army—better now. Python explained that fungal spores are in everything. In the air they breathe, on the flowers and plants that animals eat. The spores help Alphorian life to stay healthy.

But they also mean that the Whisperers have a ready connection to every living thing on the planet. Everything is part of the fungal network.

And all it took for Python and the newly connected Whisperers to call the army, was to press into the animals' minds what would happen if Blaiz was not defeated. The animals hadn't needed much persuading.

Though some of the creatures still wander around the village, most are slowly heading back to their usual homes and habits. The villagers have managed to shoo the more dangerous predators away, but Solma saw a darkcat try to corner a wildervore calf yesterday. The calf's mother chased the cat off without much trouble. But it made Solma realize the power of the Whisperers, able to convince a variety of animals to overcome their instincts and work together. To fight for something bigger.

If she thinks about it too hard, her head hurts.

Warren smiles at his friends. "Yenn's got to stay," he says. "She's teaching the new honeybee Keeper how to look after Indigo's hive."

Yenn wrinkles her nose at this. "He needs to calm down," she says. It takes Solma a moment to realize she's talking about this new honeybee Keeper, a child with the same insect affinity that she has. "He's too flighty. He keeps worrying them."

Solma laughs. "He'll get there," she says. "You all will."

She watches Warren and the others scurry away, then checks the sun. She should head back, too. A lot must be done today, and she doesn't want to face it.

"I miss you, Bell," she says. It's the first time she's said it aloud and tears well in her eyes. The ache she's been ignoring for days becomes so potent she can hardly breathe. "I miss you and I need you."

A breeze stirs a cluster of foxgloves, disturbing the fuzzy bumblebee feeding there. She wriggles free of the flower, covered in pollen, and zooms to Solma. She hovers over Solma's shoulder for a bit before landing. Patiently, she runs her legs over her abdomen, scooping and packing the pollen against her back legs. The sun glitters off her crystalline eyes. Solma smiles through her tears. The bee fires her engine, powering off into the sun.

It's time for Solma to go, too. She kisses the tips of her fingers and brushes her hand across the mound of Bell's grave. "Sleep well," she says.

Head down, she trudges towards the village.

Sand's End is a flurry of activity. No-one notices Solma, which is fine. She's not sure how many more condolences she can take, how many more times she can smile at people who clasp her hands and tell her they're glad to have her home. Or the dark glances of those angry few who still agree with Blaiz. Because there are some.

Solma knows this struggle isn't over. It's just on hold for a while.

She bypasses the orchards and wanders through the village centre. Fei and Oritch workers aren't in the fields today but patching up damaged houses and clearing debris. Some of the stronger Aldren, adept with herbs and medicines, have set up a clinic under an awning, and are busy treating wounds.

A few of the Yuen old enough to help are making themselves useful. A small group of them pause in their mending of a door to wave at Solma as she passes. She waves back but can't bring herself to smile.

She's been putting this off for nearly a week now. A week since Blaiz died and the Gatra surrendered. A week since Norsen took temporary custody of Sand's End, calling a council to discuss what happens next. There was a lot of shouting, as Solma recalls. A few of Blaiz's old allies and enemies turned up, too, either demanding compensation, or threatening to destroy the nests unless Sand's End handed them over. Norsen dealt with that swiftly, ejecting those particular visitors from the village and ensuring that his Gatra escorted them far away. But it meant the task of relocating the insects became more urgent. The Keepers and Whisperers started work immediately. Solma's hardly seen Warren over the last week. Her young, idealistic brother has suddenly grown up. At nine-years-old, she's watched him commanding troops of purple-clad Keeper kids as if he was born to this. Wherever he goes, insects swarm around him. He's always got at least twenty bees somewhere on his person. There's light in his eyes, now. Purpose. Though Solma knows he cries at night when he thinks she's asleep. She hears him murmuring Bell's name. But the minute she stirs, he falls quiet, as if this is a grief his sister can't help wi th.

Solma takes a detour round the back of the village so she can check in on the Whisperers. They've made camp there, between the village and the managed forest. But they'll be leaving soon. They have a new mission now; find and train the new Keeper children as their powers emerge. There's also the small matter of The Seasons, who weren't happy when Sidewinder and Urutu defected, or when many of the other Whisperers followed a few days later. But Solma remembers what Cobra said as they'd sat around an evening fire, Solma changing the bandage on Cobra's wound.

"It's time to do things differently," Cobra had said. She was pale, still, and exhausted. But there was a determined light in her eyes. "The villagers haven't trusted us for a long time, and why should they? We turn up when we please, we spirit their kids away, and our customs are kept secret. Alphor is changing. We need to change with it."

Solma thinks on those words as she stands at the edge of the village, watching the activity in the Whisperer camp. She spots Urutu kneeling with Ignis. Their heads are together and Urutu helps Ignis burn a tiny patch of land, before he then digs his own hands into the ash and raises fresh grass from beneath. Since his father's death, Ignis has been quiet. Urutu took charge of him, trying to teach him how fire can be a force for growth as well as destruction. To show Ignis he has a place in the future they are trying to build.

Solma hopes the Whisperer is right, but she can't help those old feelings of mistrust for the boy who stole her brother. Maybe Ignis has changed but she can't bring herself to open her heart to him yet.

Still, she watches for a moment, and smiles when a little flower struggles up from amongst the ash Ignis has created. The fire boy's face lights up and he leans closer, watching as the delicate petals open. Close to him, Urutu grins, too. He's explaining something, and Ig nods along, happy to be taught. Then, Urutu places a gentle hand on Ig's shoulder. Ig flinches, goes rigid, as if expecting violence. Urutu hesitates, waiting for the boy to relax, then slowly, deliberately, draws him into a hug.

Solma sees Ig's eyes over the bulge of Urutu's arm; wide and violet and confused. Unsure how to handle this affection. This *love*. Then, slowly, he lifts his own arms and hugs his uncle back.

Solma leaves them be. She turns and continues round to the glasshouses, where the boy she's been avoiding for the last week will be helping Gerta to fix damage from the battle. Her gut curdles at the thought of what she must do. She wishes she could talk to Bell. She can almost hear her aunt's voice in her head.

Get it over with, girl. You ain't no coward.

And she will.

She just isn't looking forward to it.

By the glasshouses, it's quieter. Gerta and a few Aldren, too infirm to help with the village clean up, are out here. Some have brought rickety chairs or stools to sit on while they mend clothing or tend to Yuen too young to be left alone. Older Yuen, busy harvesting, scurry in and out of the glasshouses.

Gerta marches up and down, leaning heavily on her cane, while she hurls orders. She's sporting a hefty bruise on one temple and the eye beneath is swollen closed. Still, she struts along rows of ripe vegetables, hollering instructions as if the battle has given her new energy. Solma smiles. She's unbreakable, this woman.

Gerta spots Solma and raises her cane in greeting.

"There you are, girl!" she croaks. "Been expecting you."

Solma flinches but clasps the hand Gerta offers. The old woman looks her over appraisingly.

"You got taller while you been away," she says. Solma laughs. "And," Gerta continues, tapping Solma's prosthesis with her cane, "we need to adjust that again. You sit down and give it to me. I'll look at it while you do what needs to be done."

Solma's not happy with that. If Gerta has her leg, she can't run from this. She has to stay, see it through.

But Gerta's frowning and, reluctantly, Solma nods. She follows the old woman to where two empty wooden chairs have been placed by the glasshouses. Solma sits, unstraps her prosthesis, and hands it to Gerta.

"Good," Gerta says. "Won't take long. I'll get the boy."

She shuffles off, and Solma has nothing to do but wait and listen to the hammering of her own heart.

Movement to her right and Solma sees Maxen sit in the chair beside her. She swallows against the anxiety scratching at her throat. He doesn't look at her but stares at the ground, hands balled into fists on his lap. His blond hair falls into his pale eyes. The bee-sting scars on the right side of his face are hidden from view and, looking at him in profile, he's the same boy she fell for two years ago. The same boy she trusted and thought loved her in return.

How much has changed since then?

She takes a breath to speak, but Maxen gets there first.

"I know what you're going to say," he mutters. Solma raises an eyebrow, waits. "You're going to tell me to leave."

Solma says nothing, just gazes out over the burned landscape.

He's right. And despite the bitterness in his voice, she's thought hard about this. She's not backing down.

"Yeah," she says. "You got to. It's the only way."

Maxen frowns. "You can't make me leave," he says. "It's my village, now Dja's ..."

He clamps his mouth shut and looks away. Solma resists the urge to touch his shoulder, to comfort him.

"It ain't no-one's village, Maxen," she says. "That's the point. That's how it's got to be now. That's what everyone wants."

Maxen scowls but Solma's practised this. She's adamant. A week ago, when the fires had been put out and Blaiz's scattered army had been subdued, Maxen tried to enter the Steward's house. The door was barred by Gerta and an army of Aldren brandishing canes, brooms, broken bits of door. They refused to let him inside.

But they parted like a tide for Solma and Olive. The two soldier girls and their Whisperer friends carried the bodies of Bell and Roseann into the house, ferrying the wounded after them. Fei and Oritch helped stretcher those too hurt to walk, and the Aldren set about installing a hospital in the house. The village had spoken. Maxen wasn't their leader anymore. Solma's not sure *he* knows that, even though Gerta hasn't let him out of her sight since the battle. The soldiers that had been his to command now stand guard over him. He's a broken thing, half-deranged from shooting his father. Solma's not sure why he did it, in the end. She doesn't think he knows either, but she's sure, now, that the only way for him to work it out is to l eave.

"I'll die out there, Sol," he says at last. His voice is pleading. Like a kid. Solma shakes her head.

"You won't," she says. "Cobra and Mamba said you can go with them."

She doesn't mention that they only agreed to this after an extensive argument.

Maxen raises his eyebrow, disdain curling his lip.

"The *Whisperers?*"

Solma meets his gaze. She clenches her fists, mainly to curb the temptation to slap him. Not that he doesn't deserve it a hundred times over.

"Yeah," she says. "The Whisperers. The people who took me in when you and your Dja chucked me out. The people who loved me, became my family. And if you harm any of them, Maxen, I swear on the Earth under my feet, I'll—

"Alright," Maxen snaps, holding up his hands in surrender. "I get it."

They fall silent. Solma watches a beetle. It's the same species that spits caustic acid, which she now knows, from Bell's books, is a bombardier beetle. It trundles quietly between grass stems, intent on its own business. Maxen watches it, too, a dark expression on his face.

"What if I refuse?" he asks.

Solma raises an eyebrow. "That a choice you gave me?" she asks.

Maxen snorts. "You ain't the Steward," he points out.

Solma shrugs. "Neither are you, now," she says. "Anyway, I reckon it's time Sand's End don't have Stewards anymore. Gerta and the Aldren are talking about an election, like they used to do in the old-world."

Maxen lets out a mirthless laugh. "The old-world," he sneers. "'Cos they're such beacons of hope and perfection."

Solma glares at him. "You're one to talk."

They fall silent again. A peacock butterfly lands on Maxen's knee. He tenses but makes no move to shoo it away.

"Please don't make me go, Sol," he whispers. Solma glances up to see tears standing in his eyes. She bites her lip. She made up her mind about this days ago. She has to be strong. For her village. For her family.

"I agreed with Gerta and Olive," she says. "And the village voted on it. I can't go back on my word." He starts to protest but she holds up a hand. Remarkably, he falls silent. "Thing is, we also agreed the exile don't have to be forever. But you got some learning to do. You ain't seen nothing outside this village, Maxen, and that ain't good enough. You got to learn about the world and the people in it. You got to see deserts and mountains. You got to survive droughts and blizzards. You got to meet the world's poorest people and see how they live. Then you got to walk through the richest villages and feel the injustice of it. You got to help rebuild houses destroyed by floods or fires or war. You got to help nurse sick children and bend your back in the fields, reaping crop. If you do this, and if it teaches you, then you can come back. Not as a Steward. Never that. But we'll take you back."

Maxen stares at her, horror shining in his eyes.

"But that'll take *years!*" he splutters. Solma almost laughs.

"Yeah," she says. "It will. That's the point. You need to be away from Sand's End. And Sand's End needs to be away from you—far away—if it's gonna heal."

Maxen frowns. The butterfly on his knee flexes her jewel-like wings and flutters off, flashing in the afternoon sun. Maxen watches her go. "When do I leave?" he asks. Solma steels herself.

"Tomorrow," she says, and holds up her hand again to still Maxen's splutter. "You travel with the Whisperers. You pull your weight. You be gentle with the kids. And you remember Ana can shoot an arrow down a rifle barrel from a hundred feet away. I've given her permission to kill you if you try anything."

She didn't mean for her voice to get so fierce, but she can't help it. Maxen doesn't say a word.

"One more thing," Solma says. "One of the ponies—the stallion—is special to me. You be kind to them both, but if I hear you treated him with anything less than utmost respect, I'll kill you myself. Got it?"

Maxen stares at her wordlessly.

"Good," Solma says. She spots Gerta returning with her adjusted prosthesis. The old woman waits, leaning on her cane, while Solma straps her leg back on.

"You tell him?" she croaks, glaring at Maxen. Solma nods. "Good," Gerta says. "Then he can get back to work."

Solma doesn't look at Maxen as she stands. But she feels his eyes on her back, she feels the confusion and hurt in him and thinks he's got no clue. No clue what it's like to wander the world, weighed down with shame and fear. But he will.

Forty-Six

THE DOORS TO THE council hall open. Villagers, Whisperers, Keepers and Norsen's Gatra spill into the late morning sun. Solma takes a deep breath and forces herself to release the tension she's been holding in for the last two hours. Like most of the meetings in the last few days, this one was heated and emotional. Almost everyone in Sand's End lost someone to the fighting. People are angry. The village population is depleted and while this lessens the burden on their stores, it means fewer hands to work the land. It has taken time to convince the more grief-stricken villagers that revenge is not the answer. That marching on the villages that supported Blaiz will only re-spark the Hive War they narrowly avoided. Solma's got a feeling she'll be having those conversations for a while yet. Wounds that deep heal slowly if they ever heal at all.

Finally, though, they have agreed on a council to run the village in the absence of a Steward. It's temporary, for now, but Solma was surprised to find herself on it, along with Olive, Gerta, Aldo, and representatives from the Fei and Oritch castes. The elected councilors vary in age and experience, but Solma was pleased to find that they all spoke with reason and perspective. It gave her hope. Still, the work isn't over yet. Not for Sand's End. Not for Alphor.

She feels a hand on her back and turns to find Olive, smiling. Solma loops her arm round Olive's waist and pulls the other girl close, kissing her. It feels good to do that, now, when the future looks safer, brighter. Olive laces her fingers through Solma's hair and they stand for a moment, leaning against each other.

"You manage to get the insects to safety?" Solma asks. It's the first time they've had a moment to themselves since Olive returned that morning. Though her work with the Keepers is done, for now, She and Aldo have also been working with the village Gatra. They're establishing a new order. Solma's no fool, she knows the village guard is not obsolete. The insects might be returning, but the world will take time to heal. There will be other enemies. Like the grasslands and forests, humans won't change overnight.

Olive nods. "Hopefully, they'll stay safe," she says. Solma leans her cheek against Olive's collarbone.

"When are the Whisperers leaving?" she asks. Olive kisses the top of her head.

"Soon," she says. "The village wants to say goodbye. There's a gathering by the glasshouses. We should go."

They make their way through the village, hand in hand, stopping occasionally when concerned villagers hail them for advice. Solma tries her best to be reassuring. She's not sure she's doing a great job of it. Anxiety scratches her throat every time she utters the words, *it'll be ok.*

How can she know that? But she sees relief in the eyes of those listening as they grasp her hand and thank her. She shakes her head and sighs when no-one's looking.

"I can't do this," she mutters. "I can't lie to them."

Olive squeezes her hand. "You ain't lying," she says. "People got to believe in this future we're building. You're helping them do that, Sol, and you're doing a great job."

Solma raises an eyebrow, but Olive's in earnest. They continue in silence, heading to the edge of the village, where almost everyone is now gathered.

Solma never thought she'd see her own villagers hugging her Whisperer friends, chatting with Norsen and the Keeper children. A group of Yuen have gathered to pat Poppy and Burdock. Solma sees Ana lift a little girl up to she can stroke Burdock's velvety nose. She grins at the sight, at the smiles passed between peoples who once distrusted each other. Cobra is hugged and kissed as villager after villager wishes her well, begs her to return next spring. She grimaces as hands brush her injured shoulder, but accepts the affection with that patience and grace Solma loves her for. Gerta has Krait's tiny hand in hers while Habu and King gabble at her. She grins at them, cupping Habu's chin as he talks. She's grown fond of those kids, and the Keeper kids, too. Watching it lifts Solma's spirits.

The one person who hangs back from the hugs and goodbyes is Ignis. He stands sullenly beside Burdock, stroking the pony's flank. Solma hesitates when she sees him, but Olive nudges her.

"Go on," she says. "I'll be right here."

Solma trudges forward. It's only when she gets closer that she realizes Ignis isn't alone. Warren is with him, a hand on the other boy's shoulder. Taipan is there, too, digging her bare toes into the earth.

"Hey, War," Solma says, pulling her brother into a hug. He leans in, holding her tightly.

"Hi, Sol," he says. He pulls back and smiles at her. "You come to say goodbye?"

Solma touches his face. He's grown taller in the last year. His hair, once the red-gold of fresh wheat, is darkening. There's a flush to his cheeks. Solma's heart aches to see that his skin is now marked with scars. He's growing up in that harsh, hurried way that children always do in Alphor.

"Yeah," she says. "First, though, I came to talk to Ignis."

Ignis looks at her nervously. He's kept to himself since the battle, never straying far from the Whisperer camp where he's been in Urutu's care. He's been quiet and subdued, but eager to help wherever he's been asked. Every so often, Solma's caught sight of him in the village, mending doors or re-thatching roofs. He's helped in the fields, swept away ash. *Ash from his own fires.*

Solma shakes her head to loosen that thought. She's tried not to hold on to that, but it's difficult. When she looks at him, she struggles not to see the sneering boy that stole her brother. Vulkan's son. A Fire Maker. A villain.

But when Ignis looks at her, it's obvious he's struggling not to think of himself that way, too. He's a well of shame. And she knows what that's like. She puts a hand on his shoulder.

"You gonna be ok?" she asks. Ignis looks at the ground and nods.

"Yeah," he murmurs. "My Uncle's gonna look after me. I'm gonna travel with him and he'll teach me to use my ... my gift."

It's obviously as strange for him to speak of his abilities that way as it is for Solma to hear it.

"Yeah?" she says, smiling. "That's great."

They're quiet for a bit.

"Thought we might go back to my village," Ignis mumbles. "Maybe see my ... my Ma."

Solma doesn't know what to say to that. Instead, she gives his shoulder a brief squeeze.

"I got a lot to do," Ignis says, "before ... you know."

Solma does know, but she's not going to say it aloud. Before she'll be able to forgive him. Before she'll trust him. But she knows the weight of that, so she's got no desire to rub it in.

"Sure," she says. "But ... good luck. The Whisperers will take care of you. And me'n Warren, we're grateful for what you did ... in the end."

Warren shuffles his feet nervously. Solma turns her attention to him, realising he's been fidgety the whole time she's been talking. She raises an eyebrow.

"What's with you, eh?" she asks. "You been avoiding me the last few days?"

Warren bites his lip. Irritation flares briefly in Solma's gut. She's tired and battered, grief-stricken, just like he is. Why won't he talk to her? Doesn't he know there's nothing in the world she won't help him with? Nothing in the world—

Understanding hits Solma all at once. She reels, the breath struck out of her.

"You're going, too," she says quietly. "You're leaving."

Warren's green eyes flick up to meet his sister's. Tears draw tracks down his face. He nods. "I got to, Sol," he says softly. "There's a new power in Alphor's kids and ... I gotta help. I gotta find them, teach them, help them understand what's happening. I'm the only one who can. It's gotta be me."

Solma kneels in front of him. "On your own?" she demands. "Who's gonna take care of you? You're only nine, Warren, you're—"

"Sol," he says, holding her hands tightly. "It's gonna be ok. I'll be with Cobra and Mamba and Ana. I'll have Tai. I'll come back. I'll always come back. But this is bigger than you and me now, ain't it?"

It always has been. And this day was always going to come. The day her brother, grown beyond his years, walks away from her. She's held him so tightly since their parents died and she's not sure she knows how to let go. The sobs bubble from her throat before she can stop them. Warren wraps her in a hug as she cries against him. He hushes her, strokes her hair. "It's ok, Sol," he says. "It's gonna be ok."

And it hurts that *he's* comforting *her*. It hurts that she's begging him to stay and he's gently, calmly, telling her he can't. That if the change they hope to make is going to spread, he has to be out there in the world. It's the only way.

And then she isn't just crying for Warren. She's crying for Bell, too. And Roseann. And the many villagers they lost to the battle. And the years she spent traveling, and the shame she carried. She cries for Blume, that beautiful first bee who changed everything. She cries for Vulkan, too. And Blaiz. She cries for the fact they weren't brave enough to change. And for how they broke everything.

At last, the tears stop. Solma pulls away from Warren, wiping her eyes. Her face feels puffy and now she has a pounding headache.

Warren touches her face. "I'll be back, Sol," he says. "You gotta trust me, yeah?"

Solma manages a smile. "I trust you," she tells him. "You're so much braver than me. You always have been."

Warren grins, tears falling freely down his face. Beside him, Burdock tosses his head, startling Ignis. Solma looks up to see Cobra waiting quietly. She opens her good arm when Solma stands, gathers her friend into a hug.

"I'll miss you," Cobra says into Solma's hair. "And I'm so proud of you."

Solma nods but doesn't trust herself to speak. A hush falls on the gathered crowd and now they stand, watching solemnly. The Whisperers ready themselves. The kids climb onto the cart. There's a murmur of shock when Warren climbs up alongside Taipan. Solma, though, sneaks a look at Gerta and sees the old woman looks unsurprised. Figures.

Urutu and Sidewinder come to find Ignis, and Urutu places a gentle hand on the boy's shoulder. Solma notices that, for once, Ignis doesn't flinch at the touch. Instead, he leans into his uncle, and Urutu's eyes glaze with grateful tears. Solma knows Sidewinder plans to head back to the Whisperer camp with the many Whisperers that came to fight with her. Urutu and Ig, though, will travel west. They'll stay with Mamba's troupe for a while, then separate and head to Ig's old village. To his Ma.

Norsen and his Gatra lead the Keeper kids out of the crowd, too. They'll also travel west with Mamba's Whisperers for a while, then head back to their own village. Aldo suggested they take one of the solar trucks with them. It's a good idea. They pile into the truck now and Norsen takes the wheel, his Gatra falling into formation around it.

Solma knows Norsen plans for the Keeper children to spread their gift across the continent. He and Solma talked about it at length. They agreed that, first and foremost, these were *children,* many orphaned, driven from their homes or escaped from villages that tried to hold them hostage, like Maxen did with Warren. They had become soldiers, fighters, saviours. And now, they need safety and love before anything. As they grow in age and confidence, things will change. But this generation of brilliant, broken youngsters need a chance to heal themselves before they can heal the world.

Solma feels Olive approach and wrap an arm round her. Soft breath tickles her ear as Olive whispers.

"He loves you, Sol. And so do I. Always."

The Whisperers give one last wave and move off. Burdock holds his ground for a moment, turning to stare at Solma. But Ana encourages him on. With a toss of his head, he follows. The villagers move forward, waving, the Yuen chasing the cart for as long as their legs will carry them.

Solma keeps staring at Warren's face. She tries to imprint it in her mind, to keep those green eyes, that gentle smile safe in her memory. She knows, though, that the next time she sees him, he won't look like that. He'll be taller, older. He'll be stronger and wiser. He won't need her anymore. And that hurts. It hurts so much she clutches her stomach and struggles to breathe. Olive pulls her close.

"It's ok, Sol," she says. "It's ok."

The crowd gradually grows bored and disperses. There's still work to be done, after all. The Gatra have patrols to run, there's windfall to gather in the orchards. Many houses still need fixing. They can't stand and stare at the horizon forever.

So, it's only Solma and Olive still there when a strange sound makes Solma glance up. A high-pitched, erratic note cuts the air. A frantic but beautiful sound that makes Solma's heart lift in a way she doesn't understand. A defiant cry in the otherwise silent skies. And Solma know it means, *I'm here! I'm here!*

"What is that?" she whispers, afraid the noise will stop at the sound of her voice.

Olive's fingers tighten around hers. Solma glances over to see the girl she loves awash with awe.

"It's a bird, Sol," Olive whispers. "The birds are coming back."

Solma shields her eyes, peering at the top of the nearest glasshouse and ... there it is! Small and delicate, impossible as the future, its wings are bright, midday blue and its belly feathers, a fluffy sunburst yellow. It's so tiny, yet its song fills the air. Solma feels tears sting her eyes. She grips Olive's hand as the bird hops to the edge of the glasshouse roof, trills a note and takes off, its song mingling with that of the last summer bees.

Song of the Bumblebee Queen: Clover's Daughter

MY MATING FLIGHT IS a dance and a battle at the same time. I am sun-touched, my body full of nectar. I am strong. It barely takes effort to outmaneuver the little males who think they should father my nest. Up-starts. They chase me in a cloud of desperate buzzing. Their engines fire in a thousand different keys, but all making the same plea.

Choose me! Choose me!

I don't choose any of them. Not yet. They must catch me first.

We zoom in and out of the sunlight that dapples the forest, dipping beneath tree branches, between ferns, grown tall in the autumn sun. I lift above the canopy, battle the wind. The breeze means nothing to me. But I want to see if the drones can keep up. Midday warmth on my fur fills me with energy. My flight engine rumbles, deep and proud, as I hang in the air, just long enough for a few males to think they might catch me. I shoot off again just as they draw close. I hear the note of dismay in their song.

Wait!

Wait indeed! A virgin queen waits for no-one! Want to mate? Have to catch me first. I dive through the cover of green leaves, darting around wide tree trunks. I put a taunt in my song.

Who's worthy? I ask.

And the desperate males clamor, *Me! Me! Me!*

But, one-by-one, they fall away. Exhaustion overcomes them, or hunger. They land, spent. The cloud of suitors slowly diminishes until only a few dozen remain. The strongest.

Now I fly faster, my wing muscles vibrating a deep, determined note against the summer air. But they're on my tail, closer and closer. It takes all my wit to outrun them. I duck and dive, loop around them. I let them think they've caught me, then blast away, buffeting them with the wind from my wings. Another falls away, losing the race. And another.

There are so few, now, that I hear the individual notes of their song. A few of them beg for my attention.

Pick me! It should be me!

As if I'd ever let myself be caught. My future nest deserves better. My mother did not let herself get caught on her mating flight. No, she outran those drones for as long as she was able until only the strongest, the most tenacious—my father—caught her. That's how a nest survives. The strongest begets the strongest. A weak father means a doomed nest. No less than the best genes will make my daughters.

There's one male, near the front of the group, who doesn't beg and taunt. His attention is fixed firmly on the prize. Me. All his energy goes into powering those impressive wing muscles. I dance a little in the air to get a look at him. He's big, even for a drone. His fur is a lustrous gold, his antennae long and twitching. His eyes glitter in the summer sun. I listen for the deep vibration of his song in the air, matching my own engine note to it.

I like him.

And because I like him, I test him. I fly faster. Higher. He stays on my tail, even as the other males fall away. I twist and swerve and dodge. I feel his legs brush the fur on my back and I charge on, slipping from his grasp. I hear the frustration in his song, and I'm buoyed with lightness. An energy, like the first rays of sunlight warming the land. Perhaps it's what humans might call joy. Excitement. Love, even.

This male will be the one. I know it. But he's got to prove it. He's got to *earn* it. He's the last one left, and he chases me up through the forest canopy and down again. We plunge into a tangle of brambles, dodging ferns, dancing round the heads of confused rodents that nip at us. We're too fast. We burst out of the forest and into the sun, racing each other over the grass.

At last, I feel his legs clamp around me. I fight to break free but he's strong. Strong enough to hold me close, strong enough that the race is over. He's won. And I am his prize. But I have won, too. Because his genes will make powerful daughters, a healthy nest.

It's over quickly. Passionless and brief, and then, exhausted, his grip loosens. He falls away, barely alive. I hear the final, feeble buzz of his song as he tumbles into the grass.

With my future tucked safely in my body, I wander up the grasslands, following a winding path, until I find a small cluster of birch trees surrounding a mighty ash. There are flowers here. Poppies and borage and clover. I land and dip my tongue into the flower hearts, drinking deeply. I am strong but I must get stronger. My mother was one of many virgin queens who left her own hatching nest, one of only a few that survived the winter hibernation.

And I will survive, too. I will drink my fill of sweetness, then burrow deep and sleep while the land above is ravaged by winter cold.

And next spring, I will wake, having outlived my mother, my sisters, carrying the hope of our species inside me. The skies will be silent of our song for a few months, but we will come back.

I take off, blasting my engine so my song carries across the grasslands. I feel light and strong, not just from the mating flight, not just from the nectar. But with something a little like happiness. Like hope.

Do you want to read more?

Did you enjoy reading Ignis' journey? Did you love Solma and Warren's battle for freedom? You can discover the next book in this series, check out extra content about the world of Silent Skies, and sign up to my readers' club, where you'll receive newsletter updates once per month and get a gift ebook. You can also help other readers discover this story by leaving a review online.

You can do all this by scanning the QR code below. Or visit:

https://subscribepage.io/rlfssseriespage

See you there!

Also By Rebecca L. Fearnley

The *Silent Skies* Trilogy **(Complete)**
The Last Beekeeper
The Hive Child
War Song of the Wild
The Snake's Nest
The Nowhere Chronicles (**(In Progress)**
Doorway to Nowhere
The Darkling Thief
The Howling Mare
A Song of Forgetting
The Shadow and the Scream
Flight of the Bone Crow
A Fearsome, Lonely Heart
Under a Tortured Mountain
The Girl in the Nightmare Tree
A Soul for a Secret
The Rage-Scaled Serpent

Thanks To...

Any writer will tell you that a book doesn't get written without the support, faith and guidance of many, many people. I'll start with those who've made this book the physical thing that it is. To my editor, Lara, thank you for your brilliant and thorough feedback and for showing such faith in the story and for staying with me through this series. Thank you to my wonderful cover designer, Stefanie, at Seventh Star Designs, for your beautiful artwork in which this story lives.

Thank you also to my wonderful writing group, Lou, Georgia and Daisy, who've beta read this book and continued to push me to be the very best writer I can be, cajoling me through my fear and celebrating my successes. Thank you to my dear friend, Tess, who read this book in its early form, offering her thoughts and being constant with her support. Thank you again to Lucy, Carly from Limb Power and Dave

Goulson, whose sensitivity and accuracy readings for *The Last Beekeeper* informed my writing for *War Song of the Wild*. Thank you to the wonderful Sue, librarian at one of my residency schools, who has championed and supported me for years now, and whose endless support with *The Last Beekeeper* has helped it find many new readers!

Thank you to my family. To both my parents, who've remained stalwartly certain that I will succeed in my lifelong writing dream and have supported me in every way possible. Thank you to my brilliant siblings for listening to me cry, panic or celebrate down the phone and talk round in circles when I was feeling particularly overwhelmed. Thank you to my partner and life teammate, David, for your constant patience, faith and reassurance. I know you've had to tell me it will be fine a million times. I almost believe you now.

And lastly, but by no means least, thank you to you, my readers. The people who breathe life into this story. I hope it touched your heart. I hope it made you dream. My story continues to live on through you, and for that I am truly, deeply grateful.

About Rebecca L. Fearnley

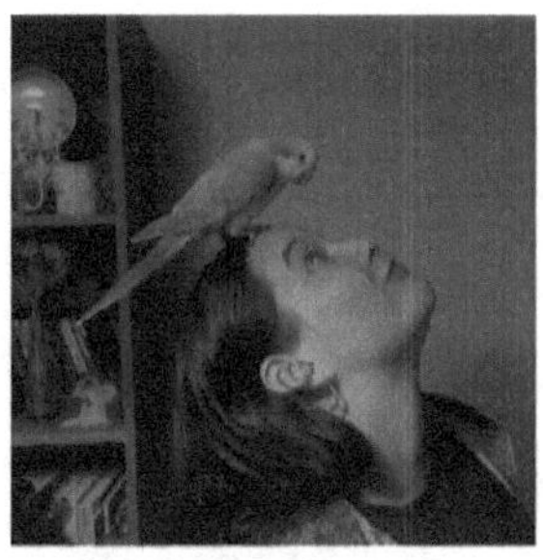

Rebecca has been obsessed with two things since she learned to walk and talk: stories and animals. Luckily, the two seem to be very compatible. In addition to writing, Rebecca is also a teacher and, in 2018, decided that she wanted to write quality books for the young people she works with. Her books tend towards themes of respect for the environment, protecting the planet and the new generation challenging the old to face up to their mistakes.

She lives in Reading with her unusual little family, which includes herself and her partner, a friendly little mini-lop rabbit (called Cleo) and a gregarious and feisty quaker parrot (called Maya).

www.ingramcontent.com/pod-product-compliance
Lightning Source LLC
Chambersburg PA
CBHW030834190726
48285CB00004B/1209